"The author knows abou[illegible] ...ul Pioneer Press

Dead Astern

"A great, bounding thrill ride . . . *Dead Astern* is the book Agatha Christie might have written if she'd loved the sea and had known how to trim a sail. Jenifer LeClair offers readers an engaging tale that is a strong, seagoing version of the locked-room mystery. With several well-plotted twists, lots of riveting scenes on the bounding main, and plenty of fascinating sailing information along the way, *Dead Astern* is an exciting excursion sure to please anyone willing to sign on for the voyage."

—William Kent Krueger
New York Times Bestselling Author

Apparition Island

"With a mastery of details and a sailor's sense of land and sea, LeClair has given us another memorable story on an eerie island off the coast of Maine . . . a real gift for those who like their mysteries straight from the sea."

—Steve Thayer
New York Times Bestselling Author

"LeClair handles the island's rugged terrain and its rugged inhabitants equally well."

—*Publishers Weekly*

"Jenifer LeClair provides her fans with another thrilling investigation in a consistently excellent series."

—*Midwest Book Review*

"LeClair skillfully brings the setting into the mind's eye with wonderfully descriptive detail."

—*Foreword Magazine*

Cold Coast

"Brie is so likable and the plot so involving, it's not surprising this series has won several awards."

—Mary Ann Grossmann
St. Paul Pioneer Press

"This engaging police procedural vividly captures the Maine background. . . . The eccentric Mainers add depth to a fabulous step-by-step investigation."

—*Midwest Book Review*

"*Cold Coast* is superbly written. The characters are easy to follow and well developed. . . . Brie is a strong female protagonist but in an endearing way, not the stereotypical hard-nosed female law enforcement officer. The descriptions of the harbor and the coast are exceptionally vivid. . . . 5 Stars—excellent read!"

—*Reader Views*

"Tense . . . keeps the reader guessing until the final outcome . . . full of wonderful descriptions of life on a sailing vessel."

—*Armchair Reviews*

Danger Sector

"If you love sailing, grab this title and prepare to be immersed. . . . A strong sense of place and a fine little closed-room drama make this seafaring read a real pleasure."

—*Library Journal*

"Intelligent and well-written . . . The strong, smart protagonist is Minneapolis homicide detective Brie Beaumont."

—*St. Paul Pioneer Press*

"Recommend this agreeable mixture of adventure and crime."

—*Booklist*

"There is something compelling about the sea, particularly when it claims a murder victim. LeClair weaves a yarn that draws in the reader from the first page."

—*Midwest Book Review*

"LeClair combines police procedure, finely-honed investigative skills, psychological insights, and suspense . . . in this haunting story of unrequited love, deceit, and murder [that] involves all five senses. A creative imagination, a love for sailing, and gifted communication skills combine to make Jenifer LeClair a top-notch storyteller."

—*Reader Views*

Rigged for Murder

"A winning combination of psychological thriller, police procedural, and action adventure. It's a five-star launch for [LeClair's] aptly named sea-going series. . . . Tightly written and intricately constructed, LeClair's *Rigged for Murder* is first-class storytelling in a setting so authentic you can hear the ocean's roar and taste the salt from the sea."

—*Mysterious Reviews*

"An engaging New England whodunit."

—*Midwest Book Review*

"Brie [Beaumont] is smart and competent, and she uses her brain and not her gun. . . . Jenifer LeClair offers another appealing main character in *Rigged for Murder*, first in her Windjammer Series."

—*St. Paul Pioneer Press*

"A strong plot, non-stop action, and first-class character development combine to make this an exciting, page-turning adventure novel."

—*Reader Views*

"A debut mystery that is so well written you will hunger for more . . . well-developed characters and superbly good writing."

—Once Upon a Crime Mystery Bookstore

"*Rigged for Murder* is an exciting mystery with a little romance thrown in. The setting for this novel is unique and gives the reader insight into life aboard a sailing ship."

—*Armchair Reviews*

"The characters have depth and movement . . . LeClair gets the sea and the sailing just right."

—*Books 'n' Bytes*

"*Rigged for Murder* is a fast-paced story which rings true both aboard and ashore on island communities. The characters are real, the situations are downright scary, tension is palpable."

—John Foss, Master/owner,
Schooner *American Eagle*, Rockland, Maine

DEATH IN THE BLOOD MOON

ALSO BY JENIFER LECLAIR

The Windjammer Mystery Series

Rigged for Murder (Book 1)
Danger Sector (Book 2)
Cold Coast (Book 3)
Apparition Island (Book 4)
Dead Astern (Book 5)

DEATH IN THE BLOOD MOON

JENIFER LECLAIR

FOG HARBOR PRESS
St. Paul, Minnesota

This book is a work of fiction. Names, characters, places and incidents either are products of the author's imagination or are used fictitiously. Any resemblance to actual events, or to actual persons living or dead, is entirely coincidental.

Fog Harbor Press
4411 Wood Duck Drive
St. Paul, Minnesota 55127

Cover Design: Rebecca Treadway / ATRTINK

Library of Congress Control Number: 2018914609

LeClair, Jenifer.
Death in the blood moon: a novel / by Jenifer LeClair – 1st ed.

ISBN 978-0-578-42432-3

10 9 8 7 6 5 4 3 2

Printed in the United States of America

For Will Sandstrom, Chief Deputy,
Cook County Sheriff's Office

Thank you for all your help.

"The truth is rarely pure and never simple."

—Oscar Wilde

Chapter 1

Brie Beaumont stood at the kitchen window of her second-floor apartment in the Longfellow neighborhood of south Minneapolis. She was thinking about John. Missing him. The old spreading oak tree in the backyard blazed red in the early morning light. The tree was at least as old as the ninety-year-old duplex where she had lived for the last twelve years. Well, almost twelve years. The past six months she had been on the coast of Maine aboard a sailing schooner. After those months at sea, it felt strangely disorienting standing in her kitchen rather than on a pitching deck, hearing the wind rattling the glass in the worn sash rather than roaring along *Maine Wind's* great canvas sails.

The blustery late October wind shook the old tree, sending showers of vermillion leaves onto the tiny backyard. Branches reached in all directions, reminding her of her life that had now traveled far beyond this house, this city, and the Minneapolis Police Department where she had served as an officer and detective for the past fifteen years.

She turned from the window. The air felt stale, smelled musty. The cracked linoleum floor needed washing, and the dark wood floors beyond the kitchen wanted sweeping. The layout of the apartment was little changed from when the first residents had inhabited it back in the 1920s. She walked into the dining room, suddenly aware of how much TLC the place needed—how little like a home it felt. She had never cared about a fancy environment. Her work had been everything. Until it wasn't.

On the dining room table a six-month backlog of mail sat in piles. A single sheet of white paper lay like a deflated ghost on the edge of the table. Brie walked over and stared down at it. Three stark words haunted the page—the letters cut from a hodge-podge of magazine fonts.

YOU'LL Be Sorry!

The irony of the message almost brought a smile to her face. *Be* sorry? She was well acquainted with sorrow—needed no future rendezvous with the emotion to make it more real. Nineteen months ago her partner, Homicide Detective Phil Thatcher, had been gunned down as the two of them responded to a call. She had been shot in the same incident and had barely survived, but it was Phil who had left a wife and young son bereft of husband and father. She had been left with PTSD and survivor's guilt. The case had gone cold.

Her eyes traveled to the right-hand side of the table where three more sheets of paper and three envelopes lay, all with the same absurd lettering, all postmarked over the past two and a half months, but each with a slightly more threatening message. Whoever had sent the letters obviously didn't know she had been out of state for six months or he wouldn't have been so persistent. *He or she,* Brie thought, correcting herself. The letters could just as easily have come from a woman. But for whatever reason, her gut told her it was a man.

Her gaze traveled on to the handmade quilt that hung on her living room wall. The one thing of real beauty in her apartment. Her Granny Beaumont had made the quilt. Placed and stitched each of the squares of vibrant red and cream and blue and sent the quilt to Brie the year she had graduated from college. Her eyes rested there, drawn into the intricate design as down a rabbit hole whereby one might enter a different world. One without cranks and criminals and malcontents. She knew she had to report the letters to the department. She was scheduled to return there in a week. Could it wait until then? No, she knew it couldn't.

She went to her bedroom closet where she kept a stack of evidence envelopes and brought one of them back to the dining room. Using a tweezers, she deposited the letters and corresponding envelopes into the evidence envelope. She sealed it up, wrote her shield number, date and time, and where the letters had been collected, as she would with any other piece of evidence, and left the envelope on the table.

The sound of a car in the driveway next to the house drew her attention. She had planned to spend a few days up North with her mother before facing the decisions she had to make about her life here and her future with the MPD. She decided she would call from the road and report the letters to the department and bring them in when she returned. They had sat in a stack of mail in her landlady's apartment downstairs for several months. A few more days wouldn't matter.

She walked back to the bedroom, picked her duffel bag up off the floor, grabbed her heavy jacket from the bed, and headed back through the kitchen and out the back door. The tang of fall filled the air. The smell of dry leaves, the sweetness of rotting apples, fallen from the tree next door; the sharp notes of wood smoke from backyard fires. She turned and locked the deadbolt and made her way down the open wood stairs to the back yard. Her mother was just climbing out of the car.

"Hey, Mom." Brittle leaves crunched underfoot as she covered the ground in a few long strides. She dropped her stuff on the ground and gave her mother a big hug. Edna Beaumont felt unusually frail in her arms.

After a few moments they stood at arms' length, assessing each other. Brie saw immediately that there were more lines on her mother's lovely face. But the blue eyes still burned as brightly as her own. *Loss has a way of diminishing exteriors,* she thought, *but the inner spirit, the real stuff of our being, is not so easily eroded.* She noted that this was not a thought she would have had six months ago.

Her mother was studying her reciprocally. "You look wonderful, sweetheart. So tan. From being at sea, I guess. I don't think I've ever seen you looking so healthy."

"Thanks, Mom, I think. You look good, too."

"Now, Brie, detectives should always tell the truth."

"You've been through a hard time, Mom." She left it at that for now. "Mind if we take your Jeep? It's more comfortable than my jalopy."

Brie drove an older model Ford Escape, which was fine for getting around the city but lacked some of the creature comforts of her mother's fancy Jeep Cherokee.

"Climb in," her mom said. "But I think I'll let you drive. That is, if you still remember how to steer a car."

"I haven't been at sea that long, Mom," Brie quipped. "Still, it feels like more than six months. In some ways, it feels like I was always there. Like a whole separate life was lived out in the past six months."

"A whole new path unfolded for you," Edna said. "One that I believe you needed to find. Maybe were meant to find. Now, I know you don't buy into that kind of thinking . . . still, there will be much to talk about this week."

Brie didn't comment, but she smiled to herself. *Things change. Sometimes in very surprising ways.* Her mother would surely be surprised at some of the upheavals in her thinking over the past months.

Edna walked around to the passenger side of the Jeep. "I want to know about John."

"If you'll teach me how to make your homemade spaetzle, I'll tell all."

"Sounds like a bargain. You're on." Edna climbed in and shut the door.

Brie started the engine and backed down the driveway and out onto the street. They headed west and turned north onto Hiawatha. They followed Hiawatha Avenue for about three miles to where it merged onto 35W, east of the new Vikings stadium that could have taken to the sea bearing two of each creature, so ark-like was its appearance. During this time of year, the Vikings were busy there, "Defending the North."

West of the stadium sprawled the mighty metropolis of Minneapolis. Brie thought about her colleague at the department, Detective Garrett Parker. He had helped her remotely with the murder case on Granite Island when she and the ship, *Maine Wind*, were marooned there during a gale in May. She remembered his words. "You're a city girl, Brie. Come home." At the time, she had scoffed at his characterization, but as she looked around at the soaring architecture, she realized there was no denying the fact. They say you can't change the spots on a leopard, but maybe in her heart she had always belonged somewhere else.

Farther along they crossed the new 35W bridge, a sleek, beautiful cement structure—a tribute to modern-day engineering. It was the replacement for the old eight-lane steel truss arch bridge that had fallen into the Mississippi River in August of 2007, killing 13, injuring 145, and shining a harsh national spotlight on the dangerously deteriorated condition of U.S. infrastructure.

Beyond the Mississippi, Highway 35W, or "35 Dub" as it was colloquially referred to, curved and carved its way north and just a mile or so beyond St. Anthony, bent east in a sharp 90-degree swing. It traveled through western Roseville, a nearring suburb north of St. Paul, and then bent due north again, heading out of the cities. Twenty miles farther on, near the small city of Forest Lake, 35W merged with 35E—St. Paul's north-south highway.

Beyond Forest Lake, Twin Citians would sit back and get into their open road groove, knowing they had left the last vestiges of the major metropolis behind them. Even though she'd been gone for six months, Brie could feel the familiar shift, as if they had passed through some invisible wall beyond which the unwinding process began. The laying down of city life and preparing for the wonders of the North.

Brie rolled her shoulders and relaxed into the leather seat. She glanced over at Edna. "I'm really sorry I couldn't get to Robert's funeral, Mom." Her mother's second husband had died suddenly in August of cardiac arrest. Robert and Edna had lived in Santa Fe, and at the time it happened, Brie had been deeply embroiled in a complicated case she was working with the Maine State Police on the far reaches of the Maine coast near the Bay of Fundy.

"It was impossible for you to come. I know that."

"Still, I should have been there for you."

"It's all right, dear. The boys were both there. And Ariel came from Colorado. That was very kind of her. I know you probably asked her to come."

"When I told her what had happened and that I couldn't get away, she wanted to go. She's so fond of you, Mom. Remember she lost her own mother to cancer when we were in college—the same year Dad died. That was what really cemented our friendship. We were both grieving and trying to press on and keep going in school. We buoyed each other up during that difficult time and have ever since."

"It was a comfort to have her there," Edna said.

"Do you think you will stay in Sante Fe, Mom, or move home?"

"Do you think you will move to Maine or stay here?"

"I asked first, Mom."

Edna sighed. "I don't know, Brie. I'm tired. A part of me would like to stay there, in Santa Fe. The path of least resistance and all that." She looked out her window as the landscape rolled by. "I have no real ties there, though. It was Robert's place. I guess I'm a Minnesota girl at heart. I like the winter and the seasons."

They were silent for a time. Above Cambridge, farmland stretched out on both sides of the highway. Wide flat fields, weathered barns with their hip roofs, and simple frame farmhouses. Brie felt as if she could see all the way to the Dakotas, the landscape was so flat. It seemed odd after living in Maine for the past six months, where the landscape rose and fell in high hills and deep valleys, where the land rolled like a stormy sea. But flat as the topography was, as they rolled off the miles, there was a sense of climbing, slowly climbing mile upon mile. And if one focused on the road, there seemed to be a slight but constant rise to it.

Edna turned and Brie could feel her eyes, sense the questions she wanted to ask. "I guess it's too soon to know what you're going to do," she said.

"Well, yes and no. Obviously, if I decide to return to Maine, there are things here I would have to take care of. The decision about my job—about returning to the department—is more pressing."

"Let me ask you something," Edna said. "Can you imagine yourself not returning to Maine? To John?"

"Well, when you put it like that . . ." Brie stopped, unsure of what she wanted to say. John was captain of the schooner *Maine Wind*, the ship she'd crewed aboard for the past six months. The two of them had become close during her time on the ship. He had become her lover and confidante, and they had survived a number of dangerous situations, which had only brought them closer.

"Is there love?" Edna asked.

Brie didn't answer immediately, but finally said in a quiet voice, "Yes, Mom, there's love."

"That's good," Edna said. "That makes me happy." She looked out her window. "Fear drove you away the first time. This time, if you go back, it should be because of love."

"What makes you think that, Mom? What makes you think it was fear?"

"Wasn't it?"

The words stretched between them, first a river, but slowly widening into a gulf.

"Why do you say that, Mom?" Brie asked again.

"Because I know what that kind of fear feels like."

"No you don't, Mom. You've never been shot. Lost your partner. Seen him die in front of you. Knowing it should have been you that died."

"Maybe not. But I know the fear that things will never be the same. That no matter what you do, you can never get back to where you were. I know that fear."

Brie sat respectfully for a time. Her father had died suddenly when they, the three children, were still in high school and college. And now, without warning, Edna had lost her second husband. Brie realized her mother knew about sudden death and grief and separation.

"I'm sorry, Mom. Of course you know. I guess I've felt so lost in the past year and a half. . . ." Her words trailed off. "Maybe that's why I didn't try harder to get to Robert's funeral. If so, it's a sad excuse."

"It's okay, honey. You need to learn to forgive yourself. Let's just stay in the now. It's the only place for peace."

Brie smiled. "You've been talking to Ariel, I see."

"Nope. That's coming from me," Edna said. "I haven't been on this earth for sixty-six years and learned nothing, you know." She turned and studied Brie for a moment. "Being lost isn't all bad. Forces one to wander around in new territory. Look what you found in the past six months."

Brie suddenly felt an odd urgency to ask her mother all the things she never had; to learn the parts of her mother's life she knew nothing of. She reflected on the fact that it takes a long time to grow up—that even in her thirties the process seemed to progress. *Maybe we don't grow up so much as out,* she thought. *Out of ourselves and into others.*

"It's good to be here with you, Mom. I'm glad we did this." She looked over at Edna but turned away when she felt tears fill her eyes. Edna must have seen, though, because she reached over and patted Brie's leg.

"I'll always be around, Brie. Even some day when I'm gone and you think I'm not there, I'll be there."

Brie smiled and brushed away a tear. "Okay, now that's Ariel talking, for sure."

Edna laughed. "Well, maybe a little. She gets to you with her wisdom."

"Hey, Mom. Hinckley coming up. You up for a couple White Castles?"

"Can't break with tradition. Let's take the exit."

Brie, like all Minnesotans, knew the tragic history of this place. The small city of Hinckley, which sits just off I-35 one hour north of St. Paul, was named after Isaac Hinckley, president of the Philadelphia, Wilmington, and Baltimore Railroad. The area was one of the first great logging sites in Minnesota. But long before the loggers arrived, the Ojibwe had settled in the area, where they trapped and hunted and traded furs at the local trading posts. The territory had been heavily forested with old-growth white pine, a resource that eventually drew European settlers, the logging industry, and the railroads—industry that encroached more and more on the indigenous people.

On September 1, 1894, after a summer of intense drought and high temperatures, the unimaginable occurred. A number of small fires started by loggers along the railroad tracks, to burn what they called "slash," led to a conflagration that morphed into a fierce firestorm, destroying everything in its path. The massive firestorm burned over 400 square miles, with temperatures that rose to over 2000 degrees Fahrenheit. In the yards of the Eastern Minnesota Railroad, the wheels of the cars fused to the tracks. The firestorm that came to be known as the Great Hinckley Fire consumed six towns and left over 400 fatalities in its wake.

As if reading Brie's thoughts, Edna said, "Did you know that the Union soldier who killed John Wilkes Booth after Booth assassinated Abraham Lincoln died right here in the great Hinckley fire?"

"I did not know that, Mom, but it's pretty fascinating."

"His name was Thomas Corbett, but he was known as 'Boston' Corbett."

Brie smiled. It had been a long time since she'd heard her mother spout history facts.

Edna had taught high school history after college and up until Brie's older brother was born. After Tom Beaumont's death, she had gone back to teaching to support the family. Minnesota history had been a special interest of hers.

"I'm afraid I only know the broad strokes of Minnesota history, Mom. But here's something. Did you know that the Ojibwe here in Minnesota descend from the Algonquin peoples of the Atlantic coast, as do the Passamaquoddy and Penobscot Nations in Maine?"

"That's interesting, Brie. How did you learn that?"

"From Joe Wolf, the medical examiner who works with the Maine State Police. He's a member of the Penobscot Nation."

The exit was coming up, and Brie took it. She turned left, and they crossed over the highway heading for the gas station and White Castle on the other side of 35E.

"I need to stop in the restroom," Edna said.

"That's fine, Mom. I'll top off the tank and then we'll hit the drive-thru."

Brie needed to notify someone at the Minneapolis Police Department about those letters lurking in her dining room. As soon as Edna was out of the car, she brought up Detective Garrett Parker's number and put the call through. She walked back, carded the pump, and started the gas.

Garrett answered on the third ring. "Homicide. Parker."

"Hey, Garrett. It's Brie."

"Well, hello, Brie. This is a surprise. Maine or Minnesota?"

"Minnesota. I got back a few days ago. I figured you would have gotten the word. I notified the commander a couple of weeks ago."

"So, are you back for good?"

"Well, I'm back for now, Garrett."

"And what does that mean?" he asked.

"Just what it sounds like. I haven't made any decisions about anything. I'm taking a few days up North with my mom. I need to spend a little quality time with her. She just lost her husband in August."

"I'm sorry to hear that. How's she doing?"

"She's doing okay. Mom's a survivor. Still, I know this will be good for her. We haven't seen a lot of each other the past couple years.

"Listen, Garrett, I just got my mail last night. My landlady has been keeping it for me. Mostly junk, since my bills are all on auto pay. But something showed up that I need to report."

"What's that?" Parker asked.

"Threatening letters."

"How many letters, Brie?"

She could hear the concern in his voice. "Four. Just a short sentence on each, but the messages get more threatening."

"What do they say?"

"The first two say, 'You'll be sorry.' The third, 'You're going to pay,' The fourth, 'You can't stop what's coming.'"

"Handwritten or typed?"

"Individual letters, cut from magazines. Like a scene from a B-movie, if you ask me. Probably just some crank."

"That may be, but you're a cop. Easy for some nut to put a target on your back. What do the postmarks show?"

"That's the weird part," Brie said. "They were mailed from different locations around the state."

"Huh. Over what period of time?"

Brie saw Edna heading for the car. She waved and pointed to her phone, then walked away from the car so she couldn't be overheard. "The first one came in August, the second in September, and the last two were both mailed in October."

"Shows an escalation," Garrett said. He repeated the words, "You'll be sorry."

"Sorry for what, though?" Brie asked.

"If we knew that, we'd know where to start looking."

"The phrase implies that I've done something wrong."

"In the eyes of this perp, you obviously have. So maybe it's someone you put away. Someone who's now free and going after retribution."

"Except that most of the perps we put away aren't coming out any time soon."

"Well, that's true enough," Parker said.

"Look, Gare. I've gotta go. Just following protocol—reporting the incident. We'll sort it out when I get back to the cities."

"You want me to go over to your place and pick up the letters?" Parker asked.

"No. I'm returning to the department next week. I'll bring them in then. See if forensics can find anything."

"Well, okay, Brie. Watch your back, though. You never know these days."

"I always do. Thanks, Garrett."

"Enjoy your time with your mom."

"Will do." She ended the call and headed back to the car. She took the pump out, replaced the gas cap and climbed in behind the wheel. "Ready for some sliders, Mom?"

"Ready as rain," Edna said.

They pulled into the drive-thru and ordered a bagful of little White Castle burgers, headed back across the freeway, and took the northbound entrance.

Chapter 2

North of Hinckley, the landscape changed. Now the road rose with serious intent, and farms gave way to solid forests of pine and birch—the boreal forest. They had crossed some invisible line where the habitat shifted suddenly. Here it was too cold for successful farming. Here the land turned wild, rolling north toward the Laurentian Divide—the Continental Divide—that ran east to west, across the top of Minnesota. Across the Arrowhead, as it was known. Beyond the divide, waters flow north to Hudson Bay, but south of the divide wild rivers surge over ancient igneous bedrock, plummeting precipitously toward Lake Superior.

They crossed the wide expanse of the Snake River. The Snake always looked like it was about to flood, spread out as it was in a broad, calm flowage. But this fall it had pushed its boundaries to the limit following a relentlessly rainy spring and summer. Farther up the road they met the Kettle River—of entirely different temperament than the Snake. The Kettle ran narrow and fast as it boiled down through Kettle River State Park.

Though Brie had traveled this road for decades, somehow this time felt different. She saw everything with new eyes. Eyes more sensitized to the beauty of the natural world. Eyes that had spent time out of the fray, engulfed in the immutable vastness of the sea.

Beyond the town of Moose Lake the hills began to fold, giving vistas from the high points, and just beyond Mahtowa, the first gray domes of Canadian Shield granite began breaking ground in the wide, forested median that lay between the north and southbound lanes of the highway. The farther north they went, the more their conversation turned to the past, as if the fact of traveling this road again together had opened some portal to a realm of shared memories. They talked about Brie's school days and Edna's teaching days after Tom Beaumont had died. They laughed about Brie's odd assortment of boyfriends and the few ill-fated suitors who had tried to approach Edna when she was in the struggle of her life to keep the family ship on course and comfort her grief-stricken children. They remembered the trials of those early months and how the struggle had melded the four of them into one strong entity—a true family that lifted every burden together. And they laughed about too many dinners of macaroni and cheese and fish sticks, and the bare bones existence they'd had to lead until they found their financial footing.

Before they knew it, they were approaching Duluth, the road rising with ear-popping diligence, getting ready for the big drop into Duluth. After their trip down memory lane, Edna drifted off to sleep. Brie was watching a car in her rear-view mirror, back the road a piece. She thought she had seen that car behind them before they had exited at Hinckley. It looked like an older model Toyota, a common make, so this could be an entirely different vehicle. The color was a nondescript shade of beige. She recognized her wariness as fallout from her call to Garrett about the letters. *Don't go looking for trouble, Brie,* she thought to herself.

At the high crest of the hills, on the outskirts of Duluth, Brie took the exit for Skyline Drive and Spirit Mountain. As she sat at the top of the exit ramp, she noticed the beige Toyota continue north on 35 and disappear over the hill. She heaved a mental sigh of relief, turned right, and wound down a short hill to the Holiday gas station and store.

When she turned off the car, Edna woke up. "Are we there already?" she said, joking. Edna knew this exit well.

"Just making a pit stop, Mom." Brie unbuckled and climbed out of the Jeep, then stuck her head back in. "Want anything? Candy bar?"

"No, I'm, good. I'll just stretch my legs a bit."

Edna stepped out of the car, and Brie headed toward the door of the store. The temperature was a good ten or fifteen degrees cooler than it had been in the Twin Cities, and when she came back out of the store a few minutes later, she noticed Edna had opened the hatch on the Jeep and pulled a wool sweater out of her suitcase.

"Feels like the North," she said, and Brie saw a twinkle in her mom's eyes for the first time since they'd left the city. Edna was a nature girl to her core, and she was glowing in anticipation of the wild beauty they were about to enter. She pulled the sweater over her head and extracted her beautiful mane of hair that, except for being gray, was so like her daughter's.

Brie reached in the back seat and snagged her jacket and slipped into it. That morning she had worked her long blonde hair into a French braid. She zipped the jacket and flipped the braid to the outside. "It'll be cold enough for a fire tonight," she said.

"We'll hope the big lake is rolling," Edna said. "No better sleep than listening to that."

They climbed into the car, headed back up the hill to the freeway entrance, and got on the road. Almost immediately, they came around a curve, and mighty Duluth harbor spread out in panorama far below them, and they began their descent into the Lake Superior basin. Brie still remembered their first trip to Duluth when she was ten, and her mother regaling her and the boys with all the amazing facts about this bustling seaport that sat smack dab in the middle of North America. Duluth is one of the leading bulk cargo ports in all of North

America and also holds the distinction of being the largest and farthest-inland fresh water seaport.

Rail trestles crisscrossed the highway—rails that had carried millions of tons of ore from Minnesota's Iron Range to Duluth to be shipped east to the great mills that had made the steel that built the cities that had made America thrive.

Across the tail of Lake Superior the Bong and Blatnik bridges arced away toward Wisconsin and the south shore of Superior. Roads and highways wove over and under one another, a tangle of futuristic design in the old port city.

Off to starboard a whole flotilla of red and green tugboats —the signature colors of the Great Lakes Towing Company— sat ready to guide the big freighters in and out of the harbor.

Farther along, they passed Canal Park, where freighters entered Duluth Harbor through a deep canal. The north end of the canal was anchored by twin lighthouses bearing red and green harbor lights to mark the ship channel. The canal also formed a breakwater for the storms that pounded in from the northeast across the 300-mile expanse of Superior.

At the other end of the canal, Duluth's iconic Aerial Lift Bridge stood like some creation wrought from a giant erector set. Massive counterweights lifted the bridge deck to a dizzying height of 135 feet, allowing the prodigious freighters to pass beneath.

Highway 35 wound through a tunnel and up a hill, where it terminated at the intersection of London Road. Brie turned right, and they drove north along London Road—Duluth's avenue of the rich and famous. Here the city's wealthy industrialists—timber and iron ore barons, banking and investment capitalists, shipping and rail magnates—had built their houses and mansions along Superior's beautiful shore.

Glensheen Mansion, built by Chester and Clara Congdon between 1905 and 1908, had been the most famous residence on London Road. Chester had made his fortune in the mining industry, and although he'd died in 1916, the mansion had remained inhabited by the Congdon family until the infamous murder of Chester and Clara's daughter, Elizabeth Congdon, and her nurse in 1977. Elizabeth's adopted daughter, Marjorie Congdon, and her husband, Roger Caldwell, had been arrested for the murders, although Marjorie Congdon was later acquitted.

Edna was observing the mansion and grounds as they drove past. "Such a sad ending for a magnificent place."

"You mean the murders, or the fact that Glensheen is now a museum?"

"The murders, of course," Edna said. "I can well understand why the family gave the property to the State of Minnesota."

"I've read about the case in depth," Brie said.

"I can imagine it would fascinate any homicide detective."

"I'll tell you, Mom, if you ever want to read a profile of a first-class sociopath, that's the case to study," Brie said. "Marjorie Congdon may have been acquitted, but there's little doubt that she was the driving force behind the murders."

"Well, I don't know everything about the case, but I know that Marjorie Congdon's life of crime didn't end with the death of her famous mother."

"She was suspected of murders, arson, and various kinds of fraud for decades after the murders at Glensheen mansion. And you know what?"

"What?" Edna asked.

"As of 2018, she was still out there. And old age hasn't reformed her. She was convicted of trying to steal funds from another resident at the assisted living home where she resided."

"I've read that a sociopath can never be cured or reformed," Edna said.

"That's the official thinking on the matter," Brie said. "Best to stay far away from anyone with those tendencies."

"I'll remember that, dear." Edna paused and studied Brie. "I suppose you speak from experience."

"Being a cop, I've met my fair share of them. But that's enough of this glum discussion, Mom."

"Okay. Let's talk about that spaetzle. How would you like to make some for dinner?"

"That'd be great. I can learn the recipe." Old Mrs. Hoffmeister, their neighbor in St. Paul when Brie was growing up, had taught Edna how to make authentic German spaetzle—tiny dumplings made from thick dough and cooked in boiling water.

"But don't we need that little contraption you used to make the spaetzle?" Brie asked.

"Now, don't get too excited, but I brought that little contraption along. It's called a spaetzle maker. Clever, eh?"

"Clever." Brie smiled.

"We'll need to pick up some flour and eggs, though."

"We can grab those on the way up the shore."

At the end of London Road, near Kitchi Gamme Park, Highway 61 bent off to the left. This short piece of expressway was the quick route to Two Harbors, thirty miles away. But the Scenic Lakeshore Drive to the right was, well, just what its name implied—very scenic. Brie didn't hesitate. She turned right. She'd seen lots of different names on various maps for this piece of two-lane road: Old Highway 61, Northshore Drive, and Congdon Boulevard. None of that mattered. Everyone referred to it as the scenic route. It terminated at Two Harbors just like the expressway did, but the saying "It's not about the destination, it's about the journey" best defined why a traveler might choose one over the other. Mighty Superior lay so close in places it felt like one could almost reach out the window and dip up a cup of its cold, clear essence.

Furthermore, there was only one way to get to Russ Kendall's Smoke House. and that was via the scenic route. Russ Kendall's was one of those pilgrimage spots on the North Shore. Once you'd been converted to Russ's smoked fish, you were going back, period.

Chapter 3

Above Duluth and Two Harbors, the scenery got seriously beautiful. Soaring cliffs and deep forests and always, just to their right, laid out to the south and east, the stunning sapphire presence of Lake Superior. Highway 61 ran like a fine dark ribbon through dense pine that crowded up to the road's edge.

Up, up the road climbed through glacial topography, past historic Split Rock Lighthouse into the ancient remnants of the Sawtooth Mountains. Scenic 61 carved its way through vast cliffs of basalt and limestone where the tilt of the bedrock lay nearly vertical—a sign of the extreme height of the ancient primordial mountains that had stretched from here on up across Canada.

The names of the rivers told the tale of a land stewarded by the indigenous peoples. Names like Crow, Encampment, Gooseberry, Split Rock, Beaver, Manitou, Caribou. And later, as their hold over their native lands began to slip away, the names told that story as well. Names like Cross and Temperance and Baptism.

One hour above Two Harbors, they crossed the Temperance River that flows with a vengeance down through its ancient volcanic gorge, bisecting Temperance River State Park. Just beyond the park, they entered the Superior National Forest. The scenic highway ran as much east as north, working its way toward the Canadian border. Brie was struck by the thought that the north shore of Superior was nearly a replica for the coast of Maine. Lay one map over the other and the similarity would be surprising. Same angle of ascent—east by north—same rocky coastline, Canadians to the north and cold blue water stretching away to the horizon. There was no question in her mind that Maine's likeness to this part of her native state was another reason she felt so at home there.

They passed through the tiny village of Tofte, and now the Sawtooth Mountains with their jagged tops stretched away across the northern horizon like the teeth of some giant's cross-cut saw, and Superior sprawled out to the south and east, content in its dominance over all things northern Minnesota.

"So, did you want to do anything today, Mom? Or just get settled into the cabin?"

"Would you mind if we made it a low-key day? I've been traveling a lot the past few days, and I'll admit to feeling a little ragged around the edges."

"That's fine, Mom. We'll get unpacked and take a walk down by the shore. After dinner, I'll build a fire."

"That sounds perfect," Edna said.

They fell silent again, watching the beauties of the North Shore stream by. Autumn colors were still in play along the shore, where the thermal effects of the big lake kept the temperature consistently ten degrees warmer in fall and winter. The reds of the oak and maple had faded, but fiery sumac still blazed among brown and tan grasses that had died off for the season. Deep green pine played a counterpoint to tall, slender white birch. The birch still held tight to their yellow leaves, and when the wind moved through the forest and the late October sun struck them, those leaves shimmered like gold coins.

"In your letters—and by the way, Brie, it's so nice to receive an actual letter occasionally," Edna said.

"Just doing my part to preserve a lost world, Mom. One where everything isn't delivered in sound bites and acronyms."

There was a part of Brie that longed for the simplicity of another time. The kind of simplicity and peace that seemed lost in today's frenetic, neurotic world. She wondered how many other cops had these kinds of escapist longings.

Edna was talking again. "You mentioned working with the Maine State Police and that you liked the people you worked with."

"I do. It's different from the Minneapolis PD."

"How so?

"Well, the biggest difference is that the Maine State Police are not just troopers. The Major Crimes Unit is the investigating body for homicides throughout the state, including Maine's islands. The Portland and Bangor Police Departments also investigate homicides, but those are the only three agencies in the state that conduct homicide investigations.

"I first became involved with the Maine State Police when I investigated a murder aboard ship while we were anchored off a remote island during a gale in May. There's no police presence on the islands in Maine, and in visiting the islands aboard *Maine Wind* I've had cause to be drawn into several cases throughout the season. A funny thing seems to happen when you're the only one around who resembles law enforcement."

"I can well imagine that," Edna said. "But there has to be some form of police on the islands. Sheriffs maybe?"

"Nope. Well, I take that back. I know of one exception. There's a Knox County Sheriff stationed on Vinalhaven Island. That island has a year-round population around eleven hundred, and it goes much higher in the summer."

"But what do they do?" Edna asked. "I mean on the other islands?"

"They police themselves. And believe me, Mom, they like it that way. Many of those islands off the coast are a world apart. The old timers still call it 'Going to America' when they board a ferry for the mainland."

Edna laughed at that.

"It's a different kind of place, Mom. I'm not telling you anything, though. Dad was a Mainer, for heaven's sake. You've been there plenty of times while we were growing up, when we used to visit Granny Beaumont."

"That's true," Edna said. "But we never visited the islands. Except for that one trip to Monhegan when you were twelve."

"I remember that. I got sick on the ferry. So anyway, like I was saying, Mom, someone goes missing from one of these islands, and you happen to be there, and you're a cop. It's easy to be drawn in. That's what happened in May and again in July, and it brought me in contact with the Maine State Police. Lieutenant Dent Fenton of the Major Crimes Unit became aware of the work I had done in those cases. Then in August, we anchored in Tucker Harbor, away down East near the Bay of Fundy. During a hike ashore, we found a body in the woods. Grisly scene. Throat slashed."

Edna cringed, and Brie caught the reaction with her peripheral vision.

"Sorry, Mom."

"That's all right. I know it's the world you have to deal with."

"Tucker Harbor is a coastal village on the mainland. The county sheriffs were the first responders, but the Maine State Police were also called in because the cause of death was undetermined. Anyway, that was the case that cemented my relationship with the Maine State Police. Lieutenant Dent Fenton asked if I would work the case with them, and I was deputized. Detective Marty Dupuis and I took the lead in the investigation and reported back to Dent Fenton. It was that case that kept me from attending Robert's funeral."

"It couldn't be helped," Edna said.

"I'll tell you, Mom, in our wildest dreams, none of us could ever have guessed where that case would lead."

They had just passed the turn for Lutsen Mountains, the premier ski area in the Midwest and the oldest resort in Minnesota. Lutsen was established in 1885 by Charles Axel Nelson, a Swedish immigrant who rented rooms to pioneers. Over 130 years, generations of Nelsons had built Lutsen into a small kingdom.

"Clearview Store is coming up soon," Brie said. "We'll stop there and get some supplies for meals." They had decided not to worry about packing food since they'd both just gotten back to the cities.

"They should have everything we need," Edna said.

A few miles up the road, Brie turned left. Built in the 1930s, Clearview General Store and a small group of businesses were strung together by an old-fashioned, covered boardwalk and comprised the heart of Lutsen village, or "our downtown," as the locals called it. Tiny Lutsen Post Office anchored the right-hand side of the walk next to the general store, and there was a small coffee house down toward the other end.

Brie parked in front of the boardwalk. As she got out of the Jeep, a beige Toyota sailed by on the highway. Brie noted the similarity to the car she'd seen behind them below Duluth. The sun reflected off the driver's side window, making it impossible to see the person behind the wheel. *There are a million beige Toyotas out there,* she told herself. *Don't go looking for trouble.* But the detective in her quickly disregarded that advice.

She and Edna headed into the store. The small checkout counter sat to the right of the door. There were several short rows of canned and dry goods, and a row of coolers along the back of the store held the perishables. Brie and Edna each picked up a basket and started down one of the aisles. They gathered up oatmeal, eggs, and coffee for breakfast, lunch meat and bread, a couple of steaks for dinner plus the makings of a salad, and the flour and milk they would need for the spaetzle.

The store stocked a small selection of wine, and they selected a bottle of pinot noir. They surveyed their baskets, making sure they had all the staples. Up at the register they added a couple of candy bars to the mix. The clerk rang everything up and bagged the groceries. Edna insisted on paying for everything, and she and Brie gathered up the bags, thanked the clerk, and headed outside. The wind had picked up, and it buffeted them as they made for the Jeep and tucked the groceries into the hatch.

"How about some coffee, Mom?"

"That sounds great." Edna rubbed her hands together, either in anticipation or to warm them up. Brie wasn't sure which. They walked down the boardwalk to the coffee house. Inside they ordered up a pair of mocha lattés. Brie paid for the brews, and they chatted with the barista while they waited for their order.

"Up for the week?" asked the girl, whose nametag read Sonia.

"That's right," Edna said. "Today's Monday. We're heading back on Sunday."

The girl studied Edna for a moment. "So you weren't in here yesterday?"

"Nope," Edna said. "Just drove up from the cities today."

"Huh. There was a woman in here yesterday, could have been your twin," Sonia said.

"Well, they say everyone has a double out there. What do they call it?"

"A doppelganger?" Sonia offered.

"Sounds like something from a horror movie," Edna said.

"You know, it does." Sonia giggled at that.

"I'm vacationing with my beautiful daughter here." Edna put an arm around Brie's waist and gave her a squeeze.

"Ah, Mom," Brie said and suddenly felt sixteen again. But she marked the loveliness of the moment, which she wouldn't have done at sixteen.

"Well, you two sure look like mother and daughter," Sonia said. She smiled at Edna. "Two beauties."

"That's very kind. Thank you, dear," Edna said.

The lattés arrived in front of them, and Brie and Edna each took a sip and let out a simultaneous "Ahhh."

"So, doing any hiking while you're up North?" the dark-eyed Sonia asked.

"You bet," Brie said. "One day we're planning to drive up to Grand Portage State Park on the border. See the high falls on the Pigeon River. Mom hasn't been up there in quite a few years."

"Oh, you have to go. The high falls are spectacular this year, what with all the rain we've had," Sonia said.

"Otherwise we'll be hiking some of the parks closer by. Temperance, Tettagouche, Split Rock," Edna said.

"Well, enjoy the beautiful weather. This time of year it can turn on a dime."

"We will, and thanks for your hospitality," Edna said.

"Stop in again."

"I think you can count on that," Brie said. She and Edna were big into their coffee, and Brie, in her months aboard *Maine Wind,* had pretty much doubled down on the habit. Coffee, not rum, was the poison of choice on the North Atlantic. At least aboard their ship.

They headed out the door and back to their car for the last short leg of their trip. The cabin awaited.

Chapter 4

The cabin lay another ten miles north by east. Brie and Edna sipped their coffee contentedly as the final miles ticked by. To the west of Highway 61, the sky had become overcast, but a deep blue firmament still held forth over the lake, as if the gods had drawn some line of demarcation that allowed Superior to make its own weather. And in fact, this was the case. The big lake *was* a weather maker and would often keep fronts and weather systems at bay as its great watery presence cooled the air in summer and, conversely, warmed it in fall and winter. So the temperature a mile or two inland was consistently ten degrees warmer or cooler than the terrain along the shore. On the ridge above the town of Grand Marais, this thermal effect allowed oaks and maples to flourish, hanging onto their red and orange leaves well into October.

They started down a long incline, and Edna immediately said, "There's the sign."

Partway down the hill, Brie began to brake in preparation for the ninety-degree turn onto the gravel road. They made the turn and proceeded slowly, stopping at an intersecting gravel road. Across the road a carved wood sign read "Cedar Falls Cabins." The road wound down through a spruce forest and dead-ended at the site of four log cabins, each secluded in its own little world of cedar and spruce trees. An extra spur of gravel ran down to their cabin, which sat on a rocky promontory above the lake—so close to the water that when the gales pounded in, the breakers would send spray onto the cabin windows.

"Well, here we are," Brie said. "Welcome to heaven."

"You can say that again."

They opened the doors of the Jeep and heard the lake thundering onto the shore below the cabin and booming up into the rocky cove where Cedar Creek emptied into the lake.

"Let's go see the lake," Edna said.

She and Brie scrambled down the narrow, rocky trail below the cabin. Spruce, cedar, and mountain ash grew around the cabin, and small ground plants and shrubs—columbine, devil's paintbrush, and mountain maple—held their own down to the breaker line that lay fifty or sixty feet from the lake. Beyond that only moss and lichen survived out on the smooth shelf rock where the waves rolled in. Brie turned up her collar, and Edna pulled the hood of her jacket up and snapped it and fished a pair of gloves out of her pocket.

Breakers curled in, turquoise in the late afternoon sun, and the air was filled with their booming as they rushed up into the two rocky coves that lay at either end of the property. Farther back from the lake, the rocks bore a more chiseled appearance. But their jagged character gave way to smooth, rounded surfaces near the water's edge, where thousands of years of wave action had sculpted their watery contours.

Brie and Edna climbed up and down the rolling contours of the shoreline, occasionally jumping over a small rivulet that traversed the rock on its way to the lake. Brie was amazed at how nimble her mom was for her age. She had Brie's slender, wiry frame and had always been athletic. Nonetheless, Brie worried about her being alone again. The Fates had not dealt Edna an easy hand.

The air smelled of moist cedar, and the noise of the lake was so great that, to communicate, they had to get close to each other. Edna leaned in toward Brie. "The beauty and wildness of it takes your breath away."

"I always carry this place with me in my mind and heart. And every time I come here, it's just as magnificent and untamed as I remember. It never disappoints."

"It's only humans that disappoint. Never nature," Edna said. "And like all the truly wondrous places, this one seems to constantly outstrip itself in beauty."

They turned and walked back toward the cabin, taking a short detour to stand on the rocky promontory that overlooked the cove where Cedar Creek rushed down its black basalt gorge and emptied into Lake Superior. The cove was an agate hunter's haven. The lake constantly turned over the contents of the shore and spit up new pickings with each passing storm. This one small cove had offered up countless treasures over the years, but there was no venturing down there today. With the lake running so high, the rocky beach had been completely consumed by the waves.

The sun was dipping toward the distant hills of the Sawtooth range off to the southwest as Brie and Edna headed back toward the cabin to unload the car and make dinner. Brie noticed a car pulled up next to the first cabin down at the far end of the property. Smoke curled from the chimney to disperse in the wind, and she smelled the sharp tang of a wood fire. The other two cabins appeared to be unoccupied.

They got their bags and the groceries out of the Jeep and headed up onto the covered porch that ran alongside the cabin. The door was unlocked, and they carried everything inside. Brie turned on the overhead light in the kitchen and put the bag of groceries on the counter. Beyond the small kitchen a living room with big windows gave an unobstructed view of Superior to the south. On the west side of the room the windows looked out over the cove where Cedar Creek emptied into the lake. Brie walked to the front window. Storm clouds were advancing over the lake from the north, and the wind outside was picking up—starting to keen through the pine.

She turned from the window. "Good night for a fire, Mom."

At the back of the living room a rustic fieldstone fireplace with a raised hearth sat at an angle, filling the corner of the room. The perfectly fitted stonework covered the sides and front of the fireplace all the way to the roofline. Brie knew this fireplace well. It had a good draft, and with the wind tonight, they'd have a roaring fire going in no time. But first things first. She picked up her duffel and headed down the hall.

There were two small bedrooms at the back of the cabin, one on the left and one to the right. Edna had taken the first bedroom, where she always slept when they were here. Her window looked out over the cove, and when the lake was in a calmer mood, one could hear the creek burbling down through the gorge. Depending on the season and the amount of rain, the creek could be more like a small river, running swift and fast and dropping over a series of falls a short ways upstream from its mouth.

Edna was at the bedroom window, taking in nature's show beyond the glass. Brie stopped in the hall and studied her for a moment, and her heart filled up, happy to have this time with her mom. Theirs was a close relationship, fraught with none of the angst that plagued so many mothers and daughters. No one supported her more than her mom, but Edna also had a way of letting her figure out her own life. Never pressing her too much about matters of the heart.

Brie took the bedroom across from Edna's. She set her duffel on the double bed, took out her clothes, and put them in the dresser drawers. It took all of two minutes to stow her extra jeans, tops, underwear, and socks. She left her pajamas on the bed, took off her jacket and hung it on a hook on the back of the door. She had left a pink cashmere sweater on the bed, and she pulled this over her head for an extra layer of warmth.

She found Edna in the kitchen, putting the groceries in the fridge. She had left the eggs, flour, and milk on the counter. "Ready to get started on that spaetzle?" she asked.

"Sure," Brie said. "But maybe I should get the coals going in the grill for the steaks. It'll take them about twenty minutes to be ready."

"Good idea," Edna said. "I'll get a pot of boiling water started for the spaetzle."

"Maybe we should take the steaks out and let them warm up a bit," Brie said.

Edna smiled. "You seem to have developed some cooking confidence."

Brie laughed. She was the queen of take-out and frozen dinners, if ever there had been one. "It's all George's fault," she said.

"The cook on the *Maine Wind*?" Edna asked.

"Yup. He's mended my evil ways and taught me that cooking isn't really all that intimidating."

"Well, I tried to do that," Edna said.

"I know, Mom, and I used to like to help you in the kitchen, but in my adult life, I've kept such weird hours with my job . . ." She didn't finish the thought.

"Well, and almost nobody cooks that way for themselves. We cook for others."

"Isn't that the truth," Brie said rhetorically. "George never sails with a mess mate, so I got the chance to help him in the galley regularly. Over my five months aboard, I completely lost my fear of food prep."

"And you said you cook everything on a woodstove," Edna said. "I find that amazing."

Brie laughed. "At first, *I* found it plenty dangerous. You know, wooden ship, woodstove. Seems ill-advised, right? But it's not. It's a very controlled environment, and the cooks on the ships really know what they're doing with those stoves. And the food? Amazing. You wouldn't believe it, Mom. Everything homemade—breads, pastries, pies. You name it."

Edna shook her head in amazement. "It's nice to see you so passionate about something other than your police work," she said.

"You know, Mom, in a certain way I think that ship saved my life. I was in bad shape when I went to Maine, and I found a family."

"Sounds like you found more than that." Edna smiled at her. "But you scoot out and start those coals. I have to teach you how to make the spaetzle so you can show George the next time you see him." She opened a drawer to her right and handed Brie a box of matches.

Brie headed out the door, feeling more at peace than she had the last few days. Just talking about the ship and her life there brought deep happiness. She found a bag of charcoal in the corner of the porch and carried it and the small Weber grill off the porch and set them down on the gravel driveway. She poured in the briquettes, squeezed on a little lighter fluid, and struck a match to light the charcoal. She stood there until the flames had died down and the briquettes started to smolder, then headed back inside.

In the kitchen, Edna had pulled a large crockery bowl out of one of the cupboards. She handed Brie an apron she'd found in one of the drawers. "You're going to do the whole thing," she said. "That way you'll remember."

"Okay," Brie said. She pulled the apron over her head and tied it behind her back. The water was just starting to boil, and the lid was making little ratta-tat-tat noises as it released its steam.

Edna shut off the fire under the pot. "We're not ready for that yet," she said.

"So where do I begin?" Brie asked.

"Start by measuring your dry ingredients into the bowl."

At Edna's direction, Brie measured out flour, salt and pepper, and some nutmeg that Edna had found in the spice cabinet above the counter.

"Now crack two eggs in this bowl, beat them up, and measure out a quarter cup of milk. That's everything."

"Really?" Brie said. "That's it?"

"That's it."

Brie cracked the eggs and whipped them up with the milk and, at Edna's direction, stirred them into the flour until the dough formed.

Edna brought the water back to a boil and put the spaetzle maker on top of the pot. It looked like a flat grater with large holes, with a small square box attached to the top. The box on top slid back and forth.

"We used to roll the spaetzle by hand when we were kids," Brie said.

"Old Mrs. Hoffmeister, our German neighbor who taught me how to make this when I was first married, thought the only proper way to make spaetzle was by hand. And it was a good activity for you kids. But this little machine keeps the dumplings nice and light."

Brie scooped the dough into the spaetzle maker and slid the box back and forth so the dough fell into the water in small pieces. Edna melted butter and chopped parsley to put on top. In just a couple of minutes the spaetzle was cooked. Brie let Edna take over and headed out the door with the plate of steaks. The coals were ready, and she put the steaks on the grill.

She noted the lights were on in the cabin down by the creek, and she could see a man moving around inside the cabin. She wondered if he was a fisherman. Cedar Creek had some deep pools just upstream from the mouth and was rich with trout. She had noted over the years that fishermen liked to stay in that particular cabin and would be out early and late fly fishing in the creek.

After a couple of minutes, she turned the steaks and went back inside. The dining table sat in the front corner of the living room right by the windows. Edna had set two places with stoneware dishes and had lit a candle in the center of the table. Brie found the corkscrew and opened the bottle of pinot noir they had bought and set it on the table with some wine glasses. The spaetzle was in a covered serving dish, staying warm on the back of the stove. Brie lifted the cover and sniffed. The creamy yellow dumplings glistened with the butter and parsley. She smiled and put the lid back on.

"There's a platter warming in the oven for the steaks," Edna called out.

Brie put on a hot mitt, got the platter out of the oven, and headed outside to get the steaks. She flipped on the porch light as she went out the door. It was nearly dark. When night descended in this place, it meant a kind of total darkness few city folk could imagine. On a clear night with a moon, the great lake would become so bright one could nearly read by the light. But tonight was overcast. The darkness this night would be absolute.

The thought *Anything could happen* ran through her mind, accompanied by a chill that made its way down her spine. In a reflexive cop move, she glanced around the terrain. They were definitely off the map. She pulled out her cell phone. No bars. She wasn't surprised. She never got reception here. Nor was there any such thing as wi-fi. And no phone in the cabin. She shook off the feeling. She had always felt safe here. Safer than almost anywhere else. Of course, that was before her partner Phil had been killed on a dark and moonless night. But she reminded herself that that had happened in the heart of Minneapolis in a drug-riddled neighborhood, not in the north woods.

It was another reason she loved the ocean, though. Out there, nothing but a big sea could sneak up on you. There was a kind of safety about it, ironically enough. Safety from the wrong kind of humanity. *At least in Maine waters,* she thought. *No murderous pirates in Maine waters.* The same could not be said for the oceans in certain other parts of the world.

She put the steaks on the platter, covered the grill and headed back inside.

Chapter 5

Edna had put together a simple salad and was tossing it with some Italian dressing. Brie set the steaks on the table and poured two glasses of wine. Edna brought the salad, and they plated it up and started eating it while the steaks rested.

"What should we do tomorrow?" Edna asked as they munched their salads.

Brie smiled. "I have a surprise for you, Mom. I chartered a sailboat in Silver Bay for a day of sailing. I did a little research online and found a guy who still has his boat docked in the marina there. He does charters, and I arranged to have him take us out, weather permitting. We board at Silver Bay Marina tomorrow morning at ten-thirty."

Edna set her fork down. "That's wonderful, Brie. I haven't been sailing in many years. Will it be just us aboard?"

"Yup. I told the captain I had crewed on *Maine Wind* the past five months and would be happy to help if needed."

Edna's eyes sparked with excitement. "Tell me about the boat."

"It's a brand new Marlow Hunter 40. I read up on the model before I booked the sail. She's quick to the helm and will make ten knots in a fresh breeze."

"That's fast for a cruiser," Edna said.

"These aren't the Hunters of old. The company was sold and the boats redesigned for more stability when sailing to weather."

"Well, let's hope the *weather* cooperates," Edna said. "The lake is looking pretty wild tonight."

"But that can change quickly. We'll hope the clouds blow over and we have fair sailing tomorrow."

Edna raised her glass. "To tomorrow then."

They clinked glasses, and Brie served a steak onto each plate while Edna dished up the spaetzle. Then they dug in. Brie started with the spaetzle. "It's delicious, Mom. Every bit as good as I remembered."

"Well, now that you know how, you can make it any time," Edna said.

The steaks were a perfect medium rare, and they lingered over their meat and wine and spaetzle, watching the waves roll in and the light slowly fade to gold out over the lake. Forty minutes later they cleared the table, and while Edna made coffee and cleaned up in the kitchen, Brie laid a fire in the fireplace. Then they settled down in two comfortable rocking chairs in front of the fire. The chairs had wide wooden arms, and their dark green upholstery perfectly fit the room's rustic feel.

Edna placed mugs of coffee on the table between the rockers and pulled out a small bundle of knitting she was working on. "Helps me focus on the present," she said. "I haven't knitted in years, but this has been good therapy since Robert died."

Brie pulled her legs up in the big chair and folded them Indian-style. She picked up her mug of coffee and cradled it in her hands, feeling the warmth. For a time the only sound was the crackling of the birch log fire and the click of Edna's knitting needles. And outside, the booming of waves on rock and the whispering of wind around the eaves.

After a while, Edna said, "I'd like to know more about John, if you're willing to tell me."

"Sure, Mom. There's nothing to hide. He's a good, hard-working man with a deep love for the sea and his ship."

"You know you'll always be in competition with that ship, don't you?"

Brie sighed. "I don't see it that way, Mom. It doesn't have to be a competition. Maybe it was with Dad. I remember the financial stress that keeping the sailboat up used to cause, but this is different. The sea and that ship are John's living. It's not a hobby."

"Well, maybe that's true," Edna said. "But do you not find it at all ironic that you have ended up with a Maine sea captain?"

Brie sat silent for a moment. How, in all the months she had spent in Maine forging a relationship with John DuLac and his ship, had she not considered the parallels to her father?

"Dad was a sailor and a Mainer by birth," she finally mumbled.

Edna laughed. "And you're just now thinking about that?"

"Well, you know, Mom, I didn't go to Maine looking for a sea captain or a job. It all just kind of happened. It was because of my police work that I went there, and it was because of police work that I ended up staying aboard *Maine Wind*. Now, I have to admit I'm drawn to the sea, and that has a lot to do with Dad, obviously. And obviously I went to Maine because I know the place and because Granny Beaumont is still there." But she had to ask herself how she, a cop steeped in the psychology of human action and interaction, could have overlooked the obvious parallels. Was she in fact looking for the father she had lost at twenty? Was that why she sometimes felt like she had known John forever?

Edna seemed to sense her consternation and judiciously changed the subject. "How's Grandma Nellie doing?"

Nellie Beaumont was Brie's paternal grandmother who lived in Cherryfield, Maine. A lovely, kind, youthful woman of eighty-five, she still gardened and cooked and walked three miles every day.

"I visited Granny three times this summer," Brie said. "Once when I first got to Maine, and two more times when I had a day off during the sailing season. She seems as spry as ever. Uncle Pete checks in on her every couple of days." Uncle Pete was the bachelor uncle—her dad's brother who had never married and still lived in Cherryfield, where Brie's dad had grown up.

Tom Beaumont had left there at eighteen to attend the University of Minnesota, where he had majored in geology and met and married Edna Johansson. After college he had worked as a field geologist for Northshore Mining, one of the largest iron mining companies in Minnesota. He had spent a lot of time away from home on the iron range in northern Minnesota.

Being from Maine, Tom Beaumont had been drawn to Lake Superior like a moth to a flame. Eventually he and Edna had managed to purchase a cruising sailboat that the family kept in the marina in Duluth. That was where Brie had gotten her first taste of blue water sailing. She sat silently for a time, thinking about those years, staring deep into the fire as if it were some portal to the past. Thinking about her dad and her mom, the joys and struggles they'd had.

"It must have been hard having Dad gone so much. Having to raise us kids by yourself much of the time."

Edna put her knitting in her lap and looked at Brie. "Well, you know it somehow worked out, as things do. You kids and I became such a unit, and you know, I think that helped when your dad died so young. We were already used to weathering the storms together. You three always helped me get through the rough patches.

"But your dad wasn't gone all the time, Brie. During the winter he often worked on research at the university."

"I remember that," Brie said. "Those were nice times. Everyone at home together. Maybe that's why winter has always been my favorite season."

"Maybe it will be summer from now on," Edna said. "Hard to sail *Maine Wind* in winter."

Brie smiled at that, but after a moment her face became serious. "John told me that if I move to Maine, it can't be because of him."

"Huh," was all Edna said.

"I asked him what would be so wrong with that."

"And what did he say?" Edna asked.

"That I might come to regret it. What do you make of that, Mom?"

"He doesn't want to feel responsible if things don't go well," Edna said.

"Well, seems to me that how things go depends a lot on whether you believe life just happens to you or you make it happen," Brie said.

"Which do you think he believes?"

"I don't know. For me, I had always believed you make your life. But then when Phil was shot and killed and I nearly died, I began to question all of that. It's taken me a long time to work my way back around to what I used to believe. And I'm not there yet, but closer than I was a year ago."

"John's almost forty, isn't he?

"He turns forty in a few weeks," Brie said.

"I think commitment gets scarier the older one gets," Edna said. "We tend to think a lot more about the ramifications instead of just diving in."

"John had a tough go of it as a kid," Brie said. "His mom had MS, and his dad died when he was sixteen. John quit school and went to work at the Bath Iron Works, where they build the Navy ships. He's told me it was no place for a kid his age, but his dad had worked there, and he was able to get a job that paid enough to support his mom."

"Well, that certainly explains a lot," Edna said. "Poor guy. He must have felt completely overwhelmed. One minute he's a kid, and maybe things aren't great but at least he has a mom and a dad. Then the next minute his whole world falls apart, and he's catapulted into a life of crushing responsibilities."

"And he knows his mom will only get worse—that he has no real power."

"It would have been terrifying for a boy that age," Edna said.

"I guess it explains a lot about his fears about us," Brie said. "And then there's the fact that I'm a cop. I have a dangerous job. Maybe he's afraid he'll lose me too."

"Have you asked him that?"

"Not in so many words."

"Maybe you should," Edna said.

Brie got up to stoke the fire. She moved the screen aside and added three good-sized logs to the fire bed. A million sparks flew up the chimney, and the birch bark ignited immediately above the glowing bed of embers.

"So how did John come to be master of the *Maine Wind*?" Edna asked.

"Well, see, that was the silver lining—the other side of the coin, so to speak. At the Bath Iron Works, he met Ben Rutledge, who was a naval architect. Ben must have seen right away what a terrible situation John was in. He took John under his wing—became a mentor to him. You should see them together, Mom. They're like father and son.

"It was Ben who restored *Maine Wind*, and when he retired from the Navy as a middle-aged man, he put her into the windjammer trade up in Camden. Ben had also bought a small boatyard where *Maine Wind* was restored. John went to work for him, learned the ropes, learned the sea. Over time he got his captain's license and eventually became a master mariner and the owner of the *Maine Wind*."

"It's a wonderful story, Brie. Now I feel like I know your young man a bit. And I can't help but like him."

"He's not so young though, Mom."

"Well, age is relative, you know. To me he's young," Edna said. "And what about John's mother? Is she still alive?"

"No, she died when he was thirty-three."

"Wow," Edna said. "So he hasn't had very many carefree years, has he?"

"Would you like to see a picture of him?"

"You bet."

Brie scrolled through some pictures on her phone, stopped at one, and handed the phone to Edna. It was a shot of Brie standing beside John at the helm of *Maine Wind*. She had asked Scott Hogan, the mate, to take the picture as they sailed home on their last voyage.

"You both look so happy, Brie. In fact, you look joyful."

"It was a hard trip, Mom. We were glad to be going home," she said, with a twinkle in her eye.

"Yeah, right," Edna said. "I think there's a little more going on here than that."

Brie just smiled and shrugged. "I guess so."

"He's so handsome."

"He is. It scared me a little at first. I don't always trust guys that are that good looking. But John is so self-effacing, once you get to know him, you barely notice his looks."

Edna burst out laughing at that. "God forbid you should notice those."

Just then the wind sent a big branch onto the roof with a loud thud. Brie jumped.

"Wind's picking up," Edna said, noting her reaction. "Are you okay? Is something troubling you?"

"I'm okay. It's part of PTSD. Since I was shot, I startle more easily, react more to loud noises."

"You sure that's all it is, Brie?"

She stared into the fire for a few moments, deciding whether or not to tell Edna about the letters she'd received.

"I'm sure, Mom," she finally said.

Edna studied her quietly for a few moments. "So why is this decision to move to Maine, to be with John, so hard? You said the two of you love each other. What's really holding you here, Brie?"

Brie let out a long sigh but didn't respond.

"Is it the fact that your partner's murder was never solved? Is that why you feel you can't leave?"

"I did leave, Mom. I've just been gone for six months."

Edna gave her the look that only a mother can give her offspring. A look that held wisdom, authority, understanding, but a look that also said *I won't be trifled with.*

Brie regarded Edna for a moment in silence before turning back to the fire. She'd had only nightmare-like flashbacks of that night, up to the point when the shot had been fired. Beyond that she remembered nothing. By the time backup had gotten there, the shooter was long gone. Detective Phil Thatcher was dead, and her life hung by a thread.

While she had lain in the hospital, clinging to life, the case of Phil's murder had slowly gone cold. She wondered now, if the case had been solved, what effect that might have had on her psychologically. The fact that her partner had died and no one had been brought to justice tormented Brie immeasurably and undoubtedly contributed to the PTSD she battled. Maybe Edna was right. Maybe decisions now would be easier if the facts and evidence surrounding Phil's death had not been so murky.

The property where Phil Thatcher was shot had been in foreclosure, but it was a known drug house. Ultimately it was thought that Brie and Phil had interrupted a robbery—some perp looking for drugs or money hidden at that address. If that was the case, it left a field of suspects as impossibly wide and numerous as the gang members who trafficked drugs in that part of Minneapolis. The department had tirelessly worked their small army of CIs—confidential informants—but to no avail. In the end the case had gone cold, but not as cold as the stone Brie carried in her heart—the truth that her colleagues in Homicide could not crack this most important of cases.

Edna had gone back to her knitting. Brie set aside her regrets for the time being, got up and went to retrieve a book from her duffel bag. She came back out and curled up with it in the rocker. They stayed there for a couple more hours, communing in silence, till the fire burned down and Edna had a serious attack of yawning.

"We should hit the sack, Mom. If the weather's good tomorrow, we need to leave here by nine-thirty to get to Silver Bay in time to board the sailboat."

"That's all the convincing I need." Edna tucked her knitting into its bag, gave Brie a hug, and headed to her bedroom.

Brie poked around at the fire, making sure the embers were out. She put the screen across the fireplace, checked the front door and headed for bed.

Later in the night, she woke to the sound of a cedar bough softly brushing against the roof, like a ghost walking through her dreams. A benevolent ghost, perhaps, one come to free her from the nightmares she sensed she had been having. For a while she lay there, listening to the soft sound on the roof, using it to sweep away her concerns, and eventually she drifted back into a deep, dreamless sleep.

Chapter 6

Brie woke at seven, showered, and put the oatmeal on to cook. By 9:30 she and Edna were heading down the road toward Silver Bay. It took the better part of an hour to get there from the cabin. The sun was out, and the diamond blue waters of Lake Superior sparkled with a million facets. Superior, the great weather maker, had conjured up a perfect day for them to go sailing.

At 10:20 they parked the Jeep and made their way down a short hill and out one of the docks at Silver Bay Marina. They found *Northern Exposure*, the sailboat Brie had chartered, in its slip near the end of the dock. Brie paused on the starboard side and called out, "Ahoy there."

Within seconds a gray-haired and bearded man stuck his head out the companionway. "You must be Brie Beaumont."

"Permission to come aboard, Skipper."

"Come right ahead. I'm Terrance Weathers."

"Good name for a sailor." Edna extended her hand. "I'm Edna Beaumont, Brie's mom."

"And a sailor, I hear."

"Well, yes. But not for quite a while."

He waved that away. "I'll get you back in the swing of it. You'll be at the helm in no time."

Edna smiled. "That would be glorious."

Weathers had them stow their daypacks in one of the seat lockers topside and then showed them around the boat. *Northern Exposure* was a gorgeous vessel with twin helms, a comfortable, copious cockpit and, below decks, a lovely saloon with an overhead skylight, sleek galley, and small but workable chart table with instrument panel and radio. With the weather today, though, Brie doubted they'd be spending much time below decks.

"I've stocked the fridge for a nice lunch later on," Weathers said. "We'll find a sheltered anchorage along the way."

They headed back topside, and he gave them each a PFD to put on. "I thought with the prevailing winds from the north today, we'd sail up toward Palisade Head and Shovel Point. We'll have to head offshore a ways to pick up the wind, but we can tuck back into calm waters later and anchor for lunch in one of the coves toward the eastern end of Tettagouche State Park."

"Sounds like a great plan," Brie said.

They wasted no time getting underway. Brie let go the bow and stern lines and hopped aboard, and they motored out of the marina east by south, away from shore so they could catch the wind.

"The forecast is for fifteen- to eighteen-knot winds and three- to six-foot seas. But off the windward shore, we won't see that much of a swell," Weathers said.

They motored out for a half mile or so, until they began to catch the offshore breeze. "You want to take her into the wind, and I'll raise sail?" Weathers asked Brie.

"Sure."

Weathers handed the helm over to her and went forward to raise the mainsail. Brie steered to port and *Northern Exposure* responded, heading upwind. She watched the telltales on the mast, and when they were dead into the wind, she held course and Terrance Weathers hauled up the main and then the jib. He made his way back to the helm, and Brie handed off the wheel. They fell off onto their heading, and at the skipper's order, she trimmed the jib by cranking the winch on the starboard side of the cockpit. *Northern Exposure* heeled to starboard and began to pick up speed.

"Nice job," Weathers told her. "You're an able hand."

"Thanks, Skipper," she said. "I used to sail on Superior with my family, but that was years ago. I've learned a lot aboard *Maine Wind* this season and have had a chance to brush up my sailing skills."

"They've done a marvelous thing with that windjammer fleet in Maine," Weathers said. "The preservation of all those historic schooners. Fiberglass is okay and easy maintenance. But there's nothing like a well-designed wooden boat for beauty and seaworthiness."

"Did you know that wooden schooners once plied the waters of Lake Superior?" Edna asked.

"I know that sailing schooners were used in the fur trade and later in the fishing trade in the seventeen and eighteen hundreds," Weathers said. "Eventually steam and motor-powered vessels took over. But the schooners had their heyday on the big lake."

Edna was surveying the shoreline in the distance. "There's Palisade Head." She pointed to the northeast.

"We should be off the headland in about twenty minutes," the skipper said.

Every sailor knows that the wind tends to pick up around 10:30 in the morning, and today was no exception. Their speed had been steadily increasing, and they were now galloping along at 9.5 knots and taking light spray over the starboard bow. Edna produced a navy blue watch cap from her pocket and pulled it on. Brie had given it to her that morning as a gift. The hat had a *Maine Wind* insignia embroidered on it.

Fall color still blazed along the shore in patches of bright red and yellow, and the trunks of the birch stood like bleached bones against an impenetrably blue sky. Off to starboard, Superior sprawled out in cold, cobalt magnificence as far as the eye could see. The offshore breeze carried the scent of pine and cedar that everywhere crowded down to shore's edge. In the distance Palisade Head thrust its sheer cliff face hundreds of feet above the depths of Superior. Within twenty minutes, they reached the waters below the headland.

Palisade Head stands near the western boundary of Tettagouche State Park. Brie had learned about its geologic history from her dad. Formed by a rhyolite lava flow over a billion years ago, Palisade Head had resisted a billion years of erosion and several onslaughts by Ice Age glaciers over the past million years. And while Superior's storms constantly assaulted the cliff face, it had stood largely unchanged for eons.

Terrance Weathers, like all skippers, kept binoculars near the helm.

"May I?" Brie asked.

"Be my guest," Weathers said.

Brie stepped over to port and focused the glasses on Palisade Head—its sheer face and bald dome that rose high above the water. She had been up to the top and knew there was a parking lot and lookout for the public there.

As her glasses came to rest on a person standing atop the headland, she gave a start. He also had binoculars, ones that were trained on them, and for an unsettling moment their gazes met. She noticed he had a scar that ran from his left cheekbone at an angle down to his jaw. He quickly turned and studied the shoreline to the south, but Brie was left with an uneasy feeling and couldn't help thinking about the threatening letters on her table at home and about the car she thought she'd seen on the drive north.

She studied his profile through the binoculars and then his face when he briefly lowered his binoculars and turned his head back in their direction. The thought that she might inadvertently have placed her mother in any kind of danger was exquisitely painful to her. Since the death of her partner, such scenarios held a kind of terrifying sway over her psyche.

She shook off the feeling, though, and scanned the waters around them. They were the only boat out here. Wasn't it normal that tourists up on the headland would be looking out over the water at them? When she turned the glasses back on the headland, the man had moved away from the cliff's edge and out of sight. She watched for a few minutes, but he did not reappear.

Weathers worked *Northern Exposure* a little closer to the shore and brought her onto a reach and encouraged Edna to take the helm. Edna stepped behind the wheel and placed her hands at ten and two and spread her feet for balance. Brie noted the smile that slowly crept onto her face as Edna got comfortable with the feel of the boat.

They sailed along the wild shores of Tettagouche State Park. Sheer cliffs were punctuated by sea caves, whose dark and mysterious mouths beckoned, and by occasional rocky coves. Brie lifted the glasses and studied the shore. A family of hikers made their way northeast along the trail heading up toward the end of the point.

They sailed past Shovel Point, keeping the headland off their port beam. Brilliant turquoise-colored water flanked the eastern side of the headland.

"Shovel Point is known for its disjunct plant communities," Weathers said.

"What does that mean?" Brie asked.

"Disjunct means disjoined. They're arctic plant populations that are relics of the Wisconsin Glaciation and have somehow survived for thousands of years in the cold lake-supported microclimate."

"I've seen ligonberries growing up there."

"A good example of an arctic tundra species," he said.

The wind remained steady, and a few miles beyond Shovel Point they anchored in a small, secluded bay for lunch. Terrance Weathers went below and heated up a pot of wild rice soup. He had procured hearty ham and Swiss cheese sandwiches on rye from a deli along the shore. Brie and Edna helped get everything plated up and carried lunch topside, while the skipper started a hot pot of coffee.

After lunch they set their course on an arc southwest that would take them below Silver Bay to view Split Rock Lighthouse from the water. Weathers handed the helm off to Brie, and with the wind clocking at 20 knots, they reached the waters below Split Rock Lighthouse by two-thirty. Brie and Edna got out their cameras to capture the scene.

The lighthouse, which was built in 1909 to place a much-needed beacon along the perilous north shore of Lake Superior, has always been known for its starkly beautiful setting atop a sheer 130-foot cliff. On this October day, its yellow brick exterior glowed gold in the sun against a field of blue sky and water. Brie studied the lighthouse with its unusual octagonal shape and picturesque windows.

"As you must know, Lake Superior is known for its gales, and particularly its November gales," Terrance Weathers said. "But the storm that hit in November of 1905, called the Mataafa Blow after the *SS Mataafa* that sank during its fury, was maybe the greatest of the gales. In the end the hurricane-force storm claimed twenty-eight ships, most of them along the dark and frigid north shore of Superior between Duluth and Port Arthur, Ontario. The U.S. Congress was finally forced to allocate funds for this much-needed lighthouse."

"As I recall, the pressure to act came from the Pittsburgh Steamship Company—the shipping arm of the U.S. Steel Corporation—that owned some of those vessels," Edna said.

"Huh. That sounds about right," Brie said. "When the big boys lose money, then something finally gets done."

"Sadly, that's the way the world rolls," Weathers said. "The value of human life juxtaposed with the dollar. Mariners were easily replaced, but ships and iron ore sunk to the depths of Superior . . . well, that's another kind of motivation." He studied the light. "There were no roads along the north shore when the light was built. So everything needed for construction had to be brought by water and hauled up the cliff you see there. A true feat of human ingenuity."

They spent some time photographing the historic lighthouse—arguably Minnesota's most famous landmark—and then Captain Weathers set course back to Silver Bay. Weathers once again offered to let either Edna or Brie take the helm, but they said they were good and went forward to sit in the bow and enjoy the sailing.

By three-thirty, they were entering the marina. They tied off in the slip, and Brie and Edna stepped off the boat onto the dock and thanked Captain Weathers for the wonderful day on the water.

"I hope you'll come aboard again," he said.

"We'll plan to do that," Brie said.

With that she and Edna headed up the hill toward their car. Brie took her phone out and saw that she had reception. She thought about calling John. She hadn't talked to him since yesterday morning, before she and Edna had left Minneapolis. But it had been a long day, and she knew Edna was probably eager to get back to the cabin. She decided she would drive into Grand Marais later on. It was only a few miles from the cabin. She could pick up some supplies and talk to John then. She put her phone away, and they climbed into the car and headed north out of Silver Bay.

Chapter 7

The October sun was already languishing toward the western horizon, eager to reach its haunt just beyond the Sawtooth Mountains. Brie and Edna drove in silence, drinking in the beauty around them, tired from the sailing, content to let the miles roll by undisturbed. Brie was thinking about the long history of the great lake and its mariners, from the indigenous peoples—makers of the great canoes paddled by the voyageurs in the fur trade—to the sturdy wooden schooners, and finally steam-powered vessels and great freighters that would haul the ore scoured from the heart of the iron range, where vast open wounds called pit mines would one day scar the landscape.

She was thinking about other things as well. Things that she had stuffed down for too long. A cop's murder—her partner's murder—and the unforgivable, enigmatic reality that this most important of cases had gone cold.

She had not been allowed to work the case since Phil Thatcher had been her partner. And even though her colleague, veteran detective Garrett Parker, had been assigned to the case, it didn't help her angst about being ostracized from the investigation. But that was department protocol, against which she had no recourse. So in the end, she had been helpless to save Phil's life and powerless to solve his murder. That had ended up being a powerful cocktail for despair. Despair that had finally driven her to take a leave of absence.

Before she knew it, they had clocked forty miles. She saw the Clearview Store ahead on their left.

"Should we stop for coffee, Mom?"

"I wouldn't turn it down," Edna said.

Brie turned in and parked the car. "I'll run in and get it. You just stay cozy here."

"Thank you, Brie. I appreciate that." Edna had grabbed the car blanket from the back seat when they left the marina and had burrowed underneath it as they'd started for home.

"Black or something fancy?" Brie asked.

"How about some chai tea?" Edna said.

"Sure thing," Brie headed into the coffee house and in about five minutes was back out with the brews. She handed a cup across the car to Edna, deposited her own in the cup holder, and climbed behind the wheel. As they rolled the last few miles back to the cabin, Brie sipped her coffee, letting it percolate into her bloodstream. It warmed her through but also brought an invigorating rush to her tired body, the kind that only a strong caffeinated beverage can deliver. By the time they pulled off onto the gravel road leading to their cabin, she was feeling revived, ready for a hike instead of a nap. Edna, despite the tea, appeared ready for a nap.

"I think I'll walk down to the cove, Mom. Look for rocks. You want to come down there with me?"

"It's been a long day on the water. I think I've had my fill of the elements today," Edna said. "I'm going to take my tea inside and curl up in a soft chair with a good book. But you go right ahead."

"What should we make for dinner?" Brie asked.

"Why don't we just warm up some soup and have some nice bread and cheese with it?" Edna said. "Easy peasy."

"Sounds perfect," Brie said. She headed down the trail toward the cove, where Cedar Creek burbled through its mysterious black gorge and emptied into Lake Superior. The fisherman had left that morning, so she had the cove to herself.

The sun had already dipped far enough that the cove was in partial shade, and rock hunting is a pursuit best carried out in good light. Even so, Brie scoured the edge of the water where the lake constantly lapped in. Wet rocks look like polished rocks, revealing their colors, and in the case of agates, the banded layers by which they are recognized.

She worked her way back and forth along the verge for a while and finally jumped across the creek at its narrowest point and scoured the shore on the other side. But the lake was starting to roll in, and she wasn't wearing the rubber boots she usually pulled on for rock hunting. So she gave up the hunt, hiked back up the steep trail out of the cove, and made her way along the edge of the woods down toward the lake.

Superior had come to life before a stiff wind working in from the northeast. Large waves showed turquoise in the sun just before they broke on the sloping gray granite. Granite that had been rounded and hollowed until it took the very shape of the mighty waters that had carved it. The percussive booms of waves on rock were a constant—a sound that worked its way into the soul, reminding one that there were bigger things than the petty concerns that seem to dominate life. Particularly life in a big city. Like the sea, Lake Superior always reminded her that the big picture is what really matters—what brings peace.

As she came clear of the trees, she was surprised to see Edna a ways down the shore, squatting on her haunches, staring into a pool of water held captive by a hollow in the rock. She started to call out but knew her mother would never hear her over the noise of the waves, so she made her way methodically along the rock, climbing up a ledge here and there, or jumping over a rivulet that was making its way down to the lake. When she got closer, she called again.

"Yo, Mom."

The woman turned and stared for a moment and finally waved. Brie worked her way closer, and it was only when she was almost up to her that she realized it wasn't Edna at all. But the similarities were remarkable. Same gray hair cut in a blunt shoulder-length haircut. Same facial profile and lithe frame. Even a gray jacket not too different from the one Edna had worn that day.

Brie made her way up to the woman. "I'm sorry," she said, "but from a distance I mistook you for my mother, who I'm here with."

"Well, that's all right," the woman said, and even the twinkle in her blue eyes was reminiscent of Edna. "My name's Halley. Halley Greenberg." She held out her hand, and Brie took it.

Brie introduced herself and then asked, "Are you staying here at the cabins?"

"Yes, my husband and I are staying in *Sea Smoke*." She nodded toward the cabin on the far end of the property. "We come this time every year. My husband's gone fishing for a couple of days with a friend of his who lives up here. They're up on Devil Track Lake." Halley looked out over the water.

"So you're by yourself," Brie said, wondering if she might be lonely.

"Yes, but I rather like it," Halley said, turning back. "I'm a writer, so I don't mind my alone time."

Brie got the impression Halley might be used to her husband being gone.

"I'm working on an article right now, and I actually welcome the peace and quiet. My husband will be back in a couple of days, and we'll have the rest of the time here together. We're here for nine days in all."

Brie nodded and smiled. "You look so much like my mom, it's a little spooky."

"Really?" Halley looked surprised by the revelation.

"I'm not exaggerating," Brie said. "In fact, yesterday, when we were on our way up, the barista at the coffee house down the road asked my mom if she had been in the day before. When we said no, she said a woman that looked just like her had been in. That must have been you."

"Guilty as charged," Halley said. "I've stopped down at that coffee house a couple of times when I needed a break from my work."

"Is your husband a writer too?" Brie asked.

"Oh, no. We're quite different in that way. He's an attorney, a federal prosecutor for the U.S. District Court in Duluth."

Brie nodded. She thought about telling Halley she worked for the Minneapolis PD but decided not to go there. More often than not, telling someone you're a cop brings an abrupt end to a conversation, as if people don't know how to act around you once they know that. So they chatted a little more about the area and how long they had been coming to the cabins, and Halley admitted that, even though they could afford something much fancier, there was a mystique about this place that always drew them back.

"It's truly off the map," Brie said.

"That's it," Halley agreed. "In our over-connected world, no one can get to you here. I love that about this place."

They talked for a few more minutes about some of their favorite places on the North Shore. Finally Halley said, "Well, I should be getting on. It's been very nice talking to you." She started to walk off and then turned back. "I'd love to meet your mom. Do you think she'd mind if I stopped and said hello?"

Brie waved her hand. "She'd love that. We're in Spindrift." She turned and pointed along the shore to the cabin that sat on the promontory overlooking the lake.

Brie walked down to the edge of the lake and sat on the smooth rock in the late afternoon sun. The sound of the waves calmed her, bringing peace that seemed to open her mind. She could see a path rising before her, and that path was fast becoming the only one she could conceive of walking. When she'd returned to Minnesota, it was not with the thought of solving her partner's murder. Her idea had been to spend some time with her mother, empty her apartment, submit her resignation to the department, and return to Maine and John. She had worked with the Maine State Police on several cases and knew there would be an opening for her there.

But once home, something had seemed wrong with that plan. It was Edna who had shined a light on her troubled heart. She realized now that she had to make a stand. She had to uncover the truth, or the ghosts of that terrible night in North Minneapolis, when Phil was murdered, would always haunt her and would eventually erode any relationship she might have with John.

She lay back against the sun-warmed rock and turned her mind back to that fateful night when Phil had died, trying for the thousandth time to get a clear picture of what had unfolded. Trying to remember. Even though, over the past nineteen months, she'd had many flashbacks and dreams of that night, the actual details of the shooting were hazy at best—the effect of traumatic injury on memory. So she suspected her memories were no more than a hodgepodge of the real and the unreal. Bits of actual remembrance intertwined with pieces her mind had fabricated. To separate out the truth would be the challenge.

After the shooting, she had worked with a police psychologist, who at Brie's request had tried hypnotic regression on her. But it was too soon after the incident, and the attempt had not gone well. It was almost as if, at the moment she was shot, a switch had been thrown—a kind of psychic reset button—and she had started over as a changed being. If only she could press some metaphorical key, do a system restore, and take herself back to the reality that had existed before that night.

But of course, that was impossible. And her wiser self knew she shouldn't wish for that. Because of what had unfolded that night, her life had moved in a different direction—one that had revealed itself to be rich with possibility. During her time at sea, she had contemplated all of this many times and had realized that out of the darkness had come light. So she'd learned to accept what had happened and to forgive herself for somehow failing her partner.

But she now realized that *that* forgiveness would never hold. Not for a lifetime. To truly rise from the ashes of that night, she had to crack the case. Find Phil's murderer and bring that person to justice. Only then would she be free to turn the page on the next chapter of her life.

She looked around her with a bit of sadness, wondering if she would visit this most mystical of places again. Her love of big water had been born here. Sailing on Superior with her family had given her a passion for the open water. This lake and its memories were sunk deep in her soul.

A large wave crashed in and rolled up the smooth granite, then scuttled back into the deep with a hypnotic whisper. Maybe she should go back to the psychologist. If she could somehow return to that fateful night, view it in real time, there might be clues.

She climbed to her feet, her mind filled with questions. She started up the rocky shore, thinking about the decision she had come to. Wondering how it would play out and whether or not . . .

CRACK . . . an earsplitting shot ran out. Brie dove onto the rocks and flattened herself there, recognizing the report of a high-powered rifle. A fraction of a second ticked by. *CRACK.* A second shot exploded in the echo chamber of granite terrain. The air vibrated with the sound. Brie held her ground for just a second, trying to locate the point of origin of the shots. Then she was on her feet, racing up the rocks toward the cabin, jumping across cracks and rivulets. Her heart pounded a drumbeat in her ears, and she tasted bile in her mouth. The taste of fear.

Chapter 8

Brie ran as fast as the terrain would allow, but the world around her seemed to move by in slow motion. Her field of vision had narrowed, and her hearing became more acute. As she came up the rocks below the cabin, she took shelter behind a large cedar tree and listened for a moment or two. From her vantage point she could see the shoulders and head of a woman's body lying prone on the ground. *Please God, don't let it be Mom.* Edna bore such a resemblance to Halley Greenberg that, from where she stood, Brie could not tell who lay there.

After one more tick of time, she bolted from behind the tree and charged through the underbrush between her and the victim. She knew she was exposing herself, but she had to get to the woman on the ground. As she came up to the victim, she went to her knees and could see from the profile that this was Halley and not her mother. Tears stung her eyes. *Thank God,* she thought, and felt immediately guilty for the thought.

As she felt for a pulse on Halley's neck, she glanced toward the woods to the north, where her cop-sense told her the shots had come from. She knelt next to the victim just long enough to know there was no pulse and then bolted into the cabin.

"MOM!" she shouted. She took in the room at a glance. "Mom!"

"Here, Brie."

She heard Edna's voice coming from the bedroom and darted in there. Edna was on the floor, away from the sight-lines of any windows, her knees pulled up to her chest.

Brie went to the floor and hugged her. "Are you okay, Mom?" She could feel her shaking.

"I'm okay," Edna said. "When I heard the shots, I peeked out the window in the bathroom. I saw Halley lying there. We had just met. She seemed a lovely person." Edna sobbed and Brie hugged her a bit tighter. "I wanted to go to her, but I remembered what you had taught me. That if I was ever in a situation like this to stay inside and find a safe place away from any windows."

"You did just the right thing, Mom."

"There were two shots. I was so worried you might have . . ." Edna let out a giant sob.

"I'm fine, Mom." She pulled out her phone and saw she had no bars. "I'm going to run up to the caretaker's house and use the phone in the guest office to call 911. You stay right here."

Edna started to protest, but Brie was already on her feet, headed for the other bedroom, where she retrieved her gun from its lock box. She put the Glock 9 in its holster, clipped it onto her jeans, and headed for the door. She grabbed the key off the hook by the door and locked the door on the way out. She stood on the small porch and listened for a couple of seconds, then raced off the porch and up the road, giving Halley's body a wide berth.

Up the hill and a short distance along the gravel road, the caretaker's house sat in a small grove of jack pine and cedar. It took Brie maybe twenty seconds to cover the distance running flat out. She bolted in the side door of the house, where there was a small guest area with a countertop that held a calendar, some paper and pens, and a desk set telephone connected to a landline. She took a second or two to catch her breath, then dialed 911.

A dispatcher answered on the third ring. "Nine-one-one. What is your emergency?"

"There's been a fatal shooting at Cedar Falls Cabins on Highway 61. A woman is dead. Please send law enforcement. An officer is on the scene."

"I'm dispatching a deputy now from the Cook County Sheriff's Office. Are you the officer on scene?"

"Yes."

"Are you in any danger?"

"I don't know."

"What is your name?"

"Detective Brie Beaumont."

"Please stay on the line with me until you hear the squads arriving."

Brie did as ordered, responding to the dispatcher's questions about the victim, and in a matter of minutes she heard the sirens from the approaching squads.

"I hear them coming," she told the dispatcher. "I'm going to return to the scene." She ended the call and headed out the door and back down the road and waited at the bottom of the curve a short distance from where the body of Halley Greenberg lay.

The first squad arrived within minutes and proceeded with care down the road. When Brie saw the SUV, she signaled by waving an arm. The squad bearing the Cook County Sheriff's logo ground to a stop on the gravel. As the door opened and the deputy put his leg out, Brie caught the glint of steel in the late day sun. Then the deputy was out of the car and moved toward her with such ease that, had she not seen that glint of steel, she never would have guessed the man approaching had a prosthetic leg. Brie placed him at around six feet, maybe a little taller. He had very dark hair—parted down the middle and as close to black as hair could be—a straight nose and high cheekbones. She thought he might be Native American. She placed his age at around forty-five. He was dressed in the brown and tan uniform worn by the Cook County deputies.

"Chief Deputy Claude Renard," he said. He had his ID wallet in hand and held it open for her to see, but his eyes had already traveled to the victim and rested there.

"Brie Beaumont. I called 911."

"The dispatcher said there was an officer on the scene. Is that you?" His voice was surprisingly soft. Not the volume, but rather the quality of it. Like wind moving through trees.

"Yes," Brie said. "I'm here vacationing with my mother." As she said it, a look of alarm flashed in the deputy's eyes, and he glanced again at the body lying to their right.

"She's not my mother," Brie said, "for which I'm very grateful. And to answer your question, I'm a detective with the Minneapolis Police Department." She produced her ID from her back pocket and handed it to him.

He looked at the ID and then studied her for just a moment, and she saw that his eyes, which at first had appeared almost black, were actually blue. The deepest blue she'd ever seen. They were old eyes, not in chronology of years but in life lived. The eyes of one who had seen a lot, felt a lot.

"What happened here?" he asked. The question was so unabashedly simple for what seemed a completely inexplicable sequence of events.

"I had just met the victim a short while before, down by the lake." Brie's eyes slid past him and rested on Halley's body. "Her name is Halley Greenberg. She's staying in the cabin down there." Brie turned and pointed along the shore.

"Where is your mother?"

"She's inside the cabin there." Brie nodded down the driveway toward their cabin. "Halley had said she wanted to stop in and meet my mother, and I had pointed out our cabin to her. So I assume she and Mom had been visiting inside and that Halley had just left the cabin."

"Where were you when the shots were fired?" Renard asked.

"I was down on the shore, sitting on the rocks. I was just getting up to come back to the cabin when the first shot was fired. It came from a high-powered rifle."

As she said this, Claude Renard turned his head and studied the woods to the north, in the same direction Brie guessed the shots had come from.

"You said the first shot. How many were fired?"

"Two."

"So we have to assume the first shot missed."

"That would be my guess," Brie said.

No more than a minute or two had elapsed since the deputy's arrival, and now she could hear more squads approaching.

The deputy keyed his radio. "One-two-eight to County. I'm at Cedar Falls Cabins on Highway 61. We have a possible active shooter scenario. Please notify St. Louis County. We're going to need their SWAT team. We'll also need a crime scene team from the BCA in Bemidji. Break."

The voice of the dispatcher came back. "Copy that, One-Two-Eight. Notifying St. Louis County and the BCA now. Break."

"I'd also like you to contact Ned Trainer with the DNR Field Office in Duluth. Tell him we need him to come and bring his dog."

"Copy that. Break."

"Call me back with an ETA on SWAT and the crime lab team and Officer Trainer. Break."

"Copy, Sheriff. Out."

Brie was curious as to why the dispatcher had called him "Sheriff" since he'd identified himself as Chief Deputy Claude Renard. It was a question for later, though.

"What about the medical examiner?" she asked.

"We only have one medical examiner in the county, and he has a regular practice as well. So in the case of a death or a homicide, the deputies are trained and authorized to photograph, process, and transport the body. All autopsies for Cook County are performed by the Anoka County Medical Examiner's Office."

Brie nodded. Anoka County was thirty minutes north and west of Minneapolis. It was interesting to see how law enforcement rolled outside the Twin Cities. This was a big state, and county law enforcement had a lot of bases to cover. She knew cooperation with other agencies was essential. She'd seen the same thing in Maine on the cases she'd worked with the Maine State Police over the past few months.

The next squad on the scene, also from the Cook County Sheriff's Office, was just pulling down the road toward the cabins. Renard held up a hand to stop the car a ways from where he and Brie stood. He walked over to the driver's side and spoke to the deputy.

"Hank, take your squad back up to the top of the drive where the road enters the property and set up a barricade. No one but law enforcement comes down here."

Brie could see the deputy nod.

"Once enough deputies are on scene up there, I want you to check any of the surrounding properties and evacuate any residents. We're treating this as a possible active shooter scenario. St. Louis County SWAT has been called in. Once you have enough deputies up there, send one of them back to the law enforcement center to bring the body transport vehicle.

"Eventually, I'll need two officers down here to secure the crime scene. I'll radio you when I want them sent down."

The deputy nodded again, then backed his cruiser up to where he could turn around and disappeared up the road.

As Renard walked back toward Brie, a call came across his radio. It was dispatch telling him the crime scene team was on the way from Bemidji. ETA three and a half to four hours.

"Let's glove up and see what we've got here," Renard said. He walked to his squad and took some latex gloves out of a box in the back. He handed a pair to Brie, and they both gloved up. They moved over to Halley's body, and Renard knelt down on one knee next to her. Though it was clear she was gone, he still checked for a pulse. "No exit wound," he said. "Probably a hollow-point round."

It wasn't a question, but Brie nodded automatically from where she stood.

Deputy Renard rolled the victim onto her left side and studied the wound. Brie could see a large pool of blood beneath the body. The front of Halley's jacket was almost entirely consumed by the deep red stain.

"Direct shot to the heart," Renard said. He gently laid the body back down. He stood and moved over to his squad and took out a roll of crime scene tape and a camera with a telephoto lens. "BCA will take a raft of pictures when they get here. But we'll need to remove the victim's body long before they arrive, so I need to get pictures of the body and its placement in reference to the surrounding area, and also take some fixed-point measurements."

He handed the crime scene tape to Brie, and she stood back and let him work.

"Tell me about Ned Trainer and his dog," she said after a few minutes.

"Ned's a wildlife officer with the DNR. His dog Nellie's a gun dog and a damn good one. She's trained to sniff out firearms, gunshot residue, even spent shell casings." He lowered the camera and looked toward the woods in the distance. "I'm hoping she'll be able to locate on the shooter's position."

Brie nodded. "That could tell us a lot."

"If they find shell casings, we can compare them to others on record in the database," Renard said. "See if the weapon has been used in the commission of another crime."

He finished taking pictures. Then he took a small canister from his pocket and sprayed a dot of white paint on the ground just above the victim's head.

"Her phone is in her back pocket there," Brie offered. "There should be a contact number for her husband on the phone."

"Good thought," Renard said. He walked over to his car, put the camera inside and came back with an evidence envelope. He cataloged the item on the envelope, then reached down and removed the cell phone from Halley Greenberg's pocket. He turned the phone off, placed it in the envelope and took it back to his squad. Then he and Brie ran the crime scene tape in a wide radius around the cabin and Halley Greenberg's body. Brie knew the crime scene actually encompassed a far greater area, from up on the road all the way down through the woods that lay to the north of them.

"Is there an owner or caretaker present on the property?" Renard asked.

Brie turned and pointed up the gravel road. "The caretakers' house is up there. That's where I called from. I don't think either of them is home. They both work other jobs."

Renard pulled a small notebook and pen out of his pocket. "Could I get their names?" he asked.

"Sure," Brie said. "William and Ann Swenson. Theirs is the small cedar-sided house up the road on the right." She pointed again although the house was not visible from where they stood. "I'm sure they'd be down here if either of them was home. There are contact numbers for them in the office."

After they finished, Renard turned to Brie. "You said that Ms. Greenberg was staying in the cabin down there." He nodded in the direction of the cabin at the far end of the property. "I assume that would be her car next to the cabin."

"I assume so," Brie said. "She told me she was here with her husband but that he had gone fishing for a couple of days with a friend up on Devil Track Lake."

"Huh. Interesting," Renard said.

Being a cop, Brie could easily read his thoughts. *Wife is shot while husband is away fishing. Convenient.*

"Let's get that plate number and run it." Renard was already heading toward the vehicle in his long-gaited stride with Brie at his side. As they got close enough to see the plate, Renard took out his notebook and wrote down the number of the Honda CR-V. "I don't suppose you happen to know if the husband had his vehicle up here as well?"

"Sorry, I don't. A couple on vacation, though, I'd think they'd travel in one car. But with the fishing plan, it's hard to say." Brie stepped past him and onto the front stoop of the cabin, where she tried the door. "It's unlocked," she called over her shoulder.

Chapter 9

Renard stepped up beside Brie and opened the door of Halley Greenberg's cabin. "Let's see if we can find a phone number or address for where the husband is. One way or another, I want to deliver the news of his wife's death in person. See how he reacts."

Brie nodded, knowing that the first interaction with a person of interest or suspect is critical. Unless one is an Academy Award-winning actor, it's hard to fake shock and grief and carry it off convincingly. So those initial moments following a tragic disclosure can be highly enlightening for a shrewd detective or investigator.

They glanced around the cabin. It was different in design, but about the same size as the cabin Brie and Edna were staying in. Beyond the picture window in the living room, the lake was alive. Each wave rolled in to break on the rock shelf with a boom and scuttle away with a whisper. A constant crash and shoosh—nature's white noise. Sunset was starting to stain the sky in hues of gold and pink. A large cast-iron Franklin fireplace filled one corner of the living room. The doors on the front of the stove were open, and live embers still radiated heat into the room.

"I'll look around out here," Renard said. "Why don't you check the bedrooms?"

Brie nodded and disappeared into the first of two bedrooms. She opened the closet and found no clothes hanging there. She checked the drawers on the nightstand and then moved to the second bedroom. She immediately saw a small red leather address book on top of the dresser.

Renard's voice came from the kitchen. "I've got a name and phone number here."

Brie walked out to the kitchen with the address book.

Renard held a small piece of paper in his hand. On it was penciled "Tom's place" and a phone number with a 2-1-8 area code.

Brie opened the address book and started paging through to see if the number might show up attached to an address. When she got to the Ns, she struck pay dirt. "Here it is, Deputy."

Renard looked over her shoulder.

"Same phone number under the name Tom Norsted. The address is a P.O. box in Grand Marais."

"Let's go back to my squad. I want to run a search in the county records for this Norsted fellow, see if I can get a fire number for his place up on Devil Track Lake." He took the paper with Norsted's phone number on it, and he and Brie headed out the door.

They walked to Renard's squad. "Climb in, Detective, and let's see what we can find on the husband."

Brie went around to the passenger side, and they got into the front seat. Renard brought up a screen on the mobile computer and typed in the plate number of the Honda CR-V. He clicked a key and up popped the DMV registration for Jacob J. Greenberg along with his driver's license photo. Renard jotted down the information and then brought up another screen and typed again. "County property records," he said. "I'm looking for that fire number for the Norsted property." He clicked a key and ran a finger down the screen. "Here it is." He jotted the fire number in his notebook.

Brie and Renard climbed out of the squad. He tapped his small notebook. "The Norsted property on Devil Track Lake is about a thirty-minute drive from here. But before I head up there, I'd like to speak to your mother, since she was the last one to see Ms. Greenberg alive."

"That's fine," Brie said. "She's waiting in the cabin. She's terribly shaken by what has happened." Brie paused and looked at Renard. "There's something I have to tell you before we go in there."

"Yes . . . what is it?" Renard waited, and there was an aura of absolute patience about him that Brie found somehow comforting and a bit unsettling.

She chose her words carefully, as if there were a price on each one. "My mother bears a rather striking resemblance to the victim. When I approached Ms. Greenberg down on the rocks this afternoon, from a distance, I thought she was my mom. Of course, that's before I met her or knew she was staying here, so my mistake was a natural one. Still . . ."

Renard studied her for a few moments, the question in his mind already obvious to Brie.

"Do you think your mother might have been the intended victim?" he asked.

Brie stood silent for a few moments, knowing she had to tell him about the threatening letters she had received. A situation that promised to complicate this investigation.

Finally she said, "I believe it's a possibility."

"Why do you think someone would be targeting your mother?"

Brie let out a sigh. "I've been receiving these letters." She went on to tell him about the four threatening letters she had received over the past two and a half months. She also told him about her recent leave from the MPD, about the death of her partner nineteen months ago, and about being shot herself.

"I've just returned from Maine in the past few days and only became aware of the letters the night before last when I went through my back mail. I did report the letters to someone at the Minneapolis PD, and the plan was to investigate the situation when I got back to the department. Maybe start by seeing if anyone I'd helped put away might have been paroled recently."

"Does your mother know about the letters?"

Brie looked into the deputy's indigo eyes. "No," she said. "I didn't want her to worry about me. She just lost her husband two months ago." She stared off toward the lake, not knowing what to say next.

"The fact that this is your cabin and not the victim's raises the possibility that the shooter *could* have been targeting your mother. And if, as you say, they look alike, it ups the possibility that he might have mistaken one woman for the other. Here's the rub, though. There is no way to know that Halley Greenberg was not the intended victim. The case of her death will need to be investigated as if she was."

"I know that," Brie said. "And the fact that her shooting occurred while the husband was away fishing has to be considered suspicious."

"I agree," Renard said. They walked down the road toward Brie's cabin, and he took his notebook back out. "So let me get this straight. Ms. Greenberg was down by the shore when you approached."

"That's right."

"So you didn't see if she came from her cabin?"

"No, when I noticed her, she was already on the rocks below the cabins. She must have come from her cabin, though."

"So let's assume that the shooter sees Ms. Greenberg enter your cabin. It's possible he was watching her from the time she left her own cabin and headed down toward the shore. In that scenario she would be the intended target. Or maybe, for whatever reason, he only sees her leave your cabin. In that case we might have to assume that your mother was the target."

They had stopped at the end of the driveway, and Renard studied the lay of things. The door was on the side of the cabin, and a small covered porch ran along that side of the cabin. Directly across from the door a trellis was mounted to the porch railing and ran from the roof down to the porch floor. The trellis was covered with leafy vines that still held their foliage. Renard nodded toward it. "Depending on the shooter's line of sight, that trellis could have obscured his view."

Deputy Renard jotted some notes, then turned and surveyed the terrain to the north. "If we can find the shooter's position in those woods, we'll be able to determine if he had a clear firing line on either of these cabins from that position." He turned back to Brie. "I'd like to interview your mother now."

Brie nodded and they started toward the cabin. The sound of a car coming down the road stopped them.

"That will be one of the deputies with the body transport vehicle," Renard said.

They watched as a white truck with a top over the bed came into view. It wound slowly down the road and stopped behind the chief deputy's squad, and a deputy exited the driver's side of the truck. A man also stepped from the passenger side of the truck and came toward them. He wore khakis, an open-neck plaid sport shirt, and a navy blue jacket. He was a man of slight stature both in height and girth and wore large black-framed glasses that seemed to overwhelm his fine features. Brie guessed his age at around sixty.

"Doc Mosley was just dropping off some paperwork when I went to pick up the truck. When I told him what had happened, he asked to ride along."

"Hello, Sheriff," Mosley said as he came towards them, and Brie wondered again why folks kept calling Renard "Sheriff."

"Howdy, Erb," Renard said. "This is Detective Brie Beaumont from the Minneapolis PD. She's vacationing here and was on the scene when the shooting occurred."

"Doctor Erbert Mosley." He extended his hand to Brie. "I'm the medical examiner for the county."

Brie shook his hand. "Pleased to meet you, Doctor."

"You can call me Erb," Mosley said. "We're not all that formal up here."

Mosley had light blue eyes that seemed to send out little flashes of light when he smiled. His hair was a mix of curly brown and gray that was thinning significantly and, for whatever reason, the curliness of it made the balding factor more apparent.

Brie nodded. "Erb it is, then."

They walked over to the victim, and Mosley knelt down on the ground. He sat back on his heels and surveyed the body.

"It looks like a single gunshot wound to the chest," Renard said. "Detective Beaumont said the shots sounded like they came from a high-powered rifle."

Mosley nodded. "Can you help me turn her on her side, Claude?"

Renard knelt on his good knee and rolled the victim onto her left side. Doc Mosley studied the wound for a few moments and then nodded for Renard to turn the body back over. The ME stood up and surveyed the woods to the north as Renard and Brie had both done.

"Do we have a time of death?" he asked.

"It was eight minutes after five when I got to the victim and checked for a pulse," Brie said.

Mosley turned back to them. "I know it's not required, but I'll make out a report on my observations of the scene and forward it to the Anoka County ME's office. I assume the BCA is on the way?"

"They're about three to three-and-a-half hours out," Renard said. "I'll call down a second deputy to help you bag the body and get it into the vehicle." He keyed his radio and talked to Hank, who was stationed up at the entrance to the property, and told him to send down a deputy to assist with the body.

Mosley nodded. “Thanks, Sheriff.”

“I’ve got an interview to complete, but good seeing you, Erb.” He and Brie turned and walked toward the cabin where Edna Beaumont was waiting.

Chapter 10

Brie and Chief Deputy Renard stepped onto the small porch and walked to the door. They both turned to assess the visibility of the spot from the woods to the north—the direction they thought the shots had come from. It seemed the view from that direction was almost totally obstructed by the trellis and the trees surrounding the cabin.

"It's hard to say what the shooter might have seen through a high-powered scope," Brie said.

"That's true, but there's a lot of cover here."

She turned and knocked on the cabin door to let Edna know they were coming in. She waited just a moment and then opened the door with the key she had in her pocket.

Edna was just putting her knitting aside when they came in. She sat in one of the rockers in front of the fireplace that held glowing embers but no fire. Brie assumed Edna had built a fire after they got home from sailing, and with all the drama that had unfolded, it had burned out.

As soon as they entered, Edna stood and came toward them.

"Mom, this is Chief Deputy Claude Renard." She turned to Renard. "This is my mother, Edna Beaumont."

"Pleased to meet you, Ms. Beaumont." He held out his hand to her. Edna shook it, and as she did, Brie could see Renard taking stock of Edna, undoubtedly noting the more than passing resemblance between her and Halley Greenberg.

"I'd like to ask you some questions if that's all right," Renard said.

"Of course," Edna said. "Please come and sit down." She gestured toward the rockers in front of the fireplace, and Renard moved toward them. Edna turned her chair to face his and the deputy did likewise. Brie got one of the dining chairs from across the room and set it down so the three chairs formed a triangle of sorts.

Renard took out his notebook and pen and started in. "Ms. Beaumont, your daughter has told me she met the victim, Halley Greenberg, down by the shore and that after talking to her for . . ." He turned to Brie.

"About fifteen minutes," Brie said.

Renard nodded. "After fifteen minutes, they parted, with Ms. Greenberg saying she wanted to stop up here and meet you. Can you tell me what happened next?"

"I was surprised when I opened the door," Edna said. "I was expecting Brie, and there stood a stranger. But Halley quickly introduced herself and said she was staying in the cabin down at the other end of the property."

"So she knocked on the door?" Renard asked.

"Yes. Just a couple of knocks. When I heard them, I assumed Brie had forgotten to take the key or accidentally locked the door."

"You were saying that Ms. Greenberg introduced herself."

"That's right. She said she had met Brie down on the shore and wanted to stop up and say hello. I told her I was pleased to meet her and invited her in. I was just making tea and asked if she'd like some."

"Did you notice the resemblance Ms. Greenberg bore to you?" Renard asked.

Brie felt her stomach clench at the question. She wanted to protect her mother from the reality that there was a woman lying dead just outside their door who looked a lot like her.

Edna's expression changed slightly, and she studied the deputy's face. "I did notice that we looked a bit alike, she and I, and I thought about the girl at the coffee house down the road who said there was someone who looked just like me who'd been in the shop the day before." Edna turned to Brie. "Did you think about that when you met her?"

"I did, as a matter of fact," Brie said.

"Did that happen today?" Renard asked.

"No, it was yesterday, the day we drove up," Brie said. "We stopped at the coffee house down by Clearview Store. It was the barista there that asked if Mom had been in the day before. The girl's name is Sonia."

Renard made some notes in his notebook and proceeded. "What frame of mind was Ms. Greenberg in when you met her today?" he asked Edna.

"She seemed just fine. She told me her husband had gone fishing for a couple of days with a friend of his."

"Did she seem upset by that situation?" Renard asked.

"Not at all. She said she welcomed the peace. Said she was a writer and was trying to finish a project she was working on."

Edna gazed at the embers in the fireplace, and Renard watched her but said nothing. He just waited for whatever might come next, with that same patience he had shown Brie out on the road. When Edna looked back at him, he studied her for a moment, possibly trying to read between the emotional lines.

"Did Ms. Greenberg seem afraid in any way?" he asked.

Edna hesitated a moment. "No, just lonely, I thought."

"You're sure it wasn't fear?" he asked.

"Deputy, I've buried two husbands. I know what lonely feels like."

Renard nodded respectfully.

Brie hesitated, not sure whether she should break into the interview. Renard must have caught her expression because he turned to her and said, "Did you have something you wanted to add, Detective?"

"It's okay if you call me Brie," she said. "But, yes. I got the impression that she might be used to her husband being gone, but beyond that, she seemed pretty upbeat—happy to have her time to herself."

"You can enjoy your time alone and still be lonely," Edna said. "My guess is, you may be near the age of Halley's children, and so she automatically slipped into what I would call Mother Mode."

"What's that?" Brie asked.

"It's where you present a brave front, like everything is fine and will be fine in the future, when inside you are riddled with fear and doubt."

"Sounds a bit like PTSD," Brie said.

Renard turned and studied her. It was a look of complete solidarity, the kind that could only come from one who deeply related. Brie's eyes traveled down to his prosthetic leg for just a second. She was beginning to understand.

Then Edna was speaking again and the moment was lost. "I believe all mothers suffer from a certain amount of battle fatigue. The difference is the battles are emotional."

"I think you are right about that, Ms. Beaumont."

He allowed a respectful pause before continuing his questions, and in the silence, they could hear the constant crash and retreat of the waves outside the cabin window.

"Did Ms. Greenberg talk about her husband at all? Possibly say what he did for work?"

"I asked her that. She said he's a federal prosecutor for the U.S. District Court in Duluth."

Brie nodded. "She told me the same thing."

Renard wrote in his notebook, then looked up at Brie. "That's a job where you can make some enemies," he said.

"So this is a definitely a homicide," Edna said.

"I think there's little doubt of that," Renard said.

"And you think someone with a grudge against Halley's husband may have gone after her."

"It's one possibility, Ms. Beaumont. But there may be another side to this." He paused for a moment and looked at Brie. "Now might be a good time to tell your mom about the letters."

Edna turned and studied Brie, alarm firing in her blue eyes. "What is he talking about, Brie?"

Brie stood and put two logs on the glowing embers in the fireplace. She stayed there for a moment, watching them ignite before turning back to Edna. "I didn't want you to be alarmed, Mom. I didn't think the situation could possibly impact our trip up here." She went on to tell Edna about finding the four threatening letters the night before they were due to drive up North and what the letters had said. "You see, I'd just gotten my mail back from my landlady. I reported the situation to the department, and the plan was to look into it when I returned to the department next week."

Brie could see that Edna was wasting no time assembling the pieces of the bizarre puzzle. She studied Deputy Renard first and then Brie. "Do you think I might have been the target of this shooting? Do you think he saw Halley coming out of my cabin and shot her mistakenly?"

Brie sat on the arm of her mother's chair and put an arm around her. Edna was quivering, as if low voltage electricity ran through her. "I don't think we have enough information yet to make that assumption, Mom."

Renard looked at Brie for a moment before speaking. "The thing is, Ms. Beaumont, we can't rule out that possibility. So I think we need to make a plan for your safety."

"Does that mean we have to leave here?" Edna asked.

"We'd have to anyway, Mom. This is now a crime scene. But the fact is, until we know who the intended target was, this is not a safe place to be."

Edna nodded slowly, the seriousness of the situation beginning to register with her. "Maybe I should return to New Mexico."

"I'm not sure that would be a good idea, Mom. You live alone down there. Until we know what's going on here, I think we need to come up with a different solution."

"Do you want me to pack my things?" Edna asked.

"Why don't you do that. I'll talk to Deputy Renard about what the plan will be."

Edna stood and went into her bedroom. They could hear her dresser drawers sliding open and closed.

"Let's step outside," Renard said.

Brie nodded and they headed out the door. They skirted Halley Greenberg's body and walked out onto the road. The sun had officially set, but there was still plenty of light to see by. With the sky clear, the temperature was already dropping, and Brie hugged her arms to her chest.

"I could bring her back to the cities with me and let her stay in my apartment, but it's not a very safe situation. Obviously the person who sent those letters has my address. And asking the department to post an officer there after I've been gone for six months . . ." she paused and looked at Renard. "I don't picture that going over very well. Plus, it would feel like house arrest to my mom. There's other family," Brie started to say.

"Family's not a good idea," Renard said. "If by chance your mother is the target, putting her with family might just give this guy more to shoot at."

Brie stood silently, fresh out of ideas.

"I have a thought," Renard said. "Not sure what you'll think of it, but it would certainly put your mother out of reach of harm."

"I'm listening," Brie said.

"I think for her safety, your mother needs to drop off the map. We don't know who the shooter's target was, Halley

Greenberg or your mother, but we have to assume that, for now, he thinks he killed the person he was gunning for. And maybe he did. Maybe the Greenberg woman was his target. At any rate, there's a small window of time to put your mother somewhere safe before the news of Ms. Greenberg's death gets out."

"What's your idea?"

"My father is a member of the Grand Portage Band of Ojibwe. I grew up on the reservation. When I was eighteen, he and my mother moved to Duluth, where Dad taught philosophy and Native American studies at UMD. When Mom passed away ten years ago, dad moved back to Grand Portage and built a home on the rez. He still teaches at the grade school there and is one of the tribal elders. He's a very good man, and I know he would welcome your mother. And I can't think of a safer place to put her." He paused and looked at Brie. "This may seem like the wrong kind of adventure after what has happened here, but we have to be sure Edna is properly protected."

"Well, first of all, don't let the knitting needles fool you. Mom likes adventure, so I don't think we have to worry about that. I'll have to ask her, of course, but you're right, I can't think of anywhere she'd be safer. Mom's quite the Minnesota historian, though. I'm afraid she might talk your dad to death."

"Oh, I think Dad will hold his own. We'll plan to take Edna out of here as soon as she's packed up. And if by chance she was the target, by the time the shooter realizes his mistake, she will have dropped off the map."

Brie nodded. "This is awfully kind of you, Deputy."

"No problem, Detective."

"I'll go talk to Mom. See if I can get her to cotton to the plan."

"Don't forget to pack your things as well. You can't stay here tonight."

"Right," was all Brie said. But until that moment, she hadn't thought about the fact that she, too, would have to leave.

The sound of a car crunching down the gravel road got their attention. "That will be Ned Trainer with his dog, Nellie. Once SWAT arrives, they'll head up into the woods to the north, see if Nellie can locate on the gunman's position."

Ned drew his SUV to a stop a ways up the road, and his dog bounded out the driver's side after him. "Howdy, One-Step," he called out.

Renard caught the expression on Brie's face—a mix of puzzlement and disbelief. "I'll explain later," he said. "It's not what you think."

Brie smiled and shook her head from side to side. There was no making sense of anything that had unfolded in the past hour and a half. She headed into the cabin to talk to her mother.

Chapter 11

Brie stepped into the cabin and looked around. The feel of the place was peace personified. How could something so terrible have unfolded here? She listened silently for a few moments. Mighty Superior churned away outside the windows. A single loon yodeled from the small cove below the cabin. The smell of cedar from a stately tree just outside the door had accompanied her inside. She knew how much her mother had looked forward to this time with her, and she felt guilty that their stay was about to be abruptly halted.

"Brie?"

"Right here, Mom." She walked into the room beyond the kitchen. Edna stood at the window, looking out over the lake.

"I'm all packed," she said.

Brie nodded. "I just have to throw my things into my duffel." She turned toward Edna. "I'm sorry about all this, Mom. This is a terrible thing for you to be put through."

Edna reached out and took her daughter's hand. "This is not your fault, Brie. In fact, it may have nothing to do with you."

"That may be, Mom, but my work has been known to put others in harm's way." She looked out at the great reflective waters. The old windup clock on the mantel ticked away the seconds. "I'm not sure I want to do this anymore."

"Don't forget, Brie, that you work for the good. For the truth. What's more, you've always been like that. Even as a child you couldn't stand injustice. You were deeply troubled by teachers who were mean to children in your class." She paused and looked into Brie's eyes. "Do you remember the boy in your class that you got in a fistfight with in fourth grade because he pushed one of your classmates to the ground?"

"I remember," Brie said, still keeping her gaze on the lake. "That girl hit her head. It was bleeding. I don't know what came over me, but I was going to make him pay for what he did."

"The thing is, we all have a mission here. We can't step away from that even though we may want to sometimes. We can never let fear win out."

"I never have, Mom. But there's a cost that comes with the work. It takes a terrible toll on relationships. I've seen plenty of heartbreak on the force during my time with the MPD."

"That doesn't mean it has to happen to you."

Brie turned and gave her mom a small hug. "I have to go pack." She walked to her bedroom. She knew her mother was wise and that she meant well. But wise or not, she couldn't understand. There was simply no way to make her understand.

Brie took her belongings out of the small dresser and packed them into her duffel. Then she headed into the bathroom to collect her few toiletries and added them to the bag. She walked back into the living room to broach the topic of putting Edna up at Grand Portage with Claude Renard's father.

Edna stood at the window in the failing light. "Where do we go from here?" she asked.

"We need to make sure you're safe, Mom, until we can get a handle on what this shooting is all about. In the short term, we need a solution for tonight."

Edna nodded. "What do you suggest?"

"Actually, Deputy Renard has an idea."

"Yes?"

"His father is a member of the Grand Portage Band of Ojibwe. He'd like to put you up there with his dad, in the

Grand Portage community, if you're agreeable." She shared with Edna what Renard had told her about his father, so Edna could get a sense of the man.

"What do *you* think, Brie?"

"I think it's an excellent idea. I can't think where you'd be safer. As Renard put it, should anyone come looking for you, you'll have dropped off the map."

Edna studied her daughter for a moment. "I'd rather return to St. Paul," she said. "Stay with one of your brothers." But she must have seen something in Brie's eyes that changed her mind, because finally she said, "All right. I trust your judgment. When do we leave?"

"I'll go talk to Renard."

Brie carried their bags into the kitchen and set them near the door and then went outside to talk to the deputy.

Renard was talking to Ned Trainer. Nellie was sitting next to Ned, fairly vibrating with desire to take up the hunt.

Renard walked over to Brie. "Well?"

"Mom's agreeable to the plan."

"That's good. I called Dad. He's very eager to watch over your mother. And he suggested you stay with him tonight as well. I think it's an excellent plan. Your being there will make it easier for Edna, and I'll know both of you are safe."

Brie couldn't see anything wrong with the plan, and it solved the issue of where she might stay tonight.

"It's most kind of your father," she said. "Getting back to the shooting, though, aren't you heading up to Devil Track Lake to locate Halley Greenberg's husband?"

"Yes. I've just radioed two deputies stationed up at the entrance to the property, to come down here and secure the scene."

Halley Greenberg's body had been bagged and was on the litter about to be loaded into the truck for transport down to Anoka.

"I've notified the chaplain on call to meet me up at the Law Enforcement Center. It's on the same road we'll take to get up to Devil Track Lake. I thought your mother could wait at the Law Enforcement Center until we're done with the notification."

"Would you mind if I accompanied you when you interview Jacob Greenberg?" Brie asked.

"Not at all. In fact, since you're a homicide detective, it would be valuable to get another impression of the husband's response."

Brie nodded. "I'll go get Mom if we're ready to leave."

"Just give me a couple minutes to get the deputies up to speed."

A squad was just winding down the road toward them. The ME signaled for them to wait so they could drive the transport vehicle up the road.

Once the truck had left with the body, Renard gave the two deputies their orders with regards to securing the scene. He told Ned that the ETA on the SWAT team was about an hour and asked him to wait until SWAT arrived to take Nellie up into the woods. "Although it's unlikely, there's a possibility the shooter could still be up there, so we need to proceed with caution."

Ned nodded. "In that case, Nellie and I will wait in my car until SWAT shows up."

"Thanks, Ned. I'll check in with you later tonight. Get a report on what you find."

Ned patted his dog's head. "Come on, Nel. Let's go get some hot coffee."

Renard turned and nodded to Brie to go get Edna. Then he went and climbed into his squad and maneuvered it close to the short path that led to the cabin. In a few seconds Brie and Edna appeared with Brie walking close in front of Edna. She'd had Edna put on a ball cap, tuck her hair up inside and pull the collar up on her jacket. Renard opened the back passenger-side door and quickly ushered Edna and Brie into the back seat.

Chapter 12

Renard turned his squad around and wound slowly up the road to the caretaker's house. He stopped, climbed out and went inside. When he came out, he was putting his notebook back in his pocket, and Brie assumed he'd written down the work phone numbers for the Swensons. They continued up the road to where it intersected with the gravel access road that ran behind the surrounding properties. Cook County and Lake County Sheriff's squads were parked along the road to left and right.

Renard powered down his window and spoke to Hank. "Radio me if there are any developments here, Hank."

The deputy nodded. "Roger that, One Step."

Edna turned and looked at Brie to see if she might know why anyone would call a man who'd lost a leg "One Step," but Brie just shrugged her shoulders and gave her head a subtle shake.

"SWAT is en route. Once they're on scene, we can get the search of the woods under way."

"We'll hold the fort here till they arrive," Hank said.

Renard drove on to where the gravel road intersected with Highway 61, a short distance ahead, and turned right in the direction of Grand Marais. The clock on the dash read 6:28. Dusk was rapidly descending. The sun had fully retired by now, but cloud strata blazed gold and pink out beyond the vast waters that spread like dark gray silk to the horizon. For

Brie, the beauty of the scene juxtaposed with the horror that had just unfolded felt disturbingly dissonant.

Farther along, the road climbed through billion-year-old basalt cliffs. Around a curve the highway crested, and the breathtaking panorama of Good Harbor Bay and the coastline fell away below them. In the gathering darkness, the great forests of spruce and balsam had turned two dimensional and now appeared as jagged black silhouettes fringing the reflective waters. A red moon rose full over the darkening water. The October moon. The Blood Moon.

It was Renard who finally spoke. Words that seemed to flow from the depths themselves and from his Ojibwe roots. "The red moon speaks of what has unfolded."

A short ways beyond Good Harbor Bay, Edna said softly from the back seat, "Your surname is French, Claude. You would be of the Marten Clan. Is that right?"

Renard studied her in the rearview mirror. "You know of our clan system?"

"I do. I've read a fair amount about the history of the Anishinaabe here in Minnesota."

"My grandfather was a voyageur. He also bore the name of Renard—It's French for 'fox.' My Ojibwe name means blue fox. In Ojibwemowin, the language of my people, it is *Waagosh Ozhaawashkwaa*. It was given to me because of my blue eyes. My mother was Swedish."

Edna tried the name, and Claude helped her say it a time or two until she had it.

"You mention that your grandfather was a voyageur," Brie said. "But they were here on the lake in the seventeen hundreds."

"In Ojibwe tradition we call all our elders Grandfather and Grandmother no matter how many generations back they are."

"I can see I have much to learn," she said. "But can you tell me why your deputies call you One Step? And Ned referred to you as Sheriff."

"They are not being cruel, if that's what you think."

"I think there must be a story behind the name," Brie said.

"There is. I joined the Army Reserve back in the early nineties to help pay for college. I majored in criminology at UMD, and after that, I moved back home and joined the Cook County Sheriff's Office and eventually rose to the rank of chief deputy. A few years after that, the sheriff passed away suddenly. In the interim, I was appointed to the office and became acting sheriff. I was known for having good organizational skills, and I had this favorite saying, 'One step at a time.'"

"Ah," Brie said. "Now I see."

"So I stayed at that post until the election a year and a half later. The deputies and everyone in the town took to calling me 'Sheriff One Step.' Being Native American, I kind of liked it. There was a nice feel to it, I guess.

"I had been encouraged to run for sheriff, and later on I did, and I was elected. But within a year after the election, my unit was called up—I'd stayed in the Reserves, you see. We were sent to Afghanistan. Long story short, one day the Humvee four of us were traveling in rolled over a bomb. I lost my leg, but the soldier next to me lost his life."

"I'm very sorry," Edna said softly.

"Thank you, Edna."

"So, home I came, eventually. A wounded warrior. And here's the town used to calling me 'One Step' and all. It caused a lot of consternation until I put the word out that I'd like to keep my moniker, if it was all right with everyone. Some of the townsfolk and the boys on the force still call me Sheriff—colloquially. Some things die hard in small communities. It's okay though, I guess."

"What a charming story," Edna said. "Not the part about your leg, of course . . ."

Renard smiled at her in the rearview mirror. "It's okay. I know what you mean."

They were just coming into the outskirts of Grand Marais. Renard decreased his speed, and they made their way down the hill and along 61, which runs through the middle of the town. On the north end of town, Renard turned left onto County 12, also known as the Gunflint Trail. The road immediately started to climb, and about a quarter mile up the hill they turned left into the Cook County Law Enforcement Center. Renard pulled into the parking lot in front, climbed out of the squad, and opened the back door for Edna to get out.

"I'll be back in a few minutes," he said, ducking his head in the car.

They walked toward the front door. Edna carried a canvas shoulder bag with her that held a book and her current knitting project.

Brie took out her phone. She had reception in town here. She wanted to talk to John out in Maine and tell him what had unfolded, and she knew that by the time they got affairs settled tonight, it was going to be late. She brought up his number and sent the call. He answered after a couple of rings.

"Brie. I'm glad you called."

"Sorry it's been a bit sporadic. Reception is sketchy up here."

"That's what you've said. It sounds very remote, but the truth is, it would be just the same here if you went to northern Maine. How's Edna doing?"

"Edna is fine, but something has happened. I know those are three words nobody wants to hear."

"Tell me what's going on. Are you okay?"

"I'm fine." She told him about the shooting at the cabin and the strange situation of Edna resembling Halley Greenberg. She also told him about the threatening letters.

"My God, Brie, where are you now?"

"Mom and I are with Chief Deputy Claude Renard from the Cook County Sheriff's Office. I'm calling from his squad right now. So we are both safe. No worries. Okay?"

"If you say so, but I don't like the sound of this." He paused. "And the chief deputy knows about the letters you received?"

"Yes."

"And what if Edna was the intended victim?"

"It's our biggest concern. The chief deputy has a plan to keep her safe." She told him about Renard and his father being members of the Grand Portage Band of Ojibwe, and Renard's idea to put Edna there with his father on the reservation. "If by chance she has a target on her, by the time the shooter knows he muffed up, she will have dropped off the map."

"And what about you, Brie? I need to know you're safe."

"I'm going to stay with her in Grand Portage tonight, and tomorrow I'm heading back to the Twin Cities. The answers to those letters may lie in a previous case I've cleared. Deputy Renard will investigate the murder of Halley Greenberg up here. At this point there's too little information to know which woman was the intended target, but I can tell you that law enforcement here will rigorously pursue the investigation with the assumption that Ms. Greenberg *was* the intended target."

"When will I hear from you again?" John asked.

"I'll call you tomorrow when I get back to the cities." She didn't tell him she had decided to delve into the case of her former partner's death. That was a discussion for another time. A time when she could explain why she had to look for those answers.

"I know this will always go with the territory, Brie. But it's hard. Especially when you are so far away."

"I know, John. I'm okay, though."

There was a brief silence at the other end. "I miss you."

"I miss you, too." They ended the call, and Brie sat for a few moments reflecting on how hard this would be if the tables were turned.

Before long, Renard exited the Law Enforcement Center. He had another man with him that Brie assumed was the chaplain.

They walked to the car, and Renard opened the back door. "Why don't you ride up front with me?" he said to Brie. "I'd like to get your thoughts on this interview."

Brie climbed out, and Renard introduced her to the chaplain. "This is Father George from St. John's Church here in Grand Marais."

"Pleased to meet you, Father." She held out her hand. "Is George your first or last name?"

The padre smiled. "It's my last name. First name is James. But please, call me Jim."

"Okay, I'll try. But I've always found that hard with priests."

"I'll bet you grew up Catholic."

"I did," Brie said.

He smiled a smile that anyone would warm to and nodded his head. "That always makes it harder."

She climbed in the front seat and let Father George take the back.

Chapter 13

Renard turned left onto County 12. The historic two-lane road, also known as the Gunflint Trail, wound north for 55 miles, deep into the Boundary Waters Canoe Area Wilderness. There the road terminated near Saganaga Lake on the northeastern edge of the Boundary Waters between Canada and Minnesota.

As soon as they turned onto 12 from the Law Enforcement Center, the road began to wind and climbed precipitously, and within a couple of miles they passed the turnoff for Pincushion Mountain. One of many entry points to the Superior Hiking Trail, the overlook there was also an ideal spot to watch the hawk migrations in the fall. Brie had once spent a weekend camped here doing just that. The overlook was so high as to be nearly an aerial vantage point—a literal bird's eye view of the village of Grand Marais, far below, and its tombolo, an unusual geographic feature whereby an island, in this case Artist's Point, is joined to a mainland by means of a deposited sandbar.

They followed County 12 north for four miles and turned left onto County 8, also known as Devil Track Road, and followed it for six miles. Except for the moon, darkness had now fallen. They passed the Grand Marais airport on the right and, a little farther on, the turn for the abandoned Skyport Airport and Seaplane Base, on the east end of Devil Track Lake.

Renard nodded toward the sign. "The seaplane base closed around 1989, but at a straight nine miles long, Devil

Track Lake possesses near perfect geography for landing seaplanes."

A couple of miles farther along, Renard spotted the fire number for Tom Norsted's cabin. They turned left and followed the gravel road, their headlights boring a hole in the blackness of the forest. The road dead-ended at a simple frame cabin. Renard killed the engine, and they climbed out. Out on the lake, moonlight ghosted over the water. This time of year, this far north, the temperature plummeted once the sun set. Brie stuck her hands in her pockets for warmth as they headed for the back door of the cabin.

Renard and Brie stepped up to the door, and Father George stood just behind in the gap between them. Renard knocked hard, and within a few seconds the door opened and a bald man of average height with slightly stooped posture stood before them. Brie had seen Jacob Greenberg's DMV photo when Renard had looked up the Honda's vehicle registration back at the cabins, and she knew the man standing before them was not Greenberg.

"Are you Thomas Norsted?" Renard asked.

"That's right, Officer. What's going on?"

"Is Jacob Greenberg here, Mr. Norsted?"

Norsted's expression changed from what had been a combination of curiosity and wariness to one of alarm. "Yes, he's here. We've been fishing together the past two days."

Greenberg must have heard some of the exchange from within the cabin because he now appeared behind Norsted. He was a tall, lean man with a neatly trimmed gray beard and dark, hawkish eyes. "What's going on, Tom?" he asked.

"Could we step inside, Mr. Norsted?" Renard asked.

"Sure." Norsted motioned them into the kitchen, and when Father George stepped out of the shadows and through the door, Greenberg's brow furrowed, and his eyes moved to Renard's face and held there.

"Is there somewhere we could sit down?" Renard said.

"What's going on here, Officer?" Greenberg's voice was just short of harsh. "I heard you ask for me. Tell me what this is about. Is my wife all right?" His voice broke slightly as he asked it. "Is this about her?"

"Mr. Greenberg, I'm very sorry to inform you of this, but your wife is dead."

Greenberg's mouth opened but nothing came out as he studied Renard for a moment and then Brie and Father George. He stepped back and felt behind him for a chair. Tom Norsted took him by the arm and guided him onto one of the kitchen chairs just to the left of them. Father George sat to the right of Jacob Greenberg, and Brie and Renard took the two chairs across the table from him. Tom Norsted stood behind his friend, a hand on his shoulder.

"Tell me what happened." Greenberg searched the chief deputy's face. "Was it a car accident?"

"No. I'm sorry to have to tell you this, but your wife was shot."

"Did someone attack her?"

"No. She was shot from a distance with a high-powered rifle."

"Oh my God." Greenberg buried his face in his hands. After a few seconds he asked, "Did she suffer?"

"No," Renard said. "Death would have been instantaneous."

"Could it have been a hunter?" Tom Norsted asked.

"I don't think so," Renard said. "Deer season hasn't begun. And anyway, this has the mark of a sniper." He kept his eyes on Greenberg as he spoke.

"Why do you say that?" Greenberg asked.

Renard studied him, knowing his words would wound.

"Look, Deputy, I'm a prosecutor. Whatever it is, I need to know."

"She was shot directly through the heart."

A moment ticked by and then Jacob Greenberg bolted up out of his chair and moved over to the kitchen counter, his back to the others. He stood for a moment and then brought his fist down hard on the counter. "No, no, no, no, no." His voice crescendoed with each repetition, and he pounded his fist as if he could somehow hammer away the truth.

Silence fell over the room. Brie could smell the coffee burning on the warming plate. The overhead light in the middle of the ceiling flickered occasionally, casting harsh blue light on them, making the kitchen feel a bit like an interrogation room. The window over the sink looked into a black void. A void into which it was possible Jacob Greenberg wished he could disappear.

Father George spoke to Tom Norsted. "Could you get your friend some water, or maybe something stronger?"

Tom Norsted disappeared into the room beyond the kitchen and in a few moments came back with what looked like whiskey in a short glass. He set it on the table and then steered his friend back to the table. "Come sit down, Jacob. Have a drink of this."

Greenberg allowed himself to be guided back to the table. He took a swallow of the whiskey and closed his eyes as it slid down.

"The search is under way for the shooter's position," Renard said. "We've called in the SWAT team from St. Louis County, and we have a gun dog on the scene as well."

Greenberg took another drink from the glass. "She was at the cabin at Cedar Falls. She was working on her writing. She was happy to have the time to herself." His eyes drifted to the wall beyond Renard, and his gaze came unfocused. "We always come up here this same time of year. She encouraged me to come up to Devil Track and fish with Tom for a couple of days."

Brie watched him closely when he said that and knew that Renard would be doing the same.

"This is Detective Brie Beaumont from the Minneapolis PD," Renard said. "As fate would have it, she and her mother were staying in one of the other cabins on the property. She spoke to your wife shortly before the incident unfolded. She is also the one who heard the shot and found your wife right afterward."

Greenberg turned his hawkish eyes on Brie and studied her face for a minute. "Was she still alive when you got to her?"

"It was only twenty or thirty seconds before I reached her, but I'm sorry to say she was already gone."

"What did she say to you when you talked earlier? Did she seem all right? Did she seem content?"

"We only spoke briefly this afternoon, down on the rocks by the lake, but she told me she was alone for a couple of days, that her husband had gone fishing with a friend up here, and that she welcomed the time to work on a piece she was writing." As she spoke, Brie searched Greenberg's face for any sign that he might recognize her. She hadn't been at the cabin with her mother for three years; her brothers had come the past couple of years. She was very curious about whether Greenberg knew of the similarities between his wife and Edna, but she was on Renard's turf now, so she kept silent.

Greenberg looked at his hands and the glass between them. "I never should have left her."

Norsted, who sat to his left, reached over and gripped his forearm. "This isn't your fault, Jake. You can't blame yourself. It seems the world is full of people right now who kill for no reason."

Renard studied Greenberg with a steadiness that was nearly tangible. "Can you think of any reason someone might have wanted your wife dead, Mr. Greenberg?"

Greenberg cast an inscrutable look at Renard. "Do you think this was something other than a random act?" he asked.

"I think considering the setting and logistics of the shooting, that it's more likely your wife was targeted," Renard said.

Greenberg took a swig of his whiskey. "I'm a federal prosecutor, Chief Deputy, assigned to the United States District Court in Duluth. One can't be in my line of work without making enemies. We put away some bad people."

Renard took out his notebook and leafed through to a blank page. "Does anyone in particular come to mind?" he asked. "Have there been any particularly troubling cases in recent months?"

Once again, Greenberg's gaze traveled back to the wall behind Renard. "There was one case two years ago. The attempted bombing of a synagogue in Duluth by a group of white supremacists who call themselves 'The White Wave.' We had enough evidence to arrest, try, and convict the ringleader. I've received a number of anonymous threats in the past year that I feel connect to that case and that hate group."

Renard made some notes. "Who's the guy you convicted?"

"His name is Robert Trader."

"And where is that group's base of operations?"

"In and around Duluth. Most of them live in the city or within thirty minutes of it."

Renard wrote some more notes. "I'd like to take a look at that case file," he said.

Greenberg nodded. "I'll have it forwarded to you."

"I have to ask where you were tonight at approximately five o'clock."

Greenberg nodded as if resigned to the fact that the question was coming. "I was out on the lake with Tom, fishing."

"Do you confirm that, Mr. Norsted?" Renard asked.

"Yes I do," Norsted said. "We headed out about four and stayed on the lake till a little after six o'clock."

Renard nodded and made a note of that. "Did your wife work outside of the home, Mr. Greenberg?"

"She does . . ." He paused a moment, collecting himself. "She did some freelance writing, and she was involved with several charity organizations in Duluth."

"Could you send me a list of those, please?"

"Of course," Greenberg said.

"What happens next?" Tom Norsted asked.

"Your wife's body has been taken to the Anoka County Medical Examiner's Office. Her body will be released once the autopsy is complete. The BCA is en route and will begin their investigation as soon as they arrive at the scene. If we can find the shooter's site, it may tell us more." He left it at that, but took a card out of his pocket and gave it to Jacob Greenberg. "This has my contact number. You can't return to the cabin at Cedar Falls. It's an active crime scene right now."

"I understand," Greenberg said.

"Jacob can stay here with me until we know more," Tom Norsted said.

"You should be able to collect your car and possessions from the cabin sometime tomorrow," Renard said. "We'll let you know when." He wrote down cell phone numbers for both men. "That's all for now, gentlemen."

"We are very sorry for your loss," Father George said. "The parishioners at St. John's and I will remember you and your wife in our prayers."

"Thank you, Father," Jacob Greenberg said.

With that Brie and Father George stood and left with Renard.

Chapter 14

Renard, Brie, and Father George drove in virtual silence. Clouds had moved in and covered the moon, so the darkness outside was almost total. Only the headlights of the squad kept it at bay. Brie stared out the window into the blackness, reflecting on how suited it felt to the events of this particular night. The wind had picked up, and she was aware of movement in the dark shadows of the forest. Seven miles east, they turned onto Highway 12—The Gunflint—and began the descent toward Grand Marais. Gusts buffeted the squad, occasionally giving it a violent shake, as if spirits carried on the wind sought their attention.

In this part of the state, all roads north climb toward the Laurentian Divide, and all roads south fall sharply away from it. So down and down the road wound over the next four miles. Finally they saw the lights of the Law Enforcement Center ahead on the right. Renard turned in and drove up into the visitors' parking lot in front of the building. Father George said good night, climbed out of the back seat, and walked to his car just down the line.

Once he had left, Renard turned to Brie. "So, any thoughts on the interview before I go in and get Edna?"

Brie let out a breath that was almost a sigh. "Well, he has an ironclad alibi. But since the crime bears all the marks of a hired gun, I don't guess that means a whole lot."

"That's exactly what I was thinking."

"What about his reaction to the news of his wife's death?"

"Very hard to say. I've seen some accomplished actors in my time as a homicide detective. That said, in this case, his behavior seemed genuine."

"I sense a 'but' in the tone of your voice."

Brie turned and looked at him. "I'm just troubled by the similarity between Halley Greenberg and my mother. It seems like too much of a coincidence, and I don't like coincidences."

"And yet you can't get past the fact that here are two different groups of people coming to this resort at the same time in the fall, over however many years, and these two women just happen to look a lot alike. I can't see that as anything but a true coincidence," Renard said.

"Or maybe a situation that was ripe for the picking," Brie responded.

"I'm not sure I follow," Renard said.

"Jacob Greenberg is an attorney—a prosecutor. He knows a lot about jury trials and reasonable doubt. Let's say—and we have no motive for this at this point—but let's just say he wanted to do away with his wife. How better to create reasonable doubt than by having two women who look so much alike both on the scene at the time of the shooting?"

Renard turned his head and looked out the windshield. "An interesting theory, and one that might come into play if I find in the investigation that there were problems in his marriage. I'm also going to interview the caretakers tomorrow and see if Jacob Greenberg inquired about who would be in that cabin of yours this week."

"Seems to me, if he *is* the perp, that he'd be more careful than that," Brie said.

"It could have been couched in some innocent inquiry. Like maybe they wanted to stay in a different cabin this year."

"I suppose that's possible," Brie said.

"We'll have to see what kind of motives the investigation turns up." Renard sat for a minute, thinking. "If you want to know what gives me pause, it's those threatening letters you received. They really muddy the water. If they relate to this incident, then the letters and the fact that Halley Greenberg was shot on the path leading from your and Edna's cabin suggest a different motive altogether. One that does not involve the Greenbergs."

He paused as if considering something. "Unless you take it a step further and posit that Greenberg sent those letters to you to make it look like Edna was the intended victim."

"Wow, that would take the prize for deviousness."

"But not necessarily beyond the realm of possibility," Renard said.

Brie sat silent for a few moments, thinking again about the car she had suspected of following them on the way north. And the odd feeling she had gotten about the man on Palisade Head whom she had seen through the binoculars. Of course, both of those occurrences could be written off to hypervigilance—a reaction to the letters she had received.

"Were there postmarks on the letters?" Renard asked.

"Yes. They were sent from different locations around the state. Apparently, whoever sent them was willing to travel to protect his location from being discovered. I'll be curious to know which way the evidence is leaning in this case. It may affect how we investigate the letters when I get back to the department."

"I'll keep you informed," Renard said. "There's this other angle, too. Greenberg's involvement with the prosecution and conviction of this white supremacist, Robert Trader. These white nationalist groups are not immune to violence. I can see them going for revenge." He ran a hand through his hair. "Stupid, though. They would have to know they would be among the first to be investigated."

"Sometimes craziness comes with its own form of entitlement," Brie said.

"That may be," Renard said. "But it will be easy enough to get a warrant for their phone records and computers and pick up a scent if they *are* involved in this."

"You'd think they would have been targeting the Greenbergs' house in Duluth, though."

"It's what I would have thought," Renard said. "I'm sure we'll learn more as the investigation gets under way. I'll let you know which way the wind is blowing."

"I appreciate that," Brie said.

"But until we know more, I'd like Edna to stay put with Dad on the reservation." Renard opened his door. "I should go get her now so we can head up to Grand Portage."

"My car is back at Cedar Falls," Brie said. "I was going to head back to the Twin Cities first thing in the morning."

"Once I get you and Edna up to Grand Portage, I'm going back down to the scene of the shooting. I'll bring your car when I come back up later on tonight."

"Do you live in the Grand Portage community?"

"No, I have a house in Grand Marais."

"It's a lot of extra driving."

"It is no trouble," he said.

Once again, Brie sensed an omnipresent patience about the man. A stillness that is almost always grounded in wisdom. "Thank you, Deputy," she said.

"You're welcome, Detective."

Brie smiled at the formality between them, but somehow, it had just the right feel for the gravity of the day.

Chapter 15

Renard climbed out of the squad and headed in to get Edna. Brie leaned forward in her seat and arched her back, stretching her spine. The time on the dashboard clock read 8:05. Her stomach was starting to set up a noisy protest at the absence of dinner. She knew Edna must be hungry, too. Maybe Renard's father would have sandwich fixings on hand when they got where they were going.

In a few minutes Renard and Edna came out the front door of the Law Enforcement Center. The strong north wind hit Edna's slender body, and Brie saw her stagger to the right a couple steps. Renard stepped around her to block the wind and put an arm around her shoulder to steady her. He guided her to the driver's side of the car and into the back seat.

"How you doing, Mom?" Brie asked.

"The day is starting to feel two days long," Edna said.

"I'll bet you're hungry."

"Oh, it's all right. We don't want to bother Claude here with that."

Renard smiled at her in the rearview mirror as he made his way down the hill from the parking lot and turned right onto 12. "I'm sure Dad will have some food for you when we get to his place."

Those words consoled Brie and her rumbling stomach.

At the foot of the hill they turned left onto Highway 61 and headed north out of Grand Marais. Edna crossed her arms on her chest and leaned her head against the door. Beyond the town, an inky blackness descended on them, and Renard switched on his high beams. They drove in what felt like a tense silence, Brie and Renard intent on the road ahead and the ditches off to left and right from which a deer might materialize at any moment.

"How many miles is it to Grand Portage?" Brie asked.

"About forty miles from Grand Marais," Renard said.

They went back on deer watch, and in about fifteen miles they passed the sign for Judge C. R. Magney State Park. There the Brule River flowed wild and wooly through a black basalt gorge where half the river thundered into a rock formation known as The Devil's Hole and disappeared. There was much speculation about where the water went from there.

Five miles beyond the park, Renard slowed as they drove through the small village of Hovland, and then the road began to climb again. Brie thought Edna had drifted off to sleep, but just beyond Hovland, her voice came from the back.

"I just remembered something," she said.

Brie turned toward the back seat. "What is it, Mom?"

"Something Halley Greenberg said to me this afternoon before she left the cabin and was shot." Edna paused for a moment and then went on. "She said, 'Life beats you up, and then it beats you down.'"

There was silence for a moment, and Brie felt Renard look her way in the darkness. "What were you talking about when she said that, Mom?"

"I think I had told her that I'd lost my second husband a couple of months ago. But when she said it, it seemed self-reflective, like maybe she was talking about herself. And now, remembering it, those words seem especially haunting in the light of what's happened." Edna's voice broke as she said that.

"It's okay, Edna. This is not your fault," Renard said, his voice gentle.

"But what if that bullet was meant for me? What if Halley Greenberg died for no reason?"

"You are not the one at fault here, Mom. The shooter is the one at fault and possibly whoever hired him."

"I wish I could just go home," Edna said. "Wherever home is. I'm not even sure anymore."

It was Renard who spoke. "I know this has been a terrible thing to go through, Edna, but right now, and until we learn more about this case, you need to be somewhere safe. I know you don't know me, but I hope you can trust me. I think in the morning things will feel a little better."

There was a moment of silence and then Edna said, "I do trust you, Claude. And I'm grateful for your help, even though it probably doesn't sound like it."

"It's all right, Edna. I understand."

Brie could not say what she was thinking because it would have terrified her mother. But what she knew was that if the shooter was a hired gun and Edna was the intended target, he would not rest until the job was done. She had also noted how many times Renard had checked his rearview mirror since leaving Grand Marais. In her mind there was only one reason for his vigilance.

Five or six miles farther along, the headlights of the squad fell on the sign that informed them they were entering reservation lands of the Grand Portage Annishinaabe Nation.

"Not too much farther now," Renard said. "We'll be at the turn into the Grand Portage community in about twelve miles."

Brie looked at the clock on the dash, which read 8:40. Ten minutes farther along, she saw the lights for the gas station and Grand Portage Trading Post—the last sign of civilization before the Canadian border, ten miles away. They slowed and turned right and drove past the gas station. Down the road to the right was a small lodge and casino run by the band.

They took the road to the left that wound down the hill past the interpretive center for the Grand Portage National Monument. Brie had visited the monument before. It included the interpretive center that sat high on the hill overlooking beautiful Grand Portage Bay and Hat Point, and at the base of the hill, the reconstructed eighteenth-century fort and fur trading depot from the days of the voyageurs.

Beyond the monument and the fort, the road hugged the bay. To the right, the dark waters of Superior stretched away. In the wash of the squad's high beams, Brie saw modest homes scattered along the road.

"We're on Bay Road," Renard said. "Dad lives out toward the end of Hat Point."

Five minutes farther along, the road climbed, and they made a right turn onto Upper Road and followed it for maybe a half mile before Renard turned left into a driveway.

The outside light was on, and it revealed a small but handsome log house. Brie and Renard climbed out, and Brie helped her mother out of the back seat. Renard collected their bags from the back and started up the path. The sweet, pungent smell of wood smoke issued from the chimney at the far end of the house. A set of copper chimes that hung from the front porch sang in the wind. It was a welcoming sound. Brie put an arm around her mother and led her toward the house.

Chapter 16

Renard knocked on the door and then opened it. "*Boozhoo,* Father," he called. It was the Ojibwe word for "Hello" or "Greetings" and sounded like "boo-zhoo" with the accent on the second syllable.

"*Boozhoo,* Claude."

Brie and Edna were right behind Renard, and he ushered them forward.

"Father, this is Brie Beaumont, the detective I told you about, and her mother, Edna." He turned to them and spoke. "This is my father, Joseph Renard."

"You are most welcome," Joseph said. He gestured toward the room on their right. "Come, sit by the fire. It is a cold night." Except for the color of his eyes and white hair, which he wore in a traditional braid, Joseph Renard bore a striking resemblance to his son. They were nearly identical in height with the same broad shoulders, straight nose, and high cheekbones.

Joseph guided Brie and Edna into the living room, where a fire burned in the large stone fireplace. The air smelled slightly of sage, and a wonderful aroma issued from the fireplace, where a big iron kettle sat on a rack above the fire. The delicious smell reminded Brie of the galley aboard the *Maine Wind,* where George Dupopolis, the cook, created his heartwarming meals on the old woodstove he lovingly called "Old Faithful."

"I've prepared dinner for us," Joseph Renard said. "I thought you might be hungry."

"It smells wonderful, Joseph," Edna said. "Thank you so much for offering the refuge of your home to us."

"You are most welcome. Claude has told me a little of what has unfolded. You will be safe here."

Brie sensed a shadow descend over her mother. The chief deputy must have felt it, too, because he spoke up. "You ladies sit by the fire, and I will help Father get the table set." He lowered his voice as he and Joseph walked toward the kitchen. "I can't stay long, Father. I have to return to my deputies at the scene of the shooting."

Joseph turned and studied him. "You need to eat, Claude. You have a long night ahead of you. A meal will not take long."

"I can help," Brie said.

Joseph turned and smiled at her. "In Ojibwe tradition only the men set the table, so allow us to get things ready while you two enjoy the fire."

"I like that tradition," Brie said. She led Edna over to the fire, where they sat on a large sofa with leather so soft it felt like butter against the skin.

The walls of the living room were decorated with a variety of weavings of Native American design. A large oil painting hung over the fireplace. It depicted Grand Portage Island and the sapphire waters of the bay over which an eagle soared. Brie stood and crossed to the fireplace to look at the artist's signature. It read "Elsa Renard." She wondered if Joseph's wife had created the work.

In a few minutes, Claude Renard came into the living room and lifted the black iron kettle from its rack over the fire. "Dinner is served if you will follow me," he said.

Brie and Edna did as instructed and followed him past the half-log stairs that rose to the second floor and into the dining room. The round oak table was set with woven mats and pottery dinner plates the color of wheat. An autumnal feast filled the center of the table. There was a platter of winter squash, oven baked to a nut brown, a large bowl of wild rice with what looked like dried blueberries and cranberries, a round plate with squares of cornbread, and the big black kettle that now sat on a stone base in the center of the table.

Edna spoke. "You have gone to so much trouble on our account, Joseph. We humbly thank you."

"It is seldom I get to welcome guests to my home," Joseph said. "I live a somewhat reclusive life since I retired and returned to the reservation. Please sit, and we will pass a sacred pipe for healing and protection." Everyone sat, and Joseph took a beautifully carved wood pipe from the small table in the corner. A large ceramic bowl contained what looked like dried herbs and chips of wood.

"These are the four sacred plants or medicines. Sage, sweet grass, tobacco, and cedar. They are gifts of the Manido—the Four Directions." Joseph took a small amount of the tobacco in his left hand, held it for a moment and then placed the tobacco in the bowl of the pipe and lit it. He said a prayer in Anishinaabemowin, the language of the Ojibwe.

"If you do not wish to smoke the pipe, you may place it on your left shoulder, above your heart, before passing it. We do not inhale the smoke but let it rise to the Great Spirit and to our ancestors who have gone before us." He sat at the table and took four puffs from the pipe, letting the smoke rise each time, and then passed the pipe to Edna on his left. To Brie's surprise, Edna smoked the pipe before passing it to Claude. When the pipe came around to her, she took four ceremonial puffs before passing it back to Joseph, who stood and placed the pipe back on the small table in its wooden holder.

Brie noticed that her mother seemed calmer, as if the pipe ceremony had brought some peace to her—as if the smoke from the sacred pipe had carried her fears, her concerns, with it to the Creator, the Great Spirit that Joseph had spoken of. The one who gentles and heals all things.

Claude lifted the lid on the iron kettle and carried it to the kitchen.

"The stew smells delicious," Brie said, for the pot unmistakably held a rich meat and vegetable stew.

"Fortuitously, I had started this in the afternoon before I knew of your visit. It's a combination of beef and venison with root vegetables from my garden. I hope it will be pleasing."

There were four bowls on the table, and Claude dished up the stew and passed a bowl to each of them. The wild rice, squash, and cornbread were sent round, and they began to eat in companionable silence.

"This is my first taste of venison," Brie said. "It's delicious."

"Venison is said to taste gamey," Joseph said. "But aging it in the refrigerator on a rack for five or six days will take away its gaminess. I like to cook it into a stew with vegetables and added beef or bacon, because venison does not have much fat."

"Edna knows something of our clan system, Father. She is a historian and was a teacher, like yourself. She might be interested to learn about Grandmother and the Bear Clan."

"I know only a little of your social structure and traditions," Edna said. "But I am very interested to learn more."

"My mother was a Mide, a healer," Joseph said. "Her father was Bear Clan. They are the healers and protectors. The child takes the clan of his or her father. Claude and I are Marten clan because of our French lineage that we trace back to the French Canadian voyageurs and the fur trading days with the North West Company."

"My husband's people, the Beaumonts, Brie's paternal ancestors, migrated from Quebec down into Maine. Brie's grandmother believes there was lineage with the Cree, one of the First Nations of Canada. But I'm sorry, Joseph. I interrupted you."

"Not at all, Edna. I am most interested in what you have just said. Many of the French Canadians married with the native women. The name Grand Portage is French for 'The Great

Carrying Place.' This area is steeped in the history of the French Canadian canoemen, known as the voyageurs, and their close liaisons with the Ojibwe during the height of the fur trading era in the seventeen and early eighteen hundreds."

"I have read that millions of pounds of furs and trade goods flowed in and out of Grand Portage during that time," Edna said. "All transported by the voyageurs, first by canoe and then along the eighteen-mile carry inland to Fort Charlotte and back."

"It is hard to conceive of," Joseph said, "but after paddling their vast canoes over a thousand miles from Montreal through the Great Lakes to this spot, each man would carry a hundred pounds of trade goods on the nine-mile trek inland and the same weight in furs on the trek back from Fort Charlotte. Often they made multiple carries. It's sad to think about, but in spite of their good-natured ways, the voyageurs were virtually human pack animals."

Joseph paused and sat back in his chair. "But the French voyageurs understood and respected the ways of our people and lived in such close harmony with them that the Ojibwe assimilated them into their communities, adopting them into the tribe and allowing them to marry with their daughters. Because the children of those unions needed a clan designation, and because the affection between the French and the Ojibwe was so great, the children of French fathers were taken into the Marten Clan, the clan of the warriors."

"A great honor," Edna said.

Joseph nodded. "That is true."

Claude caught Brie's eye and smiled, seeing his father and Edna so engrossed in tribal history. He had finished his meal and excused himself, saying, "Father, I must head back down to Grand Marais." He didn't mention the site of the shooting, but Brie knew that was where he was going.

"I understand, Claude," Joseph said. "You go ahead."

Brie checked her watch and was surprised to see that only a little over a half hour had passed since they had arrived.

Edna thanked Claude for his help and kindness. "I feel a bit like I've been adopted just as the French were all those years ago."

Claude smiled at her. "You rest easy here, Edna, and enjoy your time with Father."

Brie walked to the door with Renard.

"I'll keep you informed as the investigation unfolds and we learn more about Jacob and Halley Greenberg."

"And I you," Brie said. "I'm returning to the Twin Cities first thing tomorrow morning and will begin investigating the letters and looking into past cases for leads. See if I can find anyone who might have had opportunity to target me or my family."

"I'll bring your car when I come back from the crime scene later tonight."

"Thank you, Deputy."

"You're welcome, Detective."

She gave Renard her cell number, and he entered it into his phone. "I'll be eager to know if Ned Trainer locates the shooter's site and if so, what it will reveal in the light of day."

Renard nodded. "We need that information. It may bring some clarity." With that he was out the door. Before it closed, Brie heard the wind tuning itself up, jangling the chimes on the porch. And beyond, in the blackness, waves crashing ashore on Hat Point.

She closed the door against what felt like a hostile night and walked over to the fireplace in the living room. She could hear Edna and Joseph talking to each other. They probably thought she was out of earshot, but Brie heard everything they said and smiled to herself.

"I wonder why they are so formal with each other," Edna said.

"Maybe it is out of respect for their shared occupation," Joseph said. "Or maybe it is because they are attracted to each other, and the current circumstances are not appropriate for any expression of that."

"Maybe," Edna said, and she sounded a bit surprised at Joseph's words.

She probably doesn't have the heart to tell him that I'm somewhat spoken for, Brie thought. Like all parents, she knew Joseph would hope for Claude to find a partner in life. And to her thinking, he should have no problem doing so. He was a handsome and interesting man.

"Claude seems suited to the work he has chosen," Edna was saying as Brie returned to the table.

"When Claude was young, I encouraged him to spread his wings. I told him, 'You were raised Anishinaabe. You know the sacred ways and traditions of our band. Now you can be anything you wish to be.' I believe he has chosen well. Law enforcement is a noble calling, and he is of the warrior clan, known for their bravery and skills, so it is an appropriate choice."

Joseph and Edna talked on about the history of the Ojibwe and the French at Grand Portage. Brie was glad to see that he had not asked her mother about the horrors that had unfolded back at the cabin, but her own mind had returned to the reality of a woman shot dead and to what might possibly be the motive.

She sat quietly, finishing her dinner and thinking about the interview with Jacob Greenberg, trying to go over it in detail so as to commit it to memory. She pictured the kitchen of Thomas Norsted's cabin and recalled Greenberg's expression when he had been told of his wife's shooting. She thought about what he had said, how he had moved and reacted. Was it authentic? Were his the actions of a grief-stricken husband who had just received the most terrible news that life could deliver? Brie couldn't be absolutely sure, wasn't completely convinced. And so she returned to her cop mantra—the one she had learned from her first homicide commander. *Just work the case.* It was profoundly simple advice, but over the years it had proven surprisingly effective as a tactic.

There was a lull in the conversation, and Joseph Renard rose to make coffee. Brie and Edna carried the dishes to the kitchen, which like the other rooms, had rich pine floors and log walls the color of amber maple syrup. A big double window over the sink looked out into the blackness of the night in the direction of Lake Superior.

"I think once things are cleaned up, I'll retire," Brie said. "I want to start for the cities early in the morning."

"Claude took your bags up to the spare bedroom," Joseph said. "It's to the left at the top of the stairs."

"I'll be up soon," Edna said. "I'd like to help Joseph clean up a bit."

Joseph tried to protest but got nowhere.

"Thank you again, Joseph, for your kindness," Brie said. "When Claude first mentioned his idea to have Mom stay with you, I wasn't sure, but it was a good choice."

Joseph nodded. "You go now and get your sleep." He wrote down the phone number for his landline and gave it to her. "I do not have a cell phone. It makes Claude upset, but for now, I'm sticking with my choice. I have been told by others in the band that cellular reception is almost nonexistent here anyway."

"I'll call on the landline, and I'll be checking in with you every day, Mom." With that she said goodnight and headed for the stairs.

The bedroom was simply furnished with two twin beds constructed of log frames the color of honey and covered with thick wool blankets of Native American design that had been dyed red and orange and reminded Brie of flaming autumn leaves. A simple table between the beds held a lamp made from antler bone. It was turned on and cast a soft glow around the room. The log ceiling ran at an angle up toward the roof peak, making the room feel larger than it actually was.

On the wall above each bed hung a dream catcher made from what looked like red dogwood and sinew and decorated with beautiful beads and feathers. The Ojibwe believe that the good dreams will pass through the dream catcher, but the bad ones will be caught in the web. Brie hoped it would be the case tonight. Since the death of her partner and the advent of PTSD, bad dreams were known to stalk her sleep, especially after a day such as this.

There was a bathroom to the right, and Brie stepped in and turned on the light. She reached into the shower and turned on the hot water and went back to the bedroom to get her pajamas and toiletry bag from her duffel. Back in the bathroom, she undressed and stepped into the shower. She stood for a few moments, letting the stress of the day dissolve under the hot water and taking deep breaths that always worked to unknot her shoulder muscles. After a few minutes she washed her hair and soaped up and rinsed her body. She stepped out of the shower, wrapped the soft bath towel around herself and stood in the steamy bathroom, absorbing the quiet of the surroundings, allowing it to supplant the dissonance of the day.

She dried off, climbed into her pajamas, and brushed her teeth. She wiped the fog from the mirror with her towel and worked her long, wet hair into a braid. It would dry overnight. When she stepped out of the bathroom, she found Edna sitting on her bed.

"I decided to shower tonight so I can get an early start on the road," Brie said. "That way I won't wake you in the morning."

Edna nodded. "I know I was lukewarm about this plan, but it was a good idea. And Joseph is such a nice man. I'll be fine here until you think it's safe to come home."

"I'm glad, Mom. I don't want you to feel like you're on house arrest."

Edna smiled. "Well, I don't." She unpacked a few things and went in the bathroom to wash up. "I'll shower in the morning," she said, and in a few minutes she came out, turned off the light and crawled into bed.

The clouds had broken up a bit, and the full moon shone through the window between the beds. It cast its spectral light across the log walls. For a time Brie watched the shadows fold themselves over the rounded logs all around her, and soon she was gone. That night she slept as soundly as a bear in winter, and she dreamed. It was a good dream.

A giant eagle soars above Joseph Renard's home. An eagle so large its wings reach from one side of the roof to the other. From within the dream Brie wonders if this could be the legendary Thunderbird of Native American legend. The eagle carries her former partner, Phil Thatcher, on its back. He is alive and strong and happy, and that gives her joy. From his perch astride the eagle, he sends down showers of red leaves, the color of blood. There is something written on them. Brie leans out the window to try and catch one of them, but they are driven away on the wind and carried out over the stormy waters of Lake Superior.

Chapter 17

Brie woke when the first light of dawn began to bring shape and substance to the room around her. She quietly rose from bed, feeling surprisingly rested, and crept into the bathroom, where she washed her face and brushed her teeth. A few strands of long blond hair had escaped from the braid she had carefully plaited the night before. She tucked them back in as best she could and returned to the bedroom.

Edna slept soundly as Brie pulled on jeans, wool socks, a long-sleeved tee shirt, and a navy blue hoody. She slipped her feet into her shoes and stood at the window looking out for a few moments. In the light of day, she could see that the log house sat up on a hill with a fine vantage of Lake Superior out beyond Hat Point. Superior, this morning, was all dark water and wind-strewn whitecaps, as if the Manido—Spirits of the Four Directions—that Joseph had spoken of last night had converged to stir the great lake into a spectacular frenzy.

Brie picked up her duffel and left the room, closing the door carefully behind her. She had planned to get her keys and leave quietly without disturbing anyone, but when she got to the head of the stairs, the aroma of bacon and coffee and something savory cooking wrapped itself around her like a welcome embrace. As she came down the stairs, the early morning light illuminated the painting over the fireplace in such a way that, for a brief moment, she thought she was looking through a window at an actual eagle in flight. It was a *trompe l'oeil*, a trick of the eye, whereby a two-dimensional image mysteriously morphs into the three-dimensional world. A moment later the painting was back, but the experience was real enough that Brie stood for a moment on the stairs, hoping the magic might return. She thought about her dream in the night—the immense eagle carrying her partner Phil—and wondered if the painting had somehow triggered the dream.

In the kitchen she found Joseph pouring blueberry pancakes onto a griddle and Claude turning bacon—a scene of such domestic harmony she forgot about the keys and the car.

"Good morning, Brie," Joseph said.

Claude turned and nodded. "Morning," he said, almost shyly.

"Good morning to both of you. I was actually planning to just grab my keys and go," Brie said. "Then I smelled breakfast."

"One must eat before one begins a journey," Joseph said.

Brie smiled. "I like that philosophy. I know someone in Maine who feels exactly the same way." She thought about George and his woodstove and the wonderful aromas that would waft topside as the crew did their daily chores in the early morning light of the North Atlantic.

She reflected on the fact that she was about to begin two journeys—one physical, the other metaphorical. One that would take her home, back to the department, back to where she had spent fifteen years of her life, and one that would take her into the netherworld of a specific cold case. The case of her partner's death. A probe she would have to conduct far below the radar of Bull Johnson, her homicide commander.

Then there was the matter of the threatening letters she had received and whether they connected to Halley Greenberg's shooting or were meant to be a harbinger of Edna's death. What was more, she fully expected the commander to assign her a case as soon as she stepped into the division tomorrow. Long story short, she planned to be up to her eyeballs in investigations as soon as she got home. Oddly enough, Brie welcomed the fact. She could only abide so much downtime.

The food was ready. The kitchen had a small wood table, and they gathered around it as soon as the pancakes were done. A window next to the table looked out on the forest, where two deer had just ventured beyond the fringe of spruce trees. They stood statue-still, listening, turning their large ears like radar dishes. Brie held her breath for a moment, not wanting to move. A second later the pair bounded away.

"Did you sleep well?" Joseph asked.

"Surprisingly well," Brie said, but somehow she sensed a deeper undercurrent to the question. "I couldn't help noticing the painting over the fireplace last night and again this morning as I came down the stairs. It's quite remarkable." And then almost as an afterthought she added, "I dreamt of an eagle last night."

Joseph looked at her with interest—a gaze that seemed to see into her soul. "Your dream has meaning," he said.

It didn't seem to be a question, but how could he know that the dream had been deeply symbolic?

"I don't know," Brie said. "Why do you say that?"

"The eagle has great significance to the Anishinaabe, as it does in all Native American cultures. Eagles have a special connection with visions, and it is believed that eagles can serve as messengers between humans and the spirit world. The appearance of one in a dream can have a deeper meaning. The dream may be meant to teach you something or show you a path."

Brie was silent for a moment, considering his words. Then she said, "I've never believed in such things, but I have to say I found the dream both joyful and unsettling." It was said in the most respectful way, because the fact was that Brie had changed in the past six months. She had begun to think about things she never had before, some of them downright mystical. "The eagle was huge," she said. "Its wingspan overshadowed the house—this house. And it wasn't a bald eagle, but gold in color."

Now it was Claude who spoke. "The golden eagle, also known as the war eagle, is particularly associated with warriors and courage in battle." He paused for a moment and studied her. "It may be that you are about to enter into an undertaking that will require great courage."

Brie felt slightly uncomfortable about the topic at hand but equally astonished that what both Joseph and Claude were saying seemed to link with the nature of the dream. She didn't tell them about the presence of her dead partner in the dream, nor that she was about to embark on an investigation into the case of his murder, which had never been solved. Instead she simply said, "This is all very interesting. I appreciate you sharing this knowledge with me. I will see if the eagle visits me again."

"It is a good practice to write your dreams down. Especially ones that seem to have special meaning," Joseph said. "Even though you may not understand them when they occur, their deeper meaning may be revealed to you at a later time."

"Thank you," Brie said. "I will do that." She thought for a moment. "Considering what you have told me of the significance of the eagle, the painting in the living room seems even more interesting. It almost appeared to come to life as I descended the stairs this morning."

"My mother painted it," Claude said in a voice that held all of a son's gentleness and love.

"I saw the signature last night and wondered."

"My wife was a fine artist," Joseph said. "Her name was Elsa. She was of Swedish lineage. We met in high school in Grand Marais. We fell in love—a love that lasted forty-three years. We had a wonderful life together."

Brie looked at Claude. "You told us that's how you got your blue eyes."

He nodded. "It's a part of my mother I carry with me."

"That's a lovely thought," Brie said.

They continued eating. The pancakes were made with buckwheat flour, and the tiny blueberries had melted into the cakes. They would have been delicious even without the maple syrup.

"These are wonderful, Joseph. Thank you."

"The blueberries and syrup come from our tribal lands," Claude said. "We taught the first settlers about the sugar maples and how to tap the trees and make the syrup."

"We live in a world where so much is unreal—what is called virtual," Joseph said. "Children must learn to keep touch, literally, with the earth. Without that, they become anxious. They become lost."

"I agree with you, Joseph. I was wounded. The physical wounds had healed."

"But your spirit . . ." Claude said.

"Yes," Brie said softly, "my spirit was damaged. I went to the sea. I stayed there for six months. It helped to heal me."

They ate in silence after that. Brie watched out the window to see if the deer might return. There was no mention of the crime scene that Claude had revisited last night or Halley Greenberg's shooting. In any open case, there can be no discussion of the case outside the circle of law enforcement.

"Could you drop me at the Law Enforcement Center?" Claude asked.

"Of course," Brie said. She saw they were both finished with breakfast. "If you're done, we can get started."

They cleared their dishes even though Joseph protested. "Tell Mom I'll call her later tonight," Brie said.

"I will tell her. Be safe on your journey."

"Thank you, Joseph." Brie suspected his words encompassed more than just the drive home, maybe even more than the current case. She put on her jacket. Claude picked up her duffel, and they left with Joseph waving a last goodbye and closing the door against the wind.

Chapter 18

Brie could smell winter in the air—its essence clean, fresh, crisp. It is an odd thing to contemplate winter in October, but such is the capriciousness of Minnesota's far north. Words like *nip* and *bite* come into play. The air has a nip to it, or the wind has a bite. Moisture content becomes practically nonexistent, and breath drawn in through the nose carries a dry chill that makes the inside of the nose tingle in direct proportion to the plummet in temperature.

Tiny white flakes drifted aimlessly down as she and Renard came down the steps and headed for Edna's Jeep. Frost coated the windows, telling her the temp had dropped below freezing. Claude opened the back door and put her duffel on the seat, and she climbed in behind the wheel and turned over the engine.

"Do you have a scraper?"

"Back in the hatch," Brie said.

Claude retrieved it and set to work scraping the windows. Brie would have gotten out to help, but there was only one scraper. She fished her gloves out of her pocket and put them on. She crossed her arms, tucked her hands under her armpits, and hunched her shoulders up and down—a northerners' plan for warming the core.

In a couple of minutes Renard climbed back in, rubbing his hands and hunching his own shoulders, and they backed down Joseph's driveway. They headed out along the road that took them around Grand Portage Bay and back toward the highway. The waters of the bay reflected the leaden gray sky that had settled in overnight. A few gulls—late migrators—circled out over the water.

They turned south onto 61, and within a few miles the car had warmed up. Brie was about to broach the topic of the crime scene when Renard spoke.

"With the help of Ned Trainer and Nellie, we located the shooter's site last night. BCA immediately set up a perimeter and began working the scene. Of course, in the dark we couldn't see what the shooter had a vantage of. That question will get answered today."

Brie nodded. "Any casings?"

"As of last night, no. But we'll see what has turned up overnight. You're welcome to visit the scene with me and check the line of sight."

"That's all right. I need to get headed down to the cities. I'll leave it to you to keep me informed."

Renard nodded. "I'll contact you as I learn more." He paused and looked over at her. "Edna talked a little last night about your time in Maine. Do you think you will go back there?"

"Yes, but not right away. There's something I have to do before I can feel right about going back." She told him about Phil Thatcher's case and that it had gone cold. "He was my partner, so I wasn't allowed to work the case. I can't let it lie, though. I have to find justice for him."

"It could cost you your job," Renard said.

"It will cost me my conscience if I don't. I'll never have peace."

"I understand," he said. But there was a finality to his remark, a cop-to-cop understanding, and after that no more was said.

In a little over a half hour, they entered the outskirts of Grand Marais. "I think I'll have you drop me at my house,"

Renard said. "I'd like to change my uniform before heading to the crime scene."

"Sure," Brie said. "Which way do I go?"

"My house is out on East Bay. It's a left at the light once we get into town."

There is only one traffic light in Grand Marais, and they turned left onto Broadway when they reached it. Broadway skirted East Bay and ran out to the Coast Guard station, designated U.S. Coast Guard Station North Superior, and to Artist's Point, where it dead-ended.

"It's a block or so down past the historical museum on the left," Renard said.

The Cook County Historical Museum sat just behind World's Best Donuts that anchored the southeast corner of Broadway and Wisconsin Streets in Grand Marais. It was one of the busiest and tastiest spots in Grand Marais from Memorial Day through the Moose Madness Festival, the third weekend of October, which officially heralded the end of the tourist season in this remote northern outpost.

Claude Renard lived in a tiny gray frame house with a sloping roof that backed up to the bay and looked for all the world like it had been transported directly from the Maine coast and set down here for safekeeping. It was quaint and rustically charming, and Brie was captivated by the place. To the south, between the house and a small tract of woods, sat an old but sturdy lap-strake fishing boat with a vintage Evinrude outboard motor affixed to the stern. It was perched on a trailer, ready to go, but with snowflakes drifting down, it seemed an unlikely proposition.

"I can't believe you live here," Brie said. "Ever since I started coming to Grand Marais, years ago, I've been charmed by this house. It feels like a little piece of New England."

"Is that right? Huh," was all Renard said, and Brie was left wondering exactly which part of her statement he was responding to, but he said no more. Maybe he thought she was fishing for an invitation to see the inside of the place, which she definitely was not. It was possible that beyond the charm of the New England façade lay the typical home of a busy bachelor, and that fear had momentarily gripped his heart at the thought of anyone venturing there.

The street was empty this time of the morning, so she made a U-turn and pulled up in front of the house.

Renard opened the door and climbed out. He leaned over and stuck his head back in the door. "Thank you, Detective. I'll be in touch."

"You're welcome, Deputy," Brie said. They regarded each other for a moment, and a smile simultaneously crept across each of their faces. Renard nodded and closed the car door, and as he walked up to his house, Brie pulled away.

The road climbed steeply as Brie made her way out of town and brought the Jeep up to highway speed. The strong wind overnight had stripped the leaves from the birch trees, giving an unobstructed vantage of Lake Superior. Gusts of wind lashed the car, and giant snowflakes drifted out of the iron gray sky. Gale force winds were predicted for today—the gales of November come early that Gordon Lightfoot had written about. Just the kind of storm that had taken the *Edmund Fitzgerald* down with all twenty-nine souls aboard. Swallowed by the icy waters of Superior before she ever got off a distress call.

Brie reflected on the fact that she and Edna had been out sailing just yesterday on what were then friendly blue waters. No welcoming seas today. As she took the curve around Good Harbor Bay and crossed Cutface Creek, she could see giant swells driven ashore before a relentless northeast wind. She settled into her open road lacuna, watching the drama unfolding offshore. Twelve miles down the road she pulled into the Clearview General Store in Lutsen. She topped off the tank and walked down the boardwalk to the coffee house where she had picked up brews the previous two days.

Sonia, the barista whom she and Edna had met the day they drove up, was at the counter and greeted her like they were old friends.

"Hey there. Where's your mom today?"

"Just hanging out, relaxing. I'm just picking up a few supplies." She ordered a medium dark roast, black.

"Anything for your mom?" Sonia asked.

"Nope, just the one today."

Sonia filled a cup and put a lid on it. "You guys are staying up at Cedar Falls, right?"

"That's right," Brie said, becoming uncomfortable with the questions.

"How long did you say you're staying?"

Brie looked around, feeling uneasy. "Just a couple more days," she lied. She stuffed a couple bucks in the tip jar and made a show of checking her watch. "Oop, gotta run." She picked up her coffee and headed for the door.

Sonia waved. "Well, try to kick back and enjoy your stay."

"Thanks," Brie called over her shoulder. "Have a great day."

She headed back to the Jeep and climbed in. She wondered as she turned right onto the highway if Sonia was watching, asking herself why Brie was headed the opposite direction from the cabin. She took it as a sign she was now locked into full investigative mode—that space where you cease to trust anyone who is even remotely connected to the crime or the vicinity where it has occurred.

The miles rolled by as she followed the winding road west by south along Superior. Every now and then, a strong blast of wind would rock the car, causing her to focus on the road and the elements in play, and slowly her anxiety about Edna's vulnerability seemed to dissipate. She tried to think about cases she had cleared back before she and Phil had been shot, before he had died. Cases where someone might have held a grudge.

In a big city like Minneapolis, there is a constant flow of homicide cases. As soon as one case is cleared, reports are written and the case files archived. Then it's on to the next case. Details, specifics of a case may linger in the mind for a few days or even weeks but are eventually forgotten in the flood tide of new cases. So specific people on the periphery of those cases, the ones most likely to hold a grudge—wives, parents, children left behind to cope after a homicide conviction—may be difficult, even impossible to recall without digging deep into the case files. As for the perps, most of them had been given long sentences and weren't coming out anytime soon.

A few cases came to mind as she mentally drilled down into the two years before she had taken a leave from the department. But the one case that stood out in her mind went back farther. The case of Boyle Bouchard, who had been sent up on a manslaughter charge five or six years ago. As she recalled, he was originally from up here somewhere in the Arrowhead. She made a mental note to check on his status.

Chapter 19

Brie pulled off the road in Beaver Bay and put through a call to the homicide commander at the MPD. She was scheduled to return to the department next week but wanted to let him know she was available to return tomorrow. She got his voicemail and left a brief message. She had just hung up when her phone rang. It was Claude Renard.

"Hello there, Chief Deputy."

"Hello, Detective. I've got some information on the shooter's line of sight."

Brie braced herself for what might be coming. "Go ahead," she said.

"The shooter had a line of sight to both the Greenberg cabin and to yours. As to the cabin where you and Edna were staying, the view of the front door is obscured by the trellis attached to the porch rail, but there's a clear line of sight from the edge of the porch up the path to the gravel road that runs in front of the cabins."

He paused and Brie waited, sensing he had more to say.

"This means we have two possible lines of investigation. As we discussed outside the Law Enforcement Center last night, Jacob Greenberg could potentially have hired the shooter and even sent those letters to you in an attempt to make it look like your mother was the intended victim. You told me your mother goes to that cabin the same week every year, and apparently so do the Greenbergs. Jacob Greenberg certainly could have been aware of the similarity between the two women."

"Or my mother *was* the intended victim," Brie said.

"We'll know more as we dig into Greenberg's personal life and finances."

"As to the theory about the white supremacist group, I'd think if they were behind it, the gunman would have been targeting the Greenbergs' cabin," Brie said.

"Yes, but to my way of thinking, the shooter would have been primarily targeting a person. So while he might have been watching the Greenberg cabin, he would have been focused on the movements of that person. The close similarity between the two women really muddies the water." Renard paused for a second. "The fact is, Halley Greenberg is dead, and that points to the husband as a suspect. And even though the circumstances of the shooting are bizarre, we both know that next of kin always top the suspect list."

"So, best to just work the case then. Me from my end and you from yours," Brie said. "I'll be following several paths of inquiry when I get back to the department tomorrow."

"I think that's the best course of action," Renard said. "We'll be in touch, Detective."

They ended the call.

Brie got back on the road, and near Two Harbors she picked up a radio station in Duluth. The shooting was all over the news. "Wife of a prominent federal prosecutor and Duluth resident murdered. The name of the victim is being withheld pending notifications of next of kin."

Brie heaved a sigh of relief. She wanted to get down to the cities and stash her mother's car before Halley Greenberg's name was tied to the shooting. She called a friend from the Ramsey County Sheriff's Office. Tab Stevens, short for Tabitha, was a female deputy she'd met a few years back working a case in which the MPD and Ramsey County Sheriffs had collaborated.

She gave Tab a general rundown of the current case and told her they had put Edna in hiding and asked if there might be room to stash her car at the Ramsey County Sheriff's garages in Arden Hills. The thought of asking a favor from the MPD even before she returned to duty made her cringe. Tab said she'd check it out but thought it would be fine. Brie hoped so since interagency cooperation had been touted as the new gold standard in the past decade.

Within twenty minutes, Tab called back. "It's a go with your mom's car," she said. "I'm off duty today, but I can meet you up at the Arden Hills installation when you get back into the cities."

"That's great, Tab. Thanks. I owe you."

"No problem. I'll plan to drive you back to your place after we stash the car."

"You sure about that?"

"Sure as shootin'," Tab said.

Brie laughed. "Great. I should be back in to the cities close to noon. I'll call you when I'm an hour out."

They ended the call.

Below Duluth, the snow ceased, but the low-slung gray sky still brooded over the landscape. Brie returned to her open road space, and something about the Zen nature of just rolling down the highway put her at ease. She thought about Joseph Renard's words at breakfast. "Your dream has meaning." And his recounting of the Ojibwe belief that eagles have a special connection to visions and that the eagle can serve as a messenger between humans and the spirit world. If that were the case, Phil had appeared in the dream to convey something to her—to tell her something.

Brie smiled to herself. *You're getting to be an awful lot like Ariel,* she thought. And yet the dream seemed to haunt her, but in a good way. As the miles rolled by she thought about her former partner. How well they had worked together. What a great friendship they'd had. What a hard worker Phil had been, but how he had always made special time for his wife and son.

As the miles ticked by, she slipped back to that night—the last night she had been with Phil. The darkness of the house on Upton Avenue North where they had responded to an intruder call just after midnight. The blackness as they had entered through the open front door of the house. The sudden sense of movement, Phil responding to the movement, turning his light and gun, the deafening sound of the shot as the gunman fired on Phil, and then falling, falling, as if into a black well.

Brie suddenly looked around, aware that she had been driving on autopilot while in deep remembrance of that night. The landscape rolled by as it had been, but something was different. She realized that she had remembered something—something new. Phil had turned his light and gun toward the intruder.

In all the times she had relived that night, in all the PTSD-fueled flashbacks she had experienced, this was the first time that particular detail had come clear. Prior to this recollection, there had only been darkness—total darkness as they had entered the house and the shooting had unfolded. But she knew that couldn't have been right, because they both would have been carrying flashlights.

There was more, though—something of even greater import. She had seen the shooter aim directly at Phil and fire. In all the other flashbacks over the past nineteen months, she had glimpsed movement and then Phil diving in front of her, taking the shot, and then both of them falling into darkness.

The recollection of these new details shocked her, but also gave her hope. Hope that she might possibly remember something else. She thought again about returning to the police psychologist, the one she had worked with after the shooting.

"I'm going to get to the truth, Phil," she said aloud. "I'm going to find out what happened and close the case." She waited, almost hoping to hear him say, "I know you will." But of course, her rational self knew that couldn't happen.

Still, she couldn't help thinking again about the dream with Phil astride the great golden eagle. Maybe it wasn't just a dream. Maybe it *was* what Joseph Renard had called a vision. And maybe if she believed—believed in herself and this process—she might be shown the next step. As the rest of the miles rolled by, a profound sense of peace seemed to descend over her. A peace she could not remember feeling. Not since the death of her partner.

Chapter 20

Before Brie knew it, she was approaching Hinckley, an hour or so north of the cities. It had been almost three and a half hours since she and Claude Renard had left Grand Portage. She pulled off for a bathroom break, gassed the car, and hit the White Castle drive-thru, where she ordered a cup of coffee. She pulled ahead to a small parking area and drank half of the coffee. Then she put through a call to Tab Stevens and told her she was a little over an hour out and set a time to rendezvous with her at the Ramsey County Sheriff's Office in Arden Hills, just up the road from Minneapolis.

Then it was back on the road for the last leg of the trip.

As she drove due south, flat brown farmland sprawled to east and west. A dusting of snow across the harvested fields lay like a stark harbinger of the coming season. She rolled down the road past exits for Pine City, Rock Creek, and Rush City, and within forty-five minutes she was on the outskirts of Forest Lake.

A short way below Forest Lake, she took the 35W split toward Minneapolis. Arden Hills was located north and east of Minneapolis, and its western boundary abutted 35W. The Ramsey County Sheriff's Office sat a little over a mile east of 35W on Highway 96. Within twenty minutes, Brie took the 96 exit. The sheriff's department and installations sat on the southeast corner of a sprawling tract of land—2382 acres—that had housed the Twin Cities Army Ammunition Plant.

Construction of the Twin Cities Ordnance Plant, later renamed the Twin Cities Arsenal and finally, in 1963, the Twin Cities Army Ammunition Plant, had begun in August of 1941, a sign that the United States fully anticipated being drawn into a world war—a probability that became reality just four months later. Employment at the munitions factory peaked at 26,000 in 1943, with more than half of the employees being women. Brie had never been a soldier, but still the history of the place interested her.

With each new war—Korea, Vietnam—the installation was brought back into production, and finally, in 1983, the site was added to the National Priorities List as a Superfund site due to the extreme contamination of soil, sediments, and ground water from a brew of dangerous chemicals used in the production of ammunition. Since the cleanup, the destiny of the site had hung in the balance several times, once as a potential site for the new Vikings stadium.

Brie took a left on Lexington, and just after that, another left into the Ramsey County Sheriff's installation. She drove around the facility to the municipal garages and spotted Tab Stevens sitting in her car. After they greeted each other, Brie gave Tab the key to the Jeep, and Tab got behind the wheel and drove it into one of the garages. She was back out in a few minutes, and she and Brie got into her Subaru and headed back toward 35W.

They were both quiet for a time as they rolled down through Roseville and arced west and south toward Minneapolis.

Tab glanced sideways at Brie. "Is your mom okay?"

"I think so," Brie said. She had told Tab about the threatening letters but couldn't go into any details of what had unfolded up North.

"Do you have any idea who might be behind this?"

"None," Brie said. "But I'm returning to the department tomorrow, and we'll start to dig into it."

"How are you doing anyway?" Tab asked.

"I'm doing okay. Better than I was six months ago."

"I heard through the grapevine about the leave you took."

Brie was quiet.

"I get it, Brie. For my part, I think you did the right thing."

Brie smiled. "Yeah, well, we'll see what kind of a reception I get tomorrow."

"Hey, girl. Just take it one day at a time."

"I will," Brie said.

"Let's get together some weekend," Tab said. "You come over, and we'll all watch the Vikings. Frank puts out quite a spread for the games."

"That'd be great." Brie knew that she and Tab were both hard-core, lifelong Vikings fans.

"This is our year, you know."

"So I keep hearing. We've heard it all before, though."

"You have to believe," Tab said.

"Yeah, okay."

Tab laughed. "I know it's not your way. You're a pragmatist."

"I'm working on opening that other door."

"I'll loan you a crowbar."

"Very funny."

Tab took the Hiawatha exit, and within minutes they were approaching Brie's house in the Longfellow neighborhood. Brie reminded her where she lived and directed her along the side streets until they reached the two-story duplex.

Brie climbed out and retrieved her duffel from the back seat. "Thanks, Tab. I owe you one. Do you want to come in?"

"No, I gotta get back. The kids will be getting home from school soon."

"Well, thanks again," Brie said. "I'll be in touch."

She watched as Tab pulled away and then headed around the house and up the stairs to the back door.

Brie stood in her kitchen, looking around. The idea that just three days had unfolded since she'd driven north with Edna seemed outlandish. But it was true. She walked into the bedroom and deposited her duffel on the bed and went back out into the dining room. The envelope with the four threatening letters still lurked at the edge of the table. She paused and studied it for a few moments as if it were some kind of toxic substance that needed to be dealt with, she knew not how.

She despised the fact of it being there, and yet it was hard to draw her eyes away from the envelope, as if it possessed some magical power to ruin her life and so needed perpetual watching.

Finally she walked to the kitchen and took a piece of paper from one of the drawers and started a grocery list. When troubled, choose a mundane task and press on. It was a skill she had learned over years of dealing with the kinds of trauma she met daily in her work. Bread, lunch meat, milk, cereal, lettuce, chicken breasts, laundry detergent, red wine. She smiled at that one. *Home only ten minutes and already I need a drink.*

She finished the list and grabbed her jacket and car keys. She wanted to get to the store and back home before the traffic got bad. She headed down the back stairs and got in her car. She'd turned it over the night after she got home from Maine and had been amazed that it started. She backed out of the driveway and headed for Cub Foods a few blocks away.

She made her way through the grocery store feeling like she was in a foreign land rather than the place where she'd purchased her food for the past twelve years. She noted the oddness of the situation but didn't dwell on it. She knew in her heart of hearts that while she'd been gone only six months, she had somehow in that time lived out what felt like an entire other existence.

She walked down the aisles gathering what was on her list, and things she had forgotten to write down, and within twenty minutes she was in the checkout aisle, unloading her cart. She bagged the groceries—three bags in all—and headed for the car. Fall in the cities was still on as she drove through the neighborhood streets. Despite the wind that seemed intent on stripping them away, red and orange leaves clung tenaciously to their branches, boosting the mood of the otherwise colorless and gloomy day.

Brie carried the groceries up the stairs and unlocked the door. She spent a few minutes stowing the supplies and unpacking her duffel, then collected her laundry in a basket she kept in the bedroom and headed out the back door. There was a separate entrance to the basement from the outside, and she unlocked the door, flipped on the light, and headed down an open flight of wood stairs.

Rough limestone walls gave the basement a cave-like look and feel, complete with dank smell and its own underground stream that during a bad rainfall would materialize and flow through the front wall to wend its way toward the floor drain near the washer. By this time of year, though, the tributary would usually dry up so that doing one's laundry felt less like a spelunking expedition.

The washer and dryer sat against the left wall, and there was a six-foot table for doing folding. Brie put her load in and headed back up the steps, taking them two at a time. Back upstairs she went through her closet and picked out an outfit for the next day. Black slacks, a lightweight gray sweater and flat black ankle boots with laces. She looked at her phone and noticed that Bull Johnson, the homicide commander, had returned her call while she was in the basement. She listened to his voicemail telling her that he was fine with her returning tomorrow and that, as usual, they were overrun with cases.

Brie went out onto the porch. It was accessed via French doors in the middle of the living room wall and was the feature she had always liked best about her apartment. It sat directly above her landlady's porch and overlooked the street. The porch had a tongue-and-groove floor that she had covered with a colorful area rug. A set of rattan furniture that she had picked up at an estate sale gave the space just the right feel. She opened the porch windows so the fall air could blow through the apartment. Then she stretched out on the sofa and brought up Joseph Renard's number, which was a landline. He answered on the fourth ring.

"Hello, Joseph. It's Brie Beaumont."

"I'm pleased to hear from you, Brie. Did you have a safe journey?"

"Yes. Quite uneventful," Brie said.

"That is what one would hope for under current circumstances."

"Is Mom around, Joseph? I thought I should let her know I arrived safely."

"I'll get her."

In a couple of minutes Edna answered the phone. "Hello, sweetheart. Did you have a safe trip down?"

"I did. I've just been pulling things together around here so I can return to the department tomorrow. But I wanted to check in with you since I didn't get to say goodbye. Are you and Joseph getting along well?"

"We are. He's such a kind man, Brie. He took me to visit some of the sacred sites on the reservation today. I was deeply honored by that. Tomorrow if the weather is good, we are planning to hike up to the top of Mount Rose."

"That's quite a climb, isn't it, Mom?"

"Yes, but Joseph says the views from up there are well worth the effort." She paused for a moment, and Brie sensed there was something on her mind. Finally she said, "Will you tell me what you find out about those letters you received, Brie?"

"I'll tell you whatever I'm able to, Mom. Please don't worry, though. You are safe."

"It's not me I'm worried about, Brie."

"I'm fine, Mom. I'll talk to you tomorrow."

"I'll look forward to that," Edna said.

They said goodbye and hung up.

Brie set the phone on the floor and turned her gaze to the windows. The leaves swirled helter-skelter in the wind. She was tired from the long drive home, and the sound of the wind around the eaves was just hypnotic enough that she drifted off to sleep.

Chapter 21

It was dark outside when she woke up. She picked her phone up off the floor and checked the time. Just after six o'clock. She got up and went to the kitchen and pulled out a piece of tilapia. She pan-grilled the fish in a dusting of flour and mild spices and paired it with some steamed green beans to which she added a dash of olive oil and a squeeze of lemon.

For the first time in her life, cooking from scratch seemed as natural as breathing. All thanks to George Dupopolis and her time on the *Maine Wind*. Because George cooked alone aboard ship—no messmate—both Scott and Brie were accustomed to helping out in the galley when needed. Assisting George had demystified cooking for Brie. Aboard ship everything was fresh, so everything was cooked from scratch. She had learned how to prep the food and how simple it was to make it taste great, because it *was* fresh. And she had vowed there would be no more frozen dinners for her when she got home.

She carved a thick slice of artisan wheat off a loaf she had bought that afternoon, spread it with real butter, and poured herself a glass of pinot noir. She took her plate to the living room and turned on World News Tonight on the local public television channel.

She'd just finished eating when her phone rang. She checked and saw it was John, calling from Maine.

"Hey, you," she said into the phone.

"Hey, yourself," John said. "Hope this is an okay time. You've been on my mind all day. Did you get back to the cities safely?"

"Yup. Everything's good. Edna's in a safe place. She hit it off right away with Claude Renard's father, Joseph. He used to be a teacher like Mom. After his wife died a number of years ago, he moved back to the reservation and built a home there."

"That's good to hear, Brie. This has to be hard for Edna."

"I think she's more worried about me than herself."

"Well, of course she is. You're her daughter. So, how are you going to investigate those letters you received?"

"I'm returning to the department tomorrow. I've already cleared it with the commander. I'm going to ask his permission to search through cases I've closed in the past couple of years. See if anything jumps out."

There was silence at the other end of the phone. "So you're returning to your job," he finally said.

"I have to, John. Edna may have been the intended victim in this shooting. If that's the case, I have to get to the bottom of it."

"Can't someone else investigate?"

"Only I can find the answers in those case files. The only other person who knew those cases was my partner Phil, and he's dead."

She realized it was time to break the news to him that she had decided she wasn't returning to Maine until she solved her partner's murder.

"There's more, John, and I know this part will be hard for you to hear."

"I'm listening," he said, and she could hear the gentleness in his voice but also the frustration.

"I've realized that I have to try to solve Phil's case." She paused a moment to let that sink in. "When I left Maine, my intention was to turn my resignation in to the department, close up my apartment here, and move back to Maine."

"So, what changed that?"

"You know my partner Phil was murdered."

"Of course I know that. That's when you were shot."

"And you know the killer was never found."

"You told me that when we talked about it over the summer. You said the case went cold."

"That's right. While I was lying in the hospital with a gunshot wound, unable to do anything about it."

"So you're going to try to solve Phil's case."

"Yes," was all Brie said.

There was a long silence at the other end.

"I suppose you'll be working with Garrett Parker. Make sure you give him my love," John said facetiously.

Brie smiled. "I'll do that, John." She recalled that the two of them had gotten into a heated argument when she was running the investigation on Granite Island back in May. Because of the remote location they were in, Brie had sought Garrett's help via long distance to run some background checks on the suspects. Garrett had made no bones about the fact that he thought Brie needed to come home.

"Well, he's got what he wanted. You're back there."

"Just temporarily, John. Once the case is solved, I'm leaving."

"Yeah. Does *he* know that?"

"I'll get farther with Phil's case if I keep my plans to myself."

"Why's that?"

"I'll tell you why. According to department protocol, I'm not allowed to work on his case."

"Why?"

"Because he was my partner, and I was shot in the same incident that killed him. There's conflict of interest. It's just the rules, John. And it will be easier for me to find the truth if everyone at the department doesn't know I'm on borrowed time."

"Or maybe you're going to need Parker's help with the case. Maybe you're going to ask him to cover for you."

"Really, John. That sounds a lot like jealousy. And if it is, it's unbecoming. You know my heart is with you."

There was silence at the other end. "You're right, Brie. I'm sorry. I'm acting like an idiot. It's a part of me I'm working on—the idiot part."

Brie laughed. "I'm not perfect either, believe me, and I know it's hard to be apart like this. But I have to close this chapter of my life. And, since being back here, I've realized that if I don't find justice for Phil, it will haunt me for the rest of my life. I have to do this, John."

There was another short silence from his end. "I get it, Brie. And I love that you will not walk away. That you have to do the honorable thing."

"It's about more than honor, John. It's about peace. I have to face the darkness that killed Phil—that almost killed me. If I don't, I'll never be whole again."

"What if it can't be solved, though?"

"I don't accept that," Brie said. "At least I have to try."

She heard him draw in a breath and let it out slowly.

"I know you'll find the answers," he said. "And however long it takes, I will wait."

"Thanks, John. Now, that's the man I love talking."

They chatted a little more about the off-season work going forward on the *Maine Wind*, and then it was time to end the call.

"I should go, John. I have a few more things to do before I turn in."

"That's fine, Brie."

"I'll call you tomorrow." They ended the call.

Brie got up and took her plate and wine glass to the kitchen and washed them. She headed into the bedroom. Rain was predicted for the next day, so she took her black, belted trench coat out of the closet and laid it on the chair. As an afterthought she went back to the closet and took her gray wool fedora down from the shelf, brushed it off, and tossed it on top of the trench coat. It had always been her detective's ensemble for cold rainy days in the spring and fall. Just seeing them lying there ready for action made her feel back in the groove. She set her MPD shield on the chair. She would clip it onto her slacks when she dressed in the morning. She got out her soft-sided briefcase and put the evidence envelopes containing the threatening letters into it and set it on the floor next to the chair.

She hauled her upright vacuum out of the closet and gave the apartment a good vacuuming and then a proper dusting. She opened some more windows and let the fresh air blow through while she laid things out in the bathroom for her morning shower. Then she buttoned down the windows, checked the back door, and got into her pajamas. She went to one of her piles of books in the living room and found a spy novel by John LeCarre that she had picked up at a used bookstore. She went back to the bedroom, turned on the bedside lamp, and set an alarm on her phone for the morning. Then she climbed into bed with the book. Within twenty-five pages, the book dropped to the floor. She reached over and shut off the light and fell into a dreamless sleep.

Chapter 22

By the following morning, Thursday, the inclement weather had arrived in the Twin Cities, and a drizzly rain, right on the edge of sleet, caught drivers unaware and sent cars sliding off the road. Brie made her way northwest on Hiawatha Avenue to the 7th Street exit and into downtown Minneapolis. She pulled into the Government Center parking ramp and parked in the contract section. Even with the bad weather, the commute took her less than fifteen minutes. It was the main reason she had stayed so long where she lived. She hated traffic jams.

She took the elevator down to the tunnel level and headed north toward City Hall, which housed the Minneapolis Police Department along with the mayor's office, the offices of the Hennepin County Sheriff's Department, and the jail. The tunnel brought her out at ground level at the back of City Hall, and she made her way along the west hallway to the rotunda and the grand staircase. Six dizzying stories above the rotunda, a domed skylight containing 76,000 pieces of glass glowed like an enormous green and white jewel.

Anchoring the rotunda, the *Father of Waters* sculpture symbolized the Mighty Mississippi that flows between St. Paul and Minneapolis, separating the two cities. Brie paused for a moment in the old man's presence. He had been sculpted from the largest single block of Italian marble ever taken from the celebrated Carrara quarries in Italy that had supplied Leonardo da

Vinci and Michelangelo. Commissioned by twelve Minneapolis citizens, the sculpture had been presented to the city in 1904 as a gift.

Father of Waters reclines on a Native American blanket, leaning against the paddle wheel of a river boat. But were he to rise from the river, he would stand over 15 feet tall and weigh 14,000 pounds. Brie made a tour around the venerable old fellow and then rubbed his big toe. It was said to bring good luck. Over the next few weeks, she was going to need plenty of that. Then she took the marble stairs—slightly concave from over a century of wear—up to the first floor to the Minneapolis Police Department.

Down the corridor to her left, she entered the double glass doors that led to the MPD investigative units and to the other divisions within the department. At the end of the hall she passed through two more doors and found herself back in the place she had left six months ago. Nothing had changed and yet the place felt somehow different—both bigger and smaller than it had before her departure. Bigger because the scope of the building lent a grandness to everything that resided there, and smaller, maybe, because the views from the windows, of downtown Minneapolis, seemed to dwarf the department itself.

Brie found her old cube in the Homicide Unit and peeked in. One desk was clearly in use, the other not. She wondered if she'd still be assigned to this desk. She'd come in early, before detectives on the day shift normally arrived, so she could avoid making an entrance.

She turned and looked out the windows at the city. The rain was coming down harder now. She remembered rainy days aboard the *Maine Wind* and thought about what a different view this was from the one she'd become accustomed to.

"Beaumont. Can I see you in my office?"

Brie turned and saw Commander Bull Johnson standing in the doorway to his office. She headed in that direction.

Bull Johnson didn't abide fools or liars. Coming up through the ranks, his nickname had been "No Bull Johnson" but somewhere along the line, the "No" part had been lost. Maybe because just plain "Bull" described him best. A towering black man, he led a headlong, no-holds-barred charge into each investigation. Focus and momentum were everything to him. His voice had the timbre of a Patrick Stewart, sans British accent, and while he'd never said, "Make it so," that was his constant subtext. And truthfully, in the realm of homicide investigation, there was no other way. Cases not solved in forty-eight hours would more than likely never be solved, slipping into a no-man's-land of cold cases—that vast and bleak territory from which few ever returned.

"Close the door, Beaumont," the commander said as she entered.

"Yes, sir." Brie shut the door and turned to face Bull Johnson.

"Welcome back, Detective," he said. "We're happy to have you back here."

She hoped it was true, but there was an edge to his voice that raised a question in her mind.

"Thank you, sir. It's nice to be back," she said reflexively, not knowing whether or not she really meant it. "Am I still assigned to the same desk?"

"Same desk, same locker," he said.

Brie nodded. "Thank you, sir."

"A call just came in. We've got a body up in Theodore Wirth Park. I'm teaming you up with Garrett Parker for now. As soon as he gets in, I want the two of you to head up there."

"That's a big park, sir. Do you have an exact location?"

"The crime scene is north of 55, near the bridge."

Brie nodded. "Did Parker tell you about the letters?"

"What letters?" the commander asked.

She took the evidence envelope with the threatening letters out of her briefcase and laid it on the desk. "These were mailed to me over the past two and a half months. Of course, I wasn't here to receive them, but they were among my mail I collected from my landlady when I got back home. The first two say, 'You'll be sorry.' Then the messages escalate. The third one says, 'You're going to pay.' The last one says, 'You can't stop what's coming.' The messages are composed of letters cut from magazines and pasted on plain printer paper."

"Any idea who might be behind this?" Johnson asked.

"Not offhand, sir. I'd like permission to go back through the cases I've cleared in the past couple of years. See if anything jumps out. Also check to see if any of the perps from earlier cases have been paroled."

Bull Johnson gave her a steely look. "Trouble seems to follow you around, Beaumont."

"What's that supposed to mean, sir?" She didn't like his tone of voice, but after what had just happened up North, she had to admit he had a point.

"Just this, Beaumont. Now that you're back, I want your head in the present."

"All due respect, sir, those letters are the present."

He locked eyes with her for a couple of moments. "I'll get the letters over to the crime lab. See if they can pull any prints or DNA off of them." He picked up the envelope and placed it on the left side of his desk. "Let me know if you find any leads in the case files. Anything that might give us a clue as to who sent these."

"Yes, sir."

He opened the right-hand desk drawer, took out her duty firearm and slid it across the desk to her. "That's all, Beaumont. Collect Parker and head on up to Wirth Park. Crime Lab should be on the scene by the time you get there."

"Yes, sir." She picked up the gun and holster. "Is that Parker who's sharing my cube now?"

"That's right."

She nodded and turned to go. She paused at the door, knowing she had to tell him about the shooting up North. Even if it didn't involve her mother, she had been on the scene —was the reporting officer—and so was tied to the case. She turned back around, walked back to his desk and gave him the details of what had unfolded and the paths of inquiry the chief deputy was pursuing.

Bull Johnson studied her for a few moments. "And you say this woman looked like your mother?"

Brie sidestepped that a bit. "From a distance it's possible they could have been mistaken."

"Like I said, Beaumont, trouble seems to follow you around. I'm glad you informed me about the situation, but that's off our turf. It's Cook County's investigation, and I don't want you involved in any way. Is that clear?"

"Crystal, sir."

"I want your head in this Theodore Wirth murder. Beyond that, keep me informed about any leads you turn up on those letters."

"Yes, sir." She turned to leave once more.

"Beaumont," the commander said as she had her hand on the door.

"Yes, sir," she said, turning back to face him.

"I had a call from Lieutenant Dent Fenton at the Maine State Police. He had high praise for you." He paused and studied her. "He told me about the case you worked with his team up in Tucker Harbor, Maine, as well as two other cases you were involved in there. Impressive, Beaumont."

"Thank you, sir."

"You're a fine Detective, Beaumont. I'm glad your head is back in the game."

"Yes, sir."

"That's all. Report to me later on the case in Wirth Park."

"Yes, Sir." She turned and left his office.

She stopped by her cube, but Garrett Parker wasn't in yet, so she headed for her locker to stow her shoulder bag and her off-duty weapon. She went back to her cube and pulled up a list of all the cleared cases she had worked throughout her time as a detective at the MPD. The list was long. She was poring over it and noting down case numbers on a piece of paper when Garrett Parker walked in.

"Brie! The commander said you were coming back today."

"Hey, Garrett." Brie stood up, and they gave each other a quick hug.

"It's good to have you back." He held her at arms' length. She'd forgotten what intense blue eyes he had. Today they appeared full of warmth, but she'd seen them reflect the full gamut of emotions. A slow smile spread across his face and deep dimples appeared on either side of his mouth, giving him a boyish look even though he was nearly a decade older than Brie. "I see you're already hard at work." He nodded toward her monitor. "Same old Brie."

She didn't tell him that she was here for one reason and one reason only. To close a cold case—the case of Phil Thatcher's murder—and that, without that objective, her letter of resignation would already be on Bull Johnson's desk and she'd be packing for Maine. Instead she said, "The commander wants us to head up to Wirth Park. A body was discovered there a short time ago. I was just waiting on you."

"Oh, well let's go." Parker ran a hand over his dark blond hair. It was buzzed short and set off his strong facial features.

Brie grabbed her raincoat off the back of her chair and followed him out. They took the elevator down and headed through the tunnel to the parking ramp.

"I need to thank you again for the help you gave me remotely on that case up in Maine last May on Granite Island," Brie said.

Garrett waved a hand. "Don't mention it. I was happy to help." He glanced over at her almost shyly. "I suppose you thought I was acting crazy, telling you to come home and arguing with the captain of that ship you were on."

Brie smiled. "Don't worry about it. Who knew my absence would leave such a hole?" she said, jokingly.

"You're one of our best detectives, Brie. How could your absence not leave a hole?"

Brie shrugged noncommittally.

"So the commander has teamed us up. Hope you're okay with that."

"It's okay by me," Brie said. "We've both been with Homicide for about the same number of years. You lost your partner to that whole demotion business six months before I lost mine. So I guess we've kind of been traveling in parallel orbits."

Garrett's partner, Detective Joe Rossi, had been demoted and assigned back to a precinct as a patrol officer following an Internal Affairs investigation. Rossi had worked as a narcotics investigator prior to moving to Homicide. The Internal Affairs investigation had found him guilty of not reporting his partner while back in Narco, who was taking money from a drug dealer to look the other way. His partner, Frank Gorman, had been fired and Rossi had been demoted. Rossi had eventually left the MPD, claiming he'd been treated unfairly.

"Well, we'll see what we've got up in Wirth Park," he said. "Nothing like being thrown right back into the fray."

"Probably the best way," Brie said. "Kind of like ripping off a bandage. Better to just do it."

Garrett smiled, and they continued on in silence to the elevator that took them down to the parking ramp.

Chapter 23

Theodore Wirth Park sits on the western boundary of Minneapolis and borders the suburb of Golden Valley. At a sprawling 759 acres, the park is almost the size of New York City's Central Park. The west side of the park is wooded rolling terrain. In winter cross-county ski trails weave in and out of the woods and up and down the hills. At this time of year, the trails are perfect for runners and trail bikers.

Brie and Garrett took Highway 55 west through Minneapolis for two miles. They turned right on Theodore Wirth Parkway and wound north through the park. As they approached the bridge over the ravine, they saw the police cordon. Garrett pulled the car to the side of the road behind an MPD squad, and they got out and walked to the edge of the steep embankment. The body of an African-American woman lay face up at the bottom of the ravine. Even from where they stood, Brie could see that her clothes—what looked like jogging attire—were covered with mud and leaves from rolling down the steep hill.

Crime lab techs in white zipper suits, booties, and caps worked the scene up and down the hill and at the bottom in a grid around where the body lay. A man with a large dog stood on the bridge just outside the police tape. There was a patrol officer with him. As Brie and Garrett approached the scene, an officer came toward them. They took their badge wallets out and held them up.

"Detectives Parker and Beaumont," Garrett said. "What do we have here, Officer Wenz?" he asked, reading the name tag on his uniform.

"Gunshot victim," Wenz said. He turned and nodded toward the man on the bridge. "The guy over there was jogging along here with his dog. It was the dog that found her. Looks like she went over the edge just before the bridge."

"Thanks, Officer," Brie said. She nodded toward the bridge. "Let them know over there that we'll be back up and question the guy with the dog after we talk to Doc Mortimer down there."

Brie and Garrett found a spot outside the crime scene tape and started down the hill, going sideways and watching their footing on the steep incline. The rain had stopped for now, but the wet leaves made the steep descent slippery as a bobsled run. At the bottom of the hill, they stepped into the bootie box for shoe covers and ducked under the crime scene tape.

Nevin Mortimer, one of the Hennepin County medical examiners, knelt over the body. Around the department they referred to her as Nevs of Steel, because of the horrors she had to deal with in her day-to-day work. People who had been shot, beaten, burned, knifed. And then there were the children.

When she saw them, she stood up and stepped away from the victim. Mortimer was six feet tall and rail thin with a flawless Irish complexion. Under her shower-style crime scene cap, her dark hair was pulled tightly back from her face, and she wore very large black-framed glasses that seemed to magnify her rather melancholy brown eyes.

"Brie, you're back. What a nice surprise." She nodded to Garrett. "Hello, Parker."

"It's good to see you, Nevs," Brie said. She had always appreciated working with Doc Mortimer on cases. Smart, professional and above all, as a pathologist, she was thorough beyond imagining.

They walked over to the victim. "What have we got here, Doc?" Garrett asked.

Mortimer looked down at the body. "We have a female gunshot victim. I'd say she's in her mid-twenties. Soot in and around the wound indicates that she was shot at close range. I'll know more when I do a close examination of the wound in autopsy. Lividity doesn't match the position of the body, and liver temperature places time of death at about six hours ago. So, unless our victim was out jogging at two in the morning, we might assume she was killed elsewhere and brought here. Condition of the clothes as well as lacerations and contusions are consistent with the body rolling down a steep hill such as we have here. And finally, the fact that there was no post-mortem bleeding from the lacerations indicates that our victim was already dead when she went into this ravine."

"Any ID or cell phone?" Brie asked.

"Nothing so far," Mortimer said. "But we'll do a thorough search of the body once we transport her."

"So from the looks of it, this wasn't a random shooting. She wasn't just in the wrong place at the wrong time," Garrett said.

"I'd say no. I think whoever shot her dumped her body here, hoping it wouldn't be found. The body isn't visible from the path on top," the ME said.

"I noticed that," Brie said. "You have to get up to the very edge of the drop to see her down here."

"There's a guy up on top with a dog that made the discovery."

"We saw him up there. We'll be questioning him once we're done here," Brie said.

"I'll have more details once I complete the autopsy, and I'll have all the pictures from the scene sent over to you right away."

Garrett took out his phone and walked over to the victim. He leaned in close and took several head shots. "We'll have the

Hennepin County Sheriff's Office run this through their facial recognition system. See what comes up."

"We have close-ups of the victim's face as well," the doc said. "We'll upload and send them as soon as we get back to the ME's office."

"Thanks, Nevin," Brie said. "We'll let you get back to your work."

"We'll be bagging and moving the body as soon as the photographer is done," the ME said.

Brie and Garrett worked their way back up the steep, slippery incline. When they got to the top, they walked around the outside of the police cordon toward the man who stood on the bridge with his dog. The rain had started coming down again. Brie turned up the collar of her coat and snugged down her fedora.

The guy on the bridge and his dog looked soggy and miserable. The man wore a dark blue windbreaker over his jogging clothes. He had pulled the hood up.

Brie and Garret held up their badge wallets as they approached.

"Detectives Parker and Beaumont," Garrett said.

The man nodded. "I'm Chad Stone, and this is my dog, Navy."

Brie bent down. "Pleased to meet you, Navy." Navy picked up a large gray paw and put it in her hand.

"Sorry," Chad said, pulling out a bandana and offering it to Brie. "I've taught him to offer a friendly paw when he hears that phrase."

"Quite all right," Brie said. "I started it. What is he?"

"Irish wolfhound," Chad said.

The dog was all gray with shaggy hair that partially obscured his mournful eyes. And he was huge. Seated as he was, his head came above Chad's waist, and Chad, at a wiry six-two or -three, was no shorty.

"Do you have some ID?" Garrett asked.

Stone unzipped a small pocket in his Lycra jogging pants and pulled out his driver's license and handed it to Garrett. "I always carry it," he said. "You never know."

Garrett looked at the license, then at Chad Stone and handed it back to him. "Take us through what happened this morning," he said. He took out his phone to record the interview.

"Navy and I were out for our morning jog," Chad began. "I live just on the other side of the park. We usually run down the east side of the park and then west on 55 to Theodore Wirth Parkway. Then north through the wooded part of the park to Plymouth and back east toward home. It's about a three-mile run. With the rain this morning, we were alone out here, so when we got to the west side of the park, I let Navy off leash. He's trained to stay right next to me. But when we got close to Wirth Creek and the bridge here, he took off down the hill like he'd been shot from a gun." Chad paused and looked at Brie. "Sorry, bad analogy."

"Go on," she said.

"I ran to the edge of the hill and yelled for him to come. That's when I saw the body down there. The ravine's a good thirty or forty feet deep, so I went partway down the slope and called for Navy again. He was standing next to the girl's body, whining and barking, but he came when I called him. I got him back on the leash and then called 911."

"So you didn't go all the way down to where the body was?" Brie asked.

"No, just halfway. Once Navy came, I climbed back up."

"You didn't go down to see if she needed help?" Garrett asked.

Chad looked sheepish now. "I guess I should have. But she wasn't moving. I guess my first thought was to call 911."

"What time was that?" Garrett asked.

"It was seven-fifteen. I remember looking at the time when I made the call."

Brie noted that he'd been standing out in the cold rain for almost an hour. "And how long before the police arrived?" she asked.

"The squad cars got here fast. I'd say two to three minutes." He pushed the hood off his head as if feeling slightly claustrophobic and ran a hand over his short dark hair.

Brie could see that he'd gone pale. "Are you okay?" she asked.

"I need to eat. I'm hypoglycemic," Chad said. He started to move toward the bridge rail as if he needed something to lean on.

"I've got something," Garrett said. He fished in his pocket and brought out a Snickers bar and gave it to Stone.

"Thanks, man," he said, tearing it open. "You're a lifesaver."

"Did you see anyone else while you were in this part of the park?" Brie asked.

"A couple of joggers. Other than them, just the usual traffic driving along the parkway. Maybe five or ten cars in all."

Brie nodded. "We'll need your address and phone number in case we have more questions."

She pulled a small notebook from an inside pocket of her trench coat and made a note of the address and phone number Chad Stone gave them. Just in case something happened with the recorder, she always liked to have a backup plan.

Garrett gave Stone one of his cards. "Would you like a ride home?" he asked.

"No, we'll be fine. I live just off Plymouth on the other side of the park."

"In that case, we'll let you go and be in touch if we need anything else from you."

Stone nodded. "Come on, Navy. Let's head for home."

Navy sprang up and started to do the excited dog wiggle. They headed off to the north along the path through the beauty of the park. Beauty juxtaposed on this particular day with the ugly reality of murder.

Brie and Garrett headed back to the car. This side of the park was large and densely wooded and, therefore, completely separated from the residential neighborhoods that lay along its fringes. For that reason there would be no canvassing of the neighborhood and questioning residents. There was simply no way that anyone could have seen anything.

Their best bet was to head back to the department and send the photo of the victim that Garrett had taken over to the Hennepin County Sheriff's Office. See if they could get a match using their facial recognition software—a technology not used by either the Minneapolis or St. Paul Police Departments, nor by the Bureau of Criminal Apprehension.

Garrett started the car and did a U-turn on the parkway and headed south to where it intersected 55.

Chapter 24

Brie was silent as they drove, listening to the tires track the water on the wet pavement. Listening to the rhythm of the wipers ticking in rain seconds, lulling her into a blank space that soon had her back in the dream she'd had two nights ago. Phil astride the giant eagle. She was sure there was something there. Something meaningful, symbolic. But what?

"You're awfully quiet," Garrett said. "Thinking about the scene?"

"Yeah," she said, although it wasn't true. "What do you think?"

"I'm hoping facial rec gives us a lead, or it could take some time to identify her."

"We should check any traffic cams at streets that enter the park and near the location of the body in the hour or two on either side of the doc's estimate of time of death."

Garrett nodded. "Why don't you work that angle when we get back to the department?"

He paused and looked over at her. "Did you bring in those letters you told me about?"

"I reported on the situation to the commander this morning and gave him the letters. He's sending them to the crime lab for a go-over. He gave me the okay to work through my back case files and see if anything jumps out."

"Any ideas?"

"Not offhand. But I'll be checking to see if any of the perps I put away has been paroled in the past six months." She looked out her window. "It's pretty much a needle-in-the-haystack proposition, though. It could be anyone connected to any case. I keep good notes on the cases I work, though, so maybe something will stand out."

They were just entering the downtown loop, and they drove silently back to the parking ramp and took the tunnel back to City Hall. They rode the elevator up to the first floor and made their way down the long hallway to Homicide.

They reported to Bull Johnson and filled him in on the details of the case and where they planned to start.

"First thing is to establish identity," the commander said. "That will give us our direction."

"Crime lab will be sending over the pictures, and Doc Mortimer will notify us when the autopsy is complete."

"Good," Johnson said. "In the meantime, let's get the photo you took down to the sheriff's office. Request that they put it through their facial recognition system. See if we can get an ID on this woman."

Brie and Garrett headed back to their cube.

"I know the Fourth Precinct where I used to work has a swarm of surveillance cameras," Brie said. "But I'm not sure how many we have west of there, near or in the park."

She quickly got her answer when she brought up the map of surveillance cam locations. It showed no cameras in Theodore Wirth Park, with the closest location being Glenwood and North Penn Avenues. That was too far from the park to be any help at all.

In the meantime, Garrett had uploaded the victim's image from his phone. The headquarters for the Hennepin County Sheriff's Office was also in City Hall, on the ground floor, virtually beneath the Minneapolis Police Department. Garrett picked up the phone and called Chief Deputy Michael Moretti, whom he knew well.

Moretti answered on the third ring. "Mike, Garrett Parker here. We're working a Jane Doe shooting. Vic found in Wirth Park early this morning. I'm sending you a digital image of the victim's face. Could you run it through your facial rec system and see if you get a hit?"

"No problem, Garrett. Send it down. We'll see what we can find."

Parker attached the image to a brief email he composed and sent it. "Now we wait," he said.

Brie sat down at her desk and brought up the list of her cleared cases she'd been working through. She had started noting down case numbers before Garrett had gotten in that morning. The beginnings of a list of cases her gut told her might somehow connect to the threatening letters she'd received.

They didn't have long to wait on the ID of the victim. Within a half hour, Garrett's phone rang.

"Detective Parker," he answered. "Hey, Moretti. What have you got?" There was a pause as he listened. Brie turned in her chair to listen to Garrett's end of the conversation.

"Yeah? Great. What's her name?"

Brie saw him jot down a name and a couple of facts followed by an address.

"Rap sheet, huh?" He listened to the charges Moretti read off and made notes. "Uh huh."

Brie saw him write a second name and the word "Domestics" after it.

"Yup. Got it," Parker said. "Thanks, Mike. That's what we needed."

Mike Moretti said something else at his end of the line.

"Let's do that," Garrett said. "I'm buyin', man."

Garrett ended the call and turned to face Brie. "We're in business. Moretti got a hit on facial rec."

"What've we got?"

"The woman's name is Ayesha Brown. Twenty-five. Moretti also ran the name through the DMV and got an address. North Minneapolis. The eight hundred block of Queen Avenue North."

"The Fourth Precinct," Brie said. "My old stomping ground. That's not very far from Theodore Wirth Park where we found the body."

Garrett was typing Ayesha Brown's name into the criminal database. Up popped a rap sheet for Ms. Brown.

Brie leaned in and read what was there. "Shoplifting. Possession with intent to sell. She was paroled the first time. Did nine months the second time."

"The address on her driver's license set off some bells and whistles, too."

"Domestics?"

"You got it. Three calls to that address in the past year. The boyfriend and frontrunner for Scumbag for a Day is one Lotrelle Gallagher."

They plugged in his name and up came another rap sheet. Breaking and entering, possession with intent to sell, assault. He'd been convicted three times on three different charges and had done time for each of them. He was thirty-eight years old.

They took what they had to the commander.

"Let's get a search warrant under way for that address," Bull Johnson said. "Parker, you take care of that. And let's bring this Gallagher character in for an interview. I'll call the Fourth and ask them to send an unmarked squad or two to meet you at the address."

"Let's rendezvous with them down the block a ways so he has less chance of spotting us and making a run for it," Brie said.

Bull Johnson nodded and picked up the phone to call the CO at the 4th Precinct.

Brie and Garrett went back to their cube to get the search warrant under way and to collect their coats.

Chapter 25

Within twenty minutes, they were headed back to the Government Center to pick up the search warrant and get the car. They drove up through the rain-soaked city toward North Minneapolis. Bull Johnson had requested two unmarked squads from the 4th Precinct to rendezvous with the detectives at the intersection of Queen Avenue and North Eighth Avenue so they could lay their plan of approach.

It was the dying time of the year, and in the rain, the black asphalt streets became a mirror that seemed to reflect shades of both desperation and perseverance that dwelt side by side in this part of the city. Brie stared out the window at the passing neighborhood, remembering her early days with the MPD—her days as a patrol officer in this part of the city.

This was a high crime part of Minneapolis. Drugs and gangs were a problem here as they were in analogous neighborhoods in big cities all across the country. But woven into each of those neighborhoods were stories of hope and striving. Of the strong fabric of families; parents who loved their children and soldiered on, fighting the hard fight up out of poverty so those children might have a better life. In the final analysis, it was love, plain and simple, that canceled out a kind of dystopian despair that might otherwise have overtaken this and other struggling parts of the city. Love that faced off each day with fear—the fear that drove the dark side of life here.

Garrett broke the silence. "I thought you'd be up North longer. I was surprised to see you back at the department today."

"Mom wasn't feeling well, so we decided to cut it short," Brie said. It wasn't the truth, but she wasn't about to get into what had happened up North. Not until she knew which way the wind was blowing on the Greenberg case. She was planning to call Renard tonight when she got home.

She stared out her window at the rainy city, thinking about the Greenberg woman and the disturbing resemblance she bore to her mother, Edna Beaumont. She knew Garrett would immediately connect the resemblance between the two women with the threatening letters she had received and assume the bullet was meant for Edna. For now, Brie wanted to control the direction of the investigation without getting Parker involved.

"Your mom's a charmer, Brie. Not hard to see where you get yours from."

"What?" Brie said, distracted. At the thought of Halley Greenberg, her mind had returned to the scene of the shooting and those moments down by the lake, right before she had heard the fatal shots.

"I said your mom's quite a charmer."

"Yeah, she is. But she seems completely oblivious to the fact. Maybe that's part of the charm." She was trying to think when Garrett had met her mother, and then she remembered that Edna had been at a ceremony where Brie had received a commendation. That was shortly before Phil had been killed. She had introduced her mom to some of her colleagues in the unit.

"I've told her she needs to drop the knitting. It makes her look old."

"C'mon, Brie. That's bias against knitters."

"Oh, whatever," she said.

"Hey," Garrett said, "When I worked in the Third Precinct, I knew this cop that was a knitter. He claimed it calmed his nerves after a hard day on the streets of Minneapolis."

Brie smiled at the thought of the knitting street cop. "Well, I guess I can see the therapeutic benefits."

"It's good to see you smile," Garrett said.

It dawned on Brie that after Phil's murder and her shooting, more than a year and a half ago now, her colleagues at the department hadn't seen much happiness in her.

"We'll get to the bottom of those letters, Brie. Don't let that bother you."

"I'm not," she said. "Just a lot on my mind."

She could feel Garrett studying her. The vibe felt compassionate.

A few blocks along, the tone in the car became serious and focused as they neared the address where, according to the DMV record, Ayesha Brown had lived.

As they approached the intersection of Queen and North 8th Avenues, they spotted the two unmarked squads and pulled up behind them. Brie and Garrett got out, and two uniformed patrol officers exited each of the cars. The six of them formulated a plan whereby two of the officers would go up the alley and cover the back of the house in case Gallagher made a run for it. The other two officers would accompany Parker and Beaumont up to the front door. They headed up the block to the address, which turned out to be a one-story single-family dwelling. It was neither the best- nor worst-kept property on the block. They turned and went quickly up the front walk. There was a glassed-in front porch. They all drew their firearms as they mounted the steps. One of the patrol officers tried the porch door. It was unlocked, and they filed quickly and silently in and stood, one officer and one detective, to either side of the front door.

Garrett leaned in and rang the bell.

Within a few moments a voice came from the other side of the door.

"Who's there?"

"Minneapolis Police Department," Parker said in a voice loud enough to penetrate the wood door. "We need to talk to you."

If they had expected a runner, they got the diametric opposite. The door opened immediately. The man facing them was African-American, five-ten or-eleven, completely bald, and cool as a cucumber. He gave them a broad, congenial smile that showed a mouthful of perfect teeth—so perfect that Brie wondered if they were dentures.

"Lotrelle Gallagher?" Parker said, holding up his badge wallet.

"That's right," Gallagher answered.

"I'm Detective Parker, and this is Detective Beaumont. We need to speak to you about Ayesha Brown. Could we come in?"

Brie watched him intently when the name of the deceased was mentioned. The smile receded ever so slightly, and he seemed to hesitate for a moment. Then he stepped aside and extended his hand to invite them in. The two uniforms went in first, followed by the detectives, and as soon as Brie stepped through the door, the strong odor of household cleaner hit her. She made eye contact with Parker, who must have smelled it as well.

Lotrelle Gallagher closed the front door. When he turned to face them, the smile was back in place, but at half-mast. "Ayesha, she didn't come home last night," he said, holding his hands out in an apologetic posture. "I ain't seen her since yesterday morning. She said she was goin' out shoppin'."

"So you're saying you didn't see her last night. That she wasn't here overnight."

"That's right, Detective . . . ah . . ."

"Parker," Garrett said. "And that didn't concern you?"

"Nah. She stay with a friend sometimes."

"Well, here's the thing, Mr. Gallagher. Ayesha Brown is dead."

"What you sayin'?" Gallagher's voice came up an octave. "You think I did it? I didn't do nothin' to her."

Brie noted the complete lack of response to his supposed girlfriend's death. He wasn't concerned to know how she had died. There were no tears, no apparent grief. Just the immediate segue to a defensive stance.

"We'd like you to accompany us downtown to answer some questions, Mr. Gallagher," Parker said.

"Why can't I answer the questions here? I ain't done nothin' wrong."

"That may be, Mr. Gallagher, in which case there's no harm in coming downtown for a few questions," Parker said.

"Does that mean I's under arrest?" Lotrelle's voice took on a pleading quality.

"You're not under arrest. This is just questioning," Brie said, attempting to defuse the situation.

They needed to get the crime lab folks over here stat, because if this wasn't a crime scene, she'd eat her fedora. She looked into the living room and noticed a rectangular area approximately six by eight feet that was darker than the surrounding wood floor, as if a rug had lain there recently.

She thought about Ayesha Brown's rap sheet—shoplifting, petty theft, possession with intent. She wondered how much of that Gallagher here might have coerced her into. Maybe he was just one notch above a pimp. Maybe they had argued, maybe she'd told him she was done. Sadly, to a homicide detective, this scenario was not uncommon. It was a recurring theme in the world she and Parker frequented.

She studied Lotrelle Gallagher. The smile was still in place, but the eyes told another story. They skittered from side to side as if in a frantic attempt to grasp the right thought, the right words that would set him free. And there was an air of astonishment there too, as if he couldn't believe they could have assembled the pieces so quickly.

As they ushered him out the door, Brie craned her neck toward the bedroom down the hall and thought she caught a glimpse of an open suitcase on the bed.

Officers Williams and Jansrude escorted Lotrelle Gallager to their squad at the end of the block to bring him down to Homicide for an interview. Parker's phone rang as he and Brie headed for their car. It was Bull Johnson, letting them know that Crime Lab was on the way. Parker stepped over to the squad that held Gallagher and told them to hang on a minute.

"If you want to wait for Crime Lab, see if you get a sense of what unfolded here, I'll ride down with the boys and Mr. Innocent there," Garrett said.

"I've already got a pretty good inkling," Brie said. "Did you notice the floor in the living room?"

"I saw it. Stunning how creative these guys are."

"I'll say." She turned to the two remaining patrol officers. "I want you to do a search of the neighboring area, starting with Plymouth Avenue where it exits the park and heading this direction. Check any and all commercial dumpsters big enough to dump a rug approximately six by eight feet. See if you can get another patrol assigned to help. Keep an eye out for any residential trash cans as well that may contain a rug."

Now it was her phone that rang. She saw it was Nevin Mortimer, the M.E. She held up a finger for the officers to wait while she answered the call.

"Hey, Nevs. What have you got?"

"We found a phone on the victim. That's on the way to Homicide now."

"Good. We'll get that to our digital forensics unit ASAP. Hopefully we can track her family and any friends or coworkers who might shed light on her life. The victim's name is

Ayesha Brown." Brie also gave her the victim's address, for the record.

"I'm making a note of that," Mortimer said. "The autopsy is still under way, but the foreign matter we found in the wound looks like a polyurethane foam. The kind they fill pillows with. I think the shooter may have used a pillow as a silencer."

"We're at her address now. I'll include that in the search criteria. Anything else?"

"We retrieved the bullet," Mortimer said. "It's from a nine-millimeter handgun."

Brie nodded. "Copy that," she said. "We think the body may have been rolled up in a rug before being dumped in the park."

"We collected a lot of trace from the clothing. Let me check the report." A few seconds ticked by. "Looks like there were a number of different fibers collected. If you locate the rug, we can test for a match."

"The uniforms will be searching the area. I'll let you know if they turn anything up. Crime Lab is on the way here now, and I'll be on scene with them."

"I should have the autopsy report by the end of the day," Mortimer said.

"Thanks, Nevin. I'll let the commander know the vic's phone is on the way." Brie ended the call.

She texted Bull Johnson to let him know the phone was on the way to the unit. Then she turned back to the patrol officers. "We need to expand that search to include all the dumpsters in a one-mile radius from here. We're looking for a pillow. Could be a bed pillow or a throw pillow that was used as a silencer. The murder weapon is a nine-millimeter handgun. Be on the lookout for that as well."

Garrett had written Ayesha Brown's license plate number down from the DMV record. He handed it to Officers Blake and Peterson. "Check up and down the street here. See if you see a vehicle with this plate number."

The guys were back in a few minutes. "No sign of the vehicle," Blake reported.

Garrett nodded. "We need to get a BOLO out on that vehicle."

"Copy that," Blake said. He keyed his shoulder radio and sent a call out to all units to be on the lookout for the vehicle.

"There's no vehicle registered to Gallagher," Parker said to Brie. "Chances are he used Ayesha Brown's car to dispose of her body."

"We need to locate that car," Brie said.

The officers proceeded to their unmarked squad. Garrett gave Brie his keys and then got into the squad with Officers Williams and Jansrude and Lotrelle Gallagher. Brie went to Garrett's car that was parked behind theirs and got in. She pulled away and turned the corner to park up the block in front of Ayesha Brown's house.

Chapter 26

While waiting for Crime Lab, Brie decided she'd use the time to canvass the neighbors immediately surrounding Ayesha Brown's house to see if any of them had seen or heard anything last night. She struck out at the houses on either side. She found neighbors at home at both houses, but they said they had not seen or heard anything unusual. Nor could either of them testify to whether Ayesha Brown had been at home last night. She asked about Ayesha's car. One of the neighbors didn't seem to know what kind of vehicle she drove, but the other neighbor said that Brown drove a small Ford, but he couldn't remember seeing it in front of the house last night. Brie tried the neighbor's house that sat directly behind Ayesha Brown's on the street to the west, but there was no one at home.

She struck pay dirt when she tried the neighbor directly across the street. The man who lived there looked to be in his mid-to-late seventies. His name was Clarence Tate. He knew Ayesha Brown and immediately asked why the police were asking questions about her. Brie had no choice but to tell him that Ms. Brown was dead. Clarence stooped and picked up the small dog at his feet that had lots of fluffy white hair. When he stood up, Brie saw a tear roll down his face.

"She was a really nice girl," he said, and Brie was sure that at Clarence's age, Ayesha would have *seemed* like a girl.

"She used to check in on me if she didn't see me for a day or two. Even brought me soup once when I was sick. That guy she lived with, though. Worthless. Sometimes in the summer, I'd hear her crying over there." He shook his head. "I knew he was hurting her. The police been there two, maybe three times."

Brie took out her small notebook. "Did you see or hear anything last night, Mr. Tate?"

He shook his head and searched Brie's eyes like he wanted to help but didn't know how.

"Do you know Ayesha's car?" Brie asked.

"Sho' do. It's a small white Ford."

"Did you see it last night, Mr. Tate?"

"Sho'. It was right there in front of the house. I took Winnie out to do her business around ten p.m. The car was right there." He nodded across the street.

Brie wrote that in her notebook. "And you're sure it was last night?"

"Positive. You know why? I noticed her rear tire was pretty low. I thought I'd catch her this morning. Tell her before she went to work. But when I looked out early this morning, she was already gone."

"Would you be willing to testify to all of this, Mr. Tate?"

"Sho' would."

"Did you see the car after that?" Brie asked.

Clarence shook his head. "I go to bed by ten-thirty."

Brie nodded. "You've been a big help, Mr. Tate." She gave him one of her cards. "If you remember anything else about last night, would you give me a call?"

"I sho' will." He stroked Winnie's head. "I wish I could do more," he said.

"You may be able to down the line, Mr. Tate. Thank you."

Out of the corner of her eye, Brie saw the Crime Lab van approaching from the south end of the block. She headed back across the street.

They drove past and turned around at the end of the block. The driver parked behind her car, and the van disgorged a team of lab techs with their kits. On the porch they suited and bootied up. Brie did the same and then accompanied them into the house. She pointed out the dark area of living room floor where a rug would have lain. Of course, there was no way of knowing when that rug might have been taken up, but it was a logical place for the team to start.

Brie walked through the house getting the lay of things. The property was registered in Ayesha Brown's name, so Brie knew that if push came to shove, it wouldn't have been Ms. Brown who would have been leaving, but rather Lotrelle Gallagher. The domestics on record indicated that Gallagher, for all his smiling, was a bad dude. One who had made himself a fixture in Ayesha Brown's life. She thought about the words her dad had said to her when she had first started dating. *Remember, Brie, it's easier to get into something than it is to get out of it. So choose carefully.* As a cop, she'd witnessed countless cases of people choosing poorly. And some of them didn't live long enough to correct their mistakes.

There was a short hall off the back of the living room that led to two bedrooms and a bath. She walked into the first bedroom that the couple appeared to have shared. The closet was open and women's clothes hung there. On top of the bed, open, was the suitcase she'd glimpsed earlier. It was half full. Two drawers were pulled out on the dresser next to the bed. They contained men's underwear, socks, and tee shirts. The bed looked like it had been slept in. Lotrelle Gallagher had blown his chance for a getaway by deciding to sleep. *But then murder can be exhausting,* she thought in her cop's black humor.

Lucky for them that perps tended to be arrogant—tended to think they wouldn't get caught. That kind of narcissism gave cops the upper hand. That and the other mistake perps made of thinking cops were slow and stupid and that the wheels of justice would always grind slowly enough to assure them time for escape.

Brie bypassed the bathroom, where one of the lab techs was bagging items that would contain DNA—toothbrushes, shavers, hairbrushes, bathroom cups. In what appeared to be the spare bedroom, she found a desk with an assortment of mail in a basket on top. She pulled on a pair of latex gloves and flipped through what was there. She found several paystubs with Ayesha Brown's name on them from a nursing home in Brooklyn Center. She jotted down the address and phone number in her small notebook, finding it more than a little disturbing that someone with a police record would be caring for the elderly.

There were several credit card bills in the mix, and she pulled out the statements and checked the balances. Two of the cards were maxed out, and the third was fast approaching the same fate. More fodder for tension in the relationship. There was a laptop on the desk. It was shut down. She unplugged and bagged it and the mail in separate evidence envelopes, logging the time and place the items were collected along with her shield number on each envelope. Then she walked back out to the living room to talk to the forensic team.

"Did you find any men's clothing that might have been worn by the shooter?" she asked the team leader, whose ID badge said "Flynn."

"There was a set of men's clothes in the dryer in the basement. We've bagged them. We'll bring them back to the lab to check for blood trace."

"It looks like there was a rug here." Brie nodded toward the floor. "Make sure you check the clothes and lint trap on the dryer for any fibers that might have come from a rug, although chances of finding any are probably slim since the clothes have been washed."

"Well, you never know," Flynn said. "We've found trace before on clothes that have been washed."

Brie nodded. "I'll let you get back to it. Let us know if you find any blood evidence." She gave him one of her cards.

Flynn went back to his work, and Brie headed out the door, ducking under the crime scene tape. She put the evidence envelopes in the trunk of Garrett's car and climbed in behind the wheel. She put through a call to Garrett that went immediately to voicemail. She left him a message about finding the paystubs for Ayesha Brown and said she was headed up to the Eagle Terrace Nursing Home in Brooklyn Center to talk to the staff there.

Chapter 27

One hour later Brie was headed south on Interstate 94 back towards the department. She had managed to interview Ayesha Brown's supervisor at the Eagle Terrace Nursing Home, as well as two other nurse's aides who knew her. She had also gotten contact information for Brown's next of kin. The mother and father lived in South Minneapolis.

The reports from the staff had all been good. The supervisor had praised Ayesha for being prompt and dependable and said she was known for her kindness to the residents. The two nurse's aides seemed to know her on a more personal basis. They told Brie that Ayesha had had enough of her boyfriend—one of them knew his name. Lotrelle. They said Ayesha had told them she was going to throw him out. That she wanted to turn her life around. Find a decent guy. They also said they knew the boyfriend was abusive—had not infrequently seen bruises on Ayesha. Both of them agreed to testify about what they knew. Brie had taken down their names and phone numbers and given each of them one of her cards.

She'd only been on the road ten minutes when Garrett called. He said they'd gotten Ayesha Brown's phone from Crime Lab and had found the number for her mother and father. "We were able to cross-reference the number with an address. I'm headed there now with the chaplain to give notice to the parents."

Brie filled Garrett in briefly on what she had learned at the nursing home. "I should be back there in about fifteen minutes," she said. "I'm gonna grab a sandwich at the cafeteria on my way back up to the unit, though." Her stomach had been protesting that she had skipped lunch. Breakfast was but a distant memory. It was a typical day at the MPD.

She continued south along I 94. She was thinking about the name of the nursing home—Eagle Terrace. An odd coincidence, she thought, reflecting on the dream she'd had up North. Her partner Phil and the golden eagle. The blood red leaves raining down as Phil dispersed them. Her friend Ariel would have called it a synchronicity. Brie had looked up the word one time. The dictionary had defined it as "The simultaneous occurrence of events that appear significantly related but have no discernible causal connection." She had liked the way that sounded, but she didn't put much stock in such things. However, in the past six months she had somehow begun to have an awareness of things that Ariel would have referred to as "not of our realm." That gave her hope that through some combination of diligence and, yes, even luck, she might somehow find the answers that had evaded those who had worked on Phil Thatcher's case.

The new memory she'd had on the way home from up North of the night Phil had died and she'd been shot gave her hope that more might be revealed. The memory felt like a lost piece of a puzzle, a piece that had somehow fallen between the cracks of her psyche. She wondered what else might be recovered from those corners of her mind—corners where maybe she had hidden some of the pieces because she simply couldn't deal with them at the time.

Brie exited on N. 4th Street, made her way back to the Government Center parking ramp, and pulled into the contract side of the ramp where Garrett had been parked. She pulled out her phone and sat looking at it. She decided it was time to call the psychologist she had visited with after being shot. Dr. Megan Travers had worked with her after she had healed enough from her injuries to visit the psychologist. Brie had hoped that by returning to that fated night under hypnosis, she might recover some memory that could be helpful in solving Phil's murder. But the sessions had brought her increased anxiety and had seemed to worsen the PTSD she was grappling with, so the doctor had stopped the work.

She found the psychologist's number in her phone and sent the call. The receptionist answered, "Dr. Travers' office. How can I help you?"

"This is Detective Brie Beaumont. Is Dr. Travers available?"

"She just finished with a client. Let me check."

A few moments later the receptionist came back on the line. "Dr. Travers can take your call now, Detective. I'll connect you."

"Thank you," Brie said.

A moment later Megan Travers came on the line. "Hello, Brie. I'm happy to hear from you. I heard you had taken a leave of absence from the department and gone out of state. Are you back in the Twin Cities now?"

"I am," Brie said. "And back at the department." She didn't tell her that she had returned for one specific reason—to solve the case of her partner's murder—and that once that mission had been accomplished, she planned to return to Maine.

"How are you doing?" Dr. Travers asked.

"Much better than when you last saw me. I've been in Maine for the past six months. In fact, I have literally been at sea."

"Ah," Dr. Travers said. "That would be healing for you." The doctor knew she had been a sailor.

"It was healing," Brie said. She paused for a moment, and silence stretched between them.

"How can I help you, Brie?"

"I'd like to resume the hypnotic regression work pertaining to the night I was shot."

"Are you sure? It didn't go well for you last time."

"I'm stronger now," Brie said. "And I've remembered something from that night."

"Something more or something different?" Travers asked.

"Something different."

"That's interesting," the doctor said. She was silent for a moment. "I'm willing to try, Brie, but if you begin to revert—if your PTSD gets worse—we will have to stop. What's more, I want to tell you, as I did the first time, that memories recovered may or may not be accurate. Therefore, nothing from these sessions could be used to obtain a conviction. Nor would any of the information be admissible in a court of law."

"I understand that," Brie said. "It's important to me that I do this, though."

"Let me check my schedule." Megan Travers was back on the line in a few moments. "As I recall, you prefer evenings. I have an opening next Tuesday at five-thirty."

"I'll take that," Brie said.

"Good. I'll see you then," Dr. Travers said.

Brie thanked her, and they ended the call.

It was 2: 30. Time to grab something to eat. She got out of the car and headed for the Government Center elevator. The Park Café is actually a cafeteria. Located in the subterranean limbo between the Government Center and City Hall, it serves both buildings. Brie went in and ordered a ham and cheese sandwich on rye and coffee at the counter. She grabbed a small side salad, paid at the register and sat at one of the tables in the dining area.

After she finished eating, she planned to head back up to the unit and start writing her report on the Ayesha Brown murder case. She wondered how the questioning of Lotrelle Gallagher was proceeding. The coffee was rich and hot, and she imagined the steaming vapor clearing the cobwebs from her brain. This was the time in the afternoon she always needed her caffeine fix.

Within twenty minutes she was headed back up to the department. She suspected the Brown case would be on hold until they got the autopsy report from Doc Mortimer, as well as the reports of what Crime Lab had found at the scene and what the patrol officers had turned up in their search of the neighborhoods around Ayesha Brown's house and Theodore Wirth Park.

Brie hoped that once her report was written, she could get back to the list of her past cases she had pulled up earlier, cases that might connect to the letters she had received—letters, she believed, that might somehow connect to the shooting up North. She planned to take some of the chosen case files home with her that night to work through.

Garrett was sitting in their cube, working on a report.

"How did the questioning of Lotrelle Gallagher go?" she asked.

"He's sticking to his story like glue," Garrett said.

"Claiming that Ms. Brown stayed at a friend's house last night?"

"Yeah. After going over the same ground for two and a half hours, he requested an attorney."

"Huh. Sounds like we're in a holding pattern until we get the preliminary report from Crime Lab."

"We have approval to hold him for up to ninety-six hours. By then we hope to have enough evidence to charge him."

"Ayesha Brown's co-workers at the nursing home where she worked said she was planning to dump Gallagher. 'Throw him out' were the exact words."

"They'll testify to that?" Garrett asked.

"That and more. They knew Gallagher was abusive."

Brie took off her coat and hung it on the back of her chair. She sat down and brought up a report form and started writing her report on the Brown case. She had brought her coffee with her from the cafeteria and stopped now and then to take a sip.

After thirty-five minutes, she had the report typed up. She sat back in her chair, stretched her arms and head back, drew in a deep breath and let it out. Garrett had left the cube after finishing his report, so she had the space to herself. She pulled up the list of her cleared cases she'd been looking at that morning and went back to making notes, opening files on her computer that pertained to specific cases, and compiling a list of case file numbers. Her search fell into two categories. More recently cleared cases—no more than two years old—that had involved particularly angry relatives or friends of the convicted person. And older cases where there was a chance that a prisoner might have been paroled.

At 4:20 she struck what she thought might be pay dirt. She wrote down the file number for the Boyle Bouchard manslaughter case. The record showed that Bouchard had been paroled four months ago. Even more compelling was the fact that he was currently living in Hovland, Minnesota, which is approximately twenty-five minutes from the cabin where Brie and Edna had stayed and where Halley Greenburg had been murdered.

Before shutting down her computer, Brie searched for one more case number. It was a cold case, her partner's case—the Phil Thatcher murder. She wrote the case number in a blank spot she'd left in the middle of her list. Then she shut down her computer, picked up her coat and briefcase, and headed downstairs to the Records Room.

Chapter 28

Brie's heart was still beating faster than normal even though she had driven through downtown Minneapolis and was now merging onto Hiawatha Avenue. It wasn't that she cared about being caught, exactly. After all, what was the worst that could happen? She'd be given a reprimand and told she wasn't allowed to work on Phil's case.

She had checked Garrett's desk for the file earlier in the day. Since he was the investigating detective and the case was still open, the case file should have been on his desk. But it worked better for her that the file had been in the Records Room. Spiriting it off Garrett's desk without its absence being noticed would have been riskier.

She had the feeling that the case might be in the process of descending to the deep freeze. Something that should never happen in the death of a cop. What she really cared about now was finding answers—answers that might have slipped between the cracks. To do that she had to dig down into Phil's case. So the first step had been to get her hands on the file. The next step was to make copies of everything in the file so she could return it to the Records Room tomorrow and hope no one noticed that she had ever checked it out.

To distract herself from her minor anxiety about breaking the rules on her first day back at the department, she switched mental gears and tried to remember anything she possibly could about the Boyle Bouchard case. It was so many years ago, and the only reason she remembered it at all was that it had been one of her early cases as a detective. And it had been a memorable case, mostly because, starting with his name and working one's way on down, Boyle Bouchard had been a memorable suspect.

Bouchard had been brought up on a charge of first-degree manslaughter in the shooting death of a friend of his. At that time, Boyle Bouchard had been living with this guy, whose name had long since been filed in some dark corner of Brie's memory banks. Anyway, as she recalled, the friend had borrowed and wrecked Bouchard's motorcycle. A violent fight had ensued at their apartment in Minneapolis. The friend had drawn a knife on Bouchard, and Bouchard had shot him.

As she recalled, the murder weapon had been an unregistered firearm. And to make bad matters worse, Bouchard had fled the scene rather than calling 911. Bouchard had entered a plea of not guilty, stating that it was self-defense.

She remembered Boyle Bouchard as a short, surly man with anger issues. She recalled thinking that Boyle was an apt name for him because it always seemed like he was ready to blow. The psych evaluation had put a label to it—Intermittent Explosive Disorder.

She and Phil had been the two detectives assigned to the case, but it had been Brie who had tracked him to a hideout up North, where he had gone to ground. She remembered that his anger at being convicted had been directed at her rather than his defense attorney—a public defender who might have been able to make the self-defense plea stick if he'd had more experience. To Brie, it had seemed like it should have come down as self-defense from what she had known about the case.

Bouchard had been sentenced to twelve years in prison and, according to the court records, had made parole after nine years. That had been four months ago. She had written down the phone number of his parole officer. She planned to call him tonight.

She had been deep in thought over the Boyle Bouchard case and the possibility that it could link to the letters she had received. In the meantime, her car, apparently on auto-pilot, had found its way back to her house, and she now realized she was turning onto her street. She parked in the driveway and headed up the back stairs. A light rain was falling as it had been off and on all day. What with the overcast sky and the lateness of the season, it was already getting dark. Brie put the key in the deadbolt and let herself into her flat. The air smelled fresh in the apartment after her marathon cleaning of the night before. A far cry from the dusty, stale air that had greeted her on her arrival home after six months away.

She went through to the dining room and put her briefcase on the table, glancing at the corner of the table where the letters had sat, almost as if she expected them to materialize there so as to haunt her.

She headed into the bathroom and took a hot shower, washing away the tension of the day—thoughts of Ayesha Brown's body in the park and of the victim's place of residence, all of which hung around her like some dark aura. After fifteen minutes she climbed out, feeling refreshed. She dressed in a set of cozy blue sweats and dried her hair, letting it hang long and straight around her shoulders.

She headed for the kitchen, took out a wide, flat bowl, and made herself a big salad with lots of veggies. She opened a can of yellow fin tuna packed in olive oil and used it to top the salad. She squeezed on some fresh lemon and *voilà*—dinner. She cut a piece of crusty bread to go with the salad, spread it with butter, and took her bowl in the dining room and sat where she could look out at the rain as the gray sky slowly faded to black.

When she was done with her salad, she got up and took her bowl to the kitchen. She came back to the table and pulled the stack of files out of her briefcase. She found the case file for Phil Thatcher and set it aside. Next she found Boyle Bouchard's file, took it to the end of the table and sat down. She opened the file and started looking through the reports that she and Phil had written nine years ago, as well as various evidence reports and testimony from family and friends, and from residents in the apartment building in Minneapolis where Bouchard had lived. Once she had looked through the file and somewhat re-familiarized herself with the case, she called Bouchard's parole officer, Ray Giles. The call went to voicemail, and she left a brief message identifying herself and telling Giles she'd like to speak with him about Boyle Bouchard.

Brie left the Bouchard file open on the table. She went to the other end, picked up the case file for Phil Thatcher's murder, and carried it into the living room. The desk in the corner held a computer and a printer with a copier. She set the file on the desk and began copying it page by page. It took her more than an hour. She bundled all the papers back into the file and put it back in her briefcase. Then she found a manila folder in one of the desk drawers, placed all the copies in it and left the folder on the desk.

Just then her phone rang, and she went back to the dining room to get it. She saw by the caller ID that it was Ray Giles. She answered the call.

"Detective Beaumont speaking."

"This is Ray Giles returning your call about one of my parolees, Boyle Bouchard. Has there been a problem?"

"I'm not sure," Brie said. "Are you familiar with Bouchard's case history?"

"Fairly familiar. I just gave his file the once-over before I called you."

"I'm the detective who worked the case originally. I see that he was paroled four months ago."

"That's right," Giles said.

Brie filled him in on the threatening letters, what they had said, and the odd circumstances of the shooting up North.

"Good God," Giles said. "Do you think Bouchard could be responsible for all that?"

"I have no idea at this point. His case jumped out because he's been recently paroled. Along with the fact that, during his trial and conviction, his anger seemed to be directed at me. Ironic, since I was part of the camp that thought this probably was a case of self-defense. But he had an inexperienced public defender, and the prosecutor went after Bouchard tooth and nail."

"So you think he's still dealing with righteous anger?"

"It's possible," Brie said. "But I sure don't want to jump to any conclusions. According to the jail record, he was a model prisoner and made parole the first time he came up for it. What's your take on Bouchard?"

"He always checks in on schedule. From reading his case file, I know he dealt with some form of escalating anger years ago. I suspect that didn't help at his trial. But I have to say, there's no sense of that about him anymore. Maybe he found Jesus. It wouldn't be the first time that's happened."

"Maybe," Brie said. "I plan to go up to Hovland this weekend to interview him. Look, I'd appreciate it if you don't mention that, should you talk to him."

Ray Giles agreed. They talked a bit more and then signed off. Brie sat thinking about what she had learned from Giles. Wondering whether Boyle Bouchard was really a changed man. Even though he had been her best lead, she was willing to give him the benefit of the doubt for now.

She brought up Claude Renard's number and put a call through to the chief deputy.

"Cook County Sheriff's Office," the voice said.

"This is Detective Beaumont calling for Chief Deputy Renard." She had meant to call his cell but had hit the wrong number. In a moment his voice came on the line.

"Hello, Brie."

She was surprised to hear her first name, but she went with the flow.

"Hello, Claude. How goes the progress on the Greenberg case?"

"Well, no big glaring revelations, but we have managed to eliminate certain possibilities."

"Do you have time to talk right now?"

"I do. I just got back to the sheriff's office, so now's a good time."

"I'm wondering what you've learned over the past couple of days."

"We've interviewed a group of people about the Greenbergs' marriage—friends, family members, neighbors—the usual gamut of connections. Also the people Ms. Greenberg worked with in her charity work."

"What did you learn?"

"We were told by family members and friends that they were both happy in the marriage and had been for many years. The neighbors we interviewed were in accord with that—said they never heard the couple fighting."

"How about financials?" Brie asked.

"We got a search warrant to look at their bank accounts, brokerage accounts, and credit card debt. Clean slate. Lots of money and assets. Good income, less than average debt for their bracket. So, no motive there either. Nor did there seem to be any history of depression or mental issues based on testimony of those closest to them."

"Huh. I'm just thinking back on what Mom reported that Halley Greenberg said to her in the cabin before she was shot. 'Life beats you up and then it beats you down.'"

"Those don't sound like the words of a totally happy woman, do they?" Renard asked rhetorically.

"No, they don't, but they don't necessarily mean anything either. Those words could have been said in response to something Mom told her. After all, Mom has gone through some hard times both in the past and recently."

Renard didn't respond to that, but after a few moments he said, "I also interviewed the caretakers at Cedar Falls to see if Jacob Greenberg or anyone else had called them asking about the cabin you and your mother stayed in, or if they had had any other queries about you and Edna being there."

"And?"

"They said they didn't recall anything like that."

"What about Greenberg's phone records and computers?" Brie asked.

"We're still working our way through those."

Brie shifted gears. "Anything on the white supremacist group whose leader was prosecuted by Jacob Greenberg?"

"We're been working that angle as well. It seems once the leader, Robert Trader, was sent up the river, the group kind of fell apart."

"Maybe the rest of them didn't cotton to the idea of prison food and cardboard sheets."

"Quite possible," Renard said. "My sense—the combined I.Q. of the rest of the group would make a pretty sorry batting average."

"Lemmings flock to zealots like moths to a flame."

"And often meet the same end," Renard said. "So, any progress on the threatening letters? Anything that might link to what happened up here?"

"That's why I was calling," Brie said. "I've been going through an assortment of my back cases. There's one that jumped out. It's an old case, but the guy was paroled about four months ago." Brie filled Renard in on the original details of the case and the fact that Boyle Bouchard was currently living in Hovland. A fact which Renard found very interesting.

"If Bouchard is still carrying a grudge against me, there's a possibility he could have gone after Edna in an attempt to get back at me. If he sent those letters, it means he knows where I live."

"But how could he possibly have known where you and Edna were going to be?" Renard asked.

"I have no idea," Brie said. "I guess it doesn't make a lot of sense when you think about it."

"Probably the very reason we should check it out. So far, nothing about this case makes any sense. And if Bouchard had your address, he could conceivably have tracked your movements, or hired someone to do so."

Brie couldn't help thinking about the car she'd suspected of following them on the drive up North.

"I'd like to drive up there on Saturday to interview Bouchard. I was wondering if you'd go with me, since it's your turf."

"Of course," Renard said.

"I could meet you at the Law Enforcement Center in Grand Marais on Saturday and we can head up to Hovland together. Would around eleven work for you?"

"Works for me," Renard said. "Pretty early start for you, though."

"It's okay. I'm used to an early start." She thought about her time on the *Maine Wind*. The crew was usually on deck by 5:30 a.m.

"In the meantime, I'm going to do a bit of reconnaissance on Boyle Bouchard," Renard said.

"Okay, but don't tip your hand."

"It'll be plain clothes reconnaissance," he said. "So, I'll see you Saturday?"

"Eleven o'clock," Brie said, and they ended the call.

She had been walking about the apartment as she talked to Renard. Now she went back to her stack of case files in the dining room and started looking through them, making notes here and there as she progressed. Two hours later she stood up and stretched her back. She had pretty much decided this was a hopeless endeavor. Theoretically, there were any number of relatives or friends of those perps who could have had a vendetta against her, but the field was too broad. And in all these other cases, the perps themselves were still incarcerated. She decided the only course of action was to see if the Crime Lab would come up with any evidence from the letters themselves. Pending that, her best course was to carry through with the interview of Boyle Bouchard.

She checked her watch. It was almost ten o'clock. She went and picked up the newly minted file that contained copies of everything in Phil Thatcher's case file. She checked the back door to be sure it was locked, turned off the lights in the living and dining rooms, and headed for the bedroom. She changed into her pajamas and crawled into bed with the file and started reading.

There were photographs of the scene and, hard as it was, Brie took time to study them. There were autopsy and forensic reports, and transcripts of the investigators' notes. There were the preliminary reports on the case, including a statement detectives had taken from her in the hospital three days after the shooting. There were also testimonies from neighbors in the vicinity of the house where the shooting had taken place. Phil's murder had occurred shortly after midnight on a moonless night in March. Some neighbors had heard the shot, but none had managed to see anyone leaving the house.

Eventually, Brie got to her own report that she had written after leaving the hospital. Now, nineteen months after the shooting, she read through it with interest to see how it jibed with what she had always seen in her flashbacks—the facts as she had always remembered them.

As we approached the house we noticed the door was slightly ajar. We went in, guns drawn. The inside of the house was as black as night in a coal mine. Phil Thatcher was to my left. Suddenly from that direction, I sensed movement. Then Phil moving in front of me. The deafening gunshot and muzzle flash came simultaneously. Then I was falling as if in slow motion, the floor rising toward me and everything fading to black.

She noted that the report was written in an almost dreamlike tone. It was a nearly identical description to what she had experienced time and time again since the shooting, when PTSD would send her spiraling into an unexpected flashback. She wondered if this dreamlike remembrance was some protective device used by her brain to remove her from the memory of the occurrence. To put some kind of filter or barrier between her and what had happened.

The bullet that had killed Phil Thatcher had passed through him and into Brie, lodging less than an inch from her heart. After surgery, she had lain unconscious in the hospital for nearly two days. The doctors were amazed that she remembered the incident at all. They had said that, normally, memory of the events would have ceased possibly with the recollection of pulling up to the curb outside or entering the house, but would have gone no further.

But now Brie had remembered something new, something different than what had appeared in the report or any of the flashbacks she had experienced in the past nineteen months. It gave her hope that, in time, something more might be revealed.

She put the report aside and continued on through the file. There were statements from two CIs who operated in the vicinity where the shooting had occurred. CIs, or confidential informants, work with the police in large cities. Many of them are former criminals with plenty of street cred. They swim in the same contaminated pond where officers like Brie go trolling for answers. Some are actually in paid positions with the department and some are not. But they are an essential part of the information pipeline connecting to what goes down on the streets, especially in high crime areas of the city. The beat cops often give them colorful names.

Sideways Louie was one of the CIs up in the 4th Precinct. Brie had known him ever since her days with that precinct. In addition to often being sideways to the law, he had gotten his name because he tended to never look directly at a person. What was more, Louie would often sidle up to you obliquely, in a sideways approach, somewhat in the manner of a crab. From that stance, he might lean in and share a confidence with his mouth close to your ear. But he never met your gaze straight on. And if he happened to be in front of you, he would look to one side of your head as he spoke, as if there were some imaginary entity there to whom he made address.

There was nothing of interest in the report that pertained to what Louie might have heard on the street about the murder of an MPD homicide detective that night in March a year and a half ago. He and another CI who operated in that part of town had both said they knew nothing about the shooting. Brie wondered if that had been true at the time, and if it was still true. She decided that she would track down Sideways Louie when she got back from up North and see if any new information had come his way in the past nineteen months.

It was getting late, and she wanted to get to the department early tomorrow to return the files—particularly the Phil Thatcher case file—to the Records Room. She closed the folder in her lap that held copies of everything in that file and slipped it into the drawer of her bedside table. She reached over and turned out the lamp, slid down in the bed, and was asleep almost immediately.

Chapter 29

Brie woke to a burning in her left side. Like the phantom pain an amputee sometimes feels, there was no explanation for it. The bullet wound had long since healed, but sometimes when she slept on her left side, she would feel the pain. Today, though, she guessed the cause was psychosomatic —that it had to do with reading the Phil Thatcher case file, or as it was called in police parlance, the murder book.

She got up, washed and dressed and had a bowl of cereal. By 7:15 she was en route to headquarters with four of the case files she had checked out in her briefcase. She had eliminated three of the cases after looking through them last night. The fourth file was Phil Thatcher's.

She parked in the Government Center ramp and headed through the tunnel to City Hall and then to the Records Room on the ground level. She returned the files to the officer on duty, signed the log, and took the elevator up to the Homicide Unit on the floor above. She went to her locker and swapped her off-duty firearm for her on-duty service weapon, got a cup of coffee and headed for her cube, where she took off her coat and settled in at her desk.

There was a file folder on the right side of the desk. A sticky note on the outside read, "This came through after you left, so I made you a copy." The note was signed by Garrett. She opened the folder and saw that it contained a copy of the medical examiner's report on Ayesha Brown. She took a couple sips from her coffee and started reading.

Cause of death had been a single gunshot wound to the chest. Soot in and around the wound indicated a close-range shooting. She and Garrett had already learned this from the ME at the scene where the body had been found in Theodore Wirth Park. But what followed in the report they had not known, and it added credence to their case against Lotrelle Gallagher.

During the autopsy, the medical examiner had found recent bruising on Ayesha Brown's body—arms, back, legs—signs that the victim had continued to suffer abuse from Gallagher. Brie shook her head, feeling a deep sadness. *She should have gotten out. Even if that was her house, she should have just left. Sought shelter at one of the homes for battered women. Let the courts sort out the rest.* It was doubly sad because apparently, from what her co-workers had said, Ayesha had been planning to move on, turn her life around. What she hadn't known was that that is the most dangerous time for a woman in her position. The time when most abusers kill their victims—at the time of the breakup or just afterward.

Brie read to the end of the report and was just finishing when Garrett arrived.

"Hey," she said.

"You read the report?"

"Yeah. Just finished."

"Sad, isn't it?"

"We have to get this bastard."

Garrett laid a hand on her shoulder. "We will."

She heard the understanding in his voice. Knew he was feeling the same sense of helplessness she was. In their business, homicide, they got to see the aftermath. No chance to intervene ahead of time. Stop what became more and more inevitable in a situation like this one.

The cops who caught the domestic calls tried to counsel women in these situations. Tried to get them to file charges, to physically remove themselves from the premises. Sometimes it worked. There were victories, stories of success. But sometimes it didn't. For those couples, the outcome was too often what they saw written down in front of them. The causes of death were different—the outcome always the same. One life eradicated, the other ended in a different way, because life in prison is no kind of life.

The phone in their cube rang. Garrett picked it up. He listened for a moment, then nodded. "Right away, sir." He hung up the phone. "The commander's got something on the Brown case. He'd like to see us."

Brie stood and they headed for Bull Johnson's office.

"We've caught a break," he said as they walked in. "The patrol officers conducting the search of the neighborhoods near the park and around the Brown home found a rug in a commercial dumpster with what appears to be heavy blood staining. Another team of officers found a pillow that looks like it was used as a silencer. Both items have gone to the crime lab for testing to see if they match the victim's blood type." He paused for a moment. "Who's the lead on this case over at Crime Lab?"

"Flynn," Brie said.

"Call him and see where they're at. What they know so far from evidence collected from the house."

"On it," Brie said.

"I want this wrapped up by day's end. I want this guy under arrest. As soon as you have something solid, let me know, and I'll contact the ADA."

Brie certainly knew the drill. The push to close cases within forty-eight hours was paramount. Beyond that time frame, things started to unravel—slip away—and the land of cold cases began to loom large on the horizon. The clock was ticking. In homicide work the clock was always ticking. She went back to her cube, looked up Flynn's number at the crime lab, and called him.

"Flynn here," the voice said after three rings.

"Hey, Flynn, it's Detective Beaumont over at Homicide."

"Hey, Brie. By the way, nice to have you back. I forgot to say that yesterday."

"That's okay. You were a little preoccupied. So the commander's hot to get this one closed."

"Yeah, so what else is new?" he chuckled. "Sorry, not trying to shoot the messenger."

"No problem, Flynn. What have you got so far?"

"Well, the rug and the pillow the cops found came in during the night. We're running blood types on both those items now to see if they match the vic's blood. As far as evidence found at the Ayesha Brown residence, the place had been scrubbed using a bleach solution—always a heads up right there. Even so, we found blood spatter when we used fluorescein under LED light. This morning we're testing the clothes we bagged from the dryer. Even though they were washed, the fluorescein can still reveal latent traces of blood on them."

"That's great, Flynn. I'll update the commander."

"I'll call as soon as we have something."

They ended the call.

Brie headed for Bull Johnson's office to inform the commander about what she had just learned. When she got there he was on the phone, but he motioned her in.

"Tell your guys that's good work. We need that car towed over to the crime lab garage ASAP." Johnson hung up.

"Ayesha Brown's car?" Brie asked.

"Yup. When the BOLO on Ayesha Brown's vehicle didn't produce anything yesterday, the boys over in the Fourth put the word out on the street that we were looking for the car. Wasn't long before one of our CIs reported in that word was Lotrelle Gallagher had stashed a car in the garage of one of his cronies. The CO at the Fourth immediately got a warrant sworn out for that address. His boys just found the car. Since Gallagher didn't own a vehicle, it's not too much of a stretch to assume that he used the vic's own car to transport her body."

Brie filled Johnson in on what she'd learned from Flynn about the blood evidence. "If we can match the fibers from the rug that was found in the dumpster to any fibers in the car, and if the blood's a match for Ms. Brown . . ."

Bull Johnson finished her sentence. "We can nail this bastard."

Brie headed back to her cube and brought up the case report she had started yesterday on Ayesha Brown's murder. She added today's date and began writing up the new developments in the case.

The rest of the day things moved fast, as was common in cases like this. The fact is, most criminals are a lot lazier than they should be. Some of them are smart enough, but as a group, they are just damn lazy. It's what gets them in trouble in the first place, and it's what gets them caught in the end. They see their cronies getting caught and sent to jail, but it never seems to occur to them to do a more thorough job.

Brie and Garrett went back to Ayesha Brown's neighborhood to do some more canvassing. Talk to more of the neighbors. Make sure that if anyone had heard or seen anything, they got those testimonies down in writing. They kept at it for several hours until they had exhausted the possibilities and then headed back to the department. As they were en route, a call came through from Bull Johnson. The blood and fiber evidence had come in from the crime lab. "I've got a meeting scheduled with the assistant district attorney in my office at three o'clock. I'd like you two here for that."

"We're headed back now," Brie said.

* * *

At three o'clock, Brie and Garrett met with the commander in his office to lay out the evidence for the ADA in the murder case of Ayesha Brown. While no murder weapon had been found, they were certain that the autopsy and forensic evidence, along with the testimony of Brown's co-workers and of Clarence Tate, Brown's neighbor, who had seen her car parked in front of the house the night of the murder, comprised more than enough evidence to charge Lotrelle Gallagher for the murder.

They first discussed the former domestic calls to Ayesha Brown's residence in conjunction with the autopsy report of bruising that the ME had found on Brown's body. Then there was the interview Brie had conducted with Ayesha Brown's co-workers in which they had attested to the fact that Ayesha had stated that she was going to end her relationship with Gallagher.

But the clincher was the fiber and blood evidence. Fibers from the blood-stained rug found in the dumpster had been matched to fibers found in the car and in the living room of Ayesha Brown's home. The blood on the rug had been matched to the victim as well as blood in the hatch of her car and blood residue found on Lotrelle Gallagher's clothes that had been found in the dryer of the victim's home. Even though Gallagher had attempted to scrub the scene of the shooting, latent blood splatter on the living room walls also matched the victim. Finally, they had retrieved the pillow believed to have been used as a silencer. Fibers from that pillow matched those found in the victim's wound as well as in the victim's living room.

All in all, the evidence was compelling, and the assistant district attorney agreed to the charge of murder one. Lotrelle Gallagher was arrested for the murder of Ayesha Brown. With the arrest, the Minneapolis Police Department's active role in the case ended, and the case moved on to the courts.

By the time the ADA left the department, it was nearing four o'clock. Brie and Garrett went back to their cube to finish writing their reports on the case.

"Care to join me for beer and pizza tonight? Celebrate putting this case to bed?"

Although she didn't say it, Brie saw little cause for celebration. Another woman had been brutally murdered at the hands of her partner and abuser. So while she was glad they'd processed the case with such efficiency, the troubling reality of another woman being victimized sat heavy on her heart.

But mostly she didn't want Garrett to get the wrong idea. And without reading too much into his invitation for pizza and beer, she still remembered his spat with John last May when the ship had been marooned at Granite Island.

"Thanks, Garrett," she said. "That sounds like fun, but I think I'll pass tonight. I really want to keep working on my back case files. See if I can come up with a link to those letters I received."

The dimples appeared along with his slow smile, and a note of amusement danced in his blue eyes. "All work and no play, Brie . . ."

"Yeah, I know."

"It's okay. We'll do it another time."

"That sounds great," Brie said. She probably shouldn't have said it, but it was the path of least resistance, and she took it.

She knew she should probably tell him about her plans to drive north to Hovland tomorrow to interview Boyle Bouchard. But she also knew she was walking a line—that she wouldn't be allowed to move too deeply into a case that involved her directly. So until she found out if Bouchard was fire or just smoke, she decided to keep those plans to herself.

The two of them sat down at their respective computers to finalize their reports. Garrett finished first and prepared to leave.

"See you Monday, Brie."

She turned to say something, but he was already gone. Then she heard one of the detectives, Arturo Estavez, hail him.

"Hey, Parker, wanna grab a couple brewskies?"

And the rebuttal. "You're on, Estavez. You thinkin' Grumpy's?"

It was probably a fit for his mood, Brie thought, since she had rejected his offer.

"Yeah. That'll do."

"See ya there, then."

That was the end of the exchange. Brie finished up her report, happy that Garrett wouldn't have to drink alone. She shut down her computer, grabbed her coat, and went to her locker to swap out her firearm. She headed for the parking garage and within ten minutes she was making her way through rush hour traffic toward home.

Chapter 30

Brie stopped for Chinese takeout at a little restaurant in the Seward neighborhood and then headed for home. She paused in the driveway just long enough to collect her mail from the box at the front of the house and then drove the car to the end of the driveway, went up the back stairs, and let herself into her flat.

She ate part of her moo goo gai pan and then went to her desk in the living room. She spent the next hour and a half poring over her copy of the Thatcher murder book, reading deeper into the file, as well as rereading some of the reports she had read the night before. Because she had been kept on the outside of the investigation, she'd really had little idea, until now, of how the case had played out.

Among those who had been questioned, she was interested and somewhat troubled to find an interview with Joe Rossi, Garrett's former partner. Rossi was the guy who'd worked in the Narcotics Unit before moving to Homicide, and who'd been demoted after Internal Affairs found him guilty of not reporting his partner, one Frank Gorman, who had been on the take during their time back in Narco. Brie's partner Phil was the one who had gotten wind of the situation from one of the CIs he worked with on the street and had taken the information to Internal Affairs. A year after being demoted, Rossi left the department claiming he'd been treated unfairly, when, in reality, he should have been grateful he hadn't been fired in the first place. At least that was Brie's take on it. There was a phone number for him in the file. She took out her small notebook and jotted it down, just in case she decided to contact him.

She was sitting there, thinking about Rossi, when she heard a knock on her back door. She closed the Thatcher file and slipped it into the desk drawer and picked up her gun. She crossed the dining room to the kitchen and flipped on the light outside the back door. Garrett Parker waved through the window and held up a pizza.

Brie unlocked the door and opened it. "Garrett. What are you doing here?"

"Hey, Brie. Estavez and I never got around to eating. I thought you might have skipped dinner, too, so I decided I'd stop by with a pizza."

He held up the box and a six-pack of beer and smiled his winning smile, dimples and all. He seemed pretty darn happy, and Brie wondered how many brewskis he'd had with Estavez.

"Well, come on in. There's two things cops never turn down."

"Pizza and donuts," Garrett said.

"You got it." She looked at her watch. "You must be pretty hungry."

"Gettin' there," Garrett said.

Garrett opened two beers, and they took the pizza in the living room and set it on the sofa between them. Brie turned on some music, and they dug into the pizza.

Brie really wanted to ask him about the Rossi interview she'd seen in the Thatcher murder book but couldn't, since to do so, she'd have to reveal that she was working on the case. Instead they talked shop about the case they had just cleared, and Garrett rambled on about some motorcycle jaunt he was planning to take down the river to Red Wing and Mankato with one of his cop buddies the following weekend.

At 9:00 Brie gathered up the pizza box and three empty beer bottles and carried them out to the kitchen. She figured Garrett got the hint because he stood up and followed her. She set the pizza box on the counter next to the sink and opened the cabinet underneath to drop the bottles in the recycling. When she straightened up and turned, she found herself in Garrett's arms with him about to kiss her. It startled her so much that she brought her knee up between his legs, and he collapsed to the floor with a loud groan.

She went to her knees next to him, feeling bad about what she'd done. He was doubled over in pain.

"What were you thinking, man?" she asked, hearing the disbelief in her own voice.

"I was thinking I'd kiss you," he rasped out. "I was thinking you might like it."

"Look, Garrett, it's not like that between us."

"It could be, though. We'd be good together. Can't you feel it?"

"Listen, Garrett, I think you've had a little too much beer. You're not thinking straight. I'm gonna drive you home, okay?"

"Okay." Garrett crawled up from the floor. "So, fun's over?"

"Fun's over," Brie said.

She grabbed her keys off the kitchen counter, holstered her gun, and steered him out the back door and down to her car. His car was parked in front of the house.

She backed out of the driveway and headed toward south 35W and his house. She'd been to his place a couple of times over the years for parties. He lived in the Diamond Lake neighborhood, about fifteen minutes from her apartment. Garrett was silent, but every now and then she could feel him gazing at her with a dopey look on his face.

A few minutes later she pulled into the driveway next to his house and put the Escape in park, figuring humiliation would be enough to propel him from the vehicle. It wasn't.

"Why don't you come in, Brie? We could make it a memorable night. I might surprise you. In a good way."

"You might, but it's not happening, Garrett."

"Ah, Brie, don't be so uptight. Anyone as gorgeous as you needs to get laid a lot more."

She got out and went around to his side and opened the door. He climbed out reluctantly, and she shut the door. She went back around and got behind the wheel and pulled out of the driveway. Garrett blew her a kiss and headed toward his front door. She paused to make sure he got in the door and then drove toward home. She was really glad it was Friday and she didn't have to see him till Monday. Even though that was two and a half days away, she cringed at the thought of how awkward Monday morning was going to be.

She should report him for what he'd done even though they were off-duty. But she had no desire to wreck Parker's career. And the truth was, she wasn't going to be at the department any longer than she needed to be. Once Phil's case was solved, she planned on leaving.

When she got back to her place, there was Garrett's car. She didn't want him showing up here over the weekend and wondering where she was. She had to get the car back to his place.

Her landlady's light was on. Brie hated to do it, but she went up and rang the bell. Her landlady's name was Sarah, and in a few moments she opened the door.

"What's up, Brie?"

Brie explained the situation about Garrett, too much beer, and driving him home. She didn't tell her the rest.

"I'm going out of town early tomorrow, and I'd really like to get his car back to him tonight. Could you possibly help me?"

For whatever reason, Sarah looked like she got it. And she was still dressed, both of which gave Brie hope.

"No problem," she said. "Let me grab my keys, and I'll follow you to his place."

Sarah was in her fifties—definitely not antiquated, so Brie didn't feel too bad about asking her. Thirty-five minutes later, they were back. She thanked Sarah not once but twice, and then headed upstairs to her place to pack for the weekend.

Her mind felt totally scattered after what had just gone down with Garrett. She tried to refocus, knowing she had to get packed and into bed. She needed to be on the road by 6:30 a.m. to make it to Grand Marais by 11:00. She laid out her clothes for the morning—jeans, tee shirt, sweater—and packed her duffel with a change of clothes, underwear, pajamas, and toiletries. Then she hopped in the shower and was out in less than ten minutes. She rubbed the fog from the mirror and blew her hair dry. It hung long and lank around her shoulders.

She had just climbed into her pajamas when the phone rang. It was John. The time read 10:30. She went and climbed into bed, leaned back against the pillows, and basked in the sound of his voice. She wasn't about to tell him what had just gone down with Garrett. That definitely wouldn't be a formula for getting to sleep any time soon. So instead she told him about the wrap-up of the Ayesha Brown case and that she had managed to spirit the Thatcher murder book out of the department long enough to make copies.

"Be careful, Brie. You might get fired."

"He says with hope in his heart," she responded.

John laughed. "Well, it wouldn't be the worst possible scenario."

"Maybe. But it wouldn't bring justice for Phil either."

"I know," John said in an almost apologetic tone.

They talked for a few more minutes. John told her he was thinking of going up to a friend's camp in the Rangley area for a week to do some canoeing.

"You should go," Brie said. "It would be good for you to get away from the boatyard for a while."

"There's always so much to be done, though," John said.

"But it will keep till you get back."

"You're right. That's what I needed to hear."

She told him she had to go back up North over the weekend to interview a parolee—someone she had put away years ago.

"Is this connected to the shooting?" John asked.

"That's what I hope to find out or at least get a sense of."

"You're not going in there alone, are you?"

"No. Chief Deputy Renard is going with me. But I don't need a guardian, John. I know what I'm doing."

"I know that, Brie. I just worry sometimes."

"I get it, John." A moment of silence followed. "Sorry I snapped at you." Her nerves felt raw, but she couldn't tell him why. Well, she could have, but what she really needed was to get to sleep.

"Listen, John, I may stay over in Grand Portage, visit with Mom. There's rotten reception up there, so I'll call you when I get back."

"That's fine, Brie. Don't worry about it."

They talked for a few more minutes and then said goodnight. She set the phone on her bedside table, checked the drawer to be sure she'd put her gun in there, and turned off the light. She lay there for a few minutes in the dark, thinking about the Bouchard case; thinking about Garrett with his arms around her. She wasn't sure which was more troubling. Fortunately sleep came, and she didn't have to decide.

Chapter 31

By 6:45 the next morning, Brie was rolling north out of the cities on her way to interview Boyle Bouchard, who lived in Hovland. She was scheduled to meet Claude Renard at eleven o'clock at the Law Enforcement Center in Grand Marais, and they would drive on to Hovland, twenty miles north of there.

She liked to think or at least hope that in the case of Boyle Bouchard, she wasn't grasping at straws. That there were substantive reasons to be investigating him, namely the threats he had made against her nine years ago, his recent parole, and his current proximity to the place where Halley Greenberg had been shot.

Brie had coffee in a travel mug and a couple of granola bars on the passenger seat in case she got hungry along the way. Except for a bathroom break halfway up, she planned on driving straight through. Traffic was light, it being Saturday, and before she knew it she had reached the 35W split and was merging onto 35E North below Forest Lake.

Just after she'd left work yesterday, the crime lab report came through on the four threatening letters she had received. Bull Johnson had sent the report to her attached to an email, and she had found and read it this morning before leaving. It was a dead end. There were no fingerprints on any of the letters, and the paper and envelopes were garden-variety stock, available anywhere. The postmarks were from four different spots around the state. If Bouchard had sent them, he'd have to have driven all over kingdom come to mail them or gotten someone else to do it. Still, she thought, if he is connected to the letters, seeing them might trigger a reaction in him. So, to that end, she had stopped at the department on her way out of town, visited the evidence room, and signed the letters out. They were now in her briefcase along with the Bouchard case file, which she had brought along to show Renard.

Frankly, divorced from the shooting up North and the possible connection to her mother, those letters would have had little effect on Brie. Cops live in a world of threats. They are surrounded by them every day, so at a point it can become natural for them to feel immune to such threats, in the dictionary sense of being not affected or influenced by them. The police must carry on, do their work, live their lives in spite of the intrinsic threat posed by their profession. This produces two kinds of cops—polar opposites. Those who become paranoid and those who maybe aren't careful enough, who should be just a bit more paranoid. In between these two polarities is the psychological territory where the majority of law enforcement officers reside. Do the job, serve the people, watch your back, but don't become paralyzed by what might happen.

Brie had always inhabited this territory, this middle ground, up until the day she had been shot and Phil had died. Then she had moved into a polar reality, and polar was a good name for it because, for all intents and purposes, she was frozen. She did not, could not, function. She had spent the past nineteen months trying to make her way back from that wasteland, trying to come home—not to Minnesota, but to herself. And she had succeeded, or at least had made great strides. She wasn't all the way back yet, but she had shed the proverbial boots and overcoat.

To her surprise, the next road sign heralded the approach of Hinckley. She was already an hour beyond the northernmost reaches of the Twin Cities.

Beyond Hinckley, thoughts of Bouchard, the letters, and the Greenberg case fell away. She slipped into her open road reverie, and the miles rolled by. Soon winter, deep and silent, would overtake the farms and prairies of Minnesota. Snow would turn the landscape arctic white. The sun would follow its low-slung arc along the ecliptic, sending long shadows across the land wherever any vertical disturbance—trees, fences, livestock—rose from the bleak horizontal plane. The sun would hold only the brightness of the moon, and outstate Minnesota would take on a distinctly Siberian look and feel. *You have to be born here to understand why people stay,* Brie thought. *Why, in fact, they love this land.*

But this was the between time. The crops harvested, the greens of summer gone, autumn's blazing reds and oranges faded, the brilliant blue skies and dazzling white of winter yet to arrive.

This time of year had always felt like a waiting time to Brie, and this particular year that feeling was augmented by her situation. She felt between two realities, being pulled, even geographically, in two different directions. The case of the shooting up North and the possible threat to her mother, and Phil's unsolved murder in Minneapolis. And then there was Maine, a third reality, and the fact that for the time being, she was geographically divorced from the place and the man she loved. *At least life is full,* she thought, deciding to put a positive spin on things.

Within a half hour she was nearing Duluth. Lost in her thoughts about the two cases, the time and miles had slipped by. She took the exit for Skyline Drive, turned left, and followed the signs for the Thompson Hill Information Center and rest area—possibly the most spectacular in Minnesota. The center is perched at the top of Skyline Drive at the southern entrance to Duluth and offers a spectacular vantage of Duluth harbor far below. The Hawk Ridge Observatory shares the center and is a migratory viewing area every fall for diverse species of raptors—hawks, eagles, falcons, and owls—that migrate along this major western Great Lakes corridor.

Brie parked her Escape and headed down the walk and into the center to use the bathroom. A curved wall of windows gave a grand view of Lake Superior stretching away to the eastern horizon. Brie crossed the center and walked out the door onto the observation deck. The sight of that vast expanse falling away below her made something that was tight in her chest loosen, and she took a deep breath in and let it out. The wind had whipped itself into a frenzy as it always did up here, and clouds sailed overhead, seemingly close enough to touch. After a few minutes she retreated back into the center feeling alive from the wildness of the spot. She used the bathroom and headed back to her car.

It was ten past nine when she reached the northern edge of Duluth. She took the four-lane to Two Harbors rather than the scenic route along the lake. It saved a little time since she needed to be in Grand Marais by eleven o'clock to meet Renard. Beyond Two Harbors, she rolled through the familiar villages on the road north—Beaver Bay, Silver Bay, Tofte, and Lutsen. And she kept pretty much a constant eye on the big lake, since there it was around every curve and over every rise in the road.

She rolled into the outskirts of Grand Marais just minutes before eleven and stopped at the Holiday station to use the bathroom. Then she drove to the end of town and headed up Highway 12 to the Cook County Law Enforcement Center, where she pulled in and parked her Escape.

She called Renard's cell to let him know she had arrived.

"Give me a few minutes, Detective. I'm just finishing with someone here."

"No hurry," Brie said, noting that she was back to being 'Detective.' "It's not like Bouchard is waiting for us."

"No, we're rather hoping to surprise him, I think."

While waiting, she brought up the number for Joseph Renard's landline up at Grand Portage and sent the call.

He answered on the third ring. "*Boozhoo,* Brie. It is good to hear from you."

"*Boozhoo,* Joseph. It's good to hear your voice as well." There was an interesting formality about Joseph, and Brie wondered if that demeanor was typical of all the tribal elders.

"I had to come back up North to follow up with something on the case. I'm in Grand Marais now, waiting for Claude. I'd like to drive up to Grand Portage later and visit Mom, if that's all right."

"You are most welcome, Brie. You should plan to stay overnight."

"I'll think about that, Joseph. Please tell Mom I'll see her later in the afternoon."

"Edna is upstairs, but I'll let her know you are coming."

Brie saw Claude just coming out the door. "Thank you, Joseph. I'll see you later." They ended the call.

Chief Deputy Claude Renard, aka Sheriff One Step, moved down the walk with a kind of athletic ease that belied his prosthetic leg. Brie noticed he was carrying a Kevlar vest. She figured it was for her.

She got out of her SUV and hailed him. "Hello, Claude."

"Greetings, Brie. I thought we would take my squad."

"That vest for me?"

"Darn right. This guy threatened you before. Who knows what his state of mind is today?"

She studied him for a moment, and what she saw there was the wariness of a modern-day cop but also the life experience of a former combat vet, and for whatever reason she was instantly back at the night Phil had been shot, pulling up in front of that house on Upton Avenue, telling Phil to wait for backup, him heading for the open door and her pursuing. A new memory. A new piece of the puzzle.

"Brie?"

"Sorry."

"Where'd you go?"

She shook her head. "It's nothing." But the look in Renard's eyes told her he knew exactly where she had gone.

She was wearing a leather bomber jacket against the chill of the day. She took it off, and Renard helped her into the vest. She put her jacket back on and zipped it up. She reached into the Escape for her briefcase, and they walked over to Renard's squad and got in. "I brought Bouchard's case file along so you could take a look, see what we were dealing with nine years ago."

Renard opened the file and studied the mug shot of Boyle Bouchard for a moment.

Brie remembered Bouchard as a surly little man who had antagonized everyone, chief among whom had been his attorney—a young public defender who had been assigned to his case. In the end things hadn't gone in Bouchard's favor, but he and some of his knuckle-dragging friends had continued to trumpet his innocence.

There had never been any doubt in Brie's mind that he had shot the other guy—the one who had wrecked his motorcycle and then pulled a knife on him. But the question that had always remained for her was whether, despite his aggressive demeanor, Boyle Bouchard had simply been defending himself.

"You told me when we talked over the phone that you were the arresting officer and that Bouchard had held you responsible for putting him in jail."

"That's right. It didn't make a lot of sense, but that's what he thought. And when the conviction came down, he blamed me in the courtroom in a loud and vocal manner. Could have been some male chauvinism wrapped up in the whole mess. Who knows? He seemed like a guy who might resent a woman in authority."

Renard smiled, and his cobalt blue eyes twinkled. "No shortage of that still going around. It's too bad we can't evolve a little faster."

"Isn't it, though?"

Renard took a few minutes and read through the arrest report and perused some of the rest of the file. When he was done, he handed the file back to her. "I sent one of my deputies up to Hovland to do a little surveilling of the situation. According to county property records, the house—actually, more of a rustic log cabin—belonged to Bouchard's father, Thomas, who passed away while Bouchard was in prison. He left the house, which he owned free and clear, to Boyle—apparently his only offspring. When he knew he was dying, Bouchard senior had the presence of mind to hire a property company in Grand Marais to oversee the house and pay the taxes until Boyle got out of prison."

"Huh. Sounds like he cared about his son," Brie said.

"Sounds like."

"Any idea if Bouchard is employed?" Brie asked.

"I did a little digging and found out he works for a logging company here in Grand Marais. The same one his old man worked for. Probably why they hired him. I talked to the owner. He said Boyle's not a regular yet but works when they need extra crew. Logging outfits tend to pay well, so he's probably getting by on that and whatever his dad left him."

"Thanks for doing all that work, Claude."

"Hey, if there's a chance he's connected to the shooting of Halley Greenberg, we need to know all we can about him."

Brie opened her briefcase and took out the clear zipper pouch that held the letters she had received. "I signed these out of Evidence this morning. If Bouchard sent them, we may get a reaction when I show them to him."

"Good thinking, Brie. Shall we head up there?"

"Let's go."

Chapter 32

Hovland was a twenty-minute drive from the north end of Grand Marais, where the Law Enforcement Center was located. The only drawback Brie could see to driving the squad was that Bouchard might see it and possibly "do a runner," as the Brits liked to say. But where was he going to go? Well, the answer was into the woods, since every small hamlet in northern Minnesota was carved out of the dense surrounding forest. She mentioned her concern to Renard, and he said they'd park a ways up the road and walk down.

Fifteen minutes up the road they crossed the Brule River and, just beyond there, Brie looked off to the right. Down a long road that ran toward the lake, the famous Nanibijou Lodge—a landmark on the North Shore—glowed russet red in the late October sun. The lodge had been built in the late 1920s as a private club and hunting lodge for the rich and famous. But the Crash of 1929 had ended its short but glittering run, and since that time, the lodge had struggled through many incarnations. But the natural beauty of the spot and uniqueness of the lodge's architecture and history had kept it going.

Five minutes more along the road they came to the unincorporated community of Hovland, which boasted a population of 80. The narrow two-lane blacktop that ran through the hamlet bore the name Chicago Bay Road, after the nearly mile-wide Chicago Bay that Superior had carved out. The bay actually had a double scallop shape that from the air resembled a pair of well-rounded breasts.

Renard drove to the northern outlet for Chicago Bay Road. It lay just across the Flute Reed River. Across the small bridge, Renard turned right and wound south for a ways along the Bay Road. Just before a curve, he pulled the squad off to the right side of the road.

"His place is just around the bend," he said. "We'll walk from here."

They exited the car and headed along the road. They were close to the small river and could hear it flowing over a cataract of rocks. Just around the curve a small log cabin came in view. The logs were stained brown, and at this late season, the structure seemed perfectly married to the near-November landscape. The cabin was nestled back by the river at the end of a gravel drive. A narrow, open porch, covered by a sloping green roof, ran across the front of the cabin. Brie and Renard stepped up onto the porch, and Renard knocked on the door. Brie thought she could smell something burning inside, but it didn't smell like woodsmoke—what one would expect in this neck of the woods—but rather incense.

"Do you smell that?" she asked Renard, but before he could respond, the door of the cabin opened and there stood Boyle Bouchard in what could only be described as a kind of sarong of a deep orange color.

Bouchard had the shape of a lawn gnome. His head sat directly on his shoulders, and his arms, seemingly too short for his body, stuck out at near forty-five-degree angles, making him look like a duck preparing to take flight. His head was bald, and his feet, which stuck out from under the orange wrap, were bare except for a pair of black flip-flops. He seemed to have aged much more than nine years, but it was his demeanor that made him practically unrecognizable to Brie. Bouchard looked from one to the other of them with an expression that could only be described as unflappable—the antithesis of all she recollected of his personality.

"Boyle Bouchard?" Renard asked.

"That's correct, Officer," Bouchard said. He turned his head and studied Brie for a moment. "Detective Beaumont? You haven't changed much. You still have that lovely face."

The last time she had seen him, the day he was convicted of manslaughter, he had shouted threats at her as they took him from the courtroom. Whatever Brie might have pictured, this Boyle Bouchard was about a light year away from that expectation.

"Mr. Bouchard, we'd like to ask you some questions," Renard said.

"Please come in, Officers. No reason to stand out there. It's cold today." He stood aside and held out an arm to welcome them in.

Brie was first in and could not have been more astonished if she had stepped through a portal into some exotic land. The living room had been converted into a kind of Buddhist temple, complete with a sitting statue of the Buddha surrounded by flowering plants and bowls of fruit. Incense burned in a bowl in front of the Buddha, and a cascading fountain in the corner of the room burbled away, filling the room with the calming sound of a brook in motion. Bouchard's sarong-like attire suddenly made sense. He was dressed like a Buddhist monk.

There was no furniture in the room, just an ornately woven rug on the floor before the statue. At the opposite end of the room, a low bookshelf built under the window ran the width of the wall. It was completely filled with books. On the wall to the right of the window hung a framed picture of the Dalai Lama.

No more than two or three seconds had elapsed since they had stepped through the door, but Renard was as bug-eyed as she, and they both stood there speechless. It was Brie who finally broke the silence.

"Can you tell us about all this?" she asked Bouchard, trying but failing to keep amazement at bay. The list of questions they had come to ask suddenly seemed a less-than-interesting aside.

"I can see you're surprised," Boyle said. "Most people would be. I guess this is the last thing one would expect to find in the north woods."

Brie noted the use of "one" and found that surprisingly academic for what she knew or had known of this man.

"Surprised would be an understatement," she said. She glanced at Renard and could see that he was still incapable of speech. "When did you become a Buddhist?"

"I learned about Buddhism in prison. It was there that I began following the way of the Buddha." He clasped his hands in front of him and looked from one to the other of them.

"In prison you have nothing. No one. I realized one day that I wanted to be happy in spite of my condition. But I had only known happiness through things. I guess I must have prayed in some way, although I don't remember consciously doing it. The next week I started going to the prison library and just looking around. You know, for a guy who only made it through the tenth grade, the library was like a mysterious foreign land." A small smile came to his face. "That in itself felt kind of nice.

"One day, after watching me ramble about the place several times, the librarian asked if he could help me find something. I said I was looking for a way to be happy even though I knew I had to be incarcerated.

"He directed me to some books on religion, asking if I had ever been religious. I told him not that I could remember. He gave me a book on the life of Jesus and another one about Christianity. There was a book there about Buddhism, and I asked him what that was. He said it was another way to enlightenment, and then he said—and I will never forget this—'There are many ways to enlightenment. They can all lead to happiness.' He took that book down from the shelf and added it to the other two.

"The book on Buddhism said that to find Nirvana, which I understood to be peace and happiness, you had to let go of attachment to things and to people. Since I was already detached from all of that, I thought maybe this was for me." He looked directly at Brie. "I was an angry man. I'm sure you remember. I'm sorry I directed that anger at you. I thought I needed to blame someone to feel vindicated. But along the way, I realized I only had myself to blame. I have never regretted going to prison. Without prison, I don't think I would have found the way to peace." He paused and folded his hands. "I read those first books and over the following years probably everything else in the library. I found I liked reading. I guess you could say I became a kind of unlikely scholar."

He looked from one to the other of them. "But you have come for a reason," he said. "And since I am only four months out of prison, it must be to ask me about something that has unfolded."

"Well, that's correct," Brie said. She glanced at Renard to see if he wanted to take the lead, but he seemed content to smell the incense.

"Can you tell us where you were last Tuesday around five o'clock?"

"Well, let's see. I didn't work that day. Oh, yes. I know. I was attending a book club at the Grand Marais library. It started at four and ran until six o'clock." He looked from one of them to the other and must have seen something on Renard's face, because he said, "I don't go out dressed like this. I was just beginning my meditation when you arrived."

Renard nodded at that and finally spoke. "We certainly wouldn't judge you if you did."

Boyle Bouchard looked pleased but said, "Well, it's not my desire to call attention to myself."

To Brie, that was the most revealing statement so far, because it represented something on the scale of a geomagnetic reversal in Bouchard's character.

"I can give you a list of the book club members if you would like. We meet there at the library once a month."

"That would be most appreciated," Brie said.

Behind the living room was a kitchen, and a door on the side wall of the kitchen led to another room that Brie assumed was a bedroom. Bouchard turned and walked toward the kitchen, and Brie and Renard followed him. From a drawer in the kitchen he took out a kind of ledger book. He withdrew a list of names from inside the cover of the book and handed it to Brie. There were about ten names on the list.

Bouchard looked from one of them to the other and finally said, "Something must have happened that brought you here today. Something that you believe I am involved in. Might I ask what that is?"

Brie set her briefcase on the table and withdrew the clear zipper pouch containing the envelopes and the four letters she had received. "These were sent to my residence over the past four months, a period of time that coincided with your time of parole." She watched Bouchard, who was looking at the message on the top letter. He looked almost as if he were in physical pain.

"You thought I sent these because of the threats I made that day in the courtroom. I would have thought the same in your place."

"Sadly, there's more," Renard said. "A woman was shot and killed ten miles south of Grand Marais last Tuesday. She happened to be staying at the same small resort as Detective Beaumont and her mother. The two women, Edna Beaumont and the victim, bore a striking resemblance to one another. We think Brie's mother may have been the intended victim."

Boyle Bouchard looked deeply ashamed. "It makes me sad that I would be suspected in such a heinous act, but one's past casts a long shadow."

Brie wanted to feel bad for him, but her training stopped her just short of doing so. He seemed to have turned his life around one hundred and eighty degrees, though, so she said, "Before coming up here, I talked to your parole officer. He said you'd been an exemplary prisoner and so far, a model parolee. If these folks on the list can vouch for you, then you shouldn't need to worry."

"I do have to ask if you have a firearm of any kind on the premises," Renard said.

"My father had a hunting rifle, but I turned it in when I was paroled and came to live here. You should have a record of the exchange at the sheriff's office."

"I'll check into that," Renard said.

"Just one more question, Mr. Bouchard. Did you know or have you ever heard of a woman named Halley Greenberg?"

"I neither know nor have heard of her, Deputy," Bouchard responded in his now-perfect English. "Is that the name of the deceased?"

"It is," Renard said.

"I will pray for her soul on its journey."

Renard put his pen and notebook in his pocket. "Thank you, Mr. Bouchard. We will be in touch if we need to speak with you again."

Bouchard nodded. He looked deeply sad. He showed them to the door and wished them well.

Outside, Brie and Claude Renard headed along the driveway and back to the squad.

"You think that was for real?" Renard asked Brie.

"I think that's probably as real as it gets. Anyway, not exactly something you could whip up on the spur of the moment."

"Well, I'll grant you that," Claude said.

"If you'd known Boyle Bouchard nine years ago, you'd know that was not an act he could have put on. So what's our next step?"

"Let's go back to the Law Enforcement Center. We can divide up this list Bouchard gave us and call these folks. See if we can establish an alibi."

"If he was sitting in a book club with ten people from four to six p.m., he couldn't very well have been shooting Halley Greenberg at five o'clock."

"I'd also like to check the records for that hunting rifle he says he turned in."

They drove the twenty minutes back down to Grand Marais and parked at the Law Enforcement Center. Inside, Renard let Brie use the office next to his. Brie tore the list in half and gave the top part to him, and they started calling. In about twenty minutes Brie walked back into Renard's office. He was just hanging up the phone.

"That was the last one on my list," he said. "They all vouched for Bouchard, saying he was there at the library the whole time, and two of the women even said he stayed afterwards to talk to them some more."

"Same on my end," Brie said. "There was some curiosity about why we were inquiring, but I sidestepped that. Two of the women said that Boyle Bouchard had shared his story with the group when he first joined. He said he didn't want them to find out about his past from someone else—that he wanted to be the one to tell them. Probably smart considering that rumors spread like wildfire in small communities."

"My sense of Grand Marais is that it's a little different," Renard said. "Lots of well-educated, artistic people here. It's become a bit of an arts community. All that has helped the town be less of a rumor mill. Still, a story like Bouchard's would be bound to get out. He was smart to take the initiative."

"So where do we go from here?" Brie asked.

"Well, I'd like to check on that forfeited firearm." He turned back to his computer and began typing. When a list came up, he sat and studied it for a couple of minutes. "The rifle is listed here as forfeited on June twenty-fifth of this year. That would coincide with his parole. Looks like he was under court order to turn in any firearms on the premises. The rifle was registered to Thomas Bouchard. That was his father."

Brie nodded. "So far everything he's stated has been the truth."

"Still, I'd like to stop back up in Hovland and interview a few of the neighbors near Bouchard's house."

"I can help with that," Brie said. "If he's clean, I guess that leaves us back at zero."

"Well, we know one thing. There has to be a motive. We'll keep working the Greenbergs' connections, but I think we may have a botched job here."

"Meaning you think Edna was the target," Brie said.

"I think if we can't find a motive in the shooting of Halley Greenberg, then we have to look at the other possibility. Namely, that Ms. Greenberg may have been mistaken for Edna."

"My gut has told me all along that this was about Edna and, ergo, about me.

"Speaking of which, while I was waiting for you, I called up to Grand Portage and spoke to your dad. Told him I'd like to stop up there after we're done here. He said I should plan to stay overnight. Not sure if I'll do that, but I'd like to spend a little time with Mom."

"How 'bout after we're done in Hovland, we can both drive up there?"

"Sure," Brie said. "I think I'll bring my car, though, so I can leave if I have to."

"No problem. You hungry? It's one-thirty."

"I'm starved, actually," Brie said. "I had a really early start."

"Well, let's eat."

They headed into town, pulled into the Dairy Queen and went in. They both ordered burger baskets and sodas and sat next to the windows and ate their food. They were the only ones in the place, since it was both past the lunch hour and past the tourist season. When they were finished, Claude dropped Brie back off at the Law Enforcement Center so she could get her SUV, and they headed back up the road toward Hovland.

Chapter 33

The lake blazed blue in the late fall sun, and in the autumn light all the edges of the natural world seemed to be etched with a remarkable clarity—the trees, rock formations, and low-growing vegetation a symphony of earth tones. This place was beautiful, and even in the dying time of year, it was alive with a certain energy.

Twenty minutes up the road Brie rendezvoused with Renard at the spot they had decided on, near Boyle Bouchard's cabin. They agreed to meet back at their cars in approximately one hour. Brie took the neighbors along the road to one side of Bouchard's property and Renard to the other side.

For every neighbor Brie found at home, there was one missing. Some of the neighbors had known Thomas Bouchard, the father, but didn't know Boyle or even that he was living in the cabin that had formerly belonged to his father. The neighbors who had known Boyle since he'd moved to Hovland four months ago described him as one of the most peace-loving and generally loving men they had ever known. The verdict was in, and it seemed unanimous. Boyle Bouchard, in his new incarnation, was an all-around good guy.

Brie met Renard back at their cars at the allotted time and shared what she had found.

"Same here," Renard said. "Everyone that knows him seems to love the guy. I got the same story when I interviewed his boss at the logging company yesterday. All the guys there vouched for Bouchard. I think it's fair to say that he's a changed man."

"I feel the same way. I think we can cross him off the list." She paused and looked at Renard. "The perverse part of me almost wishes there had been something there. Right now the possibilities in this case are as thin as pond ice in April. But one thing I know. I'm not giving up. There's something here to be found. We just haven't dug it out yet."

Renard smiled. "I like that bulldog tenacity. I've always found that determination is nine parts of success."

"Or as my first homicide commander used to say, 'Just work the case.'" She wanted to tell him that she was excavating the past on another front as well—working the case of her partner's murder that had gone cold over a year and a half ago. But she decided it was best to keep that totally to herself. Her biggest fear was that somehow her activities would get back to the department, and she would be told to cease and desist.

"Well, if we're done here, we can head up to Grand Portage. I'm sure Dad and Edna will be planning something tasty for dinner later on."

"Your dad seems to enjoy cooking," Brie said.

"If it's creative, it's for Dad."

"I never realized just how creative cooking could be until I was on the *Maine Wind*. You start with the fact that everything is cooked on a woodstove and move on from there. I learned a lot working with George on the ship the past five months. I learned you can start with what you have on hand and create something amazing. No need for a recipe. Not that George didn't ever use recipes, but there's a lot of freedom in learning to cook the other way."

"You have to tell me more about your months at sea. I'm fascinated by the idea."

"Maybe over dinner tonight," Brie said.

"Great. Shall we hit the road?"

"You bet."

They got into their separate cars and headed back out to Highway 61. The sun was already beginning its descent toward the western horizon as they drove north toward Grand Portage.

A few miles above Hovland, Brie crossed the Reservation River that formed the western boundary of the Anishinaabe Nation—the reservation lands of the Grand Portage Band of Ojibwe. The road between there and the Grand Portage community, though not far from the lake, was flanked by such dense forest that there were few glimpses of Lake Superior stretching away to the south. The wind was picking up, and Brie could feel it buffeting the Escape as the road climbed toward the Grand Portage Highlands.

Brie used the drive to review in her mind what she had read in the Thatcher murder book. It seemed like every lead, every interview had led to a dead end as the case inevitably descended into the deep freeze. You'd think the killer had arrived at the crime scene hermetically sealed, because the Crime Lab had found no trace of DNA. It seemed to fly in the face of Locard's exchange principal, which states that the perpetrator of a crime will inadvertently bring something into the crime scene and leave with something from it. And yet that did not appear to have happened. And that fact troubled Brie maybe beyond all others. She decided she needed to question the neighbors again who lived adjacent to the house on Upton Avenue where Phil had been shot.

In the distance she saw the Grand Portage Trading Post and gas station that stood on high ground just off the highway on the lake side. She noticed Renard fairly close behind her, and for the first time thought that maybe there was a reason for his bringing up the rear in their caravan. From where he was, he could keep careful track of any cars behind them and make sure no one was following them. It sounded paranoid, but Brie knew that, with the questions surrounding the shooting of Halley Greenberg and the strong physical resemblance between her and Edna, "too paranoid" was not even a possibility. For now, it was imperative that Edna remain off the map.

Brie slowed and turned right and followed Mile Creek Road past the Grand Portage Monument. She took a right onto Bay Road and followed it along Grand Portage Bay toward Hat Point, where Joseph Renard lived. After about a mile and a half, the road veered left and up a small hill, and she turned onto Upper Road and followed that until she saw Joseph's log house on the left. She turned into his driveway and parked, and Claude pulled in soon thereafter.

Brie got out of her car. The wind was strong out here on the point, surrounded on all sides by Kitchigami—the Ojibwe word for "Big Sea." The pine whispered loudly, and the voices of the past still seemed to carry on the wind. This was the final peninsula around which the voyageurs had paddled their famed Montreal and North canoes before making harbor at the Grand Portage, after what had been a grueling thousand-mile trek through the waterways of Canada and across the Great Lakes.

She stood for a minute, listening to the lake. It had been calm all day, but now it was starting to roll as the wind turned into the northeast. Claude came over to stand beside her.

"The seas are building out there," Brie said.

He smiled. "Here in Minnesota we call them waves, or in the Ojibwe language, *mamaangaashkaa,* for big waves. I like the sound of seas, though."

"*Mamaangaashkaa* sounds quite grand, actually."

"A big word for the big spirit that is Kitchigami," Claude said.

They headed up the stairs, and Claude knocked lightly on the door before opening it. They stepped inside, and the warmth of the house and the aroma of cooking greeted them like a congenial hug. In the living room, a birch log fire blazed in the big fireplace.

"*Boozhoo,* Father," Claude called.

"*Aaniin,* Claude. *Aaniin,* Brie."

"*Aaniin,* Joseph," Brie responded and looked at Claude.

"It means welcome," he said.

Edna appeared from the kitchen, wiping her hands on a dish towel. "Hello, dear. Hello, Claude. I'm so glad you called, Brie. I didn't know you were coming up here this weekend." She crossed the dining room and gave her daughter a hug.

"It was kind of sudden, Mom. I was following up a lead on the case. It smells wonderful in here," she said, changing the subject, not wanting to disturb the happiness that seemed to radiate from Edna. Brie hadn't seen her mother looking so calm in a long time, and she inwardly heaved a sigh of relief that Claude had suggested this solution.

"Joseph received the gift of a duck from his friend down the road. We've stuffed it with wild rice and dried fruit. It's roasting in the oven. As soon as it comes out, we'll put some corn on the cob on the grill out back."

"I can do that, Edna," Claude said. "You visit with Brie, and Father and I will set the table and put the dinner on."

"*Miigwech,* Claude," Edna said. She turned to Brie. "Joseph has been teaching me some words and phrases in Ojibwe. The language is beautiful. To me it sounds like wind blowing through the pine. Like nature's susurrus."

"Edna is very poetic," Joseph said from the kitchen. "She paints wonderful pictures with her words."

They wandered toward the kitchen, where Joseph was husking corn into a paper sack that stood between his feet. He wore jeans and a red plaid flannel shirt that set off his silver hair.

"We have fresh coffee there." He nodded toward the counter, and Brie and Claude wasted no time filling their mugs, since cops and coffee go together like peanut butter and jelly.

Brie bent down to look in the oven where the duck was roasting. It was the color of dark caramel, and it glistened in its own oil. Brie's stomach turned a somersault in celebration.

Once they had their coffee, Claude shooed them out of the kitchen so that, true to Ojibwe tradition, he and his father could do the final preparation of the table.

Brie and Edna went into the living room and curled up on the soft leather sofa in front of the fire, and Brie impressed her by repeating the Ojibwe word for "big waves" that Claude had taught her. *Mamaangaashkaa*. Whether it was the warmth of the fire or the mug in her hands or the overall comfort of Joseph's home, Brie didn't know. But she was suddenly struck by an overwhelming wave of fatigue and gave herself over to yawning. Edna suggested she lie down for a short nap, but Brie said she'd be fine after she'd drunk some of her coffee. And sure enough, once she had downed half of the rich, strong brew Joseph had made, she felt like she was slowly returning to consciousness.

Edna talked about the places Joseph had taken her around the reservation, including several sacred sites that could only be visited if one was accompanied by a member of the band.

"You look at peace, Mom."

"This is a wondrous place," Edna said. "I do feel a great peace here. Joseph is such a kind man, and there's something cathartic about hearing the lake in motion, seeing it in all its moods. It does feel like a great spirit."

"I've always felt that Superior has some kind of mystical healing power for the psyche." Brie smiled. "And as you know, thoughts like that don't come easy for me."

Brie told her that she had started working on Phil's cold case but was keeping her investigation on the down low, since she was pretty sure they wouldn't allow her to investigate the case.

"I'd think they'd be happy to have anyone who's interested working the case," Edna said.

"That's not how it works, Mom. The department doesn't allow anyone to work on the case that involved someone close to them."

"Why? What do they think? That you're going to plant evidence just to make an arrest?"

"Being too close to something or someone can cloud the judgment. The annals are full of such cases. Plenty of perps have gone free because some cop with an agenda either made evidence disappear or planted evidence to incriminate someone."

"Now, I'm not trying to be harsh, Brie, but having said that, how do you justify working on Phil's case?"

"Look, Mom, I just know I have to do this. For Phil. For me. Heck, maybe for some reason I don't even know about yet. And if I find anything really compelling, I'll take it to Bull Johnson, my homicide commander. What's the worst he can do? Fire me. I'm going back to Maine anyway. It's only Phil's case that's keeping me here now."

They were interrupted by Joseph entering the room and telling them that dinner was served. "Claude is bringing the corn in from the grill right now," he said.

The four of them assembled around the table, and the aroma of the roasted duck filled the simple dining room. Joseph had cut up the duck and arranged it on a large plate. Steam rose from the platter of grilled corn, and the wild rice stuffing glistened with plump cranberries. Joseph said an Ojibwe blessing over the food, and then everything was passed around the table. Claude had put some whole grain bread next to the corn on the grill and had brushed it and the corn with melted butter. Those three simple dishes comprised a feast fit for a king or a chief.

Later they sat around the fire, and Brie told them about some of her adventures aboard *Maine Wind*, as well as some of the cases she had worked with the Maine State Police during her sojourn there. Claude found the case she had worked on

Apparition Island particularly fascinating, because it involved a crime from so many years ago. And the fact that she had worked with Jack Le Beau, one of the original detectives on the case, intrigued him.

"It's a great story," he said. "It shows that we should never despair of a cold case."

"Jack had carried the ghost of that case with him for almost sixty years," Brie said. "Can you imagine?" She looked at Edna. "That's why sometimes you have to do what you have to do."

At Edna's prompting, Claude talked about growing up on the reservation—the joys and hardships of it—and his deep respect for, and connection to, his native roots. "That boy, that teenager lives in me every day. We are one—*bezhigwan*. He guides me."

Joseph listened silently, but his face shone with pride for his son.

In time, the warmth of the fire and the comfort of all the savory food got the best of Brie, and she drifted off to sleep, only to be awakened at some point by Edna gently prodding her and sending her up to bed. As she ascended the stairs, she again noticed the painting over the fireplace that had been done by Joseph's wife. The light cast by the fire lent a ghostly aspect to the mystical eagle, and in the shadow play of the darkened room, the majestic bird appeared to soar in and out of those shadows as if borne on some impalpable current of air.

Brie continued up the stairs to the guest room she'd stayed in just a few nights ago. It seemed like longer, but much had transpired in those few days. Edna's things were scattered around the room, and Brie set her duffel on the unused bed and pulled out her pajamas and toiletries. She changed, pulled back the covers on the bed, and went into the bathroom to brush her teeth and wash her face. She felt dog tired at this point and longed for the warmth of the bed, so she finished her ablutions quickly, turned out the light and crawled under the covers. The wind was picking up outside, buffeting the house, racing around the eaves. In the distance she could hear the great hollow sound of Superior starting its assault on the cliffs of Hat Point.

Chapter 34

The great eagle makes its approach from high above the stormy waters of Kitchigami. Soon it is over the house, circling, its immense wingspan dwarfing Joseph Renard's home. Brie hears a tremendous rush of wind as the golden raptor circles high and then descends. She rises from her bed and goes to the window. She pushes the sash up and leans out to see the great bird. The sky is awash in light from a full moon. Phil rides on the back of the giant eagle as he did before, and as the eagle circles low over the roof, he scatters the red leaves. Brie reaches out once again, but they are carried away on the wind. She can see something written on the leaves. Thrice more the great eagle circles low and Phil sends the leaves down, and finally one is caught in an eddy of air current and blown toward Brie. She catches it and holds it gently, for it is brittle. On the leaf the black writing is now visible. It says, LOOK INSIDE. She watches the rest of the leaves raining down. They all seem to have two words—the same words. LOOK INSIDE. She turns the leaf over gently as if it might bear some treasure—hold some secret compartment that she can look into. But there is nothing there. It is just a single fragile leaf. She looks skyward to see if Phil might send her a sign, but the great eagle is already moving away, soaring high over the dark and turbulent waters of Kitchigami.

* * *

Brie woke with a start. She sat up and looked to her left and saw that Edna was sleeping soundly next to her. She had seen a flashlight in the drawer of the bedside table earlier. She slid the drawer open and turned on the flashlight, keeping her hand over the lens to tamp down the amount of light. She stood and went to the dresser where she'd laid her small notebook and pen. In the dim light, she opened the notebook to a blank page and wrote the words LOOK INSIDE. Exactly as they had appeared on the leaf in the dream.

She stood looking at the words, feeling the chill of the pine floor beneath her feet. What could the words possibly mean? She remembered what Joseph had told her about the significance of the eagle to the Ojibwe. That eagles have a special connection to visions, and that it is believed they can serve as messengers between humans and the spirit world.

She felt completely out of her depth here. Was she meant to take the dream at face value? Could it possibly be that Phil was trying to communicate something to her? Or rather, was the dream prompting her to look for the answers within herself? To try harder to reconstruct the night of the shooting?

She had recently recovered memories from the night Phil had been shot, and she had scheduled an appointment with Dr. Megan Travers for next Tuesday to do another hypnotic regression back to that fatal night. Maybe the dream was encouraging her to go ahead. Maybe in the regressed state, more would be revealed about that terrible night.

She had only had the dream of the great eagle here in Joseph Renard's house. She wondered why. The Ojibwe referred to these as sacred lands, and something about this place did indeed feel almost mystical to her, and she was not one to sense such things, or so she believed.

She realized she was shaking. The air in the room was quite chilly, and her feet felt icy cold. She crawled back into bed and lay there shivering for a few minutes, seeing the great eagle in her mind's eye, hearing the rush of air beneath its immense wings. When she woke again, the early light from the eastern sky was filling the room.

Chapter 35

Brie stayed under the warm covers for a few minutes, slowly coming to consciousness. Last night's dream had still been vivid in her mind when she awoke. Rather than haunting her, though, she felt there was something hopeful about the dream. She decided it belonged in the good dream category. The dream catcher on the wall over her bed must have done its work.

After a few minutes, she crept from her bed, went in the bathroom and turned on the shower. She was out in a few minutes, dried off and toweled her hair. She combed out the wet hair, brought it over her left shoulder and worked it into a braid. She combed out her bangs and went out into the room to dress. Edna was still asleep, so Brie quietly pulled on her jeans, a snug-fitting tee shirt, and a soft, thick sweater with a cowl neck. It was old but still one of her favorites. She pulled on wool socks, picked up her hiking shoes and crept out of the room, closing the door softly after her.

She found Joseph downstairs in the kitchen with a steaming pot of oatmeal cooking away on the stove. He was busy ladling corn bread batter into a black cast-iron skillet. She decided the chances of ever being up before Joseph were slim and none. "Good morning, Briana," he said without turning around.

"Good morning, Joseph," she said, surprised he had heard her stocking-footed approach. What was more, she couldn't remember telling him her full name. But maybe Edna had.

"How did you sleep?"

"Really well," Brie said. She was deciding whether to tell him about her dream when he turned and studied her silently for a few moments.

"You have dreamt of the great spirit bird again."

To say that she was surprised at his words would be an understatement of Himalayan proportions. "Well, yes, but how could you know that?"

He gave her a gentle smile. "Sometimes powerful visions or dreams can be shared by those nearby."

She must have looked uncomfortable or dangerously out of her depth, because Joseph said, "Come, sit down."

They went to the kitchen table, and he sat across from her. "Your dreams have meaning, Brie. You may have the gift of seeing."

"But what does that mean?"

"In our traditions we feel that vital information and guidance from the spirit world is transmitted through dreams and visions. Our young people can choose to undergo a vision quest if they wish to explore this ability. It is encouraged in our tradition to seek this kind of guidance. But some have a natural gift for this 'seeing.' It is possible you are one of these."

Brie looked out the window for a few moments before turning back to Joseph and telling him what was on her mind.

"When my partner died, I was also shot and came very close to dying, I was told. It was after that I started having what I would call symbolic dreams. Often when I've been working on a difficult case."

"When you were shot, you hung between life and death. Between the two worlds. You would have drawn very near the spirit world. It is possible you brought back the gift of seeing when you returned. It is a great gift. One that can guide and also protect you."

Brie felt humbled by what she was hearing. "It *has* guided me, Joseph. I can't deny that. But to me it's also somewhat of a mystery."

"We refer to this world and that of the spirits—all of it together—as the Great Mystery."

Brie smiled. "It's as good a name for God as one could imagine," she said.

"The physicists talk about the mysteries of the universe. In our tradition we consider all those as part of the one. The Great Mystery." He smiled. "But this is very serious talk. It requires some sustenance."

He went to the oven and brought the heavy skillet with the cornbread Brie had been smelling. He cut a large wedge for each of them and set the maple syrup on the table. Then he brought steaming mugs of coffee for them.

"I am glad we had this time to talk, Brie. And I am honored that you have shared these parts of your life with me. It is a bond we will share."

"Thank you, Joseph. There is what feels like a kind of strength in what you have told me."

"The strength is not in my words, but in you," he said.

They ate their cornbread covered in maple syrup and drank the rich coffee in companionable silence. After a time, Joseph spoke. "Coffee is not part of our native traditions, but as a former student and teacher, I love it dearly."

Brie smiled. "As a cop, I love it dearly, too."

"So what are we talking about?" Claude said, entering the kitchen.

"Coffee," Brie and Joseph said in unison.

"That's a discussion I can get serious about."

Claude went to the cupboard and got a plate and bowl. He ladled up some oatmeal, poured out a mug of coffee and came to the table. He wore jeans and a light blue sweater that set off his dark hair and deep blue eyes. It was the first time

Brie had seen him dressed in normal clothes and not his uniform.

"Maybe I should wake Mom," Brie said.

"Let her sleep," Joseph said. "We were up late talking."

Claude ate his breakfast, and Joseph asked Brie if she'd like some oatmeal. She decided that would be a good plan, and while she dished up a bowl, Joseph refilled her coffee mug. She sat at the table with Claude and ate. Joseph sat with them but said he would wait for Edna to finish breakfast. For the first time, he asked how the case was going, and Brie and Claude told him there were still some ambiguities.

"I'd like Edna to stay with you here until we reach a resolution with the case," Brie said.

"She is welcome here for as long as she needs to be," Joseph said. "It is rarely that I have had such a kind, intelligent, and interesting visitor. She seems comfortable here, and we are finding lots of ways to pass the time." He looked at Claude. "I thought I would set up your mother's loom. It's been put away for many years, but I used to enjoy weaving." He looked at Claude almost as if seeking his permission.

"That sounds like a wonderful idea, Father. Maybe you could teach Edna."

"Winter comes early here because we are so far north. Once the snows fall, one can feel a little more closed in."

"You don't need to worry about that, Joseph. I saw some snowshoes hanging on the wall in the upstairs hall. Mom loves to snowshoe. Once the snows come, you'll have a time keeping her indoors."

"That's very good to know, Brie."

She and Claude finished eating, and Claude asked her if she'd like to take a walk down to the shore and watch the lake.

"I'd love that," Brie said.

"You'll want a hat and gloves," he said. "It's quite windy out today."

Brie looked out the window and saw the spruce trees bending in the wind. "It's so peaceful here," she said. "It seems you can always hear or see the wind."

"The wind is a great presence here, especially on Hat Point, surrounded as we are by Kitchigami," Joseph said.

She looked across at him. "I'm curious, Joseph. Are you a tribal elder?"

Joseph smiled. "I guess I must look old, then."

"No, it's just . . . I'm curious."

"He's pulling your leg," Claude said.

"The answer, though, is yes." Joseph smiled. "I believe I'm old enough to make the cut. There is no set age, though. The older men and women of each band are all considered Ojibwe elders. We are known as *chinshinabe*. The elders are the traditional teachers, the caretakers of the Ojibwe culture and sacred knowledge."

Brie nodded. "Thank you, Joseph. I've heard the term 'elder' but didn't know how one gets to be such."

"You just have to get old," Joseph said. "Unlike mainstream culture in America, among the Anishinaabeg, our elders are revered for their wisdom and knowledge."

"There's much that mainstream America could learn from your traditions," Brie said.

"Ready for that walk?" Claude asked.

"Ready," Brie said.

They got their jackets on, and Brie pulled a thin stocking cap out of her pocket along with a pair of gloves and put them on, and they headed out the door. There was a small decorative weather thermometer attached to one of the log uprights on the porch. It read 37 degrees.

The view from the porch over Grand Portage Bay was a stunning one, and Brie stopped for a moment to take it in. Then they headed down the wood stairs and around the house. A trail disappeared into a grove of stunted spruce trees. Dwarf forests—another remnant of the alpine climate that had existed here after the last Ice Age—were still found along the far North Shore.

The trail soon left the shelter of the spruce forest, exposing them to the frigid wind off Superior. A few giant snowflakes drifted aimlessly down as if testing the air, seeing if it was too cold to snow—a meteorological condition that often held sway during the very cold months of January and February in Minnesota.

"Being so far north, it's not uncommon to get measurable snow here in October," Claude said over his shoulder.

"Do you ever see the Northern Lights?" Brie asked.

"All the time. It's one of the gifts of the North Country."

They soon came to the end of the trail and stood looking out over the vastness that was Superior. Brie zipped her leather jacket up all the way and stuck her hands in her pockets against the wind.

"Here, I'll stand upwind," Claude said, stepping around to her left to block some of the north wind.

They stood silently for a few moments, looking out over the horizonless gray expanse. White caps covered the surface of the water as far as the eye could see.

"Wind's blowing over twenty-eight knots today."

"How can you tell?" Claude asked

"When the water looks white and foamy like that, it's a sign the wind is at Force 7—a near gale."

"I suppose sailors need to know those things."

"Sailors are ever watchful of the wind and the sky. Their lives can depend on that vigilance."

"Maybe it's a good occupation for a cop, then," Claude said.

Brie smiled. "I never thought of it that way, but you're right. Cops are programmed to be vigilant, maybe in a different way, but with the same kind of intensity."

She stood for a few minutes, lost in her thoughts. "I dreamt of the great golden eagle again last night. And of my partner Phil, who was shot."

For a time, Claude gazed out over the restless waters of Kitchigami. Brie was once again aware of that profound stillness she had come to identify with him. It was a stillness, a steadiness, that felt as ancient as these lands, this water. When he finally spoke, it was in a tone both grave and gentle.

"The fact that you have had the dream again is significant. Remember what I told you before about the golden eagle, known to us as the war eagle. It is possible a path of danger lies before you, Brie. You must be aware. You must see with the eyes of an eagle." He paused and studied her. "Do you know that the eagle has a three-hundred-forty-degree field of vision?"

"I didn't know that," Brie said. "So it can spot its prey, I would guess."

"But also so it can sense impending danger. This is a troublesome case. There is a great lack of clarity, which makes the investigation difficult. It's possible someone targeted Edna. It's also possible that you are the true target."

Brie shivered. The result of the strong north wind, or so she told herself. But something in the nature of Claude's carefully chosen words gave her pause. The ambiguities of this case and of Phil's case were beginning to haunt her ever so slightly. She felt as if she were drawing nearer to something. The symbolism of the leaves in the dream seemed to indicate that. In the first dream she had failed to catch one of the leaves, but given a second chance, she was able with great effort to capture one of them and read its message. *Look inside.* Another riddle, another enigma. And yet she knew her dreams carried meaning. The past six months had taught her that. It was as if being shot had opened some door inside her through which arcane information was now allowed to flow.

The two of them were silent for a time, listening to the breakers thundering in along the granite shore. "Claude, I'm interested in how you integrate your police training in investigative techniques, fact-based findings, and forensic science with your traditional teachings that seem to be based more on metaphor and symbolism."

He smiled. "On the surface they would seem to contradict each other, but I have always found them to work in perfect unison. It's a bit of a mystery, I guess. But here's the thing. All investigative work is really about a search for truth. First, who had motive to commit a particular crime? What is the motive? Because that is the truth that sits at the heart of each case and how it will be solved.

"Our Ojibwe teachings and traditions are meant to help us grow closer to our natural world and thereby closer to who we really are. Our traditions are really about understanding the sacred connection between humans and the natural world. When you move from that place—what feels to me like a very solid place—it seems you are able to see everything more clearly. Events in nature take time to unfold, so when we align ourselves with nature, we learn patience."

Brie realized he was describing the stillness she had sensed in him.

"That patience helps me to look more deeply into people and situations. It helps me to see the path I must take through the maze that is the investigation. In that stillness I often find the questions I need to ask. The ones that lead me to the truth."

"That was very eloquently said, Claude. You know, the past six months on the ocean, I experienced what it is for life to slow down. Maybe for the first time ever. During that time, I often found myself doing a kind of deep dive. Not into the sea, but into myself. Down there, in that place, I found clarity and I found healing. Interestingly enough, I also did some very good police work. So I guess the two are not mutually exclusive."

"If the heart is pure, all things work together for the good."

"And if not?"

Claude smiled. "That is why we need law enforcement."

They walked along the top of the hill for a ways, letting the power of the lake work its way inside them. Brie knew that for days after she left here, she would hear the great hollow murmurings of Superior as it attacked and retreated from its ancient shores.

Chapter 36

They had been out in the wind for nearly an hour, and the cold was slowly working its way into Brie's bones. What was more, she knew she had to get started home. It was nearly a five-hour drive, and she wanted to have some time later in the day to visit the neighborhood where Phil had been shot and killed. She planned to canvass the neighbors, see if anyone had been missed who might remember something from that night. She knew the chances were slim. It had been a year and a half since the shooting, but it was still worth a try. It was also possible that someone might be willing to talk who hadn't been when the incident occurred. People are sometimes frightened into silence by the thought that they might become a target if they speak. But with the buffer of time, it's always possible a person may feel safe enough to reveal what he or she knows.

"We should probably head back to the house," Brie said. "I'll need to get on the road soon."

"Of course," Claude said.

They retraced their steps along the bluff until they came to the trail that wound through the spruce and back toward Joseph's log house. When they came out of the trees, they walked side by side.

"I suppose you have someone back home?" Claude said.

Brie was surprised by the question. She turned for a moment and studied his face in profile. "Not here in Minnesota. But in Maine," she said.

"The captain of the ship."

"Yes," Brie said gently.

"I saw the light in your eyes when you spoke of him."

Brie suddenly felt at a loss for words.

"So you're going back East?"

"Only when I've solved the case of my partner's murder," she said.

"And if you can't?"

"I don't consider failure an option," she said. "I know that must sound arrogant, but I have to think that way. It's that important to me."

"Just remember what I said, Brie. The eyes of an eagle."

She nodded. "I'll remember, Claude. Thank you. And thank you for sheltering my mother. How can I ever repay you?"

"That's all been my father," he said.

"Yes, but you had the idea. And everything starts with an idea."

"That is truth," Claude said. "But to enter this realm, the idea must become an action."

They came around the side of the house, climbed the steps to the porch, and went in the door. Edna and Joseph were in the kitchen, having a lively conversation over breakfast.

"Let's get some hot coffee," Claude said.

Brie smiled. "That's an idea I can act on."

"Come sit, children," Joseph said.

They got their coffee and sat in the kitchen with Joseph and Edna. Edna's hair was still wet from her shower, and she had pulled it up into a ponytail and wore a heavy wool turtleneck sweater. There was some cornbread left, and Joseph convinced Brie and Claude to finish it off. It was such an amiable scene around the little kitchen table that Brie wished she could just hang out here and enjoy a laid-back Sunday. But she also wanted to make some progress on Phil's case today, if possible. Once she was back into the work week, time would be harder to come by.

So with that in mind, she visited for another twenty minutes and then went upstairs to pack her things. As she came down the stairs, she looked at the painting of the eagle one last time. This morning it seemed just a painting, albeit a lovely one. But it reminded her of Claude's words. "Remember, Brie, the eyes of an eagle."

Downstairs, she hugged her mom and thanked Joseph again for all his kindness.

Joseph presented her with a small pouch made from the softest deerskin and hung from a deerskin thong. "It is a medicine bundle," Joseph said. "It contains the four sacred medicines we spoke of the first night. Claude has added a feather from a golden eaglet. It is worn for protection and to bring spiritual power to its owner."

Brie felt deeply moved to be included in a tradition so sacred to the Ojibwe. She placed the medicine bundle over her head and tucked it into the neck of her sweater. "I will wear it next to my heart. Thank you, Joseph. Thank you, Claude. I hope we will meet again soon."

Claude walked out with her to the car, and they told each other they would be in touch if new information came to light either about the Greenberg shooting or the threats Brie had received. Though it is not a Native American custom, they shook hands, and their eyes met.

"It's been a pleasure working with you, Detective."

"And you too, Chief Deputy."

They shared a smile over that and gave each other a spontaneous hug. Then Brie climbed into her car and was on her way.

She followed the road around Grand Portage Bay and in a couple of miles came back up to the highway. She filled her tank at the gas station connected to the Trading Post and then got back on Highway 61 heading southwest toward Grand Marais.

For the next forty-five minutes her mind slid into neutral. The sound of the tires on the road, the view of the horizon, the feeling of rapidly moving through space as the world whizzed by. She liked all of it. And the solitude. No demands on her. Just driving. She liked it so much that often she didn't even turn on the radio. Just enjoyed the silence.

When she eventually reached the outskirts of Grand Marais, her reverie was interrupted, first by the change in speed limit, then by watching for cars turning onto the road, then by the one stop light in town, and on it went until she climbed the long curving hill and came out the other end.

Now she rolled along high above the lake, which lay to her left. She could see the great expanse of wind-perturbed water, and she knew, though she could not hear it, that Superior was roaring like some ancient beast come to life. And somehow that got her thinking about Boyle Bouchard and his self-styled Buddhist shrine in Hovland, of all places. He had seemed like the perfect fit as a suspect in the shooting of Halley Greenberg. But she had to admit, she couldn't have been more wrong, and that reinforced her realization that she was pretty much grasping at straws. Until new information came to light, trying to find leads in her myriad of closed cases was a total needle-and-haystack proposition.

A part of her had believed all along that Edna was the target in the shooting, not Halley Greenberg. Yes, the circumstances were bizarre, with the two women looking so much alike, but obviously not impossible. It certainly would be nice to establish a motive. If Edna was the target, the theory was that the attempt connected to the letters she had received and was intended to punish her. But motives can be mysterious and elusive things that sometimes only make sense to the killer. And even though Brie believed the case connected to those letters, the murder of Halley Greenberg had occurred in Cook County, so it was Renard's case to work.

She knew full well that if Edna was the target, she too could become a target. But she could watch her own back, and for now, Edna was safe. So she made the decision to focus single-mindedly on Phil's cold case. With that in mind, she laid out her plan. This afternoon, once she got home, she would recanvass the neighborhood where she and Phil had been shot. It was Sunday. The neighbors would be at home. And she would contact Sideways Louie, one of the CIs she'd worked with over the years. Unlike some of the other CIs used by the department, Louie, strange as he was, had become known over time as a source of reliable information.

At Duluth, more or less the halfway point in the trip, Brie stopped for a bathroom break at a gas station next to the entrance to 35E. She grabbed a coffee and a candy bar and got on the interstate and rolled down through the lower reaches of Duluth, skirting the harbor where freighters from all over the world come to collect their cargos of iron ore, timber, and grain. The twin harbors of Duluth, Minnesota and Superior, Wisconsin operate one of the largest grain-handling facilities in the world, shipping around fourteen million tons of grain a year from docks that stretch along forty-nine miles of waterfront.

Brie would have liked to stop in Canal Park and watch one of the great inbound freighters sail through the famous canal and under the Aerial Lift Bridge, heading into port. Or maybe an outbound freighter reversing that course on its way out to sea. Most Minnesotans have fond memories of their first childhood visit to the great inland port, and Brie was no exception. But truth be told, there were many things Brie would have loved to do but never allowed herself time for. When she stopped to reflect on the fact, it tended to trouble her. But the answer she gave herself was always that she could do it later.

Her friend Ariel had often counseled her about what she called "Being present in the present." Advice to which Brie had mostly turned a deaf ear until she had lived aboard a sailing ship on the ocean. There the present dominates to such an extent that it becomes particularly hard to think of the future. At least the future beyond that day's intended anchorage, which itself has little meaning, because one may or may not get there, depending on the wind and weather.

Below Duluth, it was a straight run down the interstate for two and a half hours to Minneapolis. She tuned in a Duluth radio station and settled in for the final leg of the trip. As the miles rolled by, the dream of the night before played through her mind over and over. Phil, the great war eagle, and the deep red leaves raining down. Red, the color of leaves in autumn, but also the color of blood.

Chapter 37

Brie pulled into her driveway back home just before three-thirty. She carried her duffel up the back stairs and let herself into her apartment. She took a few minutes to unpack and grab a sandwich, but she was already focused on what the rest of the afternoon might bring. She had read more than once the testimonies of the neighbors who lived close to the house where Phil had been shot. They had been of little help in the case, but it was a place to start.

She also needed to set up a meet with Sideways Louie. She went in the bedroom where she had left her phone and scrolled through the numbers in her log till she came to Louie's. She sent the call. After several rings, Louie answered.

"Hello." The word was so clipped it came out "Lo."

"Louie, this is Detective Brie Beaumont."

There was a moment of silence at the other end. "Thought you were gone," he said guardedly.

"Well, I'm back."

There was a monosyllabic response from the other end that sounded something like, "Huh."

"I'd like to meet with you."

Silence.

"Would tonight work?"

"No."

Brie waited a moment, but no explanation was offered.

"Tomorrow. One o'clock. Emily's."

"Okay . . ." But before she could say more, Louie hung up.

Emily's Café was a small diner-style restaurant where she and Sideways Louie had met before. It was located in North Minneapolis very close to the 4th Precinct. The cops from the 4th frequented Emily's, but so did everyone else. It was an eclectic mix of the good, the bad, and the ugly. Emily, the owner, an Italian-born American, had presided over the establishment for thirty-six years and still came in most days, sat on one of the soda fountain stools at the U-shaped counter and visited with her customers.

Brie put the meeting in the calendar on her phone and set it to remind her an hour before. Then she grabbed her keys, made sure she had her pocket notebook and headed out the door.

Twenty minutes later she sat in front of the house at 3147 Upton Avenue North. The house where Phil had died. The grass was long, and several of the windows on the second floor were boarded up. She hadn't been back to this spot since that fateful night, and it felt strange to be here now on a sunny fall afternoon more than a year and a half after the crime. After the shooting, it was learned that the house had been vacant—the property in foreclosure. But over the years before Phil's death, the place had been a known drug house and gang hangout. However, the county records showed that, at the time of the shooting, the house had been empty for over a year. After the shooting, the city had purchased the property since it was the scene of an ongoing investigation into the death of a police officer.

Brie studied the house, trying to decide what she felt. She had thought it might be anger or overwhelming sadness, but she was surprised that what she felt was nothing—a total absence of feeling. Numbness. Like someone had taken a scissors and cut that page out of her life and replaced it with a blank, wordless page. It was the kind of emotional numbness that is often the byproduct of PTSD. Action was the only antidote she knew for the inertia of that desensitized state, so she got out of the car and started toward the house immediately to the left or south of 3147.

The house had a screened porch, and when Brie came up the steps, she saw two rocking chairs there with a small table between them. She tried the porch door and it was open, so she crossed to the front door. She waited quite a while after ringing the bell, and while she waited she consulted her small notebook, where she had written the names of the neighbors she'd taken down from the case file. At the time of the shooting this house had been owned by a Mrs. Jonathan Adams.

As if on cue, the door opened and an elderly black woman with a cane smiled up at her. "Can I help you?" she asked.

"Mrs. Adams?"

"Yeees," she drew out the word. "I'm Viola Adams."

Brie showed her badge wallet and told Mrs. Adams why she was there—that she was doing a follow-up investigation of the shooting that had occurred at the house next door a year and a half before.

"Would you like to come in?" the old woman asked. "I can't stand for very long."

"Of course," Brie said, and Mrs. Adams led her into the living room. The furnishings were old, but the room was clean and bright and smelled of furniture polish.

"Would you like something to drink?" Viola asked.

"Oh, no thank you," Brie said. "I'm fine."

At that Viola let out a sigh and sat down in a straight-backed armchair and hooked her cane over the arm. Brie moved another small chair over closer to Viola and sat down.

"The police questioned me before, back when it happened. I couldn't be of any help at all, I'm afraid. I didn't wake up that night until I heard the sirens. Then I got out of bed and saw the ambulance and knew something had happened next door."

Brie settled back in her chair and let Viola talk.

"It was only a matter of time. I used to tell my husband, God rest his soul, that something bad was bound to happen over there. Unsavory types comin' there all hours of the night. Lordy. Then finally the man who lived there moved out. The place was empty. My neighbor next door said they was foreclosing on the house. I was glad about that, but worried too. You know. An empty house—now that's an invitation to all kinda mischief."

"The night of the incident there was someone in the house," Brie said. "A 911 call came through that a possible break-in was underway. When we got to the address next door, the door was ajar." She paused, realizing what she had just revealed.

Viola was elderly, but her mind was sharp as tacks. Her eyes opened wider and she leaned toward Brie. "There was a woman detective that night with the detective who died. She was shot too. That was you."

It was a statement, not a question, and Brie was not going to lie to Viola. "Yes, it was me," she said.

"Oh, Lordy, honey. That was your partner died next door."

"Yes," Brie said, her voice barely audible. "His name was Phil. Phil Thatcher." She raised her eyes to meet Viola's. "I'm just trying to find justice for him."

"I wish I could help, Detective Beaumont. I truly do." She studied Brie for a few moments. "Are you all right now?" she asked gently. "Did you heal up all right?"

Brie's eyes slid past the old woman and rested on a photograph on the wall of Viola and her family from years gone by. Her husband was there and two boys and a young girl. "The physical wounds have healed . . ." she finally said.

"But that ain't the worst of it, now, is it, child?" Viola asked.

Brie searched the old woman's eyes and found compassion there. She shook her head slowly. "No, it's not," she said. "The guilt is the worst part. Wondering why him and not me."

Viola reached over and patted her leg. "It wasn't your time to be called," she said with conviction. "There's important work you still got to do here, child."

Brie nodded. "I'll remember that, Viola." She took one of her cards out of her badge wallet and gave it to Viola. "If you think of anything, anything at all that might be of help, you call me. All right?"

"All right," Viola said. "I promise."

Brie stood to go, and Viola struggled to her feet as well.

"Do you know if all the neighbors that lived here at the time of the shooting are still here? That would be the house on the other side of 3147 and those across from and behind it."

"The house directly behind, that's renters. People comes and goes, so I couldn't say about that place. But no one else has moved out of the other houses you mentioned since then."

"Thank you, Mrs. Adams. Viola. I won't take up any more of your time."

"Well now, time's about all I got to give these days, so I don't mind."

Brie thought about the old woman's kindness. "I think you underestimate yourself, Viola."

She smiled. "You take care of yourself, child."

"I will," Brie said. "Promise." She stepped out the door and heard Viola draw the bolt on the other side. She headed across the street to continue her canvassing of the neighbors.

An hour and a half later, she returned to her car having learned nothing new. The neighbors to the north of the crime scene and across the street all claimed they'd seen no one around the house at 3147 Upton the night of the shooting. In fact, they all said that to their recollection there had been no one hanging around that property after the former owner moved out and the house went into foreclosure. Nor had anyone seen the shooter leave the house that night. All of that jibed with the original testimony of the neighbors.

Brie questioned the residents in the houses behind the property as well, hoping that someone might have seen the killer fleeing that night. That someone might remember something or feel safe enough to admit to seeing something at this distance from the crime. But no dice. The house directly behind 3147 Upton was a duplex, and just as Viola Adams had suggested, both renters had turned over since the shooting a year and a half ago. Brie would see if she could track the former residents down and re-interview them, but there was no guarantee that anything would come of it.

She sat in the car for a few minutes, thinking about the situation. She had been a detective for too long to be disappointed by the outcome. Even though it's seldom that anything new comes to light in these situations, it is still worth retracing those steps. And especially with a cold case. It keeps momentum moving in the right direction. It's all part of working the case.

There *was* something else that bothered her, though. The case file showed that the 911 call reporting a break-in at 3147 Upton Avenue North had come from the vicinity of the neighborhood. Yet none of the neighbors admitted to making that call. So who did? It was possible that a passerby had seen the door ajar or someone suspicious enter the premises and had called it in. But they had no lead as to who that might have been. Just that the call had come from a burner phone. That in itself wasn't so odd. This wasn't a wealthy area, and it was possible some of the residents used pay-as-you-go phones.

Brie started her car and drove toward home. It had been a long day. She planned to grab some dinner on the way home, kick back for the rest of the evening, and turn in early.

When she got home, she made the mistake of lying down on her porch. She woke three hours later, fuzzyheaded. It was after ten o'clock, and she felt more tired than when she'd laid down. She headed for the bathroom, took a shower, climbed into her pajamas, and went back to bed. She'd call John tomorrow. He would understand.

Chapter 38

When Brie got to her desk at the department the following morning, Garrett Parker was waiting for her. He didn't look happy.

"We need to talk," he said.

"Oh, yeah? What about?" she knew it could only be about one of two things—what had happened at her place Friday night or the fact that she was working the Thatcher murder case.

"Not here. Come on," Garrett said.

He headed out of the investigative unit and down the long hall to the corridor that overlooked the rotunda at City Hall. Brie followed him.

There were some small two-person tables along the railing where employees sometimes sat and ate lunch. Garrett sat down at one, and Brie sat across from him.

"Look," he said. "There's no point beating around the bush. I know you've been working the Thatcher cold case."

"Oh, yeah? And how do you know that, Garrett?"

He looked a bit apologetic, but just a bit. "I checked the log down in the Records Room."

"Why did you do that?" Brie asked. "Is this because of what happened Friday night?"

Garrett waved that away. It seemed he had no plans to discuss what had happened at her place.

"No, Brie. It's because I thought you might try to work Phil's case. I ran that investigation. It's my case. If you wanted information, you should have come to me. Because you were his partner, you're not allowed to work the case. What's more, you were shot in the same incident. So now you're working your own case. You could be reprimanded. You know that, right? And if you persist, you could be fired."

"You know what, Garrett? I really don't give a damn. I'm going to find justice for Phil. If you want to stand in my way or report me, go ahead, because I'm not stopping."

"Look, Brie, I know how you feel. I know how many years you and Phil worked together. I know he mentored you. You think I don't get that? But what if you did find something? The fact that you're working a case where you were shot and nearly killed could invalidate any information you come by."

"Really? You think if I brought an important lead on the case to Bull Johnson, he'd tell me he couldn't use it? I'm sure the fact that one of his detectives died and the case went cold eats at him as much as it does me."

Garrett sighed as if a part of him wanted to capitulate. "So what have you found?"

"Nothing, so far. I made a copy of the murder book and have read through all the reports and testimonies that were there. In fact, I've read everything twice. It's pretty thin, though. Yesterday I went back to the neighborhood where the shooting occurred and talked to the neighbors again."

"And?"

"Nothing. If anyone knows anything, they're not talking. But chances are they don't. The shooting took place after midnight. Most people were asleep. Several of them said they woke up when they heard the squads and the ambulance, but by then the shooter would have been long gone. One of the reports in the file said the first squad got there just a couple minutes after us." She sighed. "I told Phil not to respond to that call that night. To let the uniforms take it. But we were so close, he decided to respond. When we got there, I told him to wait for the squads, to wait for backup. Why didn't he?"

"You're right. That wasn't his call," Garrett said. "That's not a detective's territory. But that said, the instinct is to respond—to go in. Before any of us were detectives, we were patrol cops. That part of you doesn't disappear when you get your detective's shield."

"It's true. I've told myself the same thing." She looked over the railing at the Father of Waters sculpture below them. After a few moments she turned back to him. "Look, Garrett, I need to do this, and I need you to leave it alone."

He leaned back and let out a sigh, and his blue eyes seemed to soften a bit. "I'm not going to report you, Brie. That's not how I roll. But you need to keep me in the loop. Tell me what you find, if anything. And you need to remember that this is still my case."

"Agreed," Brie said.

"I'm depending on you to keep this on the down low. We could both be in trouble if the commander gets a whiff of it." A half smile gentled his face, and the dimples appeared beneath his cheeks. "It's okay to lean on someone a bit, you know. You don't have to do this all by yourself."

"Thanks, Garrett. And I really mean that." She studied his face for a moment, trying to make a decision about something. "I'm curious," she finally said. "The case file shows that Joe Rossi, your former partner, was questioned."

"That's right. He alibied out, though. He was on duty that night, working up in the Fourth Precinct."

"But I'm confused about why he was interviewed. According to the case file, the call that came into dispatch that night reported a break-in. When Phil and I got to the address, the door was ajar. That residence had been a known drug house, so even though it was vacant at the time of the shooting, the supposition was that someone might have been there looking for either drugs or money that had been hidden on the premises."

"That's right, and that was our primary focus. But we also had to look at anyone who might have had a motive to harm Phil Thatcher, and Rossi had made no bones about how he felt about Thatcher reporting him to IAD at the time that whole officer-involved drug case unfolded. He thought Phil was a rat. That he hadn't honored the Brotherhood. I heard him say once, 'That guy better watch his back,' referring to Phil. So of course we had to question Rossi. That kind of comment shows he may have had intent to harm Thatcher, who he blamed for his demotion."

Brie nodded. "I never knew he had it in for Phil like that. But if Rossi blamed Phil for his career imploding, instead of his own bad choices, well, it says a lot about his character."

"As you know, Rossi left the force after Phil's death. Apparently, our questioning him during the investigation was the last straw. He was belligerent—said he didn't need any of it. He quit the force and became a long-haul trucker."

"I knew he'd left the department about six months after Phil died. Never knew what he did after that, though."

"Listen. We should get back," Garrett said.

They headed back down the hall and into the investigative unit. Brie spent the rest of the morning cleaning up some remaining paperwork for the Ayesha Brown murder case. At twelve o'clock her phone beeped, reminding her of her one o'clock meeting with Sideways Louie. She continued with her work for another half hour and then headed out of the unit and down to her car. Garrett was off somewhere, working on something else, so she didn't have to worry about him asking where she was headed. To anyone else, it just looked like she was going to lunch.

* * *

Parker got back to the unit at one o'clock He figured he'd tell Brie to go to lunch, but she had already left. He had just sat down and brought up the report he'd been working on when the phone on his desk rang. He picked it up.

"Homicide. Parker."

"I'm trying to reach Brie Beaumont. Is she there in the unit?"

"She's out right now. Can I take a message?"

"This is John DuLac. I think you and I spoke last May. Could you tell her to call me when she has a chance? I just tried her phone, and it went to voicemail." He stopped short of mentioning that Brie had been up North and that he hadn't talked to her since Friday.

"Well, we're working here, you know. We can't drop everything to take personal calls."

"Of course. I know that. It's just that I was expecting to hear from her yesterday. I guess I'm worried." He knew he couldn't say anything about her working Phil's case. He was sure Parker didn't know about that.

"As *you* told *me* when we talked back in May, when she was on that god-awful island, her life in danger, 'She needs to find her confidence, again.' Wasn't that what you said? Well, she's doing just that, here at the unit, with me by her side. So you don't need to worry, DuLac. I've got her back. I don't plan on letting anything happen to her. She's my partner now. I plan to take good care of her."

John bristled at that. "Well, I wouldn't get too comfortable with the situation," he said.

"Oh, yeah? What does that mean?"

"Just that she may not be there as long as you're thinking." He knew Brie would have his head for saying that. He was sure she'd be playing that fact close to her vest.

"Look, sailor boy, get this straight. She's never coming back there. She's where she wants to be, doing the work she loves. And she's my girl now."

"Yeah, right. Dream on, Parker."

"No dream. She was in my arms just the other night. We talked about going to bed, but I told her we should wait. Take it slow. It's always better when one waits, don't you think? Heightens the experience."

"You're delusional, man. Brie will never be anything more to you than a colleague."

"You keep thinking that. But picture this, Captain; we'll be at her apartment, just like we were Friday night, eating pizza, drinking beer, listening to music, talking about the Phil Thatcher case, and oh, yeah, screwing our brains out."

Garrett hung up the phone, short-circuiting John's chance to say another word. He smiled to himself. "Now, that felt really good," he said under his breath. He knew there'd be hell to pay when Brie found out, but he didn't mind. She was sexy when she was angry. That fire in her eyes. Made him want to . . .

"Parker!"

Garrett, jumped. "What's up, Commander?"

"Sorry I startled you. Can I see you in my office? I want to put a few final details on the Brown case to bed."

"Right away, Sir." Garrett got up and followed Bull Johnson to his office.

Chapter 39

Brie parked a short ways down the block, where she could see the entrance to Emily's Café, and waited for Sideways Louie to make his appearance. He'd been sought out after her partner's death to learn what the word on the street was about the crime. And while she'd read that report in the murder book last week, she hadn't actually seen Louie since before Phil's death, over a year and a half ago.

As she waited, she was again thinking about his odd mannerisms. How he never met your gaze straight on, and how, if he happened to be in front of you, he would look to one side of your head as he spoke, as if talking to some imaginary person.

True to form, Louie did not approach the café in a direct manner but crossed the street slantwise, as if heading for another place altogether. From there he doubled back down the street to the corner where the small restaurant sat and moved swiftly in the door. He stood for a moment looking around to see if he recognized anyone in the place and then walked toward the back.

Brie got out of her car and headed into the café. Emily's was a cozy, welcoming place that would have fit right in out in Maine but would have been called a diner. She noticed it had been recently redecorated, with half-walls of wood beadboard, new tile floor, and upholstery. She walked back toward where Louie sat at a table, facing the rear of the establishment. There were four chairs—two on either side.

She knew not to sit directly in front of him but rather took the chair diagonally across the table. That way he could address the empty seat in front of him without craning his neck the whole time. But ultimately there was no way to avoid his disconcerting manner of talking not to her, but to the empty chair.

"Hello, Louie," she said. "Good to see you. It's been a while."

Louie nodded imperceptibly, darting his eyes over to hers for the briefest second before settling them back on the chair across from him.

The waitress named Sharon came back to take their order. She'd been working here since Brie had been stationed at the 4th Precinct.

"Haven't seen you for a while," she said to Brie. "Good to have you back. You, too," she nodded toward Louie, who sat like a statue. "What can I get you two?"

"How 'bout a couple of cheeseburgers with fries? You good with that?" she asked Louie, intentionally not using his name.

He nodded.

"Great. Let's have some Cokes with that, too. Thanks, Sharon."

Sharon headed back up front to place the order.

"Thanks for meeting me on such short notice, Louie."

"No problem," he said, playing with his silverware and napkin. "You doing all right?"

Brie couldn't have been more surprised if he'd asked her for a date.

"I'm doing all right. Thanks for asking. I'm pretty sure you heard about my partner's death."

"I heard. Heard you were shot, too."

"That's right. I don't think we've seen each other since then."

"Haven't."

"It took a while for me to heal up. After that I was on desk duty."

"Heard you left the state. How come?" He twisted the napkin.

Although he couldn't look at her, it was clear he felt concern on some level.

"Had to get my head straight," Brie said.

Louie nodded like that made sense.

"The case went cold. The case of my partner's shooting."

Louie nodded. "I heard."

"I'm working the case. Trying to find who was responsible for his death."

Louie's eyes darted in her direction. And there was the fleeting sense of alarm in those eyes. "You allowed to do that?" he asked.

"Doesn't matter," Brie said. "I'm doing it."

He fidgeted with his silverware. "Need to be careful," he said, so softly she barely caught the words.

She opened her mouth to respond, but at that moment Sharon appeared around the corner from the kitchen carrying their drinks. Brie studied Louie surreptitiously as Sharon set the Cokes down. A few minutes later she was back with their orders.

"Can I get you anything else?" she asked.

Louie shook his head.

"We're good. Thanks, Sharon." Brie waited for her to walk away, then leaned toward him. "What did you mean, Louie? About being careful?"

"Just what I said."

It was half-whispered, but she detected a note of fear in those words. She leaned closer. "Do you know something about my partner's death?"

His eyes slid sideways and rested on the wall next to him.

"I read the case file, Louie. I read your statement. You said at the time that you had no information about the shooting."

"It came out later."

"What did?"

"The word on the street about the killing."

They were the only ones at the back of the restaurant, and she was glad of the fact. "If you know something, Louie, tell me." She said it just loud enough for the words to be heard across the table.

Then Louie did something totally out of form. He slid into the chair to his left, leaned in, and looked directly at her. "It was an inside job."

Brie studied his face, trying to wrap her mind around what she was hearing. "You mean a cop?"

His nod was barely perceptible. "Someone put out a contract on your partner," he said, the words spoken so softly as to be nearly inaudible.

"Who, Louie? Do you know who?"

His eyes slid to the chair next to her. "That's all I know," he said under his breath. He glanced around nervously. "I have to go."

"Will you try to find out?"

He shook his head. "Too dangerous." He stood, palmed the burger in his left hand like a magician doing a disappearing act, and left the restaurant.

Brie watched him go. As soon as she could catch Sharon's eye, she asked her to box up her burger, gave her twenty-five dollars to cover the bill and the tip, and left the establishment.

* * *

Brie sat in her car catty-corner from Emily's. By the time she'd left the café, Louie was nowhere to be seen. He had disappeared back into the anonymity of his life. His words haunted her beyond imagining. "It was an inside job." And that nearly imperceptible nod when she'd asked him, "Do you mean a cop?" The whole thing shook her to her core.

She didn't know what she had expected to learn from him, but it wasn't that Phil had been killed by one of their own.

Joe Rossi was suddenly a nearly tangible presence, as if thinking about him might somehow make him materialize nearby. A chill ran down her spine, and she actually turned and looked around her and out the back window of the car. Joe Rossi, the former narcotics officer who'd later become Garrett's partner in the Homicide Unit. The cop who'd been demoted after an Internal Affairs investigation found him guilty of not reporting his partner back in Narco, who'd taken money from a drug dealer to look the other way.

It was Phil Thatcher who'd gotten wind of the situation and reported both men to IAD, the Internal Affairs Division. According to what Garrett Parker had told her this morning, Rossi held a grudge and had threatened Phil, saying, "That guy better watch his back." Just a few months later, Phil was shot dead. She knew from the case file that Rossi had been questioned after Phil's death and that Rossi had alibied out because he'd been on duty in the 4th Precinct the night of the shooting. But what Sideways Louie had revealed was a game changer. If Phil's death had been a contract killing, and Rossi had hired the shooter, then Rossi could have been anywhere when the hit went down. His so-called alibi would mean nothing. Another disturbing fact was that six months after Phil was shot, Joe Rossi had quit the department.

She thought about questioning Rossi but knew she would be ill-advised to go there alone. And to what avail? He'd just fall back on his alibi. And she certainly wasn't about to show her hand by telling him they suspected a contract killing had gone down. Her next choice was to bring the information to Bull Johnson, her homicide commander, but she felt she needed something more concrete before she approached him.

She sat there thinking, wondering if there was a different way to approach Rossi. Finally, she took out her small notebook and found the page where she'd written down his phone number from the case file. She punched in the number, took a deep breath and let it out, and sent the call. The number rang three times.

"Hello?" Brie heard a question in his inflection. It told her he was confused by her call but obviously curious too.

"Rossi?"

"Yeah."

"Rossi. It's Brie Beaumont."

"Hey, Brie." A pause. "Why are you calling?"

"I was out near the Fourth today, so I stopped in to see some of the guys. It used to be my old stomping ground. Don't know if you knew that."

"I didn't."

"Anyway, the guys there mentioned you. Asked if I knew what you were up to. It got me thinking."

"Huh. Is this about the case?"

"What case?" Brie asked, deciding to play ignorant, taking a chance he'd bite.

"Phil Thatcher's case. I've got nothing to say about that. They already questioned me."

"No, man. That's not why I'm calling. You know I can't work that case." She let that sit for a few moments, hoping he'd buy it. "I just thought we could get together for a drink."

"Well, maybe."

There was silence, and Brie thought she could feel suspicion right through the airwaves. She waited.

"I guess that'd be okay," he finally said.

"How about tonight? Maybe around five? You pick the spot."

"How about The 1029 Bar? It's just south of Broadway in St. Anthony, near where I live."

"Yeah, I know the place, Joe. That sounds good. Hey, I could see if Parker wants to come along."

"Nah, that's okay."

Brie much preferred doing this by herself, but was a bit surprised he didn't want to see Garrett.

"So, I'll see you then."

"See ya," Rossi responded, and they ended the call.

Brie put her phone down. Her hands were shaking. If Rossi had arranged Phil's death, put a hit on him, then she was about to sit down with the guy who was also responsible for her being shot and for all the pain and trauma she'd been through in the past nineteen months. Rage boiled inside her for Phil and, yes, for herself. She took another deep breath and let it out. She knew she couldn't go there. She had to keep her cool if she hoped to get anywhere with him. This was a game of cat and mouse. She had to be the cat. Not let Rossi get the upper hand.

She asked herself why he had agreed to meet with her. If he was behind the contract on Phil, why would he agree to meet with someone who had been Thatcher's partner? Curiosity? Fear? Maybe he thought he could find out about the case. Maybe that was why he didn't want Parker there.

But there was another possibility. If Rossi *was* behind Phil's death, maybe he hadn't intended that she'd be shot that night—the night Phil had died. Was it possible he felt guilty? If so, she'd be able to pick up on that emotion when they met. It was part of a detective's training. And if Rossi did in fact display any sense of remorse, in her mind there could be only one reason—that he had been behind the whole thing.

The burger from Emily's was on the seat next to her in its Styrofoam container. She had a few bites of it and washed it down with the bottle of water she'd brought with her that morning.

Then she started the car and drove back toward downtown. She was thinking again about Louie's words and something that troubled and amazed her in equal parts. It was the dream she'd had up North—Phil and the great golden eagle, the red leaves raining down with something written on them. In the last dream she'd finally captured one of those leaves and had seen what was written there. "Look inside." Now she reflected on that message juxtaposed with Louie's words. "It was an inside job." The similarity between the messages was unmistakable. Could it be a coincidence? Brie didn't believe in coincidence, but how was it possible? Had Phil really used the dreams to communicate with her? Both Claude and Joseph Renard would have believed it to be the case, based on what their sacred traditions taught—that information can be communicated through dreams. That dreams can be an interface between the spirit world and this one.

But Brie was thinking on another level. Wondering if there wasn't something she herself knew, maybe on some deep level. Some knowledge hidden *inside her* that had triggered the dream. She had an appointment scheduled with the psychologist, Dr. Travers, for tomorrow night. The plan was, through hypnosis, to take her back to the night of the shooting. Would the regression reveal any new information? Suddenly tomorrow night seemed a long way off. She decided she'd try the doctor and see if she could get in sooner.

She was approaching the government center. She pulled in and parked in the ramp, brought up Megan Travers' number, and sent the call. Valerie, the receptionist, answered, and Brie identified herself and asked if the doc might have any openings for that evening.

"We've had a cancellation for tonight at six-thirty," Valerie said.

"I'll take that appointment," Brie said. She was meeting Rossi at 5:00 but figured she'd have no problem getting to the doc's office by 6:30. Would the session reveal any new information? After what she'd learned from Sideways Louie this afternoon, the appointment suddenly seemed of paramount importance.

She got out and headed back up to the department. She continued on with the reports and paperwork for the Brown case that she'd been finishing that morning. As far as she was concerned, though, the rest of the day was just marking time until she could head for her meeting with Joe Rossi.

And what of that meeting? She knew it was dangerous to tread too close to a killer—if in fact he *was* a killer. She could only hope that her gut, her instincts, might lead her closer to the truth—might lend clarity to the increasingly murky and troubling case of Phil's death.

Chapter 40

Brie pulled up in front of The 1029 Bar at 4:58. She looked around but didn't see Rossi. She took a couple of breaths, centering herself, or maybe girding herself for battle, she wasn't sure which, and then climbed out of her car and headed toward the door.

She hadn't known Rossi all that well. He had been in Homicide for a few months, teamed with Garrett Parker, before the IAD investigation caused him to be demoted, but she hadn't worked directly with him during that time. Since she didn't know him well, she planned to rely on gut instinct here tonight. Let it lead her in how this meeting would unfold.

She opened the front door and stepped inside. Except for a few guys sitting at the bar, the place was empty. This being Monday, Brie figured everyone was caroused out from the weekend. Before long, she spotted Rossi at a table at the back of the establishment.

Joe Rossi was an easy six-foot-two and built like the big rig he now drove. He could have been a linebacker and maybe he had been, since his nose had obviously been broken, maybe more than once. In other words, he looked tough. That was the only word for it. It was why he had made it as a narcotics officer, where you worked undercover in the world of gangs and street drugs. Where you had to look the part to stay alive.

He stood and smiled as Brie approached, but the smile didn't extend to his eyes, which seemed to tell a different story.

They were wary and looked tired, like the eyes of one who might be perpetually on guard.

"Hey, Brie. Good to see you." He looked her up and down as if taking stock. "You look well," he said.

Brie found the use of "well," not "good," while grammatically correct, an interesting choice of words, since it implied health rather than attractiveness. Her mission tonight was to see if she got any sense of remorse from Rossi. Remorse that she had been shot when Phil was gunned down.

She held out her hand. "Thanks, Joe. You look good, too. Dropped a few pounds, haven't you?"

"Yeah, thanks for noticing. Surprising, I guess, since I sit in a truck most of the time, but I've been trying to work out when I can."

Brie nodded and climbed onto one of the tall bar chairs behind the table.

"What would you like?"

"Just a beer. Whatever you're having."

Rossi already had a brew in front of him that was half gone, and he signaled the bartender to bring another one for Brie.

"So, how's life in the trucking world, Joe?"

He shrugged. "Not too bad. I'll tell you one thing; it's a lot more peaceful than being a cop. I *do* like the peace of it. Plenty of time to think, too. I guess that can be good and bad."

Again, it was a statement she could have read something into, but she didn't want to jump to any conclusions just yet.

Brie's beer came, and Rossi ordered another one for himself.

"So, I heard through the grapevine that you took a leave from the department," he said.

"Yeah, that's right. It was a year after the shooting. I was messed up, let me tell you. It took six months to heal up from the gunshot wound, but mentally I was a mess. The PTSD hit me hard—flashbacks, dreams, overreacting to sound and movement.

The whole nine yards." She took a swig of her beer. "After a year, I took a leave and went to Maine, where my dad's people were from. Long story short, I ended up going to sea, crewing aboard a schooner for six months. It helped me."

Rossi had downed the rest of his beer as she talked. Now he leaned toward her. His eyes had changed. "I never got to say it, but I'm really sorry for what you went through. Being shot, nearly dying. PTSD's a terrible thing to live with."

Brie studied him. Were his words just cop-to-cop empathy, or did they go deeper, beyond empathy to remorse? Remorse for the unintended consequences of what he had set in motion. Brie wondered about the psychological territory they were skirting.

"I appreciate that, Joe. I won't lie to you, being shot took me down physically, but Phil's murder took me down psychologically. PTSD is bad, and it plays head games with you, but the worst is survivor's guilt. Constantly questioning yourself. Asking 'Why not me?' and 'How could I have stopped this?'"

Rossi took a long pull from his second beer and sat back.

"Phil went where he shouldn't have sometimes. That night we had just finished up at the scene of a homicide a couple blocks away when the call came through about a break-in. It wasn't our call. I told Phil to forget it, let the guys in uniform take the call, but he responded anyway. When we pulled up to that house on Upton, I told him not to go in—to wait for the squads, but he was already out of the car headed toward the door with his gun out. All I could do was back him up." She sat back and took a long drink from her beer. "Like I said, he sometimes went where he shouldn't have."

Rossi's eyes turned cold. "Well, it worked for whoever was gunning for him." He studied Brie for a few moments. "You have to let it go, Beaumont. Tell yourself you had nothing to do with what killed him."

Brie looked down at the table, feeling a chill run through her. She replayed his words in her mind: 'Well, it worked for whoever was gunning for him.' The supposition in the case had always been that Phil's death had been the result of being in the wrong place—a former drug house—and coming up against whoever had broken in. That had been the belief right up until today, when Sideways Louie had informed her that it was "an inside job."

So Rossi's words stunned her. They implied that this had been no accident, but that someone was gunning for Phil that night. In Brie's mind there could be only one reason for Rossi's speaking those words. He knew Phil Thatcher had been targeted. Had Rossi let it slip out unintentionally? Subconsciously was he tired of carrying the burden of what he had done? Or had the beer just loosened his tongue and led him to say something he shouldn't have? She decided it was time to switch gears, ask him why he'd been questioned.

"So, on the phone you said they questioned you in Phil's case. I was surprised by that. If you don't mind my asking, what do you think led to that?"

Rossi shrugged. "I suppose they knew I was mad at Thatcher."

"Mad is one thing. But mad enough to kill . . . well, that's something else," Brie said. She let it hang there between them.

Rossi's eyes shifted to her right and focused somewhere behind her. He held up a hand and signaled for another beer.

Brie decided it was time to rattle his cage.

"I'll admit I'm troubled by the lack of progress in the case," she said. "I've asked Parker about it—it's his case, as you probably know. And while he stopped short of saying they were at a dead end, that's the sense I got. But it's not acceptable. There's got to be more out there. A cop is never shot without loud reverberations on the street. Someone has to know something. Maybe I should see what I can find out."

Rossi stood up abruptly, took money from his wallet—enough to cover the whole tab—and laid it on the table. He looked at her—an unreadable look. "Don't involve yourself in the case, Brie. You've gotten to a better place. Let it lie. Let Parker handle it." With that he picked up his jacket and left the bar.

Brie got up shortly thereafter and headed for her car, thinking about Rossi's final words. Was he trying to be kind, or did those words contain some kind of veiled warning to leave the case alone? She knew one thing. If Rossi was guilty, they'd need evidence. Without some kind of a break in the case, they would never make a charge against him stick. She started her car and drove back toward the freeway.

Chapter 41

It was just after 6:00 when Brie headed west on Highway 55 toward Golden Valley and her appointment with Dr. Travers. She could have driven through town, but the freeway was faster. Within ten minutes she headed north on 169 through Golden Valley, the suburb just northwest of Minneapolis. She exited on Medicine Lake Road and found the small office park where Dr. Travers had her practice.

Megan Travers, Ph.D., had been a psychology professor at the University of Minnesota for many years. When she retired from the U at age 60, she had set up a private practice specializing in trauma counseling. Her ties to the Minneapolis Police Department had been established when she was at the U, and she had been a frequent lecturer and teacher at the police academy. Her focus was twofold. The first element was helping new officers understand how the traumas they would deal with on a daily basis would affect them and helping them to learn the coping skills and techniques they would need to survive the job from a psychological perspective. Her other focus was working with cops suffering from PTSD. When she went into private practice, the MPD quickly became her biggest client, and Brie was sent to work with her in the months after she'd been shot.

Brie parked her car in the lot. Each business had its own entrance, and she headed into Dr. Travers' office. The small waiting room was empty. Valerie, the receptionist, had left for the day, signaling to Brie that she must be the last appointment. She sat down and opened a magazine to wait.

Within five minutes Megan Travers appeared in the waiting room. She was a little taller than Brie, with a wiry frame, close-cropped red hair and large green eyes.

"Please come in, Brie. It's good to see you again."

"Good to see you too, Doc."

Travers studied her for a moment, but Brie knew that momentary assessment carried with it a lifetime of experience at visually evaluating people.

"You look well, Brie."

"Thanks," she said. "I'm in a better place than the last time we met."

"Come in and let's get started."

Behind the waiting room, there was a short hallway with a bathroom. Down the hall a few steps, the door to the doc's office was open, and they walked in. A bank of windows along the back wall looked out onto woods and a small pond. The fading light of early November had turned the pond to silver, and a few late migrating gulls rested there. No more appropriate setting than this for the work the doctor did.

In front of the windows, two comfortable Scandinavian-style chairs sat facing each other. Each had a table off to the side where a drink or notebook could be placed. Opposite the chairs sat a piece that was a cross between a sofa and a chaise where the client could recline if he or she wished. The forest green chaise was positioned so the occupant looked out the windows into the natural setting beyond. A view to calm the mind.

"For the work we will be doing tonight, I'd like you to lie here" she said, "and I'll sit next to you."

Brie nodded and stretched out on the chaise, and the comfort of the spot, combined with the sylvan view out the windows, caused her to take in a deep breath and let it out slowly.

"That's good," Dr. Travers said. "I want you to relax. I think rather than going over old ground, we will move right into the new work. I could tell when we talked the other day that your time away from the department, and at sea, has helped you better come to terms with your partner's death. I wouldn't undertake this work if I didn't feel you were stable enough to do it. The hypnosis we tried initially in an attempt to gain information about the shooting did not go well."

"What encouraged me to come back and see you is that in the past week or so, I've remembered some new details about what happened that night. It gives me hope that if you can take me back to that night through hypnotic regression, I might discover something that would help me solve the case of my partner's death."

Megan Travers nodded and pulled one of the chairs over so she could sit at an angle to the chaise and look at Brie. "Tell me what you have remembered," she said.

"Well, as you know, I've had many flashbacks to that night. All of them the same. Phil starting toward the front door of the house on Upton Avenue, the door ajar, like a gaping maw. Me going after him. Darkness as we entered the house. Total darkness. The shooter coming out of nowhere and firing, Phil diving in front of me, taking the bullet. Then falling, just falling, and darkness.

"I've always known the memories from those flashbacks could not be totally accurate because they have a dreamlike, or I might say nightmare-like quality. But I've always considered them a kind of springboard—a jumping off place to maybe recovering a more accurate memory. I don't enjoy going through them, but I've always hoped they might reveal something."

"And has that happened?" the doc asked.

"I believe so," Brie said. "What I saw didn't happen during a flashback, though, but when I was driving home from up North about a week ago. Call it highway hypnosis, but I think I was in some kind of relaxed, altered state. And all of a sudden I was back there on that night with Phil. The night of the shooting. But it wasn't like the flashback. This had the feel of a memory coming back to me."

"And what did you see?"

"When we entered, the house wasn't in total darkness as I had always seen in my flashbacks. We had our guns drawn, and we had our flashlights, which cast some light. The message being that I could have seen more than I remember, even though our flashlights were the only illumination."

"Was there anything else?"

"Yes," Brie said. "Something that amazed me. Again in the flashbacks, I'd always seen Phil dive in front of me when the gunman appeared and fired, but in this new memory clip, I saw the shooter at the last second, and I clearly saw him turn the gun on Phil and shoot. I don't know why, but in the memory it seemed intentional."

"His shooting of Phil, you mean?"

"Yes."

This is all good to know," Dr. Travers said. "It will help me direct the regression. So I assume you are hoping to both verify these new pieces of memory and possibly learn more from this session?"

"That's my hope, Doctor."

"Well then, let's get started. I'd like you to close your eyes and totally relax. Imagine any and all tension pouring out of you like sand out of a bottle. Breathe deeply. That's it. You will be safe at all times. As we travel back to that night, I want you to imagine that you are viewing everything you see from a detached place, as if you were floating up high and could look down on the scene. But you will see everything very clearly. Every detail."

Brie drew in a deep breath and let it out.

"That's it. Relax. We are traveling back now to March tenth. Not last March, but the year before. You are responding to a call on Upton Avenue North—a possible break-in. You are arriving now, getting out of the car. You are very relaxed, and viewing all that is happening from a safe perspective."

Brie got out of the car. She was surprised that though it was after midnight, she saw everything with amazing clarity. She seemed to be both part of the unfolding action but somehow detached from it as well, as if she were both participant and viewer. Phil began to move toward the house. She followed and heard her voice, almost like an echo, tell him to wait for backup. Their guns were drawn, and their flashlights were locked in a left-handed grip beneath their handguns.

Phil went in the door first, but she was right behind him. She saw a stairway ahead of them and rooms to the left and right. Phil nodded for her to go right. She hesitated just a moment, shining her light up the stairs. She felt him begin to turn away, but in that fraction of a second two things happened. She was suddenly above the scene looking down, and a man appeared from the room on the left and fired directly at the center of Phil's chest. Phil's gun fired a nanosecond later. She saw Phil go down. She felt a burning sensation in her left side, and she saw but also felt herself falling as if in slow motion, hitting the floor, the flashlight dropping out of her hand. She saw the shooter hesitate for a second and then move toward her body, squat down, and place two fingers beneath her jaw, feeling for a pulse. She saw her own eyes open for just a second or two. In that brief moment, the flashlight that had fallen to the ground illuminated his face. It was a face she had seen before, and in that otherworldly moment, she felt her mind snap a picture of it. Then the sound of sirens close by and the shooter fleeing toward the back of the house.

She was hearing a voice now. It seemed far away, but it was becoming incrementally louder all the time. It was calling her name. Telling her she was safe, telling her to wake up. And she seemed to be floating, as if deep under water, but slowly moving upward toward the light above. She felt calm, as if she had no need to breathe. And then she realized she was breathing. She opened her eyes and saw Dr. Travers leaning toward her.

"How are you feeling, Brie?"

Brie sat up and put her feet on the floor. "Fine, I think."

"I decided to bring you out because your breathing seemed to become erratic toward the end."

"How long was I under?"

"From start to finish, maybe fifteen minutes. Was it helpful? Do you feel you discovered any new information?"

"There were a number of new details this time. I felt as if I were part of the unfolding scene but also as if I were viewing it from a distance. It felt rather odd."

"That could be the mind's way of separating you from the trauma."

"I saw the shooter's face."

"Do you think you could describe it well enough to get a sketch made?"

"I'm certain of it," Brie said. She stood up. "I wonder if we could end the session here, Doc? I'm feeling really tired all of a sudden."

"Of course," Megan Travers said. "Are you okay to drive home?"

"I'm fine."

"There's a coffee house between here and the highway if you need a boost."

"I'll stop for a cup," Brie said.

"Do you want to schedule another appointment?" Dr. Travers asked.

"I'll call," Brie said, uncertain whether she actually would.

Megan Travers studied her for a moment. When she spoke, her words were gentle, but her tone carried a note of firmness. "In case I don't see you again, Brie, I want you to know that while PTSD is not curable, at least not with the tools we have right now, it is manageable. If you believe you are cured or that you have escaped it, the recurring symptoms will take a greater toll. The wise path is to embrace it as your new normal. Make peace with coexistence. If you do this, you will find the symptoms are far more manageable. Part of loving ourselves is accepting all parts of us. The day we can do that is the day we can stop running. Whether it is running away from one thing or toward another, it's still running."

Brie suddenly felt as if she had a bull's eye painted on her and the doc had hit it dead center. "I have been running, haven't I?"

"That may be, Brie, but know this. Every single thing you did after the shooting has served vital protective and unconscious reparative functions. You have nothing to apologize for. But the more you seek peace in the present—and part of that is putting down roots again—the more manageable PTSD will be."

"A tall order for a detective since so much of our work is digging around in the past."

"I understand that," the doctor said.

Brie thanked Dr. Travers for the session and headed for her car.

Chapter 42

Brie wanted to remember what Dr. Travers had just said because it was important, so she took a few moments to write it down after she got in the car. But the face she had seen in the regression, the face of the killer, was like a malignant presence emblazoned on her psyche. She was doubly haunted remembering Sideways Louie's words. "It was an inside job . . . a contract killer."

She had seen that face, and she had seen it recently. It was the face of the man on the cliffs of Palisade Head. The man she had observed through the binoculars when she and Edna had gone sailing with Terrance Weathers. The man who had seemed to be simultaneously studying them as they sailed toward the headland.

But why would the shooter, a hired gun who had killed Phil, be on that cliff up North? The only possible answer was deeply troubling. He had been hired to kill Edna and had shot the wrong woman. More disturbing still was the possibility that Phil's death, the threatening letters she had received, and the attempt on Edna's life were all somehow connected.

Maybe the gunman had planned to take the shot from Palisade Head. By the end of October, on a Tuesday, the spot should have been devoid of tourists. It would have been the perfect vantage from which to shoot. High ground, no trees or obstructions. Something must have foiled the plan. For that she was grateful beyond belief.

She thought about Joe Rossi. According to Garrett Parker, Rossi had had it in for Phil. It wouldn't have been hard for Rossi to find a gun for hire. Cops have connections to the street through CIs and other means. But now it appeared that he was also targeting Brie. If not to kill her, then to make her wish she was dead by murdering her mother. Thankfully, the plan had failed, but in the process it had taken another life, that of Halley Greenberg, and had wreaked havoc on *her* family.

The "why" of it all was completely baffling. It just didn't make sense. There had to be something she was missing. But what? All she could do was work the case and hope the truth would somehow be revealed.

Whatever Rossi's intentions had been, they would need evidence to bring him down. First step was to get the shooter's face on paper, then run the image through the facial recognition program to see if they could get a hit. They needed to run this shooter to ground. Bring him in. Possibly offer him a deal for turning evidence against Rossi.

She took out her phone and scrolled through her log, looking for a number for Gabriella Cole, a police sketch artist. She checked the time—a quarter of eight. She hoped it wasn't too late to meet with the artist. She sent the call and after a couple of rings, Gabriella answered.

"Brie Beaumont. What a surprise. Heard you were out of state."

Brie smiled. It was just like Gabby to skip the greetings and launch right into what she wanted to say. "Hey, Gabby. Good to hear your voice. You're right, I was on leave and out of state for six months. How're you doing?"

"Can't complain. Well, I could, but what good would it do?"

Brie laughed. "I hear you there. Listen, Gabby, I've got something I need your help on—a sketch that connects to the Phil Thatcher case."

"What ever happened with that case, Brie?"

"It went cold."

"That's a hard pill to swallow," Gabby said.

"Things are heating up, though. I've recovered a memory of that night—the night of the shooting. I'm wondering if you could work with me to capture the guy's face while the memory is still fresh in my mind."

"Absolutely. What are you waiting for? Get over here, and we'll get started."

"Thanks, Gabby. I knew I could count on you. Can I bring anything?"

"Nah. Just come. I'll put on some coffee."

"Great. I should be there in about twenty minutes."

"See you soon," Gabby said, and they ended the call.

Gabby Cole lived in St. Paul in an apartment building near the University of St. Thomas. An art professor by day, she moonlighted as a sketch artist for the Minneapolis PD, a job she had held for five or six years now.

Brie arrived at Gabby's apartment about ten past eight. She parked on the street, went to the front door of the brownstone and pushed the button for the correct apartment. Gabby buzzed her in, and Brie made her way up to the third-floor apartment. Gabby was waiting, leaning against the door frame with her front door open when Brie came down the hall. She was a petite woman in her forties with dark curly hair and a very pretty face. She was wearing leggings, boot-like fleece slippers, and a long tunic-style sweater. They headed inside, down a short hall and into the living room.

The room was an eclectic mix of furniture—some very old, some clearly of more modern origin. The walls were painted a soft tangerine orange, and the room was filled with interesting sculptures and framed art, many of which were etchings created by Gabby, etching being her primary medium as an artist. She carried her gift for detail and precision into her sketch work with the MPD.

"Coffee, Brie?"

"That'd be great. Thanks."

They walked into Gabby's small galley-style kitchen, and she poured Brie a robust cup o' joe from the carafe that sat on the warming plate.

"You look good, Brie. Healthy," Gabby said.

Brie told Gabby a little about where she'd been for the past six months and about living aboard the schooner *Maine Wind*.

"Wow, lucky," Gabby said. "I love the ocean. That sounds like a dream come true."

"I tried to continue as usual after Phil's death, but it just wasn't possible. Then the case went cold. They wouldn't let me work on it, of course. The PTSD got worse. After a year, I decided to take a leave. Try and find my center again."

"From what you said on the phone, it sounds as if you've recovered a valuable memory from the night of the shooting."

"I hope it is," Brie said. "I guess we'll see."

"Well, let's get started."

They walked back into the living room and over to where a table sat at a right angle to the windows. There was a desktop easel on top of the table. It was a solid piece of slanted wood with a small ledge at the bottom, and a slim drawer underneath for pencils or other supplies. Gabby set her sketch pad on the easel, and Brie pulled a chair over so she could sit next to her. Then they got down to business.

"Let's start with the shape of the head and the jawline."

"The head would be rectangular with a strong jawline. He had a cleft chin and facial scruff that wasn't quite a beard yet."

"Good," said Gabby. She started sketching in the shape of the head with a soft graphite pencil. "We'll get a rough facsimile and then we can begin to refine the image." After a couple of minutes she said, "Tell me about the hairline."

"It's one of the most distinctive features that I saw. It looked like a peninsula between two bays. I guess that sounds strange."

Gabby laughed. "Not really for a girl who's been at sea. I think I get the picture, though." She sketched in a hairline with two scalloped areas and a rounded point of hair in between. "Something like this?" she asked Brie.

"That's pretty close," Brie said. "But the scalloped areas went even a little farther up onto the scalp."

Gabby erased and resketched the hairline.

"That's it," Brie said, leaning forward.

"Good. Now tell me about the forehead and the brow bone," Gabby said.

"The forehead was not too high. I'd say it was average."

"Did it slope or was it more straight?"

Brie thought for a minute. "More straight, I think. And the brow bone protruded slightly."

Gabby plied her pencil, and little by little the image began to appear. "Let's work on the eyes next," she said.

"They were more wide set than normal, I would say. I couldn't tell the color, but I want to say they were brown. Don't know why."

"What about size?" Gabby asked.

"I'd say they were average. They seemed to fit the face. And they were more almond shaped than round."

"Good," Gabby said. "You're doing great, Brie."

Brie nodded, feeling reassured by her words.

They kept on working, and slowly an image began to stare back at Brie. An image that haunted her more than any other she'd ever seen began to materialize from the ether onto an artist's sketch book. The more details they filled in, the more confident she became that they would capture the killer's face.

Once the eyes were in place, Gabby asked more questions and then fleshed out the nose, the mouth, the ears, and finally the neck, which Brie described as thick and muscular. The nose was broad and, as a result, the face fell short of handsome, but not by much. As soon as the rough sketch was in place, Gabby began the fine-tuning, asking Brie to focus on the minutia—the small but significant details that would help capture the image exactly. Eyebrows, character lines, tone of complexion and color of hair, until Brie was satisfied that she was looking at the same face she had just seen during the hypnosis.

The process had taken over an hour, and once they were done, Gabby scanned the sketch into her computer and then printed off ten copies for Brie. She placed them in a manila folder with the original on the top. Brie tucked the folder with the original sketch and the copies into her briefcase. She thanked Gabby again for meeting with her so late when she had to teach the next day. Gabby waved that off. They said goodbye, and Brie headed back to her car and out of the neighborhood.

As she drove toward home, she realized she was starving. She'd gone directly from the department to the meeting with Rossi and then on to her appointment with Dr. Travers, and from there to Gabby's apartment to work on the sketch. She hit a McDonald's drive-thru on her way home and picked up a Big Mac and fries. George Dupopolis would surely be appalled at the slow but certain unraveling of what had been her healthy *Maine Wind* diet during her months aboard ship. She suddenly had a desperate longing for John and the ship and to see her crewmates, who had become her close friends over the time of her sojourn on the ocean. She knew she had to persevere with Phil's case, but her life back East called to her more with each passing day.

She was getting close, though. Close to the truth. She could feel it in her detective bones. Discoveries in the case were escalating, and she could feel the end drawing nearer. But she also sensed a kind of attendant danger that didn't usually accompany the solving of a homicide case, as if she were close to a hornets' nest and should retreat, but knew full well she would keep poking at it. She took it as a sign that her resolve was absolute. That she would not let Phil down. She thought of him in the dream, on the back of the great golden eagle, riding the thermals, sending down those red leaves. "We're close now, Phil," she said to herself. Unconsciously she reached up and laid her hand on the small medicine bundle that Joseph Renard had given her for protection. It sat just over her heart. "We're getting very close."

Chapter 43

Brie was just pulling into her driveway at home when something disturbing dawned on her. Something she had overlooked in describing the gunman's face to Gabby. He had a scar on the left side of his face. She had seen it clearly when she had studied his face through the binoculars the day they were out on the sailboat. How could she have forgotten about it? She turned off the car and sat for a few moments in the dark. Troubled by the omission and how she could have overlooked it, she closed her eyes and focused in on her memory of the night of the shooting that was still very vivid in her mind. For a brief moment she actually felt the killer's fingers press on her neck, feeling for a pulse, and in the memory she opened her eyes. The left side of his face was in deep shadow; the flashlight that had fallen shone on the right side of his face, illuminating it.

Brie opened her eyes. She realized that in recalling his face for the artist, she had been singularly focused on what she had just seen in the recovered memory from the night of the shooting, and on that night, in the diffuse light from the flashlight, the scar had not been visible. Now in her mind's eye she thought about the face of the man she had seen on Palisade Head. Was it the same face? She closed her eyes again, remembering that day. The sun on the surface of the lake. The feel of the boat. She was standing near the helm, looking through the binoculars. And suddenly the face she had seen swam into sharp focus in her memory—a detective's memory, trained to mentally record detail. There was the odd hairline, like two bays and a peninsula, the broad nose, the eyes set slightly wide. It was the same face. There was no mistaking it. But this time the face held no scruff of beard, and the scar was clearly visible.

She could understand now how she had omitted the detail but wondered if it would make identification harder. There was no going back to Gabby tonight to have it adjusted. It was too late. *May as well take a chance on running facial rec with the image as it is,* she thought. She knew the program primarily used bone structure—shape of head, jawline, nose, eyes—in acquiring a match. If nothing popped, she could always go back to Gabby tomorrow night and have her add the scar.

She got out of her car and headed up the stairs and let herself into her apartment. Her burger had gotten cold, so she heated it up in the microwave for a few seconds, opened a can of Coke, and sat down at the table in the dining room to eat. When she was done, she opened the folder with the artist's sketch, and the face of the gunman from that fateful night stared back at her. It was amazing how Gabby could so accurately recreate an image of a face she had never seen.

Brie decided she would visit Viola Adams tomorrow and show her the sketch. Viola was the elderly woman she had interviewed on Sunday, who lived in the house next to where she and Phil had been shot on Upton Avenue North. Over years of interviewing neighbors near crime scenes, Brie had learned that the older folks in any neighborhood are the best observers. They have time and are not as harried as working folk, and they tend to observe the comings and goings of those around them in a way that is often quite helpful to the police.

Although it was late, she gave Claude Renard a call up in Grand Marais and explained about recovering the memory of the gunman's face. She told him it matched the face of the man she'd seen on Palisade Head and that she believed this man was behind Halley Greenberg's shooting. She said she would keep him informed as she learned more.

She also thought about calling Sideways Louie—see if he might be willing to ask around the streets, find out if anyone knew this guy. But when she'd met him at Emily's Café, he had seemed quite reluctant to take any further part in the case. In fact, reluctant was too gentle a word. He had flat-out refused, and she had seen real fear there. The kind of fear that accompanies the thought of bringing down a cop—even a former cop. She decided she would wait and see what facial rec turned up. If it was nothing, she'd press Louie to help her by going to the streets. She closed the manila folder, put it in her briefcase and headed into the bathroom for a long, hot shower.

By the time she got out, it was after ten o'clock. She went out to the living room, curled up in one of the armchairs and called John. He answered right away.

"Brie, it's good to hear from you."

"Sorry I didn't call last night, John. After I got home from Grand Portage, I went back to the neighborhood where Phil was shot and interviewed the neighbors. Long story short, I laid down when I got home and didn't wake up till after ten o'clock. I felt like a walking zombie, so I took a shower and went to bed."

"It's okay, Brie. I know you have a lot on your plate."

He sounded bothered, though, or maybe hurt, she wasn't sure which. She told him what had transpired with Boyle Bouchard up North and that it had been a dead-end, albeit an interesting one. John seemed entertained by the story of Bouchard blazing his path to enlightenment in the depths of the north woods, but Brie was still picking up a weird vibe.

"Is everything okay, John? You don't quite sound like yourself."

"Look, Brie, I'm wondering, does Parker know you're working Phil's case?"

"Yeah, he knows. He found out I checked the case file out. He confronted me about it this morning. Why do you ask?"

John proceeded to tell her about the phone call and about Parker saying she was never coming back to Maine and that she was his girl, now.

"That's just a load of macho crap." Brie said. "He's delusional."

"That's what I told him. But then he went on to describe what happened last Friday at your place, supposedly. Beer, pizza, you somehow ending up in his arms, talking about going to bed."

Brie laughed out loud.

"So none of that happened? He wasn't at your place Friday night?" John asked.

"Oh, it happened. Just not the way I'm sure he described it."

"He made it sound like you came within an inch of sleeping with him."

"Well, of course he did." Brie paused for a moment, wishing she didn't have to get into this, feeling exhausted from what had been an incredibly stressful day.

"Look, John, he showed up at my place unannounced Friday night with beer and a pizza. Of course I let him in. He's a longtime colleague, and I'm trying to stay on his good side while I work the Thatcher case. We listened to some music, ate the pizza, drank a beer. That was it."

"So why didn't you tell me about this when we talked Friday? Why'd I have to hear it from him? It must have happened right before we talked that night."

"Listen, John. I had to be on the road by six-thirty the following morning. I just couldn't get into it. The last thing I wanted to do was rehash the whole thing. I knew it would upset you."

Silence at the other end.

"So you didn't end up in his arms?"

"I did, actually, and right after that, he ended up on the floor from my leg coming up abruptly between his."

John laughed. "Really?"

"It's not good to surprise a cop, you know. We have training."

He was still laughing. "Parker's obviously losing it," he said. "And it's pretty clear he's got it bad for you." He let out a sigh. "I'm sorry, Brie. I shouldn't even have told you about the phone call."

"Yeah, you should. You think I'm not gonna confront him about what he said?"

"Maybe you should just let it lie. Not even dignify it with a comment."

"Well, maybe," she said. She couldn't contain the large yawn that suddenly overtook her.

"You need to go to sleep, Brie."

"I do, actually."

They said their "I love yous" with more tenderness than usual and then said goodnight.

Brie went to the bedroom and crawled into bed, feeling overwhelmed by the day. The revelation from Sideways Louie, the meeting with Rossi and the uneasy feeling she had gotten. And finally the session with Dr. Travers and the recovered memory of the face of Phil's killer.

She reached over, turned out the light and laid there. But suddenly in the dark of the room, she was back on Upton Avenue. She was falling, the room fading to black. A few seconds later, she felt the killer's fingers against her neck. She opened her eyes and sat up in bed, feeling deeply disturbed by the memory. It didn't make sense. Why had he felt for a pulse? If it was to see if she was dead, he would have shot her again. So it must have been to check if she was alive. But why? Had he wanted her to be alive? It was a puzzle, a troubling one.

She sat there in the dark for a few minutes, trying to work out some logical explanation for the shooter's actions. She thought about Rossi's concern about her wellness and his sincere words that seemed to border on an apology. "I never got to say it, but I'm really sorry for what you went through. Being shot, nearly dying . . ."

Had Rossi arranged the hit? Had he told the shooter there was to be no collateral damage, that only Phil Thatcher should die?

It had been a long and emotionally draining day, and in spite of these unsettling thoughts, sleep began to overtake her. She slid down in bed and let herself drift away. But it was a troubled sleep, and twice in the night she thought she heard something and crept from her bed in the dark, gun in hand, to move silently through her apartment, listening.

Chapter 44

Brie was wide awake by six the following morning and decided to go out for a run before heading to the department. She sensed she should be watching her back, but she wasn't about to go into hiding. Running helped to clear her head—helped her to think, and she needed that edge right now.

She pulled on the spandex leggings she wore for running in colder months, a long-sleeved silk tee shirt that hugged her body, and a fleece jacket. She took a few minutes to stretch her legs and then headed out the door, down the back stairs, and south along the street. She could feel the north wind at her back giving her a constant nudge. The temp had dipped into the high thirties overnight. The air was crisp and cold, and a flawless blue sky crowned the early November morning.

Thoughts of the case and the image of the shooter quickly melted away, and she focused on breathing and the rhythm of her strides. Her route today took her south to 34th Street and east to the northeast corner of Longfellow Park, then around the park and back home. Approximately a three-mile loop. On the final leg she ran straight into the north wind, which slowed her pace a bit but had an overall cooling effect that felt good. She was back home in a little over thirty minutes and hopped in the shower.

Forty-five minutes later she was on her way to the department in her Ford Escape. She had worked her wet hair into a French braid, and it felt cool against her head, so she turned on the heat in the car. The rush-hour traffic flowing into the city was heavy at this time in the morning, but she lived close to the department and could avoid the freeway. So within fifteen minutes she was parked and on her way through the tunnel to City Hall.

Her shift didn't start until eight-thirty, so she had plenty of time to stop in at the Hennepin County Sheriff's Office on the ground floor of City Hall. She asked the deputy up front if Deputy Michael Moretti was on duty and got an affirmative. He called back to his desk to let him know she was waiting. Moretti was a pal, plus he had just worked on the Ayesha Brown case with them last week, running a facial recognition search.

"Hello, Brie. What's up?" Moretti closed the gap between them.

"I'm wondering if you could run another face for me?" she asked. "It's a different case from last week. A cold case. We've just had a break."

"Sure thing. That's good news, by the way. Show me what you've got."

Brie pulled the folder with the sketch from her briefcase and took out one of the copies. "I can also send you a digital image that the artist scanned of this."

Moretti studied the image. "He's got some distinctive features. We'll give it a go. See if we get a hit. Go ahead and send that digital image down as well. We've got another search we're running, so it may be a couple of hours before I have anything for you."

"No problem. Thanks, Mike."

"You got it. I'll let you know when I have the results."

Brie headed upstairs to the floor above and down the hall to the investigative unit. She had decided the time had come to let Bull Johnson know what she had turned up in the Phil Thatcher case, what she had learned from Sideways Louie and her suspicions about former detective Joe Rossi's involvement. She had no idea what to expect from him, so until the hammer came down, she tried not to think the worst. His door was open. She knocked and stuck her head in, but he wasn't there. She turned and saw Detective Arturo Estavez at his desk.

"Hey, Estavez. Have you seen the commander?"

"He sent a memo. Didn't you get it?"

"I just got in. Haven't checked my email."

"He's giving a lecture at the police academy this morning, and later he has meetings and an appearance with the mayor."

"So he may not be in today at all?"

Estavez shrugged. "Dunno."

Brie headed back to her cube and brought up her email. Gabby Cole had sent her an email with the scanned image of the sketch attached. She forwarded it to Michael Moretti. Then she replied to any other pertinent emails. It took the better part of an hour.

Garrett wasn't due in until noon, and she figured it would be at least a couple of hours before she heard back from Deputy Moretti about any match from the facial rec search. So she decided it was a good time to head up to North Minneapolis, talk to Viola Adams and show her the sketch of the shooter.

She pulled out her small notebook. She had taken down Viola's number, and while she figured the elderly woman would be at home, it was always good to check. She punched in the number and waited. It took Viola six rings to answer.

"Hello, Viola. This is Detective Beaumont. Do you remember me?"

"Sakes alive, child. We met just the other day. Of course I do."

Brie smiled. No short in Viola's circuits. "I'm wondering if I could stop by and show you something."

"Wait a second, child, I'll check my social calendar."

Brie laughed out loud.

"You're in luck," Viola said. "I have an opening."

"You're a tease, Viola. I'll head for your place now. I should be there in twenty minutes."

"It's a cold day. I'll put on some tea," Viola said with certitude.

"That sounds great. I'll see you soon."

They ended the call, and Brie took one of the copies of the sketch out of the folder and placed a large white rock she used as a paperweight on top of the folder. She folded the sketch in thirds, slipped it into the inner pocket of her trench coat and headed for her car.

Twenty minutes later she pulled up outside Viola Adams' house and headed up to the door. The wind buffeted her, and she caught the scent of something savory cooking—maybe soup or stew. It seemed to be coming from across the street, and just for a moment it made her think of George's wonderful soups and stews aboard *Maine Wind*. The porch door was open, so Brie crossed to the front door, rang the bell and waited. Within a couple of minutes, the door opened and Viola Adams ushered her in.

"Come in, child. That wind today could blow down a strong man. I made some tea. Maybe you could carry it into the living room."

"Sure," Brie said. She followed Viola through to the kitchen. The morning sun poured in the back window that faced east and filled the small breakfast nook next to the window. "What a charming little spot," Brie said. "Why don't we have our tea out here?"

"Fine by me," Viola said. "It's my favorite spot in the morning."

Brie carried the tray over and poured out two cups of tea, and she and Viola sat opposite each other.

"How is the case going, Detective?"

"Well, over the past week or so, I've started to remember a few more details from the night my partner was killed. I believe

I've recovered a memory of the shooter's face. Last night I met with a police sketch artist, and with my input, she was able to capture the face I saw in my memory. That's what I wanted to show you."

Brie took the sketch from the pocket of her trench coat that she'd laid on the back of the chair next to her. She unfolded it and handed it to Viola. "Have you ever seen this man?"

Viola took the sketch and studied it for a moment, and Brie thought she saw her expression change slightly. "I know this face," she said. "This man lived right here in the neighborhood. Down the block a bit on the other side of the street. It's been a while since he lived there."

"Can you remember if he was here at the time my partner was killed?"

Viola considered the question. "Yes. Yes, he was, and I can tell you why. I remember after the terrible happenings next door . . ." She paused and closed her eyes as if in deep reflection. "I can remember that after that night, I never saw him again. Of course, I didn't think about it right away, but later on, when I did, it seemed to me he had disappeared right around that time. And I never saw any sign of him moving out. There's always activity when someone's moving in or out. You know what I mean, Detective?"

Brie nodded. "Yes, I do."

"But not with him. One day he was just gone. Like he'd vanished in the night."

Brie thought to herself that that was probably exactly what had happened. He had killed Phil and then vanished into the night.

Viola was talking again. "I guess I should have called the police, but I'm just an old woman. I don't know as they'd put much stock in my ramblings."

Brie sighed, knowing this was not an uncommon sentiment, especially in the black community. It made her sad, though, and a little angry. Not at Viola, of course, but at the great divide that still seemed to exist almost everywhere between police and African American communities.

Viola must have read something in her expression, because she leaned across the table. "I'm sorry," she said. "I should have said something. It might have made a difference."

"It's all right, Viola. I don't know that it would have mattered. My guess is we wouldn't have caught him anyway. By the time you would have made the connection and contacted us, he was long in the wind. And it certainly wouldn't have changed what happened. But your testimony today is *very* important. Now we know that we have a witness to the fact that this guy, this killer, was living right here when the shooting occurred. And that tells us a lot."

Viola nodded as if Brie's words had brought her some solace. After that they drank their tea, and Brie asked Viola about her husband and children. She told Viola about taking a leave and living on the ocean for six months, at which point Viola's eyes got bigger and took on a faraway look, as if she were trying to imagine such a thing as life aboard a sailing schooner. Brie showed Viola the picture of her and John aboard the *Maine Wind*, telling her he was the captain of the ship.

"Lordy, child. That's a fine man. And you say he's waitin' for you? Whatcha all still doing here?"

Brie smiled. "Just my job, Viola. He knows I'll come back to him when I'm finished here."

"Well, don't wait too long, girl. Some conniving woman might decide to go after him."

"Well, I guess that would be a test of whether he really cares," Brie said.

Viola let out a "humph" as if she weren't so sure about that, which made Brie laugh.

"You're a character, Viola. It's been really nice getting to know you."

"You stop in any time you're in the neighborhood, child."

"I will, Viola. Promise."

"Better yet, you finish up this case—I know you can—and go back to your captain on the . . . what was it called, now?"

"The *Maine Wind,*" Brie said.

"Ah," Viola said. "It sounds romantic. Like a faraway place," and a light shone in her eyes as she pictured it.

Brie cleared away the tea things for Viola and washed out the cups and pot even though Viola clucked at her like a mother hen. Then they walked slowly to the door together.

Viola laid her hand on Brie's arm. "You be careful out there, child."

"I will. Don't worry." She gave Viola a hug, and they said goodbye. Brie waited to be sure she heard Viola lock the door and then headed across the porch and down the steps.

She sat in her car, thinking about what she'd just learned from the elderly woman. Sideways Louie's tip that this was a contract killing was holding more and more water. The shooter had been installed in this neighborhood with an obvious objective. To draw Phil and Brie there on some pretext. The big question in her mind was whether Joe Rossi was involved.

Whoever was behind this had done his research. Knew there was a vacant, foreclosed property on the block. Had installed the hit man just down the street and then waited for an opportunity. North Minneapolis was a high crime area, so it was only a matter of time before Brie and Phil would be sent to a nearby address. The trap was set. All it needed was bait. The phone call that fateful night reporting a break-in at 3147 Upton Avenue North had been the bait. All the perpetrator would have needed was access to a police scanner or, easier yet, to put a tracking device on Phil's vehicle, since the two of them always took his car—a fact that had been common knowledge.

Brie thought about calling Sideways Louie to see if he might circulate the sketch of the hired gun to his contacts on the street. He'd been pretty adamant about not getting further involved in the case, but maybe she could persuade him. She decided to wait, though, and see if the facial recognition search turned up any matches. She started her car and headed back to the department.

Chapter 45

Brie made her way back downtown, parked, and headed toward City Hall. She had just entered the Investigative Unit and turned left toward her cube when she saw Garrett Parker ahead of her. She saw him walk to her desk, pause for just a moment, then move the rock and open the file with the copies of the sketch inside.

"Mind telling me what you're doing?" she asked from behind him. She saw him jump ever so slightly.

He closed the file and turned slowly, and his blue eyes were equal parts fire and ice. "Who is this?" he asked, and his middle finger drummed loudly on the folder.

"I've recovered a memory from the night of the shooting." She thought he would be glad for her, but that wasn't the vibe she was getting. She supposed it was because she was stealing his thunder. Maybe he thought this would make him look bad to the commander since this had been and, technically, still was his case. But she was the only one who could possibly remember the killer's face. Phil was dead, and no one else had seen him. Only she could recover that crucial memory.

"I thought you said you were going to keep me in the loop." He looked equal parts hurt and angry.

"Look, Garrett, I just recovered this memory last night. I met with Dr. Travers, and under hypnosis I was able to go back to the night Phil died. I was able to remember more details from that night."

"I'm sorry," he said, and his face softened. "That must have been hard. Sorry I jumped down your throat."

"I went right from Doc Travers' office to meet with Gabriella Cole to see if she could capture the face I had just seen. That's what's in the file. I've given it to Moretti down at HCSO to see if they can get a match using their facial rec program."

Garrett nodded. "Anything else?"

Brie hesitated. If possible, she wanted to leave Sideways Louie out of it. For whatever reason, she wasn't eager to share what she'd learned from Louie or Viola Adams with Garrett, even though this had been his case.

"I was going to give all my findings to the commander this morning, but Estavez said he's out for most if not the whole day." She paused for a moment, knowing she had to somehow bring Parker into the loop. "Listen, Garrett, I think we need to focus on Joe Rossi. I think he's our guy."

"But he had a watertight alibi. He was on duty in the Fourth when Phil Thatcher was murdered."

"Doesn't mean he didn't hire someone to do the job."

Garrett looked stunned.

"Look, Garrett, it wouldn't be the first time a cop hired a killer, and it won't be the last either."

"We'd need some kind of new evidence to take another run at him," Garrett said.

Brie tapped the folder on her desk. "I'm hoping we've got it right here," she said. "If we can find this guy, bring him in, maybe we can cut a deal with him if he'll give up Rossi."

"Maybe," Parker said. "I guess we'll see what Moretti's search turns up." He sat down at his desk, which was positioned at right angles to hers, and got to work.

Brie opened a Word document. For the next hour she wrote down everything she'd done on the Phil Thatcher case, from recanvassing the neighbors near 3147 Upton Avenue North to detailing her two interviews with Viola Adams to her meeting with former detective Joe Rossi. She could transfer the information to an official report form later, after she had talked to Bull Johnson.

By the time she finished, it was one-fifteen. She was starving. The bowl of cereal she'd eaten that morning was long gone. Garrett had left his desk twenty minutes earlier and not returned. She didn't want to miss the call from Moretti, but she needed to get something to eat. So she headed down to the cafeteria, planning to grab a sandwich and coffee to go that she could eat at her desk.

Later in the afternoon the call came through from Moretti at the Hennepin County Sheriff's Office.

"Sorry it took a while, Brie. I got called out of the department unexpectedly."

"No problem, Mike. Did the search turn up any matches?"

"I'm sorry to say it didn't. Hope you have some other avenues to try."

"I do," Brie said. "It just makes the job a little harder. But thanks again, Mike." They ended the call.

Brie got up from her desk and walked out of the unit and down the hall to the railing overlooking the rotunda. She brought up Sideways Louie's number and put through a call to him.

He answered after several rings, and Brie wondered if he had been debating not answering at all.

"Hello."

"Louie, it's Detective Beaumont. I'm wondering if we can meet."

"I told you I don't want to be involved with this case," he said.

"I know that, Louie, but I need your help nonetheless. I've recovered a memory from the night I was shot. I saw the shooter's face. I have a sketch. I need you to circulate this to a few of your contacts that you trust. Ones who can keep it secret. See if any of them can identify this guy."

There was a long silence from the other end.

"Louie . . .?" Brie finally said.

"That must have been tough . . ."

She assumed he was referring to her remembering the shooting.

There was another long silence. "All right," he finally said. "North end of the park where we've met. Six o'clock."

She heard the line go dead. He obviously wanted the cover of darkness, and by six o'clock in Minnesota in November, he would have it. Brie pocketed her phone and headed back into the unit. She swung by the commander's office to see if he might be back yet, but he wasn't, so she returned to her desk.

Garrett was there working at his computer, and she tried to settle back into her work. But she felt restless—wondered what her next step should be or whether she was at the end of the line and needed to turn all the information over to Bull Johnson at this point.

A little while later Garrett turned in his chair. "So did you hear back from Moretti on the sketch? Did they find a match?"

"Nope. Nothing popped up in the search."

"Sorry to hear that," he said. He turned and went back to typing. But a little while later he said, "You'd think with a distinctive feature like that scar they'd get a match, if this guy is anywhere in the system."

Brie froze, feeling as if all the air had suddenly been sucked out of her lungs, and she couldn't get any more to enter. For a moment she literally couldn't breathe. What she had just heard shook her to her core, and she was glad she was facing away from Garrett at that moment for fear her face might reveal all. She slowly replayed what he had just said in her head. "You'd think with a distinctive feature like that scar, they'd get a match if this guy is in the system."

But the scar wasn't in the drawing, and no one but me and the person who hired the killer knows about that scar, she thought.

"Brie, did you hear me?" he asked.

She collected herself in that instant and turned to face him, her best poker face ever in place. "Yeah, sorry, Gare, I was thinking about something. You sure would think that, wouldn't you? But no dice. And no match."

He has no idea he's just incriminated himself, she thought.

She took some slow deep breaths through her nose, trying to still her pounding heart. *I have to get out of here. Away from him.* She was afraid if she didn't, he'd somehow psychically pick up on what she now knew. After a few minutes, she quietly slid the folder with the sketches into her briefcase, stood, and put on her coat.

"I have to go back to the neighborhood where Phil was shot. There are a couple people I didn't manage to talk to the other day." She hoped it sounded plausible, since she'd told him yesterday that she'd interviewed the neighbors.

Garrett turned around. "Want some company?" he asked.

"Nah, I got this. You keep on with what you're doing. It'll probably be a dead-end anyway." She tried to sound nonchalant. "It's nearly the end of my shift, so I probably won't be back today. I'll see you tomorrow."

"Okay, see ya."

She felt his eyes on her back as she walked away. She imagined them as lasers trying to bore into her, see what was going on inside. For the first time in a long time, she felt a sharp twinge in her left side where the bullet had tracked to within an inch of her heart—the bullet that had killed Phil. She took it as a sign that she was playing a dangerous game. A game in which she no longer knew the rules.

Chapter 46

Brie stopped downstairs at the sheriff's office and collected the copy of the sketch from Moretti. She asked him not to discuss the sketch with anyone, no matter who might ask. He agreed. He looked like he wanted to ask a question, but he didn't.

Brie headed out through the tunnel toward the parking ramp. She brought up Gabby Cole's number. It went immediately to voice mail, signaling that Gabby was probably teaching a class. Brie sent a text, asking that Gabby not respond to any calls or texts from Garrett Parker and saying that she'd explain later.

Next she texted Homicide Commander Bull Johnson. The text read: *Urgent that I meet with you early tomorrow morning. What time will you be in*? She sent the text and continued on to her car.

It was four thirty-five when she pulled out of the ramp. She'd left the department early on a false pretext, but she had to get out of there. She felt as if every moment she remained, Parker could somehow read the truth of what she knew by the mere fact of her proximity.

At this point she didn't even try to think about the "why." All she knew was that Parker was somehow involved. How deep the involvement went, she had no idea. She couldn't imagine him playing a role in Phil's death, and it seemed just as outrageous that he might be involved in a plot to kill Edna. But how else could he know about the scar on the gunman's face?

All she knew was that the old bullet wound in her side was now throbbing, as if intent on sending her some message—some warning. She checked her watch and steered the car for home. She had time to get there and still make it to the meeting with Sideways Louie by six o'clock.

Brie pulled into the driveway and climbed out of her Escape. She took the back stairs up to her apartment two at a time, let herself in, and went straight to the bedroom. She pulled her small carry-on out of the closet and started packing an overnight bag. If Parker were to realize that he had incriminated himself, who knew what he might do? She thought about the letters—*You'll Be Sorry*—and the attempt on Edna's life, which had tragically ended a different life. Could he be behind all of it? For whatever reason, her gut told her "yes," so for now, she had decided to play it safe.

Because she lived alone in what anyone would call a low-security situation, she decided it was the better part of wisdom to check into a motel overnight. Until she could get the facts to Bull Johnson, she wasn't taking any chances. First thing tomorrow she'd put all her findings in the case into his hands.

She packed a change of clothes for the next day, then went into the bathroom and collected her toiletries, toothbrush, and hairbrush and added them to her bag. She grabbed the paperback spy novel from her bedside table—anything to keep her mind off the unfolding nightmare. She looked around the room to be sure she had everything and headed out the door, locking it behind her. She put her carry-on in the hatch of the Escape, pulled out of the driveway, and headed for her meeting with Sideways Louie.

Folwell Park, where Brie had agreed to meet him—where they had met on other occasions—was about twenty minutes from her place. She took Hiawatha Avenue to I 94 west. Just beyond the Lowry Tunnel, 94 bent north. She followed it another five miles and took the North Dowling exit and turned left toward the park. A little more than a half mile along Dowling she saw the park coming up. She turned left, drove to the parking lot, shut off her car, and waited. This was their rendezvous spot. Louie would find her.

Moonlight filtered through the web of bare branches, and the maple trees, their orange leaves now just a memory, swayed across the moon, creating an eerie motion picture. Brie had always credited herself with nerves of steel, but tonight she felt edgy. Skittish from too many unexpected revelations. She thought about Phil, and just the thought of him comforted her. No matter what happened, she would never regret working this case—finding justice for Phil and giving closure to his family.

She turned and looked around, sensing that Louie was nearby. He would be watching, scoping out the surroundings, making sure she was alone. CIs were spies, plain and simple. Spies for the men and women in blue. They only stayed alive, functioning in their role on the streets, through extreme finesse. To look at Sideways Louie one would never think of him as noble, and yet Brie could think of no other word for what he did. She knew her fellow detectives and officers didn't see it that way. They saw CIs as misfits, criminals willing to work both sides of the street for profit. Brie only saw the danger, and in her book, to expose oneself to that took courage of some kind.

She heard a soft knock on the window and immediately hit the switch to unlock the door. Louie ducked into the car and closed the door. He was dressed in black with a hood pulled up over his head. Brie had turned the light control on the console to off so no light would come on when he entered the car. They sat there in the dark for a few moments, not saying anything. She could just make out his profile as light from the gibbous moon filtered through the trees.

"Thanks for meeting me, Louie."

"I wouldn't have done it for anyone else," he said, looking straight ahead.

"That means a lot," she said. She didn't think about it often, but their relationship went back. Back to her early days as a detective, more than a decade ago. Phil was the one who had gotten Louie to sign on as a CI in exchange for a reduced sentence on a drug charge, but it was Brie more than Phil who had worked with him down the years. And odd as he was, he'd never let her down. She could depend on him. She realized their relationship meant something to him, or he wouldn't be sitting in her car tonight, helping her stalk a cop who had killed a cop. She wanted to tell him about Garrett Parker—tell him to watch his back—but she couldn't. This was still an open case.

She reached in her briefcase and pulled out one of the sketches of the gunman and handed it to Louie. He leaned over, held it down low near his feet and, turning on a small penlight, studied the sketch.

"Have you ever seen him before?" Brie asked.

"Never."

"He's a ghost. We can't turn up anything on him."

Louie continued studying the sketch.

"I don't want you to endanger yourself, Louie. Do you have people on the street you can absolutely trust?"

He darted a sideways glance at her. "The words *street*, *trust*, and *absolute* don't really go together."

Brie let out a silent laugh.

"Let's say there are people I wouldn't ask, and I know who they are."

"Good enough," Brie said. "Do you have any contacts on the inside who might have a bead on this guy?"

Louie straightened up, folded the sketch, and tucked it inside his hoodie. "There's a guy I know out at Stillwater. He's LWP."

Life with possibility of parole, Brie thought.

"I'll be in touch," Louie said, and Brie sensed he was eager to be gone. He glanced behind the car, and Brie could see his leg bouncing up and down, keeping a nervous rhythm.

"I'm going back to Maine, Louie. Once this case is closed. Just wanted you to know."

His leg stopped moving, and he glanced sideways at her. "How soon?"

"Probably a few weeks."

"It's nice out there, huh?"

"It's a good place for me."

"Maybe I'll get there someday," he said.

"I want to thank you, Louie. You've been very dependable and helpful to me and others in the department at no small risk to yourself, and I thank you for it."

He nodded and mumbled, "You're welcome." But before she could say any more, Sideways Louie was out of the car and had disappeared into the night. Brie waited a few moments, then started her car and drove back toward the freeway to look for a motel where she could spend the night.

She was thinking about the pieces of the bizarre puzzle and how they might fit together. She had seen the same gunman twice, which meant that Phil's shooting was not random, as had always been the theory in the case. The theory being that a drug user or dealer was looking for money or drugs in the house on Upton Avenue North that night.

The fact of the gunman's involvement in both murders links the two crimes, Brie thought. *Parker knows the killer's face, so he's somehow connected. But Parker had no motive to kill Phil.*

Enter Rossi, who did have a motive. In her meeting with him, when she had talked about Phil Thatcher sometimes going where he shouldn't, Rossi had said the words, "Well, it worked for whoever was gunning for him." A slip of the tongue? Probably. But an incriminating one, nonetheless. Those words indicated that Rossi also knew the shooting was not random.

So what next? Parker is assigned to the Thatcher murder case. Does Parker go easy on Rossi? Deep-six some of the evidence or just not dig as hard as he could have? *Why?* Is he involved in something with Rossi? Or just standing up for the "Brotherhood"? Does Garrett Parker leverage the identity of the killer from Rossi so he can hire him?

Why? she thought. *It's always about the "why."* One of them, either Rossi or Parker, hired the shooter to do the second job. To kill Edna. But neither of them has any apparent motive.

What happens next? The shooter takes out the wrong woman. That was the current working theory, anyway. In an attempt to kill Edna, he accidentally shoots Halley Greenberg. *But what if he had gunned down the right woman? Edna. What then?*

Because of the threatening letters, they would have assumed just what they had in the beginning. That someone Brie had put away was somehow out to punish her. With her mother dead, the Phil Thatcher case would have gone to the bottom of her priority list, but she never would have given up on finding Edna's killer.

All of a sudden a picture began to take shape in Brie's mind. A picture of the "why." The motive. And Garrett Parker sat dead center in that picture. She remembered John's words about Parker from the night before. "He's got it bad for you, Brie." *Exactly how bad did he have it for her?* she wondered. *Bad enough to kill? Bad enough to put a hit on her mother?*

A whole new way of thinking about the death up North, the attempt on Edna, and the intention behind it began to unfold in Brie's mind. And while the idea seemed crazy, there was a kind of perverted logic to it. What better way to keep her in Minnesota permanently than to gun down her mother? She had to admit, Parker knew her better than she thought he did.

But what would the commander think when she presented her findings tomorrow morning? She could only guess at the shock and anger he would feel. Would there be enough evidence in either case to make an arrest? Or would not one but two killers get away with murder?

Brie spotted a Best Western motel coming up. She pulled off at the exit and parked in the lot. She took a few minutes to call Claude Renard in Grand Marais and tell him what had developed with the case. Then she got out of her car and headed into the motel with her bag. She had never been more eager to reach the end of a day. Right now, sleep seemed like her only refuge.

Chapter 47

Brie was in the commander's office the following morning by seven a.m. She wasted no time on pleasantries but laid out for him the work she had done on the Phil Thatcher cold case. Then she paused and waited for a response from him.

"I'm not surprised, Beaumont, if that's what you're waiting for. I knew when you came back here that you'd feel compelled to get involved with the case." He studied her for a moment. "Officially, I have to express disapproval, but unofficially, I've been troubled by the lack of resolution in this case." He stared past her into the middle distance. "A cop died. We have to do better than we have, or we'll all be in the crosshairs. So what have you found? And what is so urgent that you texted me about last night?"

"Most of what I've done has been replowing old ground, sir. But there is one new development." She told him that, since being back home, she had begun to recover memories from the night of the shooting, which had given her hope that she might remember something crucial.

"I went back to Dr. Travers to see if she could use hypnosis to help me remember more about the night Phil was shot. And in that state, I saw the face of the shooter." She told him it wasn't the first time she had seen that face. That it was the face of a man she had seen up North in unusual circumstances and proceeded to tell him about what had unfolded when they were sailing.

"If I've seen the same gunman twice, then Phil's death could not have been a random act, as was previously thought. I believe this is the same man who shot Halley Greenberg up near Grand Marais in an attempt to kill my mother, Edna Beaumont. In fact, I believe the threatening letters I received and the deaths of Phil Thatcher and Halley Greenberg are all connected."

"How could the two deaths be connected? That doesn't make sense, Beaumont."

"I think it does, sir, but in a rather convoluted way." She took the sketch out of her briefcase and handed it to him. "This is the face I saw with Dr. Travers. The same face I saw on that cliff up North. But when I had the artist sketch it, I inadvertently left off an important detail."

She told him about omitting the scar, and about the fact that Garrett Parker had seen the sketch, albeit briefly. "A couple hours after that, after the facial rec search came up empty, Parker turned to me and said, 'You'd think with a distinctive feature like that scar, they'd get a match, if this guy is in the system.'"

Bull Johnson sat down in his chair as if the weight of her words was too much for him.

"I had just the night before recovered the memory of the shooter's face and connected it with the face of the man on the cliff," Brie said. "This was new information." She looked the commander in the eye. "There is only one other person who could have known about that scar. A person who had hired the gunman."

Bull Johnson shook his head slowly, and anger flared in his eyes. "Garrett Parker . . . unbelievable. First Gorman and Rossi and their connection to street drugs and payoffs, and now this. So much worse."

"I don't believe Parker is behind Phil Thatcher's murder," Brie said.

"But then how would he know about that scar?"

"I think he learned the identity of the shooter from the person who put the contract out on Thatcher. What if that person, the one who put the hit on Thatcher—let's call him Joe Rossi—somehow got off easy. What if the detective working the case didn't dig deep enough? Or worse, what if he purposely led the case in a different direction? In other words, let the case go cold. And what if that detective—let's call him Garrett Parker—used those actions to leverage Rossi in some way or other."

She told the commander about the Thatcher case file not being on Garrett's desk, where she would have expected it to be, and that she had found that plenty odd. "The unsolved murder of a cop—that file should be on the detective's desk," Brie said. "The file was in the Records Room, sir. Almost like he was done with the case."

"What are you saying, Beaumont?"

Brie pulled a chair over and sat down so they were at eye level. "Look, Commander, the deeper I've dug, the more I've come to believe that Rossi is behind Phil Thatcher's death. Parker mentioned the Brotherhood to me when we talked about Rossi one day. He said Rossi had held a grudge because Phil had turned in one of our own. But I got the feeling there was a lot of righteous indignation in Parker, too, about cops who are willing to rat out other cops. Then, in working the Thatcher case, I got a tip from one of my CIs that Thatcher's murder was an inside job—a contract killing set up by a cop. Of course that pointed to Rossi, who maybe wanted revenge on Phil for Phil's part in taking him down."

Brie laid out her theory of how Rossi had installed the shooter in the neighborhood and set things up so they would be drawn to that specific house. "The house on Upton Avenue North, where Phil was shot, had been a known drug house. I believe Rossi set it up as he did to make it look like a random killing by a drug dealer. I checked the record, and Rossi was one of the responding officers at the homicide Phil and I had been sent to that night, just two blocks from the Upton Avenue address. I think Rossi saw his opportunity that night. He guessed Phil would respond to the break-in call. I believe he called the gunman, told him to get in position and wait. When we left the scene that night, the trap was sprung. At Rossi's prompting, the gunman placed the 911 call from a burner phone."

She told the commander what Rossi had said to her on Monday when she had met with him—when she'd mentioned that Phil sometimes went where he shouldn't. "His words were, 'Well, it worked for whoever was gunning for him.'"

Silence stretched between them. "We should have waited for backup that night," she finally said. "I told Phil it wasn't our call. I told him to wait for the squads. To let the uniforms take it."

"Look, Beaumont, Rossi knew Phil—knew his temperament—knew he wasn't one to stand on ceremony. He would have guessed he'd go in—would have been banking on it. And sadly, for Phil Thatcher, he guessed right. As for Thatcher's decision to go into the house that night, that was on him. You can't blame yourself.

"I can buy your theory about Rossi. I knew he'd made threatening remarks directed at Thatcher. I can even buy Parker looking the other way. Wanting in some way to let Rossi off easy. But your theory that Parker learned the identity of the hired gunman from Rossi. Are you saying Parker put a hit on your mother? Hired this guy to gun her down?"

"That's what I believe, sir. I also think he's behind those threatening letters that were sent to me. Clever touch, too, him sending the letters while I was out of town. Made it look like the sender didn't know my whereabouts."

"Why? What could his motive possibly have been?"

"I know it sounds crazy, sir. But murder and reason don't always share much common ground. And I believe Parker had what may have seemed to him a very good motive. To keep me in Minnesota." She told him what had happened Friday night and that there'd been a series of more subtle advances prior to what unfolded that night.

"It's possible you're right, Beaumont." Bull Johnson told her that he'd overheard part of the heated phone conversation between Garrett and John the day before. "It didn't make much sense then, but now it's beginning to."

"What better way to make sure I would never go back to Maine than to put a hit on my mother? I believe Parker leveraged the identity of the shooter from Rossi and then hired him to take out my mother. But the shooter botched the job."

She told him again about the striking similarity in appearance between Edna and Halley Greenberg, and that the chief deputy in charge of the case up North had come up empty for both leads and motives, possibly indicating that Halley Greenberg was not the target.

"Think about it, Commander. The letters created the perfect set-up. The natural assumption about those letters would be exactly what we thought—that the threats and my mother's subsequent death connected to someone I had put away." She leaned forward and placed her arms on the desk. "I've been a detective for a long time. That would be like finding a needle in a haystack. But Parker knows me. He knows I would have stayed here and worked that case forever. But then the gunman shot the wrong woman, so that changed the complexion of the whole affair and allowed me to focus on Phil Thatcher's case. Exactly what Parker did not want."

"So his plan backfired," Johnson said.

"That's my read of it," Brie said. "And who knows? If he hadn't been tripped up by the sketch of the shooter and the absence of that scar, we might never have figured it out."

"Unfortunately, Beaumont, I don't think the sketch will hold up in court. There's no doubt that Parker's knowing about that scar is damning, but a good defense attorney would say you subconsciously transposed the face of the guy you had seen on the cliff onto the shooter you saw during hypnosis, because you found him suspicious."

"Except there's more," Brie said. "I have a witness who identified this sketch. She lives next door to the house on Upton where Phil was shot." She tapped the sketch. "Mrs. Adams says this guy, the gunman, was living in the neighborhood when Phil was shot, but that she never saw him again after that fatal night."

"That's good work, Beaumont."

"But is it enough to arrest Rossi or Parker?"

"I don't know. I'll have to talk to the ADA. The fact that we have an eyewitness who will testify that the shooter was living in the neighborhood is big. But we need to identify him."

"Facial rec came up empty. But I have one of my CIs working the street, as well as a contact he has at Stillwater Prison, to see if anyone knows who this guy is."

"Good. We'll also need to dig into Parker's finances. See if there's any evidence of payoffs from Rossi to encourage Parker to deep-six the Thatcher case."

"What about bringing Rossi back in for another interview? Show him the sketch. See if it rattles him. Tell him it's just a matter of time before the shooter is found and arrested. See if he'll cut a deal—give up Parker."

"It might work. But being a former detective, Rossi would know we haven't got much leverage without the identity of that shooter," the commander said. "But maybe we could play one of them off against the other. See who cracks first."

Brie checked her watch. They'd been mulling over the case for almost an hour. "When is Parker due in?" she asked.

"Eight-thirty. Let me contact the ADA and lay everything out. See what he thinks about the situation. In the meantime, I'd like you to go back to your desk and write a report on our meeting and everything we've discussed."

"Will do, sir." Brie got up to leave.

"It's good work, Beaumont."

"Thank you, sir."

She had more to tell him. The more being that she was planning to turn in her resignation. But she decided now was not the time. Bull Johnson had enough on his plate.

She felt she had gone as far as she could with Phil's case, and she also felt certain that Joe Rossi was behind her partner's death. Sideways Louie's revelation had been the break in the case as far as she was concerned. But unless law enforcement was able to identify, locate, and arrest the hired gunman, and then get him to turn evidence, there was little hope of arresting Joe Rossi or Garrett Parker, or of closing either murder case.

The thought of that made her heartsick. But for now, it was where they were at. She headed back to her desk to get started on the report the commander had requested.

Chapter 48

At 8:45 a.m. Bull Johnson stuck his head into Brie's cube and asked if she'd seen Parker yet.

Brie had been lost in her work but now noticed the time. "I haven't seen him."

"Huh. Well, let me know when he comes in."

"Yes, sir."

At 9:30 there was still no sign of Parker. The commander called his phone, but it went immediately to voicemail. At 10:00 he ordered a squad to Parker's house to do a welfare check, authorizing them to enter the residence on probable cause. Bull Johnson had begun to fear the worst.

At 10:25 the officers radioed the commander, saying that they had entered Parker's residence and found no one home. They reported signs that he had packed some of his belongings and may have left hastily, as there were still dishes in the sink.

The commander signed off and called Brie and Detective Estavez into his office.

"Beaumont, I want you to track any departing flights from the airport in the past twelve hours. See if you can get access to the flight manifests and see if Parker booked a flight. Estavez, you check trains and buses. In the meantime, I'm going to get a BOLO out on his vehicle and a search warrant sworn out for his property so we can collect any credit card and bank information, as well as his computer, if it didn't go with him."

Within an hour and a half, Brie and Estavez reported to the commander. They'd both come up empty on their transportation searches.

"Damn it. He's in the wind," Johnson said. "He left the department at eight-thirty last night, so he has more than a twelve-hour jump on us."

"Maybe the BOLO will turn something up," Estavez offered.

Bull Johnson sat down heavily in his chair. "I have the feeling Parker planned carefully and well in advance for all possible eventualities."

"I should have tried to brief you last night, sir," Brie said.

"I'm not sure it would have made a difference, Beaumont."

The end of the day came and went with no hits on the BOLO on Parker's vehicle.

In the meantime, a search warrant had been sworn out, and Brie and Estavez had been sent to Parker's residence to collect his computer as well as bank and credit card statements in order to look for activity on them.

Three days came and went with neither hide nor hair of Garrett Parker. There were no hits on his credit cards, and his minimal bank balance hadn't been touched. Brie guessed that he had a stash of cash, and probably not an insignificant one. If he *was* being paid off by Rossi, he'd been savvy enough to keep his take in folding money.

Five days after Parker's disappearance, Sideways Louie contacted Brie to let her know he had information on the sketch she had given him. After she left the department that night, she met him in Folwell Park—their usual rendezvous spot. Louis told her that his contact at Stillwater prison had identified the shooter as Hans Nero—a contract killer.

"All he could give me was the name," Louie said.

Brie hoped it would be enough.

She returned to the department after her meeting with Louie. The commander was still there working, and they ran the name through NCIC. The National Criminal Information Center is a computerized database of criminals maintained by the FBI and accessed by criminal justice agencies.

They got a hit on Hans Nero. The report showed several aliases that he had used in the past. It also showed his last known country of residence as Canada. The only address on record was from years before. Apparently, Nero stayed far below the radar.

Brie filed a report with the FBI that Nero had been identified as the shooter in the murder of a police officer and the suspected shooter in the murder of a woman near Grand Marais, Minnesota. She gave the details of both cases in the report. When she was done, Bull Johnson told her to go home. There was nothing more they could do that day.

The next day they brought Joe Rossi in for an interview for the second time since the murder of Phil Thatcher. But even though the commander and Detective Estevez questioned him for several hours and tried to get him to cut a deal, he refused to budge, claiming he was innocent and that he had an alibi for the night Thatcher was gunned down.

After seven days, there were still no hits on the BOLO on Garrett Parker. His credit cards had not been used, nor had there been any activity in his bank account, which they had also flagged. At the end of that day, Brie went to the commander's office to break the news to him that she would be turning in her resignation and returning to Maine. Standing there, she somehow got the feeling he had been expecting her visit.

Bull Johnson sat down in his chair and studied her for a few moments, as if he might be deciding how to frame his words. Finally he said, "I don't like it that you're leaving, Beaumont, but I understand it. You've made connections out there with the Maine State Police. And you've found a guy, and I'm happy for you there. I really am. I think for many years you've focused on your work almost myopically to the exclusion of a personal life. Policing is a lonely business. If you find another human who's willing to live with the trials a cop faces on a daily basis—that's the gold ring, and you'd better grab for it."

"Thank you, sir. Thank you for understanding."

He nodded. "You're welcome, Beaumont. You're a very good detective, and you will be missed. And I'm grateful to you for getting to the bottom of Thatcher's murder. Even though the outcome isn't what we would have wanted, the lack of resolution in that case has haunted me."

"If there was any more I could do . . ."

He waved that away. "We're in a holding pattern right now and may be for a while. But we'll keep working with other agencies, including the Royal Canadian Mounted Police, in an attempt to locate Hans Nero, the gunman. And with Interpol, in the event that Parker has left the country."

Brie told him she would stay two more weeks until he could get someone transferred into the unit. He thanked her, and she left his office.

At the end of the day she headed for her car. The die had been cast—she'd given her notice, and a host of emotions jockeyed for position inside her. Joy that she would be returning to Maine and to John. Trepidation at leaving the career she had built here. Worry about her mother and what would become of her. Anger that Garrett had slipped through the net and might not face justice for his acts. The only one of these that could really be addressed was her mother's situation, and Brie hoped something would be resolved about that before she left Minnesota.

Chapter 49

Over the next two weeks, Brie spent her nights packing boxes and making decisions about her possessions. Most of her furniture had been acquired here and there at garage sales when she'd first moved into her apartment a decade ago. The living room had several big, cozy pieces of furniture—a sofa and two chairs that had been selected based on what she called the curl-up factor. Now, as she studied them, they reminded her of distant cousins who are somehow related but share no common ground. But one of the chairs had belonged to her grandfather, and she decided she would take that with her. There was also an antique drop front desk that she loved and decided she couldn't part with. She found a carrier who would pack the two pieces and put them on a truck going to the East Coast.

As for the rest, she talked to Sarah, her landlady, and asked if she might like to acquire the rest of the furniture for a small sum so she could offer a furnished apartment. Sarah said she liked the idea. Brie wasn't sure if she really did or if her fondness for her because she'd been such a good and long-term tenant carried the day. But either way, they struck a bargain that suited them both.

Brie packed up boxes of her books, some china her mother had given her, the quilt her grandmother had made, and her out-of-season and extra clothes. The china and quilt she would fit into her car, and she shipped the rest of the boxes to John's boatyard in Maine.

Near the end of the first week, she contacted Deputy Tab Stevens, her friend at the Ramsey County Sheriff's Office who had arranged to store Edna's car in one of their garages. She asked Tab if she could help her get the car back to her mother up North over the weekend. Tab said she'd be happy to help, so on Saturday, they met at the Ramsey County Sheriff's Office to retrieve Edna's car and headed north for the long drive to Grand Marais.

Brie had asked Tab if she'd mind spending the night in Grand Marais so she could drive up to Grand Portage and say goodbye to her mom. Tab was happy to stay over, saying that she'd like to visit some of the shops in the village. So Brie booked a room for her at the Best Western that was right in town and within walking distance to all the shops and restaurants. She left her Escape at the motel with Tab and took her mom's Jeep.

As she drove the forty-five minutes up to Grand Portage, she was thinking about how to tell Edna about Garrett Parker and Joe Rossi and their connection to the deaths of her partner and Halley Greenberg. Hard as it was, she knew she had to tell her mother that she, not Halley, had been the target and that they believed Parker had fled the state. She wondered how the whole situation might impact her mother's choices for the future, and what advice she should give Edna.

But she needn't have worried. When she got to Joseph Renard's house, she learned that Joseph had invited Edna to stay at his home on the reservation for the winter. Edna had enthusiastically accepted his invitation. Something wonderful seemed to be developing between them. Brie wasn't sure if it was love or just close friendship, but she was extremely happy for both of them. She also got a chance to say goodbye to Claude

Renard, Sheriff One-Step, and fill him in on the complexities of the case when he stopped up at Joseph's house late Saturday.

On Sunday she met Tab back in Grand Marais. They had lunch at the local café and then headed back down the road to the cities.

* * *

At the end of the following week, Brie walked out of the Minneapolis Police Department for the last time and away from the job that had defined her for fifteen years.

That night she dreamt of the great golden eagle that had visited her dreams when she'd stayed at Joseph Renard's home in Grand Portage. Her partner Phil no longer rode astride the great raptor. He had delivered his messages to her and, in the beliefs of the Ojibwe, had traveled westward to the place the soul dwells after death. In her dream Brie watched as the eagle soared above the house. The whoosh of wind beneath its great wings comforted her, soothing her mind, and she slept more deeply than she had in many nights.

The next morning she took one final walk around her apartment and then turned her keys in to her landlady. It was a cold morning, and the sky was extraordinarily blue as she drove east on I 94 out of the cities. East toward Maine.

Chapter 50

November 27
Mooselookmeguntic Lake, Maine

Brie and John sat at the table by the window that overlooked the lake. John had told her the rustic log cabin was over a hundred years old. Not unusual in Maine, where the history of the territory now occupied by the state stretched back to the 1500s. So what was a mere one hundred years?

John had rented the cabin when Brie told him she'd be coming back to Maine. Right now they were enjoying their morning coffee in silence and looking across the lake toward the mist-shrouded mountains in the distance. Outside the cabin a pair of tall, aged spruce trees creaked in the wind, as if commiserating with each other over the chilly morning temperature. The thermometer outside the window read twenty-five degrees.

Under the table, Barney snuggled against her legs. Barney was a young white Lab who had wandered into the boat yard in October and adopted John. John had searched high and low for his owner to no avail, all the while caring for the dog. Finally, he had given him the name "Barney," short for "Barnacle," since he stuck to John like a barnacle to a ship.

Brie took a sip of her coffee. Her eyes slid from the window and rested on John across the table from her. His dark hair was ruffled from sleeping, and a deep aura of happiness seemed to surround him. Or maybe it was a projection of the happiness she felt. He turned his head now, and a slow smile lit his brown eyes. She traced his handsome face with her gaze.

"Just enjoying the view," she said. "It's one I've missed."

He smiled and took her hand across the table, and they returned to the silence, as if the magic might be broken by too many words. John had laid a fire, and the flames cast shadows onto the fieldstone surrounding the firebox. The birch logs crackled and snapped, carrying on a cozy conversation that complemented the peace of the room. The old mantel clock above the fireplace ticked away seconds that mattered not. Over the past few days, time had simply ceased to exist for Brie and John.

After an hour of watching the morning light paint subtle changes across the broad surface of the water, they rose to make breakfast. Brie fried the bacon, and John cooked the eggs. The smoky aroma of the bacon made her stomach growl, and Barney, overcome by the smells, forgot his manners and stood up with his front paws on the counter next to the stove in order to get a good whiff.

They cut up some oranges they'd brought along, poured more coffee, and returned to their table by the window with their plates. John set his plate and mug down and went to stoke the fire.

"So how did you find this spot?" Brie asked.

"Well, I went online to see who might be renting a cabin at this time of year. When I saw this place, I knew it was for us. I figured a girl from Minnesota would have to be tickled by a lake named Mooselookmeguntic."

Brie laughed. "I am tickled by it. What a fantastic name. Do you know what it means?"

"I read it's from the Abenaki language. It means 'moose feeding place.' Somehow it loses in the translation, don't you think?"

"I'll say. The native languages have a wonderful music and cadence all their own, as if language were allowed to take its time just as nature does."

"That's a lovely thought, Brie." He came over and kissed the top of her head before sitting back down to his breakfast.

They ate in silence, stealing glances at the lake and each other. Brie noticed the thermometer was pushing higher as the sun climbed up in the sky. By the time they finished breakfast, it was nearing forty degrees.

"It's warming up," she said, nodding toward the thermometer. "I think I'll walk down to the lake after we clean up. Want to join me?"

"I thought I'd split some wood for the fireplace. But you go ahead. If it warms up some more, let's take the canoe out."

"Sounds great," Brie said. "I'll pack some sandwiches and coffee when I come back up."

They carried their plates to the sink, washed and dried the dishes and pans, and put them away.

Brie went to the bedroom and put a pair of leggings on under her jeans and got her heavy jacket off the hook behind the door. John was heading out the door wearing only his flannel shirt.

"Don't you want a jacket?" she asked.

"I won't need it. I'll be chopping wood."

Brie smiled at that. "Okay, then. I'll see you in a little while."

"Have a nice walk." John went out the door and headed around the back of the cabin. There was a large stump there perfect for splitting wood.

She headed for the trail that wound down the hill to the lake. The cabin sat on a large tract of land, and trails had been blazed in several directions so one could walk the land. At the foot of the hill the trail ran in both directions along the lake. The cabin was located on the eastern side of the lake with a fringe of mountains rising to the southwest. John had told her the perimeter of the lake measured 58 miles, with 27 square miles of surface area. A good-sized lake even by Minnesota standards.

Brie took the trail to the left that headed south along the shore through a stand of tall spruce. The water was deep blue this morning and shimmered in the distance like a great liquid jewel. Here and there patches of frost traced lacy designs on the forest floor where there was deep shade. Brie was headed for a point of land a ways down the shore, where there was a rustic bench that looked down the length of the lake. She and John had sat there a couple of days ago and watched a storm rolling in from the west.

She came to it in a few minutes and took up her post. She sat there for quite a while, reflecting on the chaos of the past few weeks juxtaposed with the bliss of the past few days—the joy of being with John, making love, having this time completely to themselves. Not a reality that could be sustained, but a moment in time—a bubble in which they currently floated, happy and carefree. She drew in a deep breath and let it out and put her head back so the late November sun shone on her face.

The woods were nearly silent except for the chirping of birds—the ones that wintered over. In the distance, she could faintly hear the rhythm of John's ax as he split the firewood. Then something else. The sound of a car, she thought, heading along the gravel road. Someone else coming for a late fall stay at their cabin, or possibly a forest ranger driving the road.

After a time, she stood and retraced her path along the lake. When she got to the trail that climbed up the hill, she kept going straight ahead. There was another trail a short distance along that also ran up the hill and came out a ways behind the house where John was working. As she got midway up the hill, the sound of his ax ceased, and she heard Barney barking. She kept climbing, and a short distance up the trail, she caught a glimpse of his bright blue flannel shirt. But a few steps farther along, she came in view of something that nearly stopped her heart. She felt adrenaline course through her veins. A cold sweat broke out on the back of her neck, and it seemed as if all the air had suddenly been squeezed out of her lungs.

Garrett Parker stood in front of John in the clearing, his gun drawn. Barney was barking up a storm, but John had hold of his collar, restraining him. Garrett's mouth was moving, but she couldn't hear what he was saying. Then as if by sixth sense, he turned his head and scanned the hill in her direction. She ducked down, hoping he hadn't seen any movement. John didn't know it, but that moment when Parker looked away was his opportunity to make a move. But John wasn't a cop, and without the training to take Parker down, it could have ended badly. Parker continued to scan the hill, and Brie barely breathed, fearing the slightest movement would give her away. She was glad her jacket and jeans were dark colors and that she'd pulled a black watch cap over her blond hair.

From her crouched position in the undergrowth, she thought she heard Parker say, "Move." She straightened up just enough to see the tops of their heads moving toward the front of the cabin. As soon as they had rounded the corner of the house, she started working her way cautiously up the hill, trying to control her breathing, placing each step carefully so as not to make a sound, while at the same time moving as quickly as she could.

She wasn't wearing her gun. Why would she be? The thought that Garrett would risk a clean getaway to carry out some vendetta against John seemed crazy. But there it was. And when she thought about it, his actions over the past months were the definition of crazy. What was more, it wouldn't have been hard for a detective like Parker to locate John. There weren't that many windjammer captains in Maine, and none of the others were named John DuLac.

Her gun was in the bedroom at the back of the cabin, and she knew the window had been left slightly open during the night. Once at the top of the hill, she headed across the small lawn toward the back of the cabin, staying low and out of any sightline from the windows.

Chapter 51

John hoped Brie might somehow sense that something was wrong—some foreboding that would keep her from walking in the front door of the cabin. Whatever happened to him didn't matter as long as she remained safe.

Parker gave him a shove as they came through the door. "Shut your dog in the bedroom," he ordered.

John purposely walked to the spare bedroom and shut Barney inside, knowing that if Brie somehow got wind of what was happening, she would go for her gun, which was in their bedroom.

Parker motioned for him to come to the center of the room. He took a chair from the table by the window and pushed it toward him.

"Sit," he said.

John sat, his eyes moving back and forth between the hand with the gun and the one that carried a gallon-sized metal fuel can. He'd had a chance to make a move outside when Garrett had looked toward the hill, but he'd hesitated. Now he doubted he'd get another chance.

Parker set the can down and pulled several zip ties from his jacket pocket and tossed them toward John. One of them was designed like a pair of handcuffs.

"Use one of these to secure each of your ankles to the leg of the chair and the last one to cuff your hands together."

John hesitated.

"Do it or I'll shoot your dog," Parker said.

John followed his orders.

Parker pulled a length of rope about the thickness of clothesline from the pocket of his cargo pants. John could see it had a loop in it. Garrett moved to where he was sitting, dropped the loop over his head and the chair, tightened it, and ran the line twice more around his body and tied it off. John couldn't see where the gun was, but he assumed Parker had holstered it as he worked on the rope.

He stepped back in front of John. "Tell me where Brie is."

"She's on the lake. She took the one-man kayak out." John said it without hesitation, hoping Parker would buy the story.

Parker stepped to the window and looked out on the lake. "I don't see her out there."

"She probably paddled south along the eastern shore."

"Well, it doesn't matter. It's you I'm after. I have no intention of hurting her."

John heard a softening in Parker's voice when he said that. He thought back to the argument he'd had with Parker over the phone when he'd called the department a few weeks ago. It was pretty clear that day that Parker had some kind of crazy designs on Brie, but he and Brie had mistakenly assumed that once Parker fled Minnesota he would be focused on escape, not revenge.

As if reading his mind, Parker said, "If you hadn't come into the picture, she would have been mine."

"I think you're wrong. Brie's not the kind of woman *any* man can possess. The best anyone could ever hope for would be to share a life with her. But one where she has a lot of space."

"Shut up. I've known her a lot longer than you."

"Well, if you really know her, then you know I'm right."

But Parker had decided to ignore him and instead was busying himself sloshing gasoline on the floor throughout the living room and kitchen.

* * *

Brie approached the back wall of the cabin. She could hear Barney barking frantically. She went to the window of the spare bedroom and looked in. Barney was glued to the bedroom door, raising holy hell. *Smart of John to put him in the spare room,* she thought. She moved over to the other bedroom where she and John had been sleeping and carefully peeked in the window. The bedroom door was ajar, but just a little. Garrett wouldn't be able to see her climbing in the window unless he was right near the door. She'd have to be super careful about her entrance, though. She hoped Barney would keep up his barking. It would cover any slight noise she might make.

She looked around her. There was a shed a short way from the house. She hurried over there, opened the door carefully, and stuck her head in. There was a small wooden stepladder leaning against one wall. She carried it over to the back of the cabin and opened it beneath the window. She climbed up and lifted the window sash, hoping it wouldn't stick or squeak. It slid up easily. She looked in. There was nothing under the window. She put one leg through, then ducked her body through the opening. She felt for the floor and then drew her other leg in. She stood, barely breathing for a moment, listening. She heard Garrett's voice but couldn't make out what he was saying.

She crept over to the bedside table and carefully slid the drawer open and retrieved her gun. She moved over to the door, which was slightly ajar, and pressed her back against the wall, the gun in the upright position against her chest. She listened for a moment and heard the sickening sound of liquid hitting the floor. She took a quick glance around the door frame to get a bead on Garrett. She knew she couldn't fire her gun—it could ignite the gasoline. She drew in a breath and let it out and stepped through the door, gun extended.

"Drop your gun, Garrett."

He swung around, dropping the gas can, bringing his gun up leveled at John. He came forward and put the gun to his head. "You can risk it, Brie, but are you sure I won't get the shot off before I go down?"

She kept her gun trained on him.

"Put your gun on the floor and kick it aside," he said. "Do it or your sea captain's a goner."

Brie hesitated a moment but then set her gun on the floor and kicked it toward the wall.

"Now, move over by the front door."

She did as he said. "Why, Garrett? I just want to know why. Why you would let Rossi get away with killing my partner? Why would you deep-six the case?"

"Joe Rossi was a good guy. So he made a mistake not reporting his partner and the drugs. Thatcher could have looked the other way. What about the brotherhood? So, *I* decided to look the other way. Yeah, I figured Rossi was behind Phil's death, and I was right."

"So you used that as leverage to get the name of the shooter—to hire him to kill my mother. Was that the price Rossi had to pay for your silence?"

"It's a small price to pay to avoid life in prison."

"What about the truth, Garrett? The law. Your actions are the result of righteous indignation run amok. They have nothing to do with justice. What would it come to if everyone looked the other way?"

He pressed on as if he hadn't heard that. "Rossi never meant for you to get hurt. I want you to know that. He feels deep remorse for that."

"But not for Phil's wife and son, who were left without a husband and a father?"

Parker acted like he hadn't heard that either. "After the shooting, when I saw you in the hospital, so vulnerable . . . I'd never seen you like that. I knew then I wanted to be with you. As a partner and as a lover."

"I don't think that ever would have happened, Garrett."

"Sure it would have. But then you took a leave. Left without even saying a word."

"Bull Johnson knew."

Parker waved that away as if it were a troublesome fly. "And then you met him." He prodded John with the gun. "That ruined everything. I could tell when you came back to the department that you were somewhere else."

"Could you, now?"

"Yes, I could."

"Why'd you send those letters to me, Garrett? I know you did."

"Because I knew you'd assume what you did. That it was someone you'd put away. And your mother's death would have sealed the deal. You never would have gone back to Maine. You would have worked that case . . ." He stopped mid-sentence as if he didn't need to finish. "Then that idiot gunman shot the wrong woman."

Brie had decided that Garrett had no intention of discharging his weapon. Too much chance someone would hear it and call the authorities. And he wanted plenty of leeway to make his getaway. Hence the plan to torch the cabin.

"Look, Garrett, you don't have to do this. I'll go with you. Just don't set the fire."

Parker obviously hadn't expected that. He actually paused and looked at her for a moment as if making a decision. "I'm sorry, Brie," he finally said. "But you're coming with me one way or the other." Before she could say anything, he pulled a lighter from his pocket, flicked it and tossed it into the kitchen. The floor immediately ignited.

"NO," she screamed, but Garrett was already next to her and had pushed her out the door.

He prodded her with his gun. "Up the hill. Now."

Brie knew there wasn't a second to waste, and as they moved forward, she reacted out of instinct and training. Going low and swinging her leg around, she caught Garrett at the ankles and rolled out of the way as he pitched forward. She was up in a flash and darted into the cabin.

It was a scene from hell. The floor was ablaze, and John was hopping with his chair, trying to avoid the flames. She saw his pant leg was ablaze and darted to the sofa where there was a wool blanket and smothered the fire on his leg.

"Barney," John shouted. "Get Barney!"

Brie raced to the bedroom door and beat the flames with the blanket and, shielding her hand with the wool, opened the door. Barney shot out of the room and headed for the front door. Brie caught sight of her gun on the floor. She grabbed it and stuffed it in the back of her jeans and rushed back to John. She beat down the flames with the blanket and dragged the chair and John toward the door, threw the blanket down on the floor to smother the flames, and pulled John out of the cabin and a good fifty feet away from the blaze. Within a few seconds the cabin was completely engulfed.

"Are you okay here for a minute, John?"

"Go!" he said. "See if you can catch him."

Brie raced up the driveway behind the cabin. It had taken her no more than ten or twelve seconds to get John out of the cabin, but there'd been no sign of Garrett when they emerged. He would have known she'd try to retrieve her gun and had fled—obviously giving up his plan to force her to go with him. She reached the top of the driveway just in time to see his vehicle disappearing in the distance, headed toward the main road. It looked like a black SUV of some kind, but she could tell no more than that.

Her phone was in her jacket pocket, and she'd abandoned the jacket behind the cabin when she'd crawled through the window. She turned and ran back down the driveway and headed around the blazing cabin. The jacket lay a few feet from the cabin wall, and she was able to retrieve it. She pulled the phone out, knowing there'd be no reception, but needing to go through the motions of at least trying.

She turned it on. No bars. "Damn!" She headed back to John.

John was lying on his back, still tied to the chair, and Barney was frantically licking his face.

Brie knelt next to him. "Do you have a knife on you, John?"

"No, but there's one in the glove box of the truck."

John's pickup truck was parked in a pull-off spot at the end of the driveway a ways below the cabin. She ran to the truck and found a Swiss Army knife in the glove box. She returned to John, pushed the wooden chair to an upright position, and untied the rope around his chest. Then she used the knife to cut through the zip ties on his hands and ankles. His pant leg was singed.

"Is your leg burned, John?"

"It hurts," he said.

There was a small scissors in the knife. Brie folded it out and gently cut up the outside of the pants leg. It took time, but tiny as it was, the scissor was sharp and accomplished the job. She set the knife down and gently opened the pants leg. John's leg was completely blistered down the outside.

"You've got second-degree burns, John." Barney tried to edge his way in to lick the leg. "No, Barney. Leave it!" She took his collar and led him to John's other side and told him to stay.

"I saw a first aid kit in the truck. I'll go get it and put a gauze wrap on your leg until we can get you somewhere to have it treated."

"I'm fine, Brie, Really. We need to get somewhere with phone reception. Report the fire."

The cabin was completely engulfed, and even though they were a safe distance down the hill, they could feel the heat. Fortunately, there was no wind and a wide cleared area around the cabin. With luck the fire would not spread to the woods.

"I almost hate to mention it, but the keys for the truck were inside."

"Under the tailgate on the driver's side there's a small magnetic box with a key in it."

"Oh, you smart man. I could kiss you." And she did and then helped John to the truck and put him into the passenger side. Barney jumped in the back of the cab. Brie retrieved the key, and they backed around and headed for the main road.

She handed John the phone so he could watch for a signal and drove north on 17 toward the village of South Rangeley, where she thought they might pick up a cell signal. About fifteen minutes along the road, John said they had a signal. Brie pulled to the side of the road and called 911.

She reported the fire to the dispatcher along with the fire number on the road. She also reported that the arsonist was in a black, older model SUV headed either south on 17 or east or west on 16 in the vicinity of Mooselookmeguntic Lake. She asked him to notify the Maine State Police and also gave the dispatcher a detailed description of Parker and what he was wearing. Then she brought up the number for Lieutenant Dent Fenton and put a call through to him. She told him what had just unfolded. After he got over his surprise that she was back in Maine, he said he'd get a BOLO out on the SUV with a description of Parker attached, and that he would send Marty Dupuis up to the site of the fire. They ended the call, and Brie and John headed back to the cabin to wait for the firefighters and Marty Dupuis.

By afternoon, the blaze had been put out by the Rangeley Volunteer Fire Department. Marty Dupuis had arrived partway through the firefighting and taken statements from both

John and Brie. Brie had worked with Marty on several cases after she had been deputized by the Maine State Police. She considered him a friend, and like Dent Fenton, he was surprised and delighted that she had returned to Maine. He told her he hoped they would have occasion to work together again soon.

When Marty was finished taking their statements, Brie asked if they were free to go. She told him she wanted to get John to a medical clinic to have the burn on his leg treated. One of the firefighters recommended they drive into Rangeley to the Family Medicine Center. He told her it was just ten miles from where they were.

Marty assured her that he had the situation in hand and would see that the fire was reported to the cabin's owner and that all the necessary reports were filed. So with his permission, Brie loaded John into the truck and they set off toward Rangeley.

Chapter 52

Two Weeks Later
Aboard Schooner Maine Wind
Camden, Maine

Maine Wind lay in its winter berth in Camden Harbor. As Brie and John walked out the floating dock to the ship, snowflakes drifted lazily down from a steel gray sky. The boarding ladder had been lowered over the side, welcoming them, and *Maine Wind* bobbed ever so slightly as Brie climbed the ladder to the deck. As soon as her feet touched the planks, a smile spread across her face. She was home. John climbed aboard right after her, and they shared a brief embrace.

Wonderful aromas issued from the stove pipe above the galley. It had been George's idea to stage a reunion dinner aboard the ship, and since Brie and John had been gone over Thanksgiving, this was to be Thanksgiving dinner with all the trimmings. Brie was sure of one thing—George would not disappoint.

She could hear George and Scott talking and laughing below decks, and she headed for the ladder that descended to the galley.

"There she is!" They both sent up a cheer as she came down the ladder. They shared a group hug with some involuntary hopping up and down from the joy of the moment.

"Come over here, Brie." George drew her over to the woodstove that he lovingly referred to as "Old Faithful" and opened the oven door. Inside was the most aromatic and perfectly browned turkey Brie thought she'd ever seen.

She turned to him in wonderment. "What time did you come aboard, George?"

"Oh, pretty early," he said shyly. His black curly hair seemed to glow in the light cast by the lamps hanging from the overhead. "Scott came aboard at seven-thirty, though, so I've had plenty of help getting everything prepped."

"So what can *we* do?" Brie asked.

"Well, the turkey's ready to come out, and while it sits, we'll finish the rest of the prep. Why don't you and the captain get the table set?"

George had already spread out a russet-colored, woven tablecloth and placed two stout, round candles the color of pumpkin on the table. Brie and John got the plates down from behind the plate rails and laid them out with silverware and napkins. George had brought four wine tumblers aboard, and he gave them to Brie to put on the table.

The turkey came out, and George slid a casserole of yams into the hot oven. Then he heated milk and butter on the top of the stove while Brie and Scott peeled the warm potatoes. John went topside to get the wine and the salad from the ice box on deck. Brie mashed the potatoes as George poured in the milk and butter, and then the pan went on the back of the stove to stay warm while George did the final task of making the gravy.

Forty minutes later George lit the candles, and they all sat down at the table, Brie and John on the bench fitted along the hull of the ship, and George and Scott across from them on a wood bench they pulled up to the table. This was a Thanksgiving feast worthy of George Dupopolis. The turkey was moist and tender, the stuffing aromatic with sage and onion and flavored with the turkey drippings from inside the bird's cavity.

There were yams baked with bourbon, butter, and pecans, hearty honey-wheat bread straight from the woodstove, mashed potatoes and gravy, cranberry relish, and Waldorf salad rosy with apples and cherries.

Over the next hour and a half, the wine and conversation flowed copiously. Scott and George had heard about what had happened up at the cabin, and Brie tried to give them a sense of how it had all come to pass.

"When I went home to Minnesota, it wasn't with the intention of solving my partner's murder, which had long since become a cold case. It was my mom who wisely helped me to see that maybe that was exactly what I needed to do before I could feel free to start a new life here in Maine. She knew the guilt I had carried because I'd survived the shooting and Phil hadn't. Everything else that happened over the next month—a bizarre and dangerous series of events—all ultimately linked back to Phil's cold case.

"And this detective who was behind the attempt on your mother's life and the attack on you and John . . ." Scott tried to remember his name.

"Garrett Parker," Brie said.

"Has he been caught?"

"So far, no. The Maine State Police, with Dent Fenton heading up the effort, have been on the case since the day of the fire at the cabin. But Parker is clearly quite skilled at going to ground."

"Do you think he's left the state?"

"I'm fairly certain that's the case," she said in a tone that seemed resigned to the fact. "But enough of this talk. Tonight is for celebrating and enjoying George's wonderful food." She raised her glass. "To George. Best cook in the fleet. Your generosity and your wonderful fare feed us body and soul."

"Here, here," John said. They all clinked glasses, and a deep happiness settled over Brie, knowing she had been returned to her maritime family.

They spent the rest of the time over dinner talking about the schedule for the following season and where they would be sailing. After dinner they all pitched in and cleaned up. George divided up the leftovers and sent large containers of food home with everyone. Then Brie, John, and Scott helped George get the extra supplies out to his truck. It was already dark as they carried everything along the float, and Brie hugged Scott and George one last time. They made a pact to meet for dinner and cards throughout the long winter that was nearly upon them.

Brie and John walked back to the ship. John closed up the hatch to the galley, and then they took a final turn around the deck. Brie stopped back at the helm. The clouds had broken up, and out beyond the harbor, the moon cast its silver net over the sea. A light wind blew out of the south, unseasonably warm. She felt John behind her and leaned into him.

"Do you think he'll try again?"

"You mean Parker?" Brie asked.

"Yes."

"I think we can't let the thought of that ruin this moment," she said. "Tonight should feel like coming home." Because the truth was that, for her, this ship and John were as much home as anything had ever been.

"You're right. This is a night to celebrate," he said.

A sudden wind stirred *Maine Wind,* and her rigging creaked and groaned. It was a familiar and comforting sound, and Brie, well, she took it as a sign, a sign that the old ship that had brought her such peace and solace, that had been a refuge for her troubled heart, was welcoming her home.

Epilogue

In February of the following year, the Royal Canadian Mounted Police arrested Hans Nero in the city of Medicine Hat, in the province of Alberta. In March he was extradited to the United States, where he was charged with two counts of first-degree murder in the shooting deaths of Detective Philip Thatcher in Minneapolis, Minnesota, and Mrs. Halley Greenberg near Grand Marais, Minnesota.

Viola Adams, the neighbor who lived next door to the house where Phil Thatcher and Brie had been shot, positively IDed the suspect as the man who was living in the neighborhood at the time of the Thatcher shooting.

The Minneapolis Police Department offered Nero a reduced sentence, with the possibility of parole, if he revealed the name of the person or persons who had hired him. In exchange, Nero gave up former police officer Joe Rossi as the person who had taken out the contract on Detective Phil Thatcher. Nero also identified Detective Garrett Parker as the man who had hired him to gun down Edna Beaumont.

Hans Nero is currently awaiting trial. Joe Rossi has been arrested and charged with first degree murder in the shooting death of Detective Philip Thatcher.

At this writing, Garrett Parker remains a fugitive from justice.

Acknowledgements

Many thanks to Chief Deputy Will Sandstrom for all his time spent in interviews over the phone and in person, helping me to understand the workings of the Cook County Sheriff's Office and Law Enforcement Center. Any errors are entirely my own or due to this being a work of fiction. Many thanks also to the staff at Grand Portage National Monument and Grand Portage State Park for answering my questions and helping me gain a sense of the Ojibwe culture and history at Grand Portage.

Special thanks to my friend Dr. Fran Williams for helping me better understand the pathology of PTSD. Special thanks also to my friend and colleague, author Christopher Valen, for his reading of the manuscript and for his keen eye for procedural details. Thanks also to my readers, Brian Lutterman, Jeanette Brown, and Craig Granse, whose insights helped me polish the final draft. And as always to my editor, Jennifer Adkins, and my cover artist, Rebecca Treadway. Many thanks for your excellent work.

The following works have been invaluable to me in the writing of this book. *Anishinaabe Syndicated: A View from the Rez* by Jim Northrup; *Blue on Blue: An Insider's Story of Good Cops Catching Bad Cops* by Charles Campisi, Former Chief, NYPD Internal Affairs Bureau; *Embers: One Ojibway's Meditations* by Richard Wagamese; *The Mishomis Book: The Voice of the Ojibway* by Edward Benton-Banai; *Ojibwe in Minnesota* by Anton Treuer; *Rez Life* by David Treuer; *The Voyageur* by Grace Lee Nute.